PRAISE FOR THE ACCIDENTAL GENIE

WINNIPEG WITHDRAWN PUBLIC LIBRARY

"A fast-paced, amusing tale starring an engaging lead couple and the return of the previous stars. Lighthearted, fans will laugh at the scenarios that the OOPS squad confronts due to Jeannie's out-of-control wishes." —*Midwest Book Review*

"The OOPS team faces a peculiar problem in the newest wisecracking and wacky novel from the always delightful Cassidy. The dialogue is fast and furious, the characters are offbeat, and the situations bizarre, but Cassidy pulls it all together for another laugh-filled adventure." —*RT Book Reviews*

ACCIDENTALLY DEAD, AGAIN

"Cassidy's quirky and offbeat series continues to be outlandish fun laced with a hint of poignancy. There's never a dull moment with this bunch!" —*RT Book Reviews*

"I really loved this book from beginning to end. From the start I fell into a daze with the characters' quips and quirks . . . This book is great at intertwining a great plot with quirky characters espousing wonderful dialogue, which just happens to be funny." —*Night Owl Reviews*

"Do yourself a favor and go buy everything that Dakota Cassidy has ever written . . . This book is not only well written, with a twisty plot and great characters, it is hysterical. HYSTERICAL! . . . The characters are over-the-top but hilarious, and you really do care about them and their situations, which makes this paranormal romantic romp even more wonderful." —*Fresh Fiction*

ACCIDENTALLY CATTY

"This light, comedic, paranormal romance delivers simple, unencumbered entertainment. A lively pace, the bonds of friendship, and bright humor aided by vampiric sarcasm make for a breezy read with charming characters and no shortage of drama. Cassidy's fans are sure to enjoy this, while newcomers will be reminded of MaryJanic￼'s or Kimberly Frost's work."

—*Monsters and Critics*

 D0965084

"I have been a fan of Dakota's since *The Accidental Werewolf*. I loved all of the books in the series, but I think this book is my favorite . . . *Accidentally Catty* is very funny, cute, and sexy."   —*Night Owl Reviews*

"A fun read with some meat to it that will have people looking at you, wondering why you're laughing if you're out in public."   —*Fresh Fiction*

ACCIDENTALLY DEMONIC

"The Accidental series by Ms. Cassidy gets better and better with each book. The snark, the HAWT, the characters, it's all a winning combination."
—*Bitten by Books*

"An outstanding paranormal romance . . . Dakota Cassidy delivers snappy dialogue, hot sex scenes, and secondary characters that are just too funny . . . A hold-your-sides, laugh-out-loud book. With vampires, werewolves, and demons running around, paranormal romance will never be the same."   —*The Romance Readers Connection*

"Dakota Cassidy's books make me laugh and laugh. They are such great fun that I always look forward to the next one with gusto . . . I totally loved this book with a capital 'L.'"   —*Fresh Fiction*

THE ACCIDENTAL HUMAN

"A delightful, at times droll, contemporary tale starring a decidedly human heroine . . . Dakota Cassidy provides a fitting twisted ending to this amusingly warm urban romantic fantasy."   —*Genre Go Round Reviews*

"The final member of Cassidy's trio of decidedly offbeat friends faces her toughest challenge, but that doesn't mean there isn't humor to spare! With emotion, laughter, and some pathos, Cassidy serves up another winner!"
—*RT Book Reviews*

ACCIDENTALLY DEAD

"A laugh-out-loud follow-up to *The Accidental Werewolf*, and it's a winner . . . Ms. Cassidy is an up-and-comer in the world of paranormal romance."
—*Fresh Fiction*

"An enjoyable, humorous satire that takes a bite out of the vampire romance subgenre . . . Fans will appreciate the nonstop hilarity."

—*Genre Go Round Reviews*

THE ACCIDENTAL WEREWOLF

"Cassidy, a prolific author of erotica, has ventured into MaryJanice Davidson territory with a humorous, sexy tale." —*Booklist*

"A riot! Marty's internal dialogue will have you howling, and her antics will keep the laughs coming. If you love paranormal with a comedic twist, you'll love this book." —*Romance Junkies*

"A lighthearted romp . . . [An] entertaining tale with an alpha twist."

—*Midwest Book Review*

MORE PRAISE FOR THE NOVELS OF DAKOTA CASSIDY

"The fictional equivalent of the little black dress—every reader should have one!"

—Michele Bardsley, national bestselling author of *Only Lycans Need Apply*

"Serious, laugh-out-loud humor with heart, the kind of love story that leaves you rooting for the heroine, sighing for the hero, and looking for your own significant other at the same time." —Kate Douglas, author of *Dark Wolf*

"Very fun, sexy. Five stars!" —*Affaire de Cœur*

"Dakota Cassidy is going on my must-read list!" —*Joyfully Reviewed*

"If you're looking for some steamy romance with something that will have you smiling, you have to read [Dakota Cassidy]." —*The Best Reviews*

THE ACCIDENTAL WEREWOLF 2:

SOMETHING ABOUT HARRY

DAKOTA CASSIDY

BERKLEY SENSATION, NEW YORK

THE BERKLEY PUBLISHING GROUP
Published by the Penguin Group
Penguin Group (USA) LLC
375 Hudson Street, New York, New York 10014

USA • Canada • UK • Ireland • Australia • New Zealand • India • South Africa • China

penguin.com

A Penguin Random House Company

This book is an original publication of The Berkley Publishing Group.

Copyright © 2013 by Dakota Cassidy.
Penguin supports copyright. Copyright fuels creativity, encourages diverse voices,
promotes free speech, and creates a vibrant culture. Thank you for buying an authorized
edition of this book and for complying with copyright laws by not reproducing, scanning,
or distributing any part of it in any form without permission. You are supporting writers
and allowing Penguin to continue to publish books for every reader.

Berkley Sensation Books are published by The Berkley Publishing Group.
BERKLEY SENSATION® is a registered trademark of Penguin Group (USA) LLC.
The "B" design is a trademark of Penguin Group (USA) LLC.

Library of Congress Cataloging-in-Publication Data

Cassidy, Dakota.
The Accidental Werewolf 2 : Something About Harry / Dakota Cassidy. — Berkley Sensation trade
paperback edition.
pages cm. — (Accidentally paranormal novel)
ISBN 978-0-425-26865-0 (pbk.)
1. Werewolves—Fiction. 2. Paranormal fiction. 3. Humorous fiction. 4. Love stories. I. Title.
PS3603.A8685A653 2013
813'.6—dc23   2013032755

PUBLISHING HISTORY
Berkley Sensation trade paperback edition / December 2013

PRINTED IN THE UNITED STATES OF AMERICA

10 9 8 7 6 5 4 3 2 1

Cover art by Katie Wood.
Cover design by Diana Kolsky.
Interior text design by Kristin del Rosario.

This is a work of fiction. Names, characters, places, and incidents either are the product
of the author's imagination or are used fictitiously, and any resemblance to actual persons,
living or dead, business establishments, events, or locales is entirely coincidental.

ACKNOWLEDGMENTS

To Cindy McCune for the absolutely amazing title *Something About Harry*. You're a joy to hang out with on my Facebook page, and I adore you! ☺

Also, Pam Elliot (my Spaz), for the awesome phrase "stranger junk." Every time I think about that muggy night when we all sat around a table in the hotel's courtyard after a long day of seeing things we couldn't unsee in NO, laughing about our amazing experiences on Bourbon Street, I think of you and giggle to myself. You're an angel, and the cutest thing evah!

More New Orleans hijinks love to my "balcony" girls. The word *moresome* is forever ours—as is the laughter! So much laughter. I'm pretty sure you ladies are how I discovered the meaning of incontinence!

Dawn Montgomery, who gave me amazing insight to this book, and also writes amazing books!

Kaz, because seriously, it's all in the details. ☺

Most of all, to my BFF Renee George, who talks me down when I'm freaked out, and is always around to help me hash out a plot when my idea tank's on empty. I love you, lady!

And for my son, Cameron, who we lovingly, jokingly call The Antichrist (we're sure, due to his genius level smarts, all the time he spends studying—quote unquote—is really a ploy to keep us distracted while he plots world domination ☺). By the time this book is published, you'll have left home for college to begin your own life. To say I'm incredibly proud of you is too little, too small a sentiment to express the amazingly funny, smart, wise, well-adjusted young man you've become.

And always, *always* know, wherever you are, wherever I am—there's this thing called Skype. You'd better show your pretty face on it at least once a week—or I'm coming for a collegiate visit all your smartsy-fartsy friends won't soon forget. LOL!

I'll miss your footsteps on the stairs. Your moody grunt "hello" when you come in from school. Your haughty disdain for everyone and everything because you're a teenager and nothing is supposed to outwardly impress you. Your grin, your laughter . . . your everything.

I love you, son. So, so much.

Dakota Cassidy ☺

THE ACCIDENTAL WEREWOLF 2: SOMETHING ABOUT HARRY

CHAPTER
1

"This *is* OOPS, correct? The Out in the Open Paranormal Support crisis hotline?" Harry Emmerson hissed into his cell phone, casting a suspicious glance around the room he was trapped in.

There was a sharp creak, one he suspected was an office chair, and then a husky voice rasped, "Dude, you deaf? That's what I fucking said when I answered. Now what's your crisis, and it damn well better be a real one or I'm gonna use my vampy senses to sniff your location out. It takes a little time, but when I hone in on you, and I will, I'll beat you to death with your very own leg. The one I amputate clean off your torso courtesy of my sharp teeth."

Harry bristled, a spike of anger shooting up his spine, making his hair—a lot of frickin' hair—stand on end. What kind of customer service was this? "How is a threat in response to my call for help in any way supportive?" he whisper-yelled into the phone, running his very hairy fingers over his equally hairy temple in exasperation.

Hairy Harry.

Hah!

"Look, pal. If you knew the kind of crank shit I deal with on a daily basis because of this damn hotline, you'd get the reason for the threat. So get to the point. Get there fast."

The woman on the other end of the line sent a vibe that was anything but soothing. It was almost antagonistic. No, there was no *almost* about this. It was definitely antagonistic, and it riled him from the tips of his toes to the frames of his, as his sister had once called them, nerd-dweeb glasses.

Under normal circumstances, he wasn't easily riled. Harry Ralph Emmerson was a problem solver, and he always remained calm whenever a quandary arose. But this problem? This wasn't a problem that could be solved with a calculator, and it didn't have a definitive answer. This problem would rile even the most patient and sage of wise men.

Harry crouched lower under the table, thankful for his flexibility, while fighting the strange onslaught of heat rushing through his veins. "Again, how is this supportive?"

"Awww," the angry woman cooed with a mocking tone. "You just missed the sensitive, squishy paranormal-counselor-with-a-heart by like twenty minutes. She skipped off to have date night with her man. Instead, you're stuck with the cranky, impatient, bitchy counselor-who-doesn't-have-a-heart. Like literally. So get on with this shit. I got a kid to go home and feed."

Harry cleared his throat and ignored the scream of his rumbling stomach. He'd just had trail mix a half hour ago. That should have held him over until dinner, but this ache in his gut was bigger than just a warning sign. It was time for dinner.

Images of heaping piles of red meat dripping in blood, with a side of more red meat dripping in blood, flickered through his mind's eye in startling detail.

Swallowing hard, he remained as focused as he could with the caged lion in his belly. "I think we got off on the wrong foot. So let me start by apologizing for any and all faux pas I mistakenly made due to the stress of my predicament. I can't promise there won't be more. I'm walking a tightrope where my sanity's concerned here, and that could make for bad judgment on my part. Please, can we begin again? First, I'm Harry, not Harold, Emmerson. Sort of like the writer, but not. My father's name was Harry, and my mother loved——"

There was an abrasive peal of a horn in his ear. Like a bike horn. "Hear that, Harry?"

He gritted his teeth. "I did." Jesus——it was still vibrating in his head.

"Good. That's my 'I don't give a shit about your life story' horn. It's from my kid's *Barbie* tricycle she won't even be able to ride for at least another five years. But her Grandpa Arch insisted she have it because he's addicted to woot.com and online shopping. Anyway, if I sound the horn——that means I don't give a shit and you move on."

Abrasive horn equaled moving on. Understood. "Got it. And you are?"

There was a grating snort, and then the woman with the steeped-in-whiskey voice said, "Well, Harry, not Harold, Emmerson, I'm Nina Blackman-Statleon——unwilling fucking paranormal crisis counselor and full-time vampire. Now, go!" She barked the order, making him cringe at how sharp and clear her voice rang in his ear.

He cleared his throat, loosening his tightening tie with his forefinger and stretched his neck, ignoring Nina's use of the word "vampire" in order to maintain the vestiges of his sanity. "I read on the Internet that you can help me with my paranormal crisis needs. Is that true?" Jesus and hell. He hoped it was true. Because if it wasn't——really, where else was there to turn? Who could you call when something like this happened?

Dean and Sam?

The lucid, almost always able to find a reasonable explanation, half of his brain said this number he'd found on the Internet and the crackpot who'd answered was all just a bunch of hooey.

Yet, despite his misgivings about vampires and demons, he'd dialed it anyway. Out of sheer desperation, and with more hair than a pack of Siberian huskies sprouting from his face, his fingers had punched in the OOPS number without ever looking back.

Because his sensible, thinking mind told him what had just occurred after he'd sipped his vitaminwater wasn't a case of hyper-trichosis. Not with the speed in which he'd been affected. It couldn't be . . .

Not to mention, he was well and truly stuck in this room— under a table. There was no getting out of here—not like this—not at the end of a workday when every one of his colleagues could see him leaving the offices in tumbleweeds of unsightly hair. He needed help to escape quickly and quietly before he was discovered—all hairy and sharp-of-tooth. This OOPS website claimed it could help. It listed all sorts of examples of how they could help.

The tapping of a finger, like the sound of a hydraulic jack in his head, recaptured his attention. "Harrry?"

He grimaced at the throb of pressure Nina's incessant thrum-ming created in his head. "Ms. Statleon?"

"Get . . . to . . . the . . . fucking . . . point!"

Harry squeezed his temple with his thumb and forefinger. "I need help. I'm trapped. Can you help?"

There was a sharp cluck of Nina's tongue and then she said, "Depends on the crisis."

"Could you be any more vague?" he snarled, baring his teeth. Oh, shit. He'd snarled. And bared his teeth.

"Could you be in a shittier position?"

Drool formed at the corner of his mouth. He swiped at it with an impatient thumb and fought the irrational, uncommon urge to hunt this woman down and rip her head off. "Meaning?"

"Meaning, I'm the paranormal crypt keeper, and if you piss me off, I'll throw the key to the crypt in the goddamn Hudson."

Four deep, willing-his-patience-back-into-existence breaths later, Harry realized she was right. "Again, as I said before, Keeper of the Crypt, I'm feeling a little out of control. Thusly, my emotions are erratic."

"Thusly?"

Harry's eyes narrowed, awed by the magnification of his eyesight. He was nearsighted, hence the nerd-dweeb glasses. "It means—"

"I know what the fuck it means, Vocab Man. I was just pointing out how dorky it is to use, you know, in *this* century."

"Thank you. Your observation is both helpful and, above all, original." Like he hadn't been accused of throwing his broad vocabulary around a time or ten million. His sister Donna called it pretentious.

"Yeah. I'm all about enriching lives. So could we get to the reason you called? I'm bored now, and when I'm bored, I get cranky. You don't want that, Harry."

Intuitively, he somehow knew he didn't want this woman named Nina cranky. "Do you have a list of credentials?"

"You mean like a certification from Ghostbusters that says we're all official paranormal helpers?"

Was this Nina of the unladylike mouth and easily stirred pot mocking him? It made him incredibly uncomfortable when he missed a joke everyone else around him seemed to get. This happened far more often than he'd like to admit. "Well, yes."

"Yeah. Sure. You wanna call the Paranormal Center for Paranormalness? I can give you my vampire ID number. Once you've got that, you're golden, dude. Then, when you give it to the team of paranormal experts on paranormalness they'll give you my shiny references from Anne Rice and Team Edward."

Okay. She was mocking him. His sigh grated on the way out of his throat. "There's no reason to be so flippant. I just want to be sure I've done my homework and I choose the appropriate organization to advise me . . . you know, for this problem . . ."

Nina's hand cracked against a hard surface, making him cringe. "Christ. This ain't Carfax, Harry. There's no one else to compare us to. It's not like you can call the Better Business Bureau and check on us or some shit. There's no other group like us around. We're it—the total shiz."

According to the Internet, Nina's shiz really was it. He began to estimate and calculate in his head the kind of money this sort of dilemma would cost. It wouldn't be cheap, he suspected.

Was he really considering utilizing the services of a group of people who claimed, not only that they were paranormal themselves, but that they could guide him to the other side of the supernatural?

Really, Harry?

Oh, hell yes, he was. There was no other alternative. He was trapped with no chance of escape, and the option of calling 911 went out the window when his hairline had drastically changed.

"Harrrry," Nina singsonged into his ear. "I'm getting bored. I explained bored, dude, right?"

Right. Bored made Nina cranky. Do not make the Nina cranky. Forewarned was forearmed. "And what do you charge for said services? By the hour? Pay as you go?"

"Well, if I was in charge, we'd charge. But I'm not. I'm just the muscle."

His ears pricked—like really pricked. There wasn't a sound around him that wasn't overly exaggerated. "The muscle?"

"Yeah, you know, like when crazy-assed lunatics are making super vampire serums and some bent-out-of-shape nutjob djinn wants to steal a title from a nice kid who was accidentally turned into a genie? I'm the muscle they send in to take care of biz."

Vampire serums and title-stealing djinns. That would take longer to process than . . . No. He couldn't process that. Harry shoved the ridiculousness of that statement aside and plowed onward. "So, Muscle, who's the brains in your organization? Maybe I should talk to him?"

Harry heard Nina's chair scrape against the floor, and it wasn't a nice scrape. It was an angry one. How he knew that, he didn't know. He only knew that now he'd done it—razzed the beast.

"What makes you fucking think the brains belong to a man, you sexist cave dweller?"

Damn. He'd offended her. If he was clueless about general fodder and a good-natured ribbing, he was even more clueless when it came to women and their sensitivities. In other words, he often had no choice but to just shove his foot in his mouth before a conversation even started. It was sure to end up there anyway if he was left to captain the Good Ship Small Talk.

So he began again. With an apology. Because his sister Donna had always said that was the best way to make nice when you'd tripped over your tongue. "I'm sorry, Nina. It was a simple slip of a pronoun. One I regret. I just thought, in light of the fact that you claimed muscle as your title, a job sure to keep you a busy little bee, there would be someone else who'd claimed the other titles."

"And you naturally thought that someone would be a man."

Sexist pig here. "How not-of-this-century of me."

"Look, I'm gonna get to the point here. First, in one way or another, we're all the muscle. We're three women with mad-ass ninja skills because we're paranormal. Not that I wouldn't cut a bitch before all this happened to me. I was tough enough already without the vampire shit added in. Anyway, sometimes we get the occasional mad-ass specialty ninja in to consult, but it's mostly just us three chicks. And I'm the only chick you got right now. And we don't charge. We're nonprofit, which means we personally bankroll this nutball scheme. And if Marty puts one more bullshit pair of shoes down on her expense report as necessary to meet and greet clients with? I'm gonna beat the feet right off her."

"Marty," he mumbled.

"Forget Marty. Just tell me what the problem is before I go all *Girl, Interrupted* on you."

"I have a lot of hair." Everywhere. Just everywhere. He held his hand up in the dim lighting and cringed as the confession spilled from his lips.

"Gillette."

"What?"

"Gillette. They make good razors. Nice and sharp. Marty and Wanda highly reco."

"Who are Marty and Wanda? And I don't think a razor's going to make a dent in this. I don't think a case of razors can make a dent in this."

"Marty the shoe whore and Wanda the peacemaker are the other two chicks in this out-of-control BFF venture to save this shit storm of a world. So what're you thinking is going on here, Harry?"

"How the hell should I know? You're the one who's supposed to have the answers," he groused, then frowned. Jesus, he was cranky. His normally even temper was fluctuating wildly.

If he'd angered Nina further, she was sparing him with her next words. "You musta thought it was something paranormal because you called a hotline that specializes in paranormal crisis. But, dude, we do clearly state you fucking need to read the checklist, click off your symptoms, and get a determination before you bother us with your trite bullshit, didn't we? It's all in bold letters right there on our website's super annoying front page with all the eyeball bleeding fonts and the big letter X across the picture of the vampires that sparkle."

Oh, if he was nothing, Harry Emmerson was thorough. "I did just as the site asked."

"Did you *really* read the checklist and click all the little buttons that nut Marty put on the website to determine what kind of paranormal crisis you're in?"

Harry winced in shame as though someone could see him. "I did."

"And what did that crazy technology say you were, Harry?"

"A . . ."

"Oh, c'mon, Harry," Nina cajoled on a cackle—one that had a hint of devilry to it. "Be a man here. Please. Because all the other dudes in crisis have been really upstanding and manly. You don't want to land in the Sissy's Hall of Fame, do you? You'll be labeled and that's never happy-clappy. So spit it out so Nina can make all your supernatural boo-boos better."

"Other men have had a crisis of this nature?" On some small, insane level, that was almost comforting to know. Of course, that information could all be an incredible hoax on behalf of this OOPS and their muscle Nina. Again, it wouldn't be the first time he'd missed blatantly obvious cues.

"Men, women—whatever. You name it, we've fucking counseled it. Now on with it, Harry Ralph Emmerson. What did the website checklist tell you?"

He paused for a moment, noting a strange hum of vibration in his ears and an even stranger pull of his muscles. It was as if they were trying to force their way out of his skin.

Shaking off the unfamiliar sensations, Harry gritted his teeth and spewed the information the website had given him. "Its determination was that I'm a werewolf. Ridiculous, of course, and I'm sure you've all spent hours upon hours laughing about some of the results for these inane assessments. So what I really need to know is, what's happening to me?" Did he really want to know?

Yes, Harry. A real man would want to know.

He nodded to himself. Right. Grrrr, manly.

"So I got a question for ya and don't lie to me either. I can smell a bullshitter like I can smell a bag of O neg—even over the phone. It's all part of the fucking vampire charm."

"No lying. Swear it, Crypt Keeper. Ask away," he ground out his assurance, clamping a free hand down on his thigh to attempt to still the shaking that had begun in his calves and wormed its way upward.

"You feelin' a little like Chewie, Harry?"

Now a *Star Wars* reference he totally got. He forced himself to say the word from his clenched teeth as sweat soaked his furry brow. "Yes." May the force be with him.

"You got some big, shiny teeth poking out of your head?"

Gripping the phone tighter in his hands, Harry replied—reluctantly, but reply he did. "Yes."

"You thinkin' about swallowin' a herd of sheep whole?"

Well, not sheep per se—maybe some cattle . . . He rolled his head on his neck then moved it from side to side, noting a sharp crack. "I'm definitely hungry." Sooo hungry.

"Does your face feel like it's gonna split the fuck apart and explode into tiny pieces?"

That made him pause. His free hand instantly went to his fur-covered jaw and then he scowled with displeasure. "More cracking wise at my expense?"

Nina snorted. "It's the only part of this fucked-up job that brings me a deep sense of satisfaction, Harry."

"So all of these signs mean I'm a werewolf?" he asked, trying to keep the awkward high-pitched keen to his voice steady just as his eyes rolled to the back of his head and his pin-striped shirt split open with a harsh rip of material while buttons flew haphazardly, pinging against the steel table he hid under.

"I'm leanin' toward a big, fat yes, Harry. Wow. Marty's gonna blow a blond gasket over this shit. Me, Harry? I'm not so excited. We've done an accidental werewolf already. I'm bored with shifters who look like dogs, full moon festivals and buckets o' Nair. I need something more, Harry. A new adventure, ya know?"

"Is boredom going to factor badly for me in your choosing to take this case?" Because he didn't know how to spice this up enough in order to entice OOPS to help him.

That worrisome thought reeled through his brain as his body began to quake, shivering in ripples of violent, jerking motions. He fought to control it, pushing back with the heels of his feet to position himself against the wall and waited for the voice on the other end of the line to answer.

Nina's next words brought a small measure of comfort. Really small. "If fucking only, Harry. Look, we need to get this freak show on the road, and if I don't help you, Wanda's gonna nag, nag, nag the living snot out of me and call me a heartless biotch. Not that I care, but I have sensitive ears. All her whining makes them hurt. Anyway, the show. So, because I'm a suspicious bitch, and you could totally be full of shite—which, BTW, will show you a side of me you'll fucking regret you've seen when you're floatin' around in the afterlife, I need more details."

He growled his discontent—low—feral. Oh, Jesus. "Like?" he spat, his back arching with a tight snap while his limbs reared upward.

"Like how the fuck did this happen?"

"I don't know, Crypt Keeper. All signs point to the vitaminwater I drank. It was the last thing I did before *thissss* happened," he gritted out, marveling that one's head really could perform spinning *Exorcist*-like acts. He knew. Because right now, his eyeballs were looking directly at the wall his *back* was pressed to.

Oh, hell.

"Harry, vitaminwater?" Nina repeated with a dull tone. "What the fuck kind of lame shit is that? If you're one of those conspiracy nuts that thinks the FDA's spikin' shit with their special juice so they can create a super race of killing machines, just remember, I can sniff you out. I'll beat yer ass just 'cus I can. Got that?"

As his head did a total three-sixty on his neck, and he was once again looking at the far wall as opposed to the wall he was flush with, he fought a sissy scream of terror.

"No tinfoil hats here. *Ssswear,*" Harry choked out, clenching his free hand on the corner of the wall to steady his wildly thrashing legs. The moment passed, and for a brief second, his body was calm.

Stretching his arms outward to ease the tight tension of muscle and skin, he said, "But I do know, this is . . . er . . . what's happening to me, is very real. If my head flopping and turning around on my neck like one of those bobbleheads is any indication."

"Shut the fucking front door!" Nina yelped just as the thrum of vibration reentered his body with an intense force of heat.

Harry, at war with the clothing peeling from his body, frowned. "Huh?"

"Dude, your head spun around on your flippin' neck? Truth?"

"Yes!" he all but roared as he lost the battle with his trousers and they split apart, falling away from his lower body, leaving small clumps of thread.

There was excitement in Nina's response—he smelled the emotion as sure as he smelled someone's AKC registered Rhodesian Ridgeback but two miles away. On a farm. Yes. It definitely lived on a farm.

"Jesus Christ and Linda Blair. No fucking way. Marty can't do that shit. I'm all atwitter, Harry. It's like Dracula's birthday and a Stephanie Meyer's hootenanny all at the same time."

"To have piqued your interest leaves me humbled and awed, Crypt Keeper. So does this mean you'll come help now?" Hell. He hoped so. If someone didn't help him soon, there'd be no sticky-hair-remover-device in the universe big enough to clean up the pile of fur he was leaving in his wake.

"Only because it sounds like you got some new whacked ability Marty doesn't, and it means I can poke the shit out of her with it. But that's the only reason, Harry. Otherwise, I'd just call Wanda to come brush out your hairy ass and throw you a sirloin. So where are you, my brotha?"

When the crunch of bone began and his fingers sprouted long, black claws, things began to get fuzzy. Heh. Fuzzy. What an ironic play on words. "Like my location?"

Nina's response was full of exasperation. "Duh, dude. Somebody has to come out and investigate this shit. But I'm gonna remind your ass one last time, so don't say I didn't warn you, if you're fucking with me—even though my vampy senses lean toward not so much—I'll kill you from a hundred paces. Like boom, baby."

The screech of metal ripped through the large room when Harry fell forward on his knees, knocking into the heavy table and toppling it. His eyes scanned the room with a hazy red film covering them, gripping the phone to his ear like a lifeline.

Nina's urgent tone jolted him from the wonder of his uncanny vision. "Dude! What the hell is going on? Give me your location!"

The last words he was able to mutter before his face did sort of split apart and he acquired a gen-u-ine muzzle were, "Pack! I'm at Pack Cosmetics!"

CHAPTER 2

"Hoo boy," Mara Flaherty heard her sister-in-law, Marty, mutter just as she jumped off the elevator. She was skimming her phone and probably the urgent tweets she'd received from Nina, who, according to Marty's text to Mara, was manning the OOPS phones.

Mara skidded to a halt, stopping just short of her sister-in-law, scanning the halls to be sure Astrid, one of her closest friends at Pack, hadn't followed her. When Marty had texted there was trouble in the lab, she'd said Mara should come alone.

She huffed a breath, peering down the maze of halls leading to Pack Cosmetic's labs. "What's with all the hush-hush? I was just down here an hour ago, and everything was fine. What's wrong?"

Marty's smooth, beautiful features scrunched up in a scowl. She gave a quick glance over her shoulder. "Are you alone? Or did Astrid and the rest of your pocket-protecting brigade tag along?"

Mara rolled her eyes at Marty's reference to the small group of women, assorted lab techs and IT whizzes, she spent much of her time with at Pack. "Everyone's gone home to complete the final piece of the puzzle in the jigsaw we jokingly call world domination." She held up a hand. "Swear it. Now what's up?"

"We have trouble, sunshine."

Mara's stomach clenched. She hated trouble—especially at Pack. She was always sure it was her fault—even when it had nothing to do with her department. "No. Please tell me it's not Doreen from production again? I told her, if she didn't quit speeding up the conveyor belts just to mess with the new employees, I'd put her in the filing room."

"Nope, it's not Doreen this time." Marty held up her phone for Mara to see, the clang of her silver bracelets slapping together making Mara smile. Her sister-in-law and all her flashy bling made Mara happy. She was always dressed brightly, her hair was always perfect, and her clothes were to die for. But most of all, Marty's fun personality had changed so much about their pack's dynamics and rigid rules that there was hardly anyone in it who didn't love her—or eventually fall in love with her.

No matter how bad a mood you were in, you could count on Marty to mother you. She was milk and cookies, a sympathetic ear, a soft vanilla-scented shoulder to cry on. She was home to Mara after four years of marriage to her brother Keegan.

Marty shoved the phone in her face. "Read."

Noting Nina's use of Twitter to convey her messages with Marty, Mara frowned. "Why does she tweet you instead of text? Aren't you worried other people will see?"

Marty's smile was sly. "Silly. Us solving a paranormal crisis right in front of all eighty-four of our followers makes for good marketing."

Mara nodded with an encouraging grin. "Wow. Eighty-four now? Last count was at thirty-six. Go, team OOPS."

Marty shoved the phone back at her. "So read."

Mara focused on Marty's phone. Her eyes went wide when she read Nina's tweets.

OOPS@MissClairol#222 "911 at Pack. Go to lab. See Hairy Harry. Rawrrr!"
    MissClairol#222@OOPS "WTF, Team Edward? Busy here. English, pls!"
    OOPS@MissClairol#222 "Situation in ur lab at Pack. Go downstairs. Meet u ASAP."
    MissClairol#222@OOPS "???"
    OOPS@MissClairol#222 "Harry Emmerson says he's trapped in Pack lab. Called me on hotline w/crisis. Go!"

What did Harry have to do with an OOPS emergency? It didn't matter. She couldn't read any more of the tweets because of the subject matter.

Harry.

Mara bit the inside of her cheek as her eyes flew to the lab doors. Please, God. Not *the* Harry Emmerson.

Marty planted a hand on her hip and peered into the doors of the dark lab, her brow furrowed. "I checked with personnel on the way down, Mara. We do have a Harry Emmerson working at Pack. In the accounting department."

Mara's nod was stiff. Yep. They had a Harry Emmerson in accounting. Harry Ralph Emmerson, to be precise. Born on May 18, 1973. Thirty-eight, six feet one, probably about two hundred pounds of fit, yummy, goodness. Size eleven shoe, FYI.

Loved all things sci-fi, running, working out at the Pack gym while totally unaware he was making all the female employees fan themselves because of his geeky hotness, lover of numbers and order, with a brain like a human calculator.

Driver of a conservative, but still attractive Jetta Volkswagen—diesel, for anyone who cared to know, and no stranger to a tennis court. The object of more fantasies amongst the unattached women at Pack than he'd ever realize—or maybe even believe. Oh, and single, single, single.

Marty waved her hand in front of Mara's eyes and snapped her fingers. "Do you know him?"

Know him . . . not in the biblical sense of her choice. No. As a valued, and one of the few human employees of Pack Cosmetics? Yes. "Sort of," she offered, vague and noncommittal, her eyes straying to the tile floor. "I see him sometimes in the cafeteria." *And in my dreams. And in my daydreams. And in all sorts of places I shouldn't.*

Marty blew out a breath. "Well, apparently, Harry Emmerson's had a little bit of an accident, and it happened here on Pack's turf. So c'mon, let's go see what the problem is." She hooked her arm through Mara's and tugged her toward the lab doors.

Mara frowned, pulling at her ID tag. An accident? She still wasn't making the connection to how Harry's Pack accident correlated to an OOPS accident . . .

Again, it didn't matter. She was never showing her face to Harry Emmerson again—not willingly anyway.

Mara clung to Marty's faux-fur vest and shook her head. "Oh, no. Absolutely not. I am not going in there." She nodded toward the darkened lab with the surrounding glass windows. Not with hot, geekified, slurpilicious, totally-oblivious-to-her-existence Harry Emmerson on the other side of that door.

Emphatic no here.

"Honey?" Marty soothed, staring into her sister-in-law's eyes. "We have to help him. It's our duty as his employers to help him. At least give me a hand until Nina and Wanda arrive. He's trapped in there. Plus, if what he says is true, he's suffered a huge trauma."

Ah, but it probably wasn't the kind of trauma her self-esteem had suffered because Harry didn't even know she existed. As far as Mara was concerned, he deserved all the trauma he got. How the trauma had happened, right here at Pack in the lab she'd just exited an hour ago, left Mara a little worried.

Which made her pause.

No. It couldn't be. She shrugged off her concern and took in Marty's pleading blue eyes. "I'm sorry he's suffered a trauma, but I'm no trauma specialist. You three are. I just work here at Pack." With Harry. Scrumpdelicious Harry.

"Mara Flaherty?"

"Marty Flaherty?"

"If you don't help me, I'll take away your lab coat and your pocket protector."

Mara waffled. Oh, noes. Not her lab coat. It was new and shiny. "That's a cheap shot. You're a mean taskmaster, Marty."

Marty's snort was sarcastic. "Nina's my best friend. Nobody does cheap shots better 'n me, honey." But Marty's eyes held sympathetic warmth when she made an obvious note of the fear her sister-in-law was displaying.

She brushed a strand of Mara's hair from her face and tucked it behind her ear. "Why don't you want to help me, sweetie? I don't get it. Whenever there's a Pack crisis, you're the first one to roll up her sleeves and help out. This isn't like you at all. So tell me what's going on."

Here's what's going on, dear SIL. I'm a dirty, dirty whore and once, long ago, and far, far away, I attempted, awkwardly, foolishly, and miserably failed, mind you, to seduce Harry Emmerson. Totally against my better judgment, and worse, mostly against Pack rules.

Since that night, she'd hidden behind her group of friends at lunch whenever possible, avoided and sometimes even run from Harry, due to her embarrassment.

Oh, God. She couldn't say that to Marty. Never, as long as she lived, would she ever confess to what happened that night at the Pack Christmas party.

So she lied. Like all washed-up temptresses did. "Um, I'm afraid? So, so afraid." Mara cocked her head in the direction of the sound of something smashing. "Whatever's going on in there sounds pretty bad. Maybe he's hurt and all gushy with blood. Ick." She made a big show of wrinkling her nose. "I hate blood."

Marty ran her tongue over her lips with a frown, her blond hair perfect and smooth under the lights of the hallway leading to the lab. "Afraid of blood. You? A lab tech and the woman who threatened to rip off her brother's head and shit down his windpipe?"

Oh, stop. She'd just been joking. All her brothers ever did was razz her about her pathetic lack of dates, and during family dinner date night, mostly because the accusation was true, she'd flipped and made one little threat while she had Sloan in a choke hold. Now they all called her the Mara-nator. Ha. Ha.

"I was just joking. Sloan and Keegan are always harping on me about mating and having babies. They got the better of me, that's all. It was just once . . ."

A low, definitely feral growl from behind the lab's doors brought both women to silence.

But not for long. Not with Marty. "You did hear that, didn't you?"

A thread of fear and a moment of startling realization accosted Mara all at once. Nuh-uh . . .

But wait. Here was a thought. If Harry were hurt, why wouldn't he call 911? How the heck had he gotten hold of the OOPS hotline? Unless . . . Oh. The connection was becoming clearer.

Can ya hear it now, Mara? She shook her head at the niggling voice. No way. She gulped, shuffling in her knee-high boots. It couldn't be. "Did Nina say what this nine-one-one is about?"

"Somehow, according to the tweets Nina's been sending me,

this Harry Emmerson ended up inside the lab, and he claims he's been turned into a werewolf. He took the test on the OOPS website and everything. Now, I don't know about you, but my ears say he sure sounds like a werewolf. And if you let your nose do the walking, this Harry smells like one. Which means he needs help."

Oh, bullshit. He was no more werewolf than she was vixen. "But Nina said she'd be here ASAP to help. She's a vampire. She runs fast. Also, might I point out, Keegan already pitches a hissy every time you and your cohorts get involved in an OOPS case. Imagine the hell I'd get if I did, too . . ." Which was ridiculous. Mara, as well as anyone knew, if Marty wanted to do it, her brother wouldn't dream of stopping her.

Sure, he groused. Sometimes he even complained out loud, but he loved his wife's commitment to saving others who'd gone through what she'd gone through, whether he liked to admit it or not.

"And you always, always listen to your brother," Marty jabbed with sarcasm and rolled her big, blue eyes. "Look, if you don't want to help, I'll go in alone. But sometimes, in situations like these, things get a little wonky. I only have so many limbs to use to my advantage. He might get loose."

A high keening wail, one that sent shivers up Mara's spine, made her grab Marty's arm. "Wait!" The moment she thwarted her sister-in-law was the moment that first ludicrous suspicion moments ago turned into a terrifying thought.

Marty shrugged her off. "I can't wait, Mara. He needs help. Jesus, it sounds like he's giving birth in there. Now let go!"

She had no doubt Marty could handle Harry. None at all. But there was a little something else troubling her . . . She tightened her grip on Marty's arm. "No!" Mara licked her lips in nervousness. "First I need to know something."

Marty's mouth pinched when Harry crashed against the door. "Hurry it up—he's going to take the door out!"

"How did this accident allegedly happen?"

"Nina said something about vitaminwater. I don't know the rest, and I don't have time to scroll through the tweets. We have to help poor Harry!"

Mara's gut clenched tight. Vitaminwater? Right. Harry liked vitaminwater. He drank one with his bologna and mustard sandwich on whole wheat every day at lunch and two when he worked out. He liked the kiwi-strawberry best.

But there was something Harry probably wasn't going to like: the fact that the alleged vitaminwater he'd mistakenly sipped from wasn't vitaminwater at all.

Because she'd grown weary of searching for her Prince Charming, Mad Scientist Mara had made a concoction for making werewolf babies sans a male werewolf—easily disguised in a bottle of vitaminwater.

If she couldn't pull off something as simple as "Operation Seduction," not just with Harry but with any man she found interesting and attractive, she surely couldn't be trusted to obtain something like a sample for artificial insemination. Not to mention the guilt she'd harbor if she used a man to create a child he didn't know about just to ease her burning desire to have children.

And in one crazy, ridiculously stupid, insane moment, single, childless Mara Flaherty had decided she didn't need a husband or pack mate to have a family. She'd make one of her own. Lots of single women did it. But lots—nay, *most*—single women weren't werewolves.

It wasn't like there was a sperm bank for paranormals. She wanted a baby that was full werewolf. She didn't know how to raise a half human, and there weren't any half-human men beating down her door anyway. No one was beating down her door. Not even a Girl Scout selling Thin Mints.

Her as-yet-unfulfilled desire to be a mother had sent her to the lab after Pack hours and sometimes long into the night to create something that would make it possible for her dreams to come true. So she made her own baby formula. At that point, she wasn't even sure it was going to work, but the ingredients of said baby-maker wouldn't harm her, either.

Just an hour ago, in the midst of preparing to transfer it from a beaker to a secure vial, Mara had realized she couldn't find any vials. A new batch of vials was four floors up. So she'd sterilized the empty vitaminwater bottle and dumped the serum into it, in order to keep it from being compromised for an extended period of time, until she could hunt down some vials.

Because just like Harry, she liked vitaminwater, too.

But then an emergency upstairs had arisen, and she'd been called away from the lab—a lab that no one was supposed to be in until tomorrow morning, long after she was gone and the evidence of her baby mama formula had been cleared.

Okay, so she'd forgotten the bottle. A bottle she'd left on the lab table just an hour ago.

A bottle Harry must have mistaken for his own.

Wow. Harry probably wouldn't like that at all.

CHAPTER 3

Wanda and Nina skidded down Pack's hall past a still stunned Mara, bursting through the doors of the lab just as Harry was about to go for Marty's throat.

Nina went for him first, fangs flashing, her snarl ringing out through the coldly white room.

"No!" Mara screamed, her heart pressing against her ribs, a high-pitched panic to her shrill cry. "Don't hurt him, Nina!"

Nina stopped short with a skid of her work boots seconds before Harry flew over her head in an arc of fur and slobbering drool, slamming into the far wall behind her. His groan matched his slide down the dented drywall, where he fell at Wanda's booted feet, clearly unconscious.

"Oh, Harry!" Mara yelped from just outside the door, then bit her lip to hide her overly concerned reaction.

All eyes landed on Mara, narrow and suspicious.

Which, she noted, was a little uncomfortable.

Marty and Wanda were the first to react, scurrying to the lab's closet to find extra lab coats to cover Harry's naked form, chatting like girlfriends might if they'd just arrived at the prom instead of an accidental turning.

Nina sidled up to her, toeing Harry along the way with a light nudge in order to check his status. She clapped Mara on the shoulder. Her eerily pale, yet stunningly beautiful face loomed down at her. "How's it going?"

Mara looked down at her white tennis shoes, pinching off a rush of tears. "Not quite the way I'd hoped my Monday night would turn out. But *c'est la vie*, right?"

Nina nodded, her cascading dark hair tucked into her signature hoodie, rippled over her shoulders. "Yeah, *c'est* whatever. Me neither, kidlet. I should fucking be at home watching *Revenge* and hanging out with Charlie."

If she could just avoid Nina's prying eyes and her all-seeing, emotion-reading mind-meld, maybe she'd go home and watch *Revenge*, too. Whatever that was. "How is Charlie?" Charlie, Nina's infant gifted to her by a genie, was one of the myriad reasons Mara wanted a baby. Charlie, and Marty and Keegan's daughter, her niece Hollis.

"She's good. Real good."

"Crawling yet?"

Nina smiled with such serene beauty, if Mara didn't know her, she'd swear she was someone else. "Nah. Seems the half of her that's a vampire is beating down the genie half of her. She's growing faster than most vampires do, or so Clay tells me, but it's slow going."

Mara nodded her understanding of the vampire aging process. Clay, mated to Casey, one of Nina's best friends and Wanda's sister, was the only other vampire in the world who had unwillingly turned offspring—that they knew of, anyway.

Naomi, Clay and Casey's daughter, had been turned as a young child way back in the days of Vikings, so they had some iffy knowledge on the subject of vampiric aging. Nina's baby, Charlie, was one of the first half-vampire infants physically born to a vampire.

Mara rocked back on her heels, fiddling with the pencil that held her thick hair up on top of her head. "So teething in perpetuity, huh?"

Nina made a face. "Teething in what?"

"It means eternity." Harry popped his darkly delicious head upward and groaned from the floor, just completing his return to human form.

Nina rolled her coal black eyes. "Look. It's your soul mate, Mara. He likes words, too. And he fucking likes 'em big."

Yet another thing they had in common. How uncanny. Oh, Astrid and the girls would just love this.

Harry groaned once more before passing out in a lump of lovely naked limbs and drywall dust.

"So, girlie," Nina drawled, unzipping her hoodie to reveal a navy blue T-shirt that read WHEN I WANT YOU TO SPEAK, I'LL RIP OFF THE DUCT TAPE. "Talk to me. And keep that shit real. Got it?"

Must. Avoid. Nina's. Eyes. Mara looked down at the white floor, following the thready gray pattern woven into it. "Yep, real. My shit's always real."

"Good. Then why don't you tell me what the frig all that screaming was about?"

"Screaming?"

One of her almond-shaped eyes scrunched up as she sucked in her cheeks. This was Irritated Nina. Only mildly so, if Mara was judging correctly. Meaning she was still safe. The Nina you didn't want to see was Irate Nina. According to numerous reports, Irate Nina was a sight you couldn't unsee.

She pushed the black hoodie off her head with long fingers. "Remember the word *real*? Sure you do, kiddo. It's the one I told you to keep this situation in. I know it ain't a big word like perpetuity, but words aren't my thing. Now fists? That's my thing." She cracked her knuckles and formed a fist to show Mara just how much her thing they were.

Mara winced, taking a step back. She might have the strength of ten humans, but she preferred talking things through rather than resolving them physically. "I just didn't want you to hurt him. From what Marty's told me, it's a delicate time in his change from human to werewolf. He didn't mean to lunge at Marty, I'm sure. He doesn't know what he's doing right now. You do. You know, with your *real* fists."

Nina smacked her lips in understanding. "So you're hot for this dude."

"So unbelievably hot."

"And he knows?"

"No. And if you tell him . . ." She'd what?

"*You'll what?*"

"Use really big words when I squeak my protests shortly before dying of humiliation?"

Nina draped an arm around Mara's shoulders, pulling her close. Mara let her head rest just above the vampire's armpit. "We're doing a girlfriend thing here, aren't we, Short-Shot? You know how I feel about that shit. It's enough with Wanda and Marty and their bullshit girl-talk. I'm not sure I want to add another chick to my 'don't rat a bitch out' list."

"*Please?*"

"Do you know what happened to Harry, and does it have any-thing to do with you?" Nina pressed.

Oh, God. "Like did I, with malice, turn him into a werewolf?" *Nice subterfuge, Mara.*

Nina's eyebrow rose as did her level of suspicion, Mara was sure. "Patience. I got like twelve point two seconds left of it. Like with *anything.* Do you know how he was turned, or did you have something to do with him turning into a fucking werewolf?"

"What would make you ask me that? Me. Quiet, geeky lab rat?"

"Because you're a quiet, geeky lab rat."

Mara did her best imitation of a scoff. "That you would even consider such a thing."

"Makes me?"

"Mean and scary?"

"And in-fucking-tuitive?"

She slapped her hands on her thighs in exasperation. "Oh, my God, Nina! What is it with you lately? It's like you're everywhere these days. Quit rooting around in my conscience or whatever you do. Just knock it off. It's spooky."

"It's called fine-tuning my vampire superpowers. It helps. Like now, when I can tell some shit's gone down that involves you and your wicken-schtick. I just don't know how the two add up—yet."

"My *wicken-schtick*? That's not even a word, Nina."

Nina twisted a loose strand of Mara's hair around her forefinger and tugged her head downward, forcing Mara's eyes upward to meet hers. "It's your lady-garden, and you're stalling."

Mara was astounded at just how fine-tuned Nina's emotion readings had become. She lifted her chin, tightening the hold Nina had on her hair, making her eyes wide and her expression vulnerable. She was hoping for the "Thumper" look. "You can read my wicken-schtick? I feel violated."

"You wanna feel beat the fuck up?"

"No. But thank you."

She released her hold on Mara, setting her upright. "I can sense that your lady parts are involved in this, in that Harry makes your libido turn to mush. Your blood was pumping a mile o' fucking minute, and your heart might'a pushed its way outta your chest given another couple of seconds. And that scream? That whiny shit wasn't from a chick who's detached and hardly knows the guy. It was one of those, 'please don't mess up his pretty hair or pop his perfect nose off his face.'"

"You think his nose is perfect?" Mara rather thought it was just a little hooked to the right, which only made her want him more.

"I think something really bad's gonna happen to you."

"I don't like bad things."

Nina leered at her, flashing her fangs. "I do."

"What a relief. Somebody has to like them. We couldn't have the bad things left unloved. It would leave an imbalance of far too much good."

Nina planted her hands on Mara's shoulders, clamping them with warning fingers. "Quit dickin' around."

Oh, there was going to be hell to pay now. No one in her pack was ever going to let her forget this once word got around. In fact, she could be prosecuted by the council. If only her excitement hadn't overruled filling her supply bin.

Mara put her cheek to Nina's cool hand and closed her eyes. "We're friends, right? We have nothing in common, that's true, but I'd like to think that because I'm related to your best friend, you'd take a hit for me—back me up, so to speak." Caressing Nina's cool skin with her very hot cheek, she smiled up at her while she toyed with the strings to Nina's hoodie, tying them in a neat bow, giving the strings a pat.

"Why are you throwin' shade, Mara? Just say it, for the love of."

How do you just say 'I made a werewolf baby potion because no one else seems to want to have babies with me but myself'? How?

"One last chance. I'll ask again. This happened how, Mara?" Nina prodded, picking Mara's cheek off her hand to jam her hands into the front pocket of her hoodie.

Wanda and Marty's heads popped up in simultaneous acts of curiosity.

Marty sent a question to Nina and Mara with nothing but her eyes. They all knew each other that well after five years of friendship.

Mara pulled out the pencil holding her hair up and brought it directly to her mouth to have something to nervous-chew. "You'll never believe it."

"Mara Flaherty, did you just use those words in front of us? *Us?*" Wanda squealed. She tucked the lab coat under Harry's square jaw and gave his shoulder a pat before climbing over the debris left from the debacle of his first werewolf shift.

Marty followed, her silver bracelets clinking together in jarring fashion, her boots clacking against the toppled steel lab chairs. She gazed at Nina expectantly. "Up to speed, please."

Nina tilted her head in Mara's direction. "Talk to werewolf junior here."

Three beautiful women, on a sliding scale of ghetto/military chic to Audrey Hepburn classic, waited.

She took a shuddering breath before she began. "So before any of you say anything, before you judge, before I rationalize, let me just give you the basics. I wanted to have a baby. No one seems to want to mate with me. That hurts. It hurts when a single pack member isn't interested in you—even after you've watched your sister-in-law turn on the charm and woo everyone from here to Albany just because she smiled, then try to do the same thing, and experience epic failure. And yes, Marty, I'm looking at you."

Marty's brow furrowed, but her eyes held a flash of hurt. "So what happened to Harry is my fault?"

Her stomach churned. No. She loved Marty—even if she wanted to be a little more like her, and the way she'd gone about that was to spew her envy in an unfavorable fashion. "No. I love you. I'm just telling you what led me to this place. It isn't just you, it's everyone like you. Women who flirt with ease."

Marty pursed her lips. "I'm a married woman. I absolutely no longer flirt."

Mara shook her finger. "You always respect your boundaries, and I know you love Keegan. What I mean is you have a charisma, a way of sucking people into your vortex without even trying. You do it all the time. With everyone. Not just men, but women, children. You could run a cult. Women like you should bottle that kind of charm for women like me."

"I'm not sure if I feel complimented or insulted, Mara."

Mara sighed. Saying this out loud for the first time just didn't sound like it had in her head. "It's a compliment. A huge one. Here's what I mean. I'm dreadful at playing the vixen. I couldn't seduce a fifth-grader out of some Chiclets. I'm just not sexy enough. I don't have that 'it' factor. I don't have any factors. I'm also not getting any younger."

"What does this have to do with what happened to Harry?" Wanda asked, her face riddled with her confusion.

Mara's voice grew husky, her eyes straying back to the floor. "Just listen. Anyway, after discovering I was probably always going to be single, I watched a lot of TV about single women, lesbian couples, and so on. People just like me who wanted children, but didn't necessarily have a partner or a vagina to achieve it. Documentary style, of course. And I decided I didn't need a baby daddy, but it's not like they have paranormal sperm banks just waiting to offer up good DNA. I knew it would be hard enough to have a baby alone, because the pack frowns on that without mates, and you all know they encourage us to keep the lines of the breed strong."

Wanda cocked her head at Mara. "They do have your average, everyday sperm banks, Mara. Did you skip that documentary on Netflix?"

Mara nodded, holding up a hand. "I know that, too. But who really knows how well the sperm donor is screened, Wanda? Did anyone know Charlie Manson was Charlie Manson until he was Charlie Manson? Also, how do we know a human's sperm and my eggs would gel? I know we have Marty as an example, but she was already turned when she and Keegan conceived. Plus, you hear all sorts of stories about men looking for their babies because they regretted donating sperm and want to see their creation. How would that work if the guy showed up at my door? Do I just say, 'Surprise! The sperm you donated made a nice little bundle of werewolf joy. Thanks for the swimmers, dude!'"

Silence. Lots of disapproving silence.

There was nothing left to do but plow ahead. Mara twisted her hands together, her chest tight. "So I decided I'd make the baby daddy myself. All I did was concoct a potion that would get me pregnant. That's it. Swear."

"Of course. You made baby juice. That's it. Swear," Wanda mimicked Mara's minimalistic take on her baby-making. "Argh, Mara! Do you have any idea how serious this is?"

Nina shook her head, her usually full lips thinned. She held up her hand to thwart Wanda's oncoming tirade. "So Harry drank your sperm smoothie?"

Mara blanched. "Yes. I'd put it in a vitaminwater bottle, fully intending to take it home and you know—"

"Break out Helga's turkey baster?" Marty asked sweetly, finally speaking.

Mara grew defensive. "I would have bought her a new one."

"Comforting, I'm sure," Marty groused. "Do you have any idea, aside from Harry, the million things that could have gone wrong with this plan? How many screws are loose up in that genius brain of yours? And before you say it, I totally get your desire to have babies. I don't know what I did before Hollis and Nina's Charlie. But if you'd come to me, it would have saved an innocent man's life, Mara!"

Wanda straightened and buttoned Mara's lab coat with motherly hands, smoothing it over her shoulders. "It's bad enough to hurt yourself, but an innocent? I think the pack's going to be far more inclined to punish you for that. You know what happens when we turn without provocation."

Remorse streaked her eyes, fear steeped her belly. "I do. There's fire and a ritual and sometimes a full moon trial. So here." She held out her hands. "Put the cuffs on me and take me to the council."

Nina slapped at her hands. "We're not gonna rat you out. We ain't no snitches. But we gotta figure out a way to help Harry adjust so he keeps right on working here like nothing happened, if we hope to keep this fuck-uppery out of the council's hands."

Wanda shook her head in an absolute fashion. "How are we going to do that? He'll smell like a werewolf. The others will know instantly!"

Right. Good noses. The lot of 'em. She was sunk now.

"Forget that right now," Marty added. "First and foremost, we need Harry's cooperation."

Nina's finger flew up in the air. "Exactly! It's also contingent upon Harry. Maybe he's a snitch, 'cus Christ knows he uses a lot of big words and comes across as a real rule follower. What if he wants to see the council and rat on you? The bits I got from reading him over the phone was this dude likes control and order."

"And you just brought chaos and disorder," Wanda moaned.

Mara blew out a breath of pent up air. "Then I'll just go to werewolf jail." She could do jail. As long as they let her have some chemistry books and some toilet paper, she'd survive. It wasn't like she had a social life she'd miss, other than lunch with her like-minded friends during work hours, and the occasional girls' night out at Subway where they brainstormed, of all things, ways to infuse antioxidants with moisturizer.

Nina rolled her eyes, thumping her on the shoulder with the heel of her hand. "We're not going to let your brainy ass go to werewolf jail. We'll convince him—or he dies. He has choices. They're just limited."

"I can't die. I have children to care for."

Four heads turned Harry's way. He'd managed to inch his way up the wall, using the lab coat Wanda had placed over his naked length to keep himself covered.

Mara's first thought was, how much had he heard? Her second? Wow. He looked rough and pale and, damn it all, still adorable. No one should be this adorable when they'd just had their body turned inside out. His dark eyes, dreamy and fringed heavily with thick lashes, scanned the four women. She couldn't place what that assessment meant, but his wheels were turning.

Then Mara cocked her head after processing his words. "Children?" As far as she knew, he was single, although that could explain why he'd rebuffed her lame advances. If he had a significant other, that would almost make her feel better.

"My sister's children. She . . . died," he murmured the words from lips that were bloodied from slamming into the wall. He used a thumb to swipe at the corner of his mouth. "About a year ago. They have no one else. So if you're the Nina I was on the phone with, while I was ultra respectful of your feministic overreactions and threats of brutality, when it comes to my niece and nephew, I'm just warning you, I'll fight back—because they need me right now. So *back off*."

Mara's heart melted. Right there in her chest, but she couldn't speak. Couldn't apologize for what he'd go through. Couldn't apologize for her part in this. Couldn't anything. Period.

Nina held a hand out to him. Mara had to give him credit. Harry didn't balk. He didn't turn his nose up at it. He didn't cringe. Harry considered. She watched him weigh his options in his mind by applying logistics and common sense to the overall situation. Just like she would have if the tables were turned.

"I'm the feminist overreactor aka Nina. Nobody's gonna hurt you, Mr. IQ. We're here to help."

Clearly, Harry decided Nina wouldn't pass off the plague to him. He put his large hand in her smaller one and let her yank him up. The raw, open wounds on his arms and shoulder from the thrashing he'd been subjected to with his first shift made her wince. Thankfully, he'd heal quickly.

As he swung upward, the sheet parted behind him, showcasing his ass. Damn. She'd known his ass would be one of the best parts about him for all those lunges he did. Mara closed her eyes and swallowed. Not the time to be thinking about Harry's body parts.

"So, Harry," Nina said, giving his hand a hearty shake before dropping it and crossing her arms over her chest. "Guess you weren't lyin'. You really are a werewolf."

Harry's broad chest rose and fell before he replied, "So, Nina, ya think?"

"Was that more cocky I heard in your tone, pal?"

Harry shook his head, dark with thick hair, and covered in drywall. "This time, I'm afraid so."

Nina slapped him on the back. "I'll let you have it for now because, dude, your life's gonna suck for a little while, but don't get comfortable, amigo. Got that shit?"

Harry nodded, assessing, calculating, thinking. "Shit got."

"Good," Nina responded. "So now we get into the crazy of what just happened. Hold on." She paused, rooting around in her hoodie's front pocket, and pulling out an OOPS pamphlet. "Read this. We'll wait while you do." She shoved the rectangle under his nose.

"Nina!" Wanda chastised, snatching the pamphlet midair before

Harry was able to grasp it. "This is not how we do things at OOPS. Go. Sit in your corner and shut it. Please." Wanda shot a finger in the direction of what was left of the other portion of the room.

"I'm streamlining, for Christ's sake, Wanda. Jesus. We spend too much damn time explaining what happened to the client. That pamphlet does it for us. Less talk, less balk," she shot back, but wandered off to the other section of the room anyway, leaning against an annihilated countertop.

Brushing at her jacket, Wanda put on her you've-got-big-trouble-but-we're-here-to-help face and smiled at Harry. She stuck out her hand, her simple wedding band gleaming under the fluorescent lights. "I'm Wanda Schwartz-Jefferson—"

Harry's hand shot up, stopping Wanda mid-introduction. His jaw, usually on the hard side, now like granite. He hiked the sheet tighter around his chest, his fist clenched, knuckles white.

When he spoke, it was as though he had to push the words from his lips. "I heard all about your vampires and genies and werewolves and whatever you did to me while I played unconscious. Or rather, what she claims *she* did to me." He hitched his jaw at Mara.

Mara opened her mouth to protest, but slammed it shut when she saw the disdain on his face. Oh, Harry was angry. She was fascinated and appalled. She'd never seen him anything other than affable and pleasant.

Harry, delicious and just a sheet away from naked, held up another finger to ensure no one would interrupt. "Scratch that. I know what was done to me. I *felt* it. Fought it like I was fighting the idea that some don't believe man evolved from apes, but the truth is the truth. I know what I just experienced. I don't necessarily understand it, but I just lived through it. You don't have to convince me of what's happened to me. I heard it all. I even saw some of it. I saw things I can't unsee—if that's even a word."

Mara shook her head. "Not a word."

Harry glared at her, leaving her feeling exposed and above all, stupid. "Unhelpful. That *is* a word."

"Sorry," she muttered, looking down at her feet. "I'm so sorry. I never meant for this to happen. I was just—"

"Baby-making," he all but accused in Mara's direction, the veins in his neck popping out with the strain of what she expected was the enormous effort to keep his composure. "I heard that, too. I'm done hearing."

"Hey!" Nina yelped at him, stomping over the pile of debris, leaving clouds of drywall dust in her wake. She jammed her face in Harry's. "Don't be an asshole to her. Aside from what she did—which, if you ask me is totally your fault, you oughta keep better track of your vitaminwater, smart-man. This is a lab. You know, where shit gets tested? For all you know, you coulda been drinking Bigfoot's piss. So you shoulda looked before you drank."

Harry's eyebrow rose. "Sound advice. I'll take that into consideration and be grateful it wasn't Chupacabra sperm. Imagine how that would have turned out."

Nina made a face, cocking her head with that "no you didn't" tilt to it. "Is that you being cocky with me again, bro? I'll eat your cocky for lunch."

"I hope it goes down easier than vitaminwater."

Nina made that rutting noise she made when she was readying for the kill. "You're gonna need us whether you like that shit or not. But if you're a jackass, I'll dust this place up with you. Turn the volume down on the asshat, genius. That ain't what's gonna help you get through this. The world's a magical, mystical place and all sorts of shit happens that no one can explain and you can't fix."

Harry's eyes gleamed with suspicion, brilliant and shiny-sharp. "How do you know I want to fix anything?"

Nina poked a finger into his thick head of hair. " 'Cus I can read your mind." Then she took those fingers and placed them on either side of her temple like she was part of some act in a circus sideshow. "What I'm hearing right now is: 'Holy shit, the chick who made a pass at me at the Christmas party, a pass I totally missed, turned me into a werewolf with some kind of baby-making formula, but if you just *think*, Harry, do your research, you'll figure out how to reverse this and everything'll be fine.' That about right? Like logic and calculus will solve this little problem you have growin' out of your ass?"

Mara made a whimpering, wheezy noise that whistled from her throat. He remembered. Of all the things to worry about right now, she was worried about how truly slutty she must have looked that night. He remembered the night of the Christmas party. Oh. God.

Harry's deep, heaving breath was of agitation. It was also divine to watch his bronzed skin ripple with all that muscle beneath it, even as she watched him fight to keep his impatience in check. "I've heard every word you said, Nina, but none of it is up for discussion. Now, forgive me, but I need to get home to my niece and nephew and relieve the babysitter. I get the feeling they won't understand why Uncle Harry's so late. Due to my new lycanthropic status, that is."

"The children," Mara whispered more as a reminder to herself. God. What had she done? There were babies involved.

"Yes. The children. Eight and five. Lost their mother and father a year ago—I'm their guardian, for all the good I do them at this point. They're lost and out of control, and no matter how much I try to regain control, they run roughshod over me. This," he ran his hand over his jaw, still quite scruffy, "is only going to add to the kind of trouble we're already having trying to bond as a unit."

Mara's heart clenched for those poor children. She knew what it was like to lose her parents at an early age. But she'd always had Keegan and Sloan. "I'll help you Harry," she offered, kicking herself for sounding so pathetically eager-beaver. "With the kids, I mean.

Your lycanthropy means you're now a part of the pack. By extension, so are the children." *Because that doesn't sound crazy at all, Mara.*

Harry's head shot upward, his gorgeous eyes sharp with sudden clarity. "*Pack* . . . So that's why the company's called Pack? You're *all* werewolves here? Jesus Christ," he muttered, backing away from them as though he'd just seen a ghost. Thankfully, the one ghost they'd had at Pack had decided to make a choice and take door number two into the afterlife.

Marty was the first to step up to the plate when she saw Mara swallowing hard, her lips unable to move. "Not everyone at Pack is a werewolf. We hire humans, too. Like you, for instance. We're an equal opportunity employer. We're careful equal opportunists, but we do have to protect ourselves from harm. Either way, we try to give everyone a fair shot. End of."

Mara's pride silently cheered Marty. Pack had insisted humans were allowed to work side-by-side with them, even if they didn't know they worked with the paranormal. It wasn't always an easy secret to keep, and there weren't a lot of humans due to precaution, but they'd pulled it off so far.

However, none of their human employees had unwillingly been turned into werewolves. Harry might openly take exception, and that could mean big trouble for Pack.

Harry was moving now—moving and gathering his shredded clothes, shaking them free of dust and glass. "I know what you're all thinking. So before you say anything, relax. I won't tell a soul about you—any of you," he said pointedly to Nina. "All I ask is that you let me go home—peacefully."

Wanda was the first to react. She always was, according to Marty. She gathered his glasses up, crumpled and twisted, wrinkling her nose in disapproval. "You know, Harry, the last thing we're worried about right now is whether you'll out us. Partially because you're one of us, and to out us to humans would only bring you big, big trouble, too. Our first priority is you. Helping you. Teaching you." She gave him her warm, motherly smile, exuding grace and that refined air she was infamous for.

But Harry wasn't having it. "I've been helped a lot today, thanks. I admit I panicked at first, and that's why I called OOPS. But now that you've all explained what this means," he swept his hand along the length of his body, "I get it. So I'm good for now. You all go back to doing what you do. I'll go off and do me. *Alone.* That means without aid." He gave Nina the warning eyeball before pushing his way past the women, hopping over a clump of drywall, and striding out the door, his sheet trailing behind him, leaving them all stunned.

Then there was a loud crash and the slap of Harry's feet on the floor. Everyone sprang into action only to stop the moment he swore and yelled, "I got this!" in a tone that said even if he didn't have it, he didn't want them to help him get it either.

After the ding of the elevator, Mara looked to the three women for guidance, her anxiety mounting. What next? In all the OOPS adventures Marty regaled, they'd never mentioned what they did if the client was unwilling to accept their help. In fact, she couldn't remember a single one of their clients not wanting their help.

Surely they weren't just going to let Harry go off on his own to deal with the changes in his body? "You're not just going to let him go home, are you? Why aren't you stopping him?"

Nina's sigh, annoyed and impatient, grated in Mara's ears. "Don't be a dumb ass. Of course we're not gonna let him do this shit alone. We're gonna let him do it with you, Miss Hot-For-Harry. Now, let's go, baby-maker. Marty, Wanda? You two follow me, okay?"

Wanda began digging in her purse for her keys and then her head popped up. "What if . . ."

"What if what?" Marty's head popped up, too, the vanilla tipped ends of her hair bouncing under the harsh glare of the lab's lights.

Wanda's eyes were wide with horror. She put a hand over her mouth, speaking between her fingers. "What if he shifts in front of the children? He's newly turned. Probably unable to control his change. Oh, sweet Jesus."

Marty and Wanda made a break for the elevator with Nina and Mara hot on their heels.

Mara's stomach churned, growling its turmoil. Her chest grew tight. "I'm sorry," she murmured again. As if apologizing was enough for the damage she'd caused.

Nina flicked Mara's hair. "Shut up. It's done. But damn all, leave it to a geek to find the lone geek in the world who's just like her, who thinks he knows it all. So not only doesn't Harry want our fucking help, but he thinks he can fix this. Like he can turn himself back into a human with all that crazy scientific shit he has running around in his big ol' brain. And trust me when I tell you, he's got all sorts of nutty-ass theories flying around in that overstuffed head of his."

"He really thinks that?" Mara asked with a squeak. Sometimes, the most logical, rational people were the hardest to convince that improbability existed. Mara began to panic. She had to fix this.

Nina nodded her head. "He really thinks that. Among other things. Goin' in with that attitude screws the whole damn process up. It's a big kink, kiddo. Acceptance, and all that jazz. I might not be so freaked out if it was just Harry to think about. But kids? We can't let anything happen to the kids. What if, like Wanda said, he frickin' changes and can't control it? Christ and a peacock—he'll freak them out. Scar them for life. You heard him. They're having trouble bonding as a unit since their folks died, or whatever fancy, hippy-schmippy therapist-like crap he spouted. I don't give a shit what Harry says. It's not just about him. If kids are involved, we gotta look out for them."

When the elevator popped open, no one spoke. Instead, in almost eerie silence, they made a break for the parking lot, following the trail of dusty drywall and bits of glass Harry had left in his wake.

CHAPTER
4

"Ding-dong. Vampire calling," Nina chirped at Harry's eyeball, peeking out at her through the small peephole in his door.

Mara almost cowered behind her when Harry whipped open the heavy door, stepping just outside it, his eyes blazing, the arctic wind blowing the tails of his mussed shirt. He narrowed his gaze at Mara. "Didn't I tell you I could handle this myself?"

Nina geared up to bluster, but Mara stepped in front of her. This was her fault. She'd own it.

Mara nodded, appeasing him the way she did everyone she'd managed to avoid confronting in her life. "You did. And I'm sure that's probably true. Because you're smart and resourceful." So smart. So cutely resourceful. "But you've also been traumatized. It's my duty to check on you during that trauma. I did this to you. If I don't check on you, make sure that you're really, really okay, I wouldn't be able to sleep tonight."

"I wouldn't want you to lose sleep over turning me into a *were-wolf*," he snapped the word, uncharacteristically baiting her.

The newly turned Harry was riding the crest of an enormous

hormonal wave, according to Marty's retelling of her accidental change. Mara tried to take that into consideration. She also tried to take into consideration the fact that her serum had been infused with more female hormones than a menopausal midlifer, and Harry was in for the ride of his male life if they mimicked a real pregnancy.

She stopped all thought. It was too horrific to consider.

Nina put her hand on Mara's shoulder, using her as leverage to lean over Mara's head and jam her face in Harry's angry one. "Dude, you're just a little too fucking aggressive for my taste. If you don't play nice and at least entertain Short-Shot's attempts to make her own kinda nice, your world's gonna get hinkier. And fast."

Harry gave Nina an "oh, yeah?" glance, one that was very unlike him. "I will not be intimidated by your threats, Crypt Keeper. She did this to me. Not the other way around. I have every right to be upset."

Mara patted Nina's hand and nodded some more. Astrid always said she was a great yes-man. "That's absolutely the truth, and now I'm trying to fix it—or make it better. I just want to help you, Harry. All sorts of crazy things are going to happen to your body, your emotions, and you need someone who knows what's going to happen to you to help you through it."

Harry played statue.

The loud blaring of the TV from just beyond his front door brought up another point—a valid one—one that might appeal to him on a more sentimental level. "And your niece and nephew, Harry . . . What about them? What if what happened to you in the lab happens again and there's no one here to shield the children from seeing it? You don't want that, do you? We can help, if you'll just let us," Mara pleaded with him, desperate to keep his children unaffected.

Harry waffled, his eyes changing from hard, shiny slivers of blue to softer hues at the mention of his wards. It was only a little, but she sensed it. Smelled it. Saw it physically affect his entire demeanor. He rolled up the sleeves of his green and black flannel shirt, rumpled and buttoned incorrectly, and repeated, "I'm fine."

Mara held up her hands as a sign of peace. "I know we've freaked you out, and I get it. But I swear to you, if you'll just use your new sense of smell, you'll be able to tell we'd never hurt you."

Now he went all skeptical, his tone incredulous. "My nose . . ."

"Yeah," Nina groused. "You're officially an ass-sniffer now, which means you can smell danger." She used her hand to push at the air under her neck, shooing it in Harry's direction. "Sniff me."

Harry almost did as he was told, rocking forward on the heels of his feet, but then he caught himself and stepped squarely back as though there were no way he was going to be caught falling for Nina's joke. "That's ridiculous."

"No, no! It's true!" Mara infused as much sincerity as she could into her reassurance. "Look, even if you can't smell that we're not dangerous, where's your sense of reason, Harry? How long have you worked for Pack now?"

Harry's eyes narrowed again, but he was still wavering. If he couldn't smell his own uncertainty about not trusting them, Mara could, and she was going to take that and run with it. "Long enough."

Now that she had a point to make, Mara was all business. If they were talking logical conclusions, she wasn't the timid wallflower she became when she put on her man-eater underwear. "And in that period of time, has anyone ever hurt you, Harry? Caused you to fear for your physical well-being? Ever?"

Again, more waffling, but he was stubbornly hanging on by a thread. "Not unless you count today. Today, I'd say my well-being was wholeheartedly and carelessly abused."

Fair. "Today was an accident, Harry. I swear it. I was careless. I thought everyone had gone home and I was alone in the lab. It was stupid and reckless of me to put something so untested and dangerous in an empty bottle of vitaminwater. But all of us, at Pack or those who are part of our werewolf pack, respect humans. Humans do work at Pack, Harry you are—were—one of them. We've had human employees retire from Pack without a hair on their heads harmed. Don't you remember Garvin Smithfield?"

"He had no hair," he said it like werewolves had ripped it from his very scalp.

Mara rolled her eyes, tucking her chin into her coat. "That wasn't because of us. Do you remember his *retirement* party? You were there. As I recall, you ate a lot of Missy Harver's taco dip. You joked about it. Said you'd be feeling it for at least a week. Garvin was a human."

Harry's wheels began to turn again.

Aha! But then Mara cringed. When he'd made mention of the heartburn he'd experience from Missy's famous taco dip, he'd been across the room with a group of his equally geeky friends from accounting, and she'd been eavesdropping because every word Harry spoke was like an angel's wings fluttering in her eardrums.

"Wait. You *heard* that?" he asked, incredulous and again wary, the lantern-shaped light beside his front door enhancing the hesitance in his eyes.

Mara tugged her half-frozen ear. "Werewolf hearing. Sorry. It happens sometimes. But the point is, Garvin worked for Pack for over thirty-five years before he retired, and he was a human." A kind, unassuming human, who'd been good friends with her father and wouldn't have hurt a soul.

Harry popped his luscious lips in a "not flyin' with me" way. "How do I know that? Maybe he was one of your people, and he hid it just like you and your sister-in-law and God knows who else. It's not like I could *smell* what he was."

"Garvin was a vegetarian, Harry. You know that. He shared his recipes all the time. We're not vegetarians. We need meat. A lot of it. He wouldn't be grazing on spinach salads at lunch every day if he was a werewolf. He'd need to eat red meat in order to keep his energy levels up."

"Like that couldn't have been a cover up?"

"Would you eat tofu just to hide you were a werewolf, especially feeling the way I know you're feeling right now? Not to mention he'd have had to deny the gnawing hunger we experience. You feel it right now. I know you do." Mara glanced down at his stomach for emphasis. On cue, it growled.

Realization struck him then. His eyes went wide like the Harry of old. "Holy shit! That's why there's steak on the menu in the cafeteria? And not just the crappy kind you'd expect in a cafeteria-like setting. You know, injected with dyes and packed in water? The good stuff."

While he chewed on that revelation, Mara nodded again, hoping to worm her way a little closer to the door. "Yes! And if you've ever really paid attention, you'll see almost all of the Pack employees eat red meat for lunch. I'm sure, as health conscious and smart as you are, you've made note of that without ever realizing you'd made note of it. Until now."

He crossed his arms over his chest, the fine sprinkling of dark hair on them part of many of her fantasies where he held her close in a hammock under a palm tree on some tropical island and told her no one else in the world was like her. Ahem . . .

"Fine," he conceded. "So a lot of people eat red meat at Pack. I don't even remember what your point was. I also find myself incredibly irritable right now. Unusual for me. So I'm having trouble focusing. Sorry. Guess it's the *werewolf* in me," he sneered.

Mara ignored his jab, focusing on her mission. Besides, Harry deserved a few pokes at her expense. She had two brothers who poked like they'd created the word. "The point was, we would never hurt you or anyone else, and you can trust us. So let us help you. *Please*."

He eyed them both, and again Mara watched uncertainty and hesitance flit across his handsome face. And then it stuck. "I said I'm fine. We're fine."

Nina's impatience exploded. "Bullshit," she hissed in his face. "Now you can either let us in, or I can let myself in. Choose, Harry. Choose well, friend. Because if you choose not to, I'll have to break things you'll have to fix, and I get the impression you're not Bob the Builder."

"You watch that?"

"Yeah. With my kid. She loves Bob. Her Grandpa Arch bought her the DVD collection."

Noting he was again relating to the enemy, Harry's jaw tightened, silently expressing his anger in that all too sexy way he'd acquired just tonight.

Nina's impatience only served to make Mara more agitated and more determined to convince him they were here in peace.

But without so much as another protest, he suddenly shoved the door open with a low grunt, revealing his inner sanctum.

The place she'd daydreamed about a million times since she'd begun to crush on him over a year ago. Her heart melted at the idea of seeing the house where she'd imagined his seductions—all with Harry as the lead, of course.

But her crush's crib hadn't included a Barbie Dreamhouse with its accessories scattered from one end of the room to the other. Nor had it included canned ravioli, dripping from the buttery soft leather couch and the hyper bouncing of a noisy, if not adorable, little boy, who happened to look a great deal like Harry, on said couch.

Mostly, it had included a lot of cheesy porn-ish music, heavy on the horn section, and Harry in his boxers, dragging her off to his red and black lairlike bedroom where he'd perform untoward, deliciously sinful acts on her person.

Harry's small house, located in the outskirts of Buffalo, was in reality a disaster. So much unlike his work space, Mara was taken aback. This wasn't the Harry she knew: in control, organized, unruffled—if not a little goofy.

As Harry picked his way across the room, he stepped on a bright red Lego, mouthing the word "fuck" while hopping around.

The little boy ignored their entry, and Harry, continuing his bid to reach the ceiling with a plastic sword as his guide. Nina approached him, shoving a pile of dirty clothes out of her way as she went, her head bobbing in time with his leaps. "I'm Nina. What's your name, little man?"

He didn't miss a beat when, without so much as acknowledging her, he said, "None of your business."

A grumble escaped Harry's throat as though he knew he needed to chastise his nephew for his disrespect, but he wasn't quite sure how to go about it. "Fletcher! Don't be rude to our . . . guests. Now stop jumping up and down and tell the lady your name."

Fletcher made a sour face at Harry's demand, his small nose wrinkling, his words petulant. "You're not my dad. I don't have to do what you tell me."

Mara watched Harry's face change from parental to pained in the blink of an eye. His internal struggle to manage this child was so agonizingly obvious it wasn't so internal. Oh, she'd done it and done it good. Not only was poor Harry struggling with his sister's children, but now he was a werewolf. *Impeccable timing for a pile-on, Mara.*

Nina grabbed onto the back of Fletcher's pajama shirt, pulling him up into the air so his feet dangled. "Your uncle said to do something. Do it, dude."

All motion stopped. His quiet defiance did not. "But you're not my uncle."

"Nope, but I am somebody who likes little dudes who have good manners. You? Your manners are in the toilet, Shorty. So, let's start all over again. Introduce yourself to me, little man, and do it right or I get cranky. You don't want to see Auntie Nina cranky."

No truer words.

Harry's feet, clad in fuzzy, black slippers, made a scuffling noise. But Mara placed a hand on his arm to prevent him from chastising the boy or even Nina. She'd seen Nina in action with not just her own little girl Charlie, but with Mara's niece Hollis and countless others at pack picnics. All animals and children adored Nina, something that never failed to amaze Mara, seeing as Nina was the crankiest of the undead, maybe even the world.

Yet, when Nina had become a mother herself, something no one thought possible, she'd become even better at child wrangling.

Fletcher hung there, doing exactly what his uncle had done earlier—weighing Nina's mood—averaging his options. "You're not giving me enough choices."

Nina popped her lips. "Funny thing about that. I don't have to. Know why?"

"Why?"

"Because I'm the adult."

Fletcher's sigh reflected his eight-year-old displeasure with Nina. "But Uncle Harry always gives us choices. Like multiple choice. We can do A, B, or C, ya know?"

"Yep. I know. That's why you're jumping up and down on the couch like a wild animal and your house is a cruddy mess, 'cus Uncle Harry gave you all those choices. Auntie Nina doesn't give choices. She gives orders. Know what those are?"

He nodded, his attention now fully captured, his bright eyes fixed on Nina and her uncanny knack for child whispering. "Like a general gives orders. That means no choices."

Nina tweaked his cheek affectionately and grinned. "That's exactly right, Fletcher. So, last chance, smarty-pants. Introduce yourself so we can be friends. You'll totally wanna be my friend because I'm out-of-this-world cool. But you're gonna miss out if you don't bust a move. So on with it. Now, please," Nina repeated with a smile not to be mistaken for leniency.

He stuck out a hand, lean and thin, with an unsure glance up at Nina. "My name is Fletcher Graham. It's nice to meet you."

Nina grinned and shook his hand, setting him back down on the sofa. "So, how about you help me clean up this mess, Fletcher Graham, while your Uncle Harry and my friend talk."

"One question?" he asked, his voice tentative and steeped in respect.

"Only if you promise to help me clean up. Who dumps ravioli on a couch, dude?"

His face fell, as if Nina's disapproval was the end of the world for him. "It was an accident. And only one question, promise."

"Go—move while you do it," Nina said, scooping up the pile of dirty laundry and throwing it into a laundry basket.

"Why are you so white?"

"Fletcher!" Harry scolded, his flushed cheeks turning a darker shade of red.

Nina held up a finger. "'S alright, Harry. I got this. You go handle . . . the other stuff."

Concern lined Harry's face. Clearly, he was still quite unsure whether he should allow Nina to handle it. So he did what any good surrogate parent would do. He began to protest. "But—"

Nina snapped her fingers together to shush him. "Got this, Harry." Then she turned to Fletcher, smiling as she waved a finger in the direction of a roll of unwound paper towels sitting on the kitchen counter. "Because I'm allergic to the sun. So I stay inside a lot. Why are you so nosy, Nosy McNose?"

Fletcher laughed, a hearty, sweet giggle, leaving Mara's insides clenching and her ears full of his happy tone. "My mom always used to say that . . ."

Their voices drifted off as he and Nina made their way down a long hall, chatting as though they'd always known each other.

"Amazing," Harry muttered, driving a hand through his hair, moving toward the kitchen connected to the family room. He began to move from countertop to countertop, removing soiled napkins and crushed juice boxes as he went, his big body filling up the small space with his scent.

Mara nodded her head in wonder, right behind him, retrieving a bottle of spray cleaner, and saturating the gob of red sauce stuck to the surface. "I guess, since Nina was the person who answered your call, your surprise that she's so incredible with children doesn't shock me. She mostly only tolerates us adults. But she loves children and animals."

Harry stopped dead in the middle of a sticky puddle of what looked like grape juice. "She's like night and day. On the phone she was rude, belligerent, and threatening. She behaved as though it were my fault I was in this predicament."

Mara ventured a glance up at him, catching his distracted wonder. "Nina can be the most difficult, obnoxious, mouthy, opinionated, angry woman I've ever known. But there's one thing you absolutely need to know about her—she's a marshmallow on the inside. Once you're in with her, you don't ever get back out. She'd take a hit for you like you're her own blood. That's just who she is. Kids and animals are drawn to her like moths to a flame. Nina's always the one in the thick of a throng of kids at any social event we've ever attended together. I promise, Fletcher's safe with her."

Harry almost smiled then he frowned when he seemed to lose track of what he was doing and the fact that he was angry with her. "He's definitely better behaved. She got Fletch to listen to her, and she didn't have to raise her voice even half an octave. Fletch doesn't listen to anyone, and he hasn't laughed-laughed like that in forever."

"So this has been a hard transition? I mean, guardianship of the kids?"

Now his focus was back on her. Harry's eyes pierced hers, sending a shiver along Mara's spine. "Hard? It's been almost unbearable for them. Everything happened so quickly. One minute there were soccer games and ballet classes three times a week, fresh cookies and brownies for snacks every day after school, balanced, healthy meals they loved, bedtime stories, and the Ice Capades. And then it all ended in a matter of seconds. They lost their home, their rooms, their nice, neat schedules, and both of their parents. As consolation, they got me—single, bumbling Uncle Harry who doesn't know a spatula from a SpongeBob."

Her heart wrenched. She knew what it was to lose both parents. If she hadn't had Keegan and Sloan, she'd never have survived. "So no other siblings to help ease the load?"

"It was just Donna and me. My dad died when we were younger. Mom was a single mother until she died. We lost her eight years ago, just before Fletcher was born."

Mara's throat tightened. "Did you spend a lot of time with them before . . . before your sister died?"

Harry picked up a wet rag and halfheartedly wiped the speckled granite countertop. "I did. I was the cool, if unexciting, Uncle Harry. We used to be friends. We did all sorts of science projects together. Sort of like a *MythBusters* for elementary-aged kids. Now I'm their authority figure and what they call a total jerk when they think I can't hear. I know nothing about giving them rules and structure. But I've been up until my eyes want to fall out of my head, reading books and researching online to help them—me—adjust to this."

Harry's war with not just the children, but himself, and his inadequacies hurt him. It was one thing to be their doting uncle, dropping in from time to time to share a meal and hang out, quite another to be thrust into the role of rule maker. Yet, he loved them enough to try and find a way, leaving Mara sick with guilt that she'd unloaded an even bigger burden on him—parenting as a werewolf who had human children.

Mara placed her hand on his, stopping the swirling motion he made with the wet rag, trying hard not to revel in his hot skin beneath her cool flesh. "I'm sorry, Harry. Please believe that. I'll help in any way I can. I know you don't totally buy that right now, but because of what I've done to you, you're part of our pack now. No one goes without whatever's needed, and if you need help with the kids while you adjust, we're here to do that."

Harry's dark, luscious head popped up. "What if I told you I didn't want to adjust? I don't believe I have to adjust. If it can be done, it can be undone."

Nina was right. Harry wasn't looking at this from the fantastical. He was looking at it from a scientific point of view. "I'd tell you you're crazy, but you'll find that out sooner rather than later. For now, how about we focus on getting the children into bed—"

A soft moan somewhere from the floor halted more discussion.

Harry poked his head over the top of the sticky butcher block island in the center of the room and looked toward the floor. He sighed, his chin falling to his chest, his eyes scrunching shut. When he opened them, he asked, "Mimi? I already put you to bed. Why did you get out? And more importantly, why are you sleeping on the floor, sugarsnap?"

Hearing him speak to the moan on the floor twisted her heart into an unforgiving knot. Mara looked over the top of the island to find a cherubic face, creamy and rosy-cheeked, her kinky-curly hair sticking up at odd angles. Her tiny body curled around a cat wearing a purple blanket over his solid black body.

"Mimi?" Harry pressed.

Mimi shook her head. "Coconut didn't want to sleep in the bed, Uncle Harry. She told me she wanted to sleep out here, near the cans of tuna."

Harry dropped to his haunches, brushing a tendril of her wild hair from her bleary eyes. "Mimi? Coconut can't talk, honey."

Sleepy and as defiant as her brother, Mimi sat up, cuddling Coconut to her chest. "She can so talk to me, and when she talked to me, she said she wanted to sleep by the tuna."

His eyes found Mara's as she leaned forward over the counter. "She hates her bedroom, but I think the real problem is she hates being in it alone," he muttered.

Ah. Here was a little girl who'd had her small world ripped to shreds, and she was acting out in her fear of her new surroundings. "Did she have Coconut . . . before . . . ?"

Harry's nod was firm, but his lips were grim.

Mimi was afraid Coconut would leave her alone in her bedroom. More simply, Mimi was afraid of being left alone period. She was clinging to the remaining constants in her life for all they were worth so they wouldn't suddenly disappear without warning.

Mara got it. She'd done the same with her dog, Archimedes. He'd been her constant companion while the illogical fear everyone around her was going to die at any moment passed.

Mara gave Harry a knowing nod, then scooted around the island and sat down on the floor, crossing her legs over each other so she'd be eye to eye with Mimi. "Hey, I have an idea. What if you took a can of cat food to your room? Do you think Coconut would stay in there with you then?"

Her Kewpie doll lips pursed. "Who are you?" she asked with a tone that read more like, "Who do you think you are?"

Mara grinned at her. "I'm Mara Flaherty. I work with your Uncle Harry. We had some work stuff to talk about, and that's why

I'm here. It's nice to meet you, Mimi, and Coconut, too." She ran a hand over the cat's back, scratching its ears.

"You have really pretty hair." Mimi reached up and wound a strand of it around her chubby finger. "It's soft and straight and really long. Mine's curly and ugly."

Mara took a strand of Mimi's dark hair and gave it a gentle tug. "I don't think so. I think it's beautiful. Do you have any idea how much I'd like to get my hair to curl like that? But it doesn't. So maybe, if you agree, of course, we can take Coconut to your room, and if you get into bed, I'll tell you all about how much I hate my straight hair, and you can tell me how much you hate your curly hair. Whaddya say?"

Mimi's eyes, large and round, glimmered with far more suspicion than any five-year-old's should. Everything was new and strange in her world as of late. Mara was only making it stranger. "I don't like my bedroom here. It's not like my old bedroom."

Harry's shoulders slumped. The disapproval of a five-year-old was enough to leave him looking crushed. Big, easygoing, calm, rational Harry had just had his knees chopped out from under him by a wee sprite of a girl.

His eyes fixed on Mara's again with an apology in them. "I'm trying. I really am. I just can't get it right," he muttered in low defeat.

Her heart churned in her chest again. She turned back to Mimi and smiled a grin full of mischief. "Well, I'd like to see this room you don't like. So if you won't come with me, I'll just have to go it alone. But I think it'd be way more fun with a friend," Mara said, her tone light and easy. Rising to her feet to back out of the kitchen, she instinctively knew Mimi's curiosity would coerce her to follow with Coconut in tow.

She made her way down the hall, guessing at which room was Mimi's. She didn't have to have a light to guide her, the glow from it was so distinct. She flipped the light switch on and winced. It was pink—so pink it hurt her eyes.

Mimi strolled in behind her, dropping a squirming Coconut on the matching pink carpet. "See what I mean? I don't like pink. In my old house, I had a purple room. Purple is my favorite color."

Harry was behind her; she felt the heat of his poor, hormone-riddled body against her spine—a spine quickly becoming buttery from his presence—and fought the urge to rub up against him like a cat.

He leaned down, his lips but an inch from her ear. "I painted it before I brought them here, just after I found out Donna and her husband . . . well, you know. I thought pink would be perfect. But I haven't had time to repaint it, with work and their school schedules."

Mara turned around to face him, finding herself at eye level with his wide chest. She took a deep breath and a step backward.

While Mimi busied herself with a cluster of dolls in the corner of her very pink room, she whispered, "You don't have to explain yourself to me, Harry. It's obvious you're doing the best you can in a really difficult situation. I can see you love them. And the pink isn't so awful—in a Pepto-Bismol kind of way." She hoped her playful teasing would make him smile like he smiled when he was sitting at his desk, playing with all those numbers he loved so much.

Harry shoved his hands into the pockets of his cargo shorts, his expression sheepish. "I have a bad eye for color."

She grinned. "I think you could win contests."

He chuckled out of the blue, warming her to her core. Then he must have realized he was consorting with the enemy. Harry's spine stiffened once more, and his eyes clouded. "Anyway, we're good. As good as we can be under the circumstances. So if you would take the Crypt Keeper and leave now, I'd appreciate it."

They'd been dismissed. He shouldn't be left alone with the kids. Not so early in his change. Again, she protested. "Harry—"

His hand flew up again, palm forward. "Please don't. I'm

warring with my civility right now, and I fear it could be a losing battle. Just take Nina and go."

"You takin' my name in vain, Harry?" Nina poked him between his shoulder blades from just outside the doorway. "My man Fletch is in bed. Sound asleep." She stuck her head around his shoulder to peek into the room. "I see we have another critter. You two go make werewolf, and I'll put her to bed, too."

Harry didn't have the chance to protest before Nina was swallowed up by the pink bedroom and headed right for Mimi. "Holy swizzle sticks, kiddo," Nina cooed at Mimi, dropping to the floor with a look of wonder in her eyes. "You have a My Little Pony? Dude, that's beyond crazy cool. Can I see?"

Without hesitation, Mimi dropped to the floor beside her, the crinkle of her footie pajamas music to Mara's ears. She nodded her curly head at Nina. "It was my mom's. Who are you?"

"Jesus," Harry muttered in obvious disgust, turning and stalking his way back toward the kitchen.

Mara trotted behind him to keep up, zipping around his large body when they hit the living room, still in semi-disarray. She stumbled over a pair of sneakers, righting herself just in time to almost crash into Barbie's Dreamhouse.

Marty's golden head popped through the front door at just that moment, Wanda's just behind it. Her eyes found Mara's. "Is it safe? Or does Harry still want us all to die slow, torturous deaths?"

Harry jammed his clenched fists into his shorts. "What is it with you women? I said we're fine. I'm fine. Why won't you just go away and leave me alone?"

Marty and Wanda slid inside, shutting the door behind them. "We're women. It's what we do. Henpeck. Look, Harry, you and I, we need to have a talk. It's obvious you're struggling." To prove it, Marty tugged on a random patch of hair sprouting from his chin. "I understand. I can help."

"Damn," he muttered under his breath. "I just shaved when I got home. Will this never stop?"

Marty gave him a look of complete understanding, her warm, blue eyes in sync with his. "I know exactly where you're coming from. I get it. I experienced several of the problems you're having and then some. Nobody gets it better than me. So if you'll just lend me your ear—"

Harry gave another of his low hums, a clear warning signal.

"Or I could sit on you and make you give her your ear," Wanda interrupted, dropping her purse on the kitchen counter with a huff. "I know what you're thinking, too. And no, I can't read minds like Nina, but it's what all of our male clientele think. You're thinking, 'If I have to, I can take her'." Wanda winked and chuckled, cracking her knuckles. "But you'd be a fool at this stage of the game to think that. I look innocent enough, but I could take on a team of Navy Seals without so much as disturbing a hair on my head." Strolling up to him, Wanda did something she rarely, if ever, did. She flashed her fangs at him, her manner especially threatening.

Harry's eyes bulged, but his lips remained firmly clamped in the "off" position.

With a long finger, Wanda dabbed at the side of her lip before saying, "I'm half vampire, half werewolf, Harry. Twice the fun of the average paranormal. You'd know that if you hadn't left Pack in such a silly huff. Stubborn is not the card to play with me, my friend. Now, either hear us out, or I'll have to muss my dress in order to make you—which, by the way, is linen and wrinkles easily. I don't like to be mussed, Harry. Don't make me muss. Also, despite the fact that I have to drink it to survive, not a fan of blood. You don't want me to make you bloody, Harry, do you? Not after you've healed so nicely since your spectacular crash into the lab's wall. Ball's in your court, Harry. Shoot to score."

Harry looked down with more astonishment at his arms and

hands, scratched and bruised but an hour ago, now almost completely healed. "Jesus," he murmured.

Marty and Wanda planted their hands on their hips and waited, almost daring Harry to defy their offer to help. The tension in the room grew thick and cloying, making Mara's heart pound. She hated tension and discord. She hated that she'd done this to Harry and created so much of it.

Harry was at it again—assessing, evaluating—until the silence choked Mara. "Why don't I make coffee or something? Do you like coffee, Harry?" she blurted. Of course he liked coffee, and the occasional cinnamon bun to go along with it. *You know that, Mara. You know everything there is to know about Harry.*

Shoving the Barbie Dreamhouse accessories aside with her foot, Mara began to head for the kitchen when Harry said, "So are you threatening me again? I thought the Crypt Keeper was in charge of threats."

Wanda's nostrils flared as she peeled off her black driving gloves. "Not always. Sometimes I do the threatening. Nina's mostly the muscle. But when I take the torch—you'd better believe it's gone too far, and I'm fed up. Now, you have children to care for Harry. Children who, according to Nina's texts, are out of control and in need of some serious guidance. How do you expect to handle not only these poor, innocent babies who've lost their parents, but a full-on shift? Because if the scene at the lab tonight was indicative of how you plan to appropriately deal with this, you've got trouble, big boy. You need someone to help you handle the change. So, yes. I'm threatening you. Because there are children involved, and there will be no scarred children as long as I'm here to prevent it. So again, I say ball's in your court, Harry. *Shoot to score.*"

Please score, Harry.

Mara had heard all about how hard it was to convince the OOPS clients of their new life-altering changes in a million stories shared over family meals and at gatherings. She'd also heard about the danger the women had been in with these cases.

Thankfully, the only danger involved here involved helping Harry adjust. She could do that. She *would* do that. It wouldn't be easy. Her crush on him was going to make it almost impossible, but then again, he was pretty cranky. Maybe he'd turn her off so much with his terse words and angry eyes she'd wash her hands of a year's worth of fantasies.

Maybe.

"Then I guess I have no choice, do I?" Harry baited, his words tight.

Mara gulped in some air, not realizing she'd been holding her breath. "Then it's settled. I'll make coffee and Marty can tell you what happened to her. Okay?" She followed up her statement with a forced smile, slipping between tension-filled bodies and menacing eyes to get to the kitchen.

Her hands shook when she began to open cabinets as Marty's voice, beginning the tale of how she and Mara's brother Keegan had met, swirled in her ears.

They often laughed about Marty and Keegan's love story. How ironic it was. How uncanny the two met the way they had. Mara could listen to it over and over. It made her sigh with dreamy happiness.

But when she flipped the tap on to fill the coffeepot, Harry wasn't laughing. He was sitting in his recliner, arms crossed at his chest, stiff and unyielding.

Clearly, Marty's quasi-charming story about some werewolf love wasn't going to penetrate Harry's wall of anger—not right now, anyway.

But she'd find a way to scale it.

If it killed her.

CHAPTER 5

Harry slipped out of his bathroom window at approximately two thirty in the morning, leaving the women of OOPS and Mara sound asleep on various pieces of furniture in his house, with Nina tucked next to Mimi's side after a nightmare.

The frozen night air clawed at his face, but it didn't sting the way it usually did. In fact, it felt refreshing to his overheated skin, soothing his bursts of unwarranted anger.

He made his way down his short driveway, rubbing his hands together, and flexing his fingers before he put his shoulder to the bumper of his Volkswagen and gave it a shove, pushing it down the driveway until it was on the road. Thankfully, the women had parked their big SUVs along the curb.

Before he nudged the bumper, he sucked in more of the cold air—still unsure. In all the werewolf talk Marty and the women had spouted, somewhere along the way he'd heard he now had superstrength, something he'd mentally planned to use to his advantage in order to keep from starting his car and waking the women, all of whom possessed super hearing.

Or something like that.

They'd offered to stay the night in case his shift happened against his will, and Fletcher and Mimi needed someone to look out for them. He wasn't thrilled about these strange women having contact with his niece and nephew.

Yet innately, he sensed they meant no harm. How or why he was suddenly a good judge of character had to be chalked up to more of the fantastical—because he'd sucked ass at it for most of his life.

He'd been screwed by the character gauge he lacked more often than not. The one that set off alarms in your gut or imaginary warning bells in your ears. Donna used to tell him all the time, not only did he miss most social cues and lack a universal sense of humor, but he sucked when judging a person's character.

At the time, he'd been convinced Donna just didn't understand that "Beam me up, Scotty" or any of his sci-fi humor could be used in almost all situations and still be funny. Of course, that's what Donna had said to him when he'd showed up at the bank to find out his ex-girlfriend, Brigitte, had drained his bank account and left him with a buck eighteen in his checking account.

An odd number to most, but to Harry—it was a message from Brigitte. She'd left him with just enough money to buy a cup of coffee in the cafeteria at Pack because he'd once said he'd die if he couldn't have their coffee, and she'd joked she'd be sure, if she ever raped their mutual account, she wouldn't let him die coffee-less.

"Okay, so point, Donna," he muttered up at the clear, cold sky. "I lose all sense of reason when it comes to a woman I like. That's why I've been sticking to my numbers and avoiding temptation. But what the hell am I supposed to do when a passel of women are the very persons I'm supposed to try to logically figure out?"

But the confidence he felt about the women and their genuine concern for his sister's kids rang true. It was different this time. It wasn't him pulling the covers over his head to hide from an inevitable clue Donna'd found—or he'd found and pretended it meant nothing when, in the scheme of things, it meant everything.

He didn't feel a shred of doubt the women from OOPS wanted to help him with the kids.

The kids . . .

They were killing him in a slow agonizing slew of defiant acts and buckets of tears. No matter what he did, he was the enemy. He missed the hell out of the days when he'd been goofy Uncle Harry, but the way they'd responded to Nina and Mara had astonished him. They were no longer the sullen, pouty, disobedient children of the past few months. Suddenly, with Nina of all the unlikely suspects, everything was colorful rainbows and cotton candy giggles.

Mimi had crawled into her bed and cuddled with Nina like she was her new best friend until she'd fallen fast asleep, and Nina dropped a light kiss on the top of her curly head before tucking Coconut in and turning off the light. Nina was the Beast-Whisperer. If that wasn't irony, what was?

It was only then that she'd returned to the snarling brute of a female he'd met via the phone, when she'd told him if he didn't get his shit together and forget about finding a way to reverse this, she'd eat his kidneys like pâté.

He'd have been jealous of the kids' reactions to Nina, if not for the notion that for the first time in such a long time, Fletcher and Mimi seemed to have found peace. Their laughter was open and free with her. Nina brought comfort and security to them in just a matter of seconds. Something he'd failed miserably at from the word go.

That hurt like hell. Yes, he blew at the little things like cutting their sandwiches into fun shapes and making smiley faces on pancakes with chocolate chips that melted faster than ice cream in July, leaving angry globs of brown in the batter.

Yes. He also blew at braiding Mimi's hair, making sure Fletcher had his science binder on Thursdays, and remembering that Saturday night was always pizza night.

He was a no-nonsense, all-business kind of guy. That they were in school on time, even if they were a little rumpled and minus a binder, didn't seem to count as love to them.

And he didn't know how to show them, prove to them, that no matter what, Uncle Harry would take care of them, protect them—love them—at all costs.

Then there was Mara. A woman he'd found so incredibly attractive since he'd begun working at Pack, and not just because she was petite and rounded, but because she was as smart, if not smarter than him. So smart, she'd made a baby serum. Damn, that needed to be admired, but it would have to happen at another time when he wasn't so appalled.

He'd kept his distance all this time for a reason—he wanted no repeats of Brigitte. Since her, he'd promised himself he'd focus on work and avoid any sort of female temptation until he at least had a savings account again.

Then Donna and her husband Caleb were killed and the kids had needed him. He didn't have time for anything else other than focusing on their best interests.

But every chance he had, he'd watched Mara from afar—at lunch, when she dropped off her budget for the lab in his department—while she was strolling on her break around Pack's manicured lawns with her posse of equally smart friends.

He watched, and he drooled, and he mourned what a jackass he was for realizing way too late she'd been showing interest in him at Pack's Christmas party last year—or at least that's what Dwyer from his department said—confirmed tonight by Nina.

And now, she'd turned him into a motherfucking werewolf. Maybe that had been the plan at the Christmas party last year? To seduce him and turn him into one of them? Maybe that was the goal within the corporation? To turn everyone into one of them? They claimed not true. But all maniacal plotters claimed the plan didn't exist, didn't they?

But then to what end? If Pack had been around for forty years— if the intent was to mass turn, why hadn't they turned everyone into werewolves by now? Why wasn't everyone on the planet a paranormal species of some kind?

He shook his head. His vivid imagination and his love of a good sci-fi story were getting the best of his powers of deduction. He didn't sense the goal was world domination—or any domination. No matter how hard he tried to dislike the women of OOPS, he just couldn't make it mesh with his gut feelings about them.

And now they were babysitting.

Mara, in particular, had been eager to offer her babysitting services while he "adjusted." Of course, that was guilt talking—not attraction. She was the one who'd done this to him—she should feel guilty. And afraid.

If he'd heard correctly, some group of people, whose name had escaped him as he'd been thrust into consciousness, weren't going to love the idea that Mara had turned an innocent into a werewolf.

But the idea that she'd been making a formula to impregnate herself left him infuriated and in awe of how brilliant she really was. Almost all of this left him in awe.

Werewolf.

Harry snorted, the cold air blowing from his mouth making puffy clouds. He wouldn't deny what had happened to him back at

Pack. There was no denying the excruciating physical changes his body had gone through back there. His bones had shifted. His flesh had separated, stretched, torn, and it hadn't killed him. He'd molted into a werewolf.

Not a wolfman who walked on two legs and had an overabundance of hair, but an animal, one that walked on four legs and couldn't speak a word but could understand everything going on around him.

He didn't understand it. He almost didn't want to—it was freakishly sci-fi. He'd even paused to wonder if his old high school friend and fellow geek, Anson Swarkowski, would be jealous. Because this was the stuff their high school fantasies were made of.

But the curious, academic side of him begged for an answer. How did someone's entire physiological makeup simply change with one bite, or in his case, one sip? And if it could change one way, why couldn't it change back?

If in fact this was all magical and mystical like Nina had declared, why couldn't he find someone who possessed the magic to reverse it? If one existed, why couldn't the other?

This is what had thrust him out into the frigid night and pushed him to find a solution.

He didn't want to be a werewolf. Maybe when he'd been twelve, this nightmare of a graphic novel would have been super cool. Okay, maybe even when he'd been sixteen and sneaking off to Trekkie conventions, it still would have been cool.

But not now. Not when he had two children he was responsible for raising. How the hell was he going to hide something like this from them? Hang on, kids. Uncle Harry has to shift into the scariest thing you've ever seen because the full moon's calling?

Add in the fact that he wanted to tear everyone's throat out with his teeth and it didn't make for a healthy role model.

And then there were the tufts of hair on his face that he'd shaved no less than three times during the course of the evening.

Sure. Nina and Marty said that would pass. His emotions would level out and he'd be right as fucking rain, in Nina's words. He'd also be part of a pack and have an alpha leader, Marty's husband Keegan, as per her welcome to the group conversation. But how did they know for sure his rampant desire to gnaw his way through Nina's throat would pass? They had one example of a human turned werewolf.

Marty. While he'd listened to the outlandish tale of her "accident" he couldn't help but wonder whether there was any hard-core, recorded proof to back up the fact that everything would be fucking right as rain. That he wouldn't experience any backlash just because Marty hadn't. What if something in him was irreparably damaged now—and just as Marty was the first case of eventual adjustment, maybe he'd be the first case of not so great adjustment?

What if.

No. He wanted this problem solved and he wanted it solved now.

Thanking whoever was in charge that he'd forgotten to lock his car when he got home tonight, he popped the door open and gave it another push until he'd rolled all the way down the small hill of his subdivision and hopped in.

Turning the key in the ignition, he clicked his phone on and looked at the ad on Craigslist again, fighting the impulse to label it ridiculous with his haughty science.

But, hello, he was a werewolf. That didn't get much more ridiculous.

Who was he to say that this witch doctor that advertised on Craigslist, touting his ability to reverse all curses, was any less real or useful than the ladies of OOPS? Who knew the ladies of OOPS would really have been useful until they actually were?

Okay, so the witch doctor didn't have a flashy website with glitter and a dozen testimonials like the women, but he'd been the only person to answer his email after a dozen or so inquiries to other alleged witch doctors and their ilk.

And he was open twenty-four-seven.

If he had any hope of getting away from those women who were convinced he couldn't change this, now was the time.

As he hit the highway, heading toward the rural area where Guido the Witch Doctor was located, he had one thought.

Holy shit. I'm a werewolf.

Bet Anson Swarkowski wishes he were me.

"OH, dude. You've done it now." Nina pinned the man in the colorful headdress, whom Mara assumed was Guido, up against a wall with one hand, holding him by his throat to secure him there. His petrified face, thin and long, glowed white in the light of his establishment's sign hanging just outside his shack.

Their arrival at Guido's House of Witch Doctoring, after a long, torturous journey through the most rural areas of Buffalo, with Nina racing at breakneck speed to get to Harry before he did something stupid, had left Mara rattled. She'd finally fallen asleep, wedged into a corner of Harry's very uncomfortable couch, only to be awakened an hour later to Nina's colorful brand of swearing at Harry's disappearance.

After skimming the history of his computer's browser, in which her favorite genius had forgotten to clear his cache, they'd found a vast array of purported witch doctors' websites and become privy to yet more information.

Not just on Harry's whereabouts, but about Guido himself. According to Darnell, the resident demon and overall teddy bear of their OOPS group, whom Nina had texted the moment they knew Harry was gone, Guido was real. He wasn't very good at what he did. In fact, some in the paranormal world compared him to a hack. Nay, Darnell had outright called him a hack.

Ting-tang-walla-walla-bing-bang.

But he was certainly real, and he did garner results. The results were just questionable and sometimes ugly. That information had sent Nina and Mara on the SUV ride from hell to get to Harry before he did something stupid.

As Mara cornered Harry, who appeared a little rough around the edges, the moment she burst through the door, she heard her heart throbbing in her ears. Something had happened. She smelled it.

She came to a halt just outside the room where this witch doctoring had likely occurred, screeching to a halt in front of his large frame. "Harry?" she huffed, fighting for breath. "In all of your," Mara threw up her hands to make finger quotes, " 'logical reasoning,' what made you think coming to see Guido the Witch Doctor was logical and/or reasonable? Setting aside his festive costume, I don't know about you, but my first clue the gentleman wasn't on the up-and-up might have been his name. Which is Guido, Harry. *Guido.* Not Mustafa, or—"

"That's *The Lion King*," Nina interjected, tightening her grip on Guido to make him stop squirming and clawing at her hands. "I know because I watch a lot of kid's shit with Charlie now. For example, *Dora the Explorer.* Ever wonder how the fuck she fits all that shit in her backpack? It's unrealistic and teaches kids to have unrealistic expectations."

"*Hakuna matata,*" Mara replied dryly, pushing her way past a large urn with vaporous tendrils of steam rising into the stale air of Guido's dank yet colorful shack to pin Harry with her angry eyes. "Either way, it just doesn't ring very witch-doctor-ish, does it? I don't want to discriminate against poor Guido, but it's a stretch. Clearly, you didn't think this through. Witch doctors heal people,

Harry. They don't reverse something irreversible. You're not cursed." And quite frankly, she was beginning to feel exceptionally slighted by his attitude toward her kind.

Harry's eyebrow rose, arching with a haughty swell he had to fight to hold onto, but fight he did. "Says you. Guido and his whiteboard say otherwise." He pointed to the large rectangle filled with prices written in scrawling red Magic Marker for Guido's services.

Mara almost gasped when she saw the eraser marks where Guido also apparently catered to your witch doctor needs on a whimlike basis.

She stomped over to the spot on the wall reserved for Guido's pricing and pointed at his list with a shaky finger. "Harry? Do you see here where he's erased TURN YOUR EX-LOVER INTO A ZOMBIE at the bargain basement price of two thousand dollars into TURN A WEREWOLF BACK INTO A HUMAN? Does that look fishy at all to you?"

Harry's chin lifted. His lovely, covered-in-a-lot-of-hair chin. "How do you know it says that?"

"Because I have amazing eyesight." She yanked the board off the wall, taking some of the cheap paneling with it, and shoved it under a perturbed Harry's nose. "See? You have amazing eyesight, too, Harry. Look with your amazeball eyes and see what he erased!"

Harry jammed his hands into the pockets of his thick, hooded sweatshirt. "He said he could lift the curse."

Mara sighed. For all of Harry's cute, he was getting on her nerves with the quest for reversion. "Harry—you're not cursed! I'll grant you, some might call it a curse. But it didn't happen because it began as a curse. It was an accident. An accident of epic proportions, but an accident no one—not a soul on this earth—can fix. I swear it. What do I have to do to make you believe me?"

Harry's jaw went stony again—reminiscent of Fletcher and his petulant attitude. "Nothing. If it can be created, why can't it be uncreated? Riddle me that, baby-maker."

"You!" Nina roared in poor, frightened Guido's elaborately made-up face. "What the hell have you done to him? And what the fuck is that smell?"

Guido, pale even beneath his witch-doctor makeup, trembled and sputtered, "Grilled cheese? Look, lady, please let me go. Don't eat me, please, please, please don't eat me! I was just doin' what I said I'd do!" He pulled at her hand to no avail, the large feathers of his headdress bobbing wildly with his struggle. "I can't breathe!"

"Then you get the point I'm makin'?" she snarled.

Harry put his hand on Nina's, the tic in his jaw pulsing. "Be a nice Crypt Keeper and put Guido down. He didn't do anything I didn't ask him to."

Mara's stomach plunged to her feet. Oh, God. He had let Guido do something. What had he let Guido do? She pulled at Nina's fingers to loosen her grip on Guido's neck while she begged Harry with her eyes. "Harry? Please tell me you didn't let Guido do anything to you." *Please. Please. Please.*

Harry's large frame stiffened as he, too, helped her tug at Nina's fingers. He rolled his wide shoulders and shrugged as he successfully pried one of Nina's fingers from Guido's neck, only to have it snap back into place. "I can't do that."

She gulped. There was no stopping the pleading look in her eyes. "Could you lie to me—just for now? I'm on empty here. I've had almost no sleep and your couch is the pits in terms of comfort. It's been a rough day."

Harry stopped pulling at Nina's immoveable hand and shot her a look of astonishment. "Yeah. It's always rough when you turn someone into a werewolf. Need a massage? Maybe a nice foot rub?"

Her shoulders slumped. "Will you always grudge like this?"

"It could be a good, long while."

"Estimated time of arrival?"

"Unknown."

More panic rose by way of an almost uncontrollable wave of chills racing along her spine. She let go of Nina's hand, too, pulling the sleeves of her jacket over her cold fingers. As per Darnell, if they didn't find out what Guido had used on Harry in exact detail, things could get hinky. "What did you let him do, Harry?"

"Why are you so worried about what I let him do if he can't really do anything to help me, Mara?" Harry taunted down at her, smug and spiteful.

Oh, this man! Her fed-up meter tilted. "Because while he can't revert you, he can give you an extra appendage, Harry," she hissed up at him, ignoring the shock on his face. "How do you feel about an extra leg? Or maybe a finger sprouting from your man garden?" *Mr. Smarty McSmart.*

Harry blanched and shook his head. "Witch doctors can really do that? He's really real?"

Nina popped him on the chest with a flat palm, the clap sharp to Mara's oversensitive ears. "Isn't that why you're here, dumb ass? Because you did the Harry again. You thought, in that big shit storm of a brain of yours, 'If werewolves and vampires are real, then why can't witch doctors be, too?' Didn't you, you big numbnuts? Jesus, Harry. Jesus Christ and Rainbow Brite."

Guilt washed over Harry's lean face. Yet he held onto his defiance like a champ, eyes flashing, fists clenched. "Maybe."

Nina was right back up in Guido's face, glowering down at him. "What did you give him, you fucking scam artist? Tell me or I'll damn well make you scream for your mother!"

Harry's reaction startled an already fragile Mara, when he gripped Nina's shoulders and ordered quite deliciously, "Let him go, Nina. *Please.*"

Nina let her head drop back on her shoulders, her eyes glowing as she took in Harry's face from her upside-down position. They narrowed. "You touchin' me, Harry?"

Mara had to admire how he stood his ground. Strong and steady, legs planted firmly, determination in his eyes.

Nina was probably the scariest person she knew, and that was before she'd become a vampire. But his conviction was sigh-worthy and completely unlike her Harry. "I am. I apologize if that's against vampire protocol, but Guido only did what I asked him to do. Nothing more. Now, please put Guido down."

Nina let her hand open, watching with satisfaction as Guido's lean body crashed to the ground in a clatter of limbs and jars of something unidentifiable.

She whipped around to eyeball Harry, but Mara jumped between them, trying with all she had to keep from placing a hand on Harry's heaving chest. Because it would be warm and inviting and . . . "Okay, let's all just calm down. Nina, this will get us nowhere. We need answers, not casts for broken limbs." She let her eyes go round with pleading, knowing it was the quickest way to Nina's weak spot.

In unison, they each took a step back.

Guido shimmied up the wall, grabbing a nearby broom, clinging to it with white knuckles when he raised it high above his head and waved it like a weapon. "You're all crazy!"

Harry snatched the broom from Guido with such dexterity even Mara was left in shock and even a little awe. "Guido—do not rile the beast. We'll leave peacefully. I'm sorry for the trouble."

But Nina snatched the broom from Harry just as quickly and held it at Guido's pointed chin. "The hell we will." She whisked the bristles of the broom under his nose. "Now what did you give him to make the bad werewolf go away, *Guido*? Cough it the fuck up— do it fast, or I'll knock your head off your shoulders like I'm knockin' a baseball into left field."

Mara snapped—like a brittle rubber band, her guilt, remorse, anguish over what she'd done to Harry sent her right over the edge she'd tried so hard to cling to. "Nina, knock it off now!" Stalking toward the vampire, she yanked the broom from her hands with such force Nina actually stumbled backward.

While catching Nina off guard with her strength was surely reason for internal applause, or possibly ducking for cover, Mara didn't have time to consider the consequences. She just wanted them to stop quarreling and figure this out calmly. "Sit! *All of you!*" she ordered, pointing to the tipped-over chairs in the middle of Guido's dingy storefront.

Nina's eyes glittered, but she did as requested.

Harry's lips had the audacity to curve into a smile—a saucy one at that. "Who knew meek, little lab rat Mara Flaherty was so take-charge?"

She threw the broom over her shoulder and glared up at him. "Who knew quiet, unassuming, numbers guru Harry not Harold Emmerson was such a complete ass?"

"Hot," Harry said with a sexy growl, snapping his likely flossed-twice-a-day white teeth in her face while dragging a chair upward to sit down.

She fought the surprise on her face. Harry was so arrogant and cocky with the change. In all the time she'd lusted for him, he'd never used the word *hot* unless he was referring to his coffee or the temperature outside. His hormones were rampant, and if they didn't get him to at least try and get a grip, trouble could ensue.

She'd seen this exact behavior in adolescent werewolves. When childhood met adulthood for a male werewolf, that pulsing rush of growth, their coming of age, was all consuming.

Posturing and pushing the limits were all part of a process out of control, needing harnessing. Harry was displaying similar traits, and if anyone knew how wild things could get, it was Mara. She'd lived through Keegan and Sloan's teenage years.

Turning to Guido, Mara narrowed her eyes, urgency spurring her fears and her willingness to press for information. "What did you give Harry to make him think you could reverse his plight, Guido? Be specific—I want every detail. And don't you dare tell me it's some kooky secret practice, spawned from a long line of witch doctoring you can't share because it's some forbidden family secret—because your family lives in Staten Island and they're Catholic, Guido. Not a Roman Catholic in the land believes in the spells and curses you say you can perform. You weren't just hatched a witch doctor. And you're definitely not the African witch doctor you claim to be. You're half Italian, half Jewish. I know because I spoke to your mother, Angelina, on the way over here. She misses you, by the way. She said if you'll just come home, she'll make your favorite ziti and meatballs. So spit it out—or I'm going to show you I'm not so meek and mild."

Guido's thin frame sank inward, slumping in the chair Nina swiftly slid under him. His face was full of sorrow. "My mom said that? I miss my mom. I really miss her ziti. Can't duplicate it to save my friggin' life."

"So why don't you just go home, Guido?" Harry asked in a sudden sympathetic tone, much more like the Harry she'd fallen "in her mind" in love with.

Guido put his bare, thin arms on the table, dropping his eyes to the rough-cut surface as though he were ashamed. "I can't go home. I can't ever go home. Look, this is how it went down. I'm just a Jewish guy from the Island who didn't know what he wanted to do with his life. Ten years ago when I was twenty-two, I was in the Peace Corps in Africa. I met this guy. He was a little unusual . . ."

"Pot, meet kettle," Nina crowed, pointing to his lavish headdress with varying colors of feathers and beads, the red paint circling his eyes, and the white slashes just under his cheekbones. "Now get to the point because all this stallin' just gives me more time to decide how I wanna fuck you up."

"This," he said, plucking at the feathers surrounding his head-dress with bony fingers, "is just for the show. People aren't going to show up and believe I can cast spells, et cetera, if I don't look the part. So I play the part."

"But you don't always cast the right spells, do you, Guido?" Nina sneered, tapping the splintered table with a finger. "My friend Dar-nell tells me you suck at this. He says you're a hack, and you've screwed the pooch more than once. So what should we expect for poor, fucked-up Harry here? He's already nothing like the dude I talked to on the phone. He's currently pushy, demanding, thinkin' he's a real lady-killer, and hormonally out of whack—not the norm for our brainiac Harry, according to Mara here, his coworker and resident fantasyland dweller. So you'd damn well better tell me what else I have to prepare for. 'Cus if you made shit worse, I need to know how hard to beat your quack ass when the time comes for punishment."

Harry grunted his displeasure in Nina's direction, but Mara placed a hand on his arm to prevent him from baiting her. "How did this happen to you, Guido?" she asked.

"You'll never believe it," he groaned.

Nina rolled her eyes in impatience. "Dude, I'm a goddamn vam-pire and they're werewolves. What the fuck kind of statement is that?"

Guido dropped his chin to his chest. "Point," he said on a sigh. "Look, the guy that handed this off to me, unwillingly on my behalf by the way, just wanted out. I don't know how he did it—I just know he did. One night, me and a bunch of guys in my group are drinkin' some pretty rare scotch in a place where water is scarce, let alone booze. You know what it's like, far away from home, you meet a guy—a native to Africa—one you think has connections, one who offers you stuff you haven't had in a year. Like hot dogs and Fritos, you get to thinkin' maybe he could hook you up." He shook his feathered head, his eyes, dark slits beneath the red makeup, held a pain that touched something deep within Mara.

Nina? Not so much. She shook her dark head. "Nope, I don't know what that's like, but you'd better get to tellin' me what it's like before I get impatient. Ask Harry how I feel about waiting."

Guido's face went slack. "The next thing I know, there were chickens and blood and a mortar and pestle and the sweat of a thousand Namib Desert beetles. At least I think that's what he called all those marching, squiggly things with a hundred legs." Guido shuddered violently. "Anyway, it was loud, there was shrieking and praying, and it felt like he was dragging my insides outside of my body, then stuffing them back in again. I blacked out. When I woke up the next morning, under the hot-ass African sun in a lump of elephant shit, people were gathered around me praying. A villager who spoke English told me the juju was now mine. I beat feet out of there I was so scared. By the time I figured out what the hell the juju was, I was on my way home to New York, and I was like witch doctor out of control. I turned a guy on the plane with me into a mute, for Christ's sake. I know it was me who did it, too. I *felt* it happen." He shook his head, his makeup-masked face full of regret. "That poor son of a bitch still can't speak because of me. I keep tabs on him, you know. Because I'm not the dick everyone in your nutbag world thinks I am."

"How altruistic," Mara muttered. "Yet you keep right on practicing."

His look matched his sarcastic tone. "Look, lady. I gotta make a living. When I joined the Peace Corps, I didn't know what I wanted to do with my life. But while I was in Africa, I figured it out. I was all jazzed to do my time and come back home and go to culinary school. I wanted to be a chef. Not some flippy witch doctor. Then this happened. I didn't ask for it. I sure as hell don't want it, but I'm not fit for public consumption because believe me when I tell you that culinary school I went to, for less than a week mind you, will never be the same. I do shit I don't even mean to do to innocent people every time I try to leave this hell. It's like I've got some kinda invisible chains on me, and when I finally break free, bad shit happens. It's not like I can just quit or go home to my mother's. What if something happened to her because of the whacked-out stuff I can't control? I'd never forgive myself. In the meantime, somebody's gotta pay the rent on this dump. I have to eat, too," he finished defensively, pushing his thin chest forward only to expose his rib cage.

"So you offer a service you know will go awry? You tell people you can help them, knowing your spells are bad?" Mara asked, incredulous.

Guido made a face at her, comical under all his stage makeup if not for the fact that he was a madman. "Oh, stop with the 'I'm so moral' look. It was you who did this to poor Harry, wasn't it?"

Harry was up and in Guido's face in a heartbeat, his long arm reaching out to clamp a hand on his thin shoulder. "Back off her, Guido."

Mara's pulse raced at Harry's defense of her. This was almost like the fantasy she had about him defending her against the evil Malfoy. Well . . . it wasn't a lot like that, but he was taking up for her honor. That was as close as she'd gotten in a year's time of infatuation.

Guido's hands shot up in the air just as Harry shoved him back into his rickety chair. "Peace, brother. I'm just pointin' out the facts, man. Look, the spells I cast are mostly just bullshit. Yeah, yeah, I take their money because like I said, I gotta eat. But I've only had three incidents. Three times where I really tried to do this right by readin' from that hokey-ass book. Shit went kooky, but they were all accidents. Kinda like your hot girlfriend and her accident."

Harry growled in response, a low hum Mara recognized as menacing.

She put her hand back on Harry's shoulder and squeezed it, telling herself it was to settle him down rather than just experience the firm, round muscle of his flesh beneath her fingers. "Finish, Guido. Hurry. I make no promises he won't shift at this point. It could get hairy—literally."

Guido gripped the edge of the table. "Since then, I just fake it. I'm not in this to hurt anyone. I make everyone sign a disclaimer, all legal-like, so I don't have to deal with the repercussions if the spell actually works. Most times, it doesn't work well because I don't know what the hell all that mumbo jumbo in that book I inherited means. Or if it does work, I can't pinpoint how I made it work. I just know I don't guarantee shit."

Harry bristled, sitting up in his chair. "So I'm guessing this means I paid you to trick me so you had grocery money? That's a lot of grocery money, man . . ."

Guido gave him a guilty look and, reaching into his pocket, he dropped a wad of bills on the table using his fingers to push them at Harry.

Mara grabbed the wad of bills with a gasp. "Guido! This is an indecent amount of money for probably nothing. Shame on you."

"So no go on the werewolf reversion after drinking what tasted like toxic waste?" Harry asked, shoving half the wad back at Guido because the Harry she knew had a good heart.

Guido toyed with the bills, finally looking at Harry, gratitude filling his eyes. "Probably not, but you never know, right? The mishaps like the mute guy happened in the adjustment phase of this crazy. Since then, I've stayed away from the general population, and I guess whatever this thing I was given is, it evened out. As long as I'm around all this stuff that was mysteriously shipped back from Africa with my personal belongings—" he pointed to the

mason jars, and dried skulls hanging from the ceiling "—the voo-
doo crap, or whatever it's called, seems to stay quiet. It's just when
I try to leave everything all behind and start a new, voodoo-free
life things go to hell in a fruitcake. So I stay to protect everyone
else. But I need to have food and shelter. I won't apologize for that."
He pulled his shoulders back tight, shooting them all a defiant look.

"So what did you give Harry?" Mara was suspicious again. And
afraid. Very afraid.

He shot a dismissive hand up. "Just some dirt from my garden,
and some fresh herbs with some banana seed oil. I think. I mix it
up with coconut milk and a Capri Sun to hide the flavor."

Harry chuckled. "You need to work harder. It was disgusting."

Mara finally felt comfortable enough to sit. She grabbed the last
toppled chair, her anger passing and sympathy setting in. How
awful to never be able to see your family again because you might
turn them into a mute—or a toad. "So what about all these experi-
ments gone wrong we heard about. If you're so innocent, how'd
they happen?"

"I've screwed up pretty royally a few times now, but it wasn't
on purpose. I really was trying to do what I'm supposed to do—my
destiny, as the villagers called it," he defended with a scoff.

Though it was with a defeated air to it. One that left Mara sad.

"But after Carl, I learned my lesson and stopped trying to fulfill
my destiny. I'd rather be a crappy witch doctor than screw up like
I did with Carl. Now, mostly, I fake it. I jump around—shake some
maracas, make stupid noises, and dance like I saw some tribal dudes
do on Nat Geo. Then I take the cash so I can afford to eat canned
ravioli and, sometimes when the greens are right, a can of tuna.
I'm livin' the witch doctor life, people."

A loud scraping noise from the back of Guido's shack startled
them all. When the noise groaned and snorted, Nina was on her
feet, leering down at Guido. "What the fuck?"

"Jesus, what is it with you and all the snarling? Relax, lady. It's just Carl."

The moaning and grunting became louder, almost enraged.

"What the fuck is a Carl?" she roared seconds before a large, grayish blue figure with stringy hair and hands the size of slabs of meat stumbled into view.

Harry was up on his feet and shoving Mara away in an instant, his strong hands forcing her behind him. "Is that what I think it is?"

Oh, sweet heaven. Mara nodded, but words eluded her. She didn't even have time to appreciate Harry's forceful touch on her body.

"It is not," Harry mumbled, shaking his head as if doing so would make it all go away.

She cleared her throat after a gulp. But it was . . . "Oh, yes. Yes, I believe it is."

"Do you think Daryl's got some free time on his hands?"

Mara's eyes widened as the thing identified as Carl, arms ramrod straight, his gait hindered by a limp, headed straight for Nina. "I'd even settle for Andrea right now. I know that sounds lame, because really her libido does most of the talking, but she was pretty righteous with a knife."

"You watch *The Walking Dead*?" Harry yelled, sounding surprised as Carl broke tables and howled a pitiful wail in his effort to get across the room.

Who didn't watch *The Walking Dead*? "Like it's my religion!" she screamed back when Carl launched himself at Nina.

Where was Rick when you needed him?

CHAPTER
6

"Carl? When Auntie Nina says stop slobbering on her, knock it the fuck off. And dude, something has to be done about your death-breath."

"We have a zombie," Harry mumbled, obviously still dazed.

Mara clucked her tongue, rooting in her purse for the keys to her front door. "We do, in fact, have a bona fide sorta zombie." Sorta because, well, there had been some glitch no one could explain when Carl became a zombie. A glitch Mara still wasn't sure she understood, and instead, decided to accept at face value.

Nina, on the other hand, had dubbed Guido unfit to parent his massive mistake gone wrong. After Guido had explained Carl was mostly harmless, and the parts of his mind still in working order liked vegetables, not brains and flesh, she'd declared Carl unkempt and mismanaged and had all but snatched him from Guido, daring him in her colorfully, loud, frighteningly scary way to tell her she couldn't have him.

Carl had latched onto Nina in much the way Fletcher and Mimi had, and when she'd tried to leave, he'd moaned and groaned loud enough to make Guido's shack of witch doctoring tremble with his unhappy distress.

After seeing the state of the room Guido had tried without much success to contain him in, and the complete disarray of his appearance, Nina was convinced Carl was helpless, trapped in a body that, while not in tip-top physical condition, was still useful and worthy.

And that had been that. She'd loaded Carl into her SUV like he was Charlie and made Mara drive so she could sit in the back and bond with him.

Nina flicked Harry's head with two fingers. "Look, Harry, I wasn't going to leave him with that asshat Guido. If it weren't for you, I'd be heading for a fucking bag of O neg and some shut-eye with my fam right now. You were the dipshit who thought you could be turned back into a human, which led us to poor Carl. Who, I might add, is a perfectly good half-assed zombie. He just needs a little fucking attention and some rules. Like all kids. So shut the fuck up and suck up your werewolf fate. 'Cus I'm tired of your pissy-ass whining."

"You brought a zombie home," Harry repeated, a mixture of horror and wonder in his voice. "Like you went to the pound and adopted a puppy."

Nina flicked another finger at him again. "He's not a full zombie, Harry. You heard Guido. He's only three-quarters dead. When Guido found him on his doorstep, dead or some such shit, and tried to fix him, he performed one of his lame-ass spells, fucked it up, and only half turned him into a zombie. Carl's just like you. Like me. *An accident.* Wanna sing 'We Are The World'?" she asked on a cackle, slapping Harry's back as they made their way along the winding, cobbled path of dormant rosebushes and various hedges leading to Mara's beloved guesthouse-turned-cottage.

Mara unlocked her periwinkle blue front door, taking no pleasure or solace tonight in the calming color she'd spent two solid "will it be welcoming enough?" weeks deciding upon. She propped the door open, letting Nina lead Carl into her house with Harry right behind them.

After Guido had assured them what he'd said earlier was true and all he'd really given Harry was a mixture of coconut milk and herbs mashed up in a grape Capri Sun, and that his intention had been to merely bilk Harry out of two thousand dollars, Nina had read Guido's mind to be sure the acrid scent they'd encountered when they'd arrived really was just a burnt grilled cheese sandwich.

Satisfied he was telling the truth, they'd driven home with Harry following close behind under Nina's eagle eye—oh, and more than one threat that if he tried to make a break for it, she'd hunt him down and eat his testicles like foie gras on toast points.

Harry—large, painfully lost, and much tamer than he'd been back at Guido's—stood in the middle of her living room, looking ridiculously out of place amongst the large planters stuffed full of silk blue, white, and purple hydrangeas.

His mouth opened as he backed up against the moss green wall with the bleached white wainscoting she'd just painted, but no words came out. He slammed his lips shut, compressing them into a tight line.

Carl gave him an awkward thump on the back and a misshapen crooked smile as Nina led him into Mara's kitchen and opened her stainless steel refrigerator in search of fresh vegetables for the zombie she'd apparently adopted.

This, much like the scenario she'd created about Harry's house, was not how she'd pictured him in hers. He definitely hadn't been a curmudgeonly werewolf, and his clothes were never on for longer than the two seconds it took to rip them off. Before ripping off hers, that is.

Harry ducked under the copper pots hanging from the thick block of whitewashed wood above his head and leaned on the counter, his beautiful eyes a little dull, probably on overload with still more paranormal crazy. "Carl is a zombie. But not a flesh-eating zombie, a vegetable-eating zombie." His words were wooden, but still calm. That was good. Calm beat sassy.

"Half zombie," Mara corrected, looking down at her feet, noting she still had some work to do on her newly installed barn wood floors. She just couldn't seem to get the right color throw rugs for it.

"Who doesn't eat people."

Her head bobbed. To Harry, this was clearly nuts. For Mara, it was just another day in the life—and in this moment, a distraction. A sweet, adorable, if not smelly one. "Right. Just vegetables, broccoli being his favorite. Lots of broccoli, according to Guido."

She lifted her eyes in time to catch Harry cocking his head. "But if he's a zombie . . ."

"Half zombie, rocket scientist. Stop stereotyping, dude," Nina quipped with a grin as Carl consumed a package of carrots, plastic wrapper and all. She thrust a napkin at him, showing him how to wipe his mouth with gentle hands.

"I don't understand," Harry responded, limp and almost lifeless, as he looked on at the scene unfolding before him.

"What's to fucking understand, dude? Guido told you—Carl was near dead and bleeding out. He was gonna die in a matter of seconds anyway. There wasn't time for nine-one-one or any of that shit. Guido just tried to save him. Decent, considering he's a shyster."

"This," Harry pointed at Carl's discolored skin and toddlerlike eating habits with a grimace, "is saving him? What kind of life can he have? Leaving him like this, with no ability to communicate and only a small portion of his brain functioning, was considered a save in your world? I don't like your world."

Nina gave him the finger, her eyes angry. "You don't like anything today, do you, widdums?" she cooed. "Guess what? That's too bad, pal, 'cus here the fuck you are. You heard what Guido said—he tried to help him. I know he's telling the truth because I read him. Carl's the result of a botched spell to save him gone wrong. An accident. Just like you, Harry Emmerson. Not all the facts add up, blah, blah, blah."

"But," Harry began another protest, one Mara was sure was filled with quality-of-life stats.

Nina's face went angry, her eyes flashing at Harry. "Who the fuck are you to decide, dude? And what's the point? Carl's here—right now. It's already done, ass-sniffer. If you don't like that I decided his life, no matter how insignificant to *you*, is worthy, ask me how much I give a fuck. Or better yet, you take him out and end his insignificance, why don't you? You got the balls for that, *Harry*? 'Cus you're gonna have to go through me to do it. Good luck, Chuck."

Instantly, Harry's face held an apology mingled with horror. "No!" he immediately responded. "That's not what I meant. I mean . . . I don't know what I mean—it's just . . . I don't get . . ."

Nina's mood instantly changed, her tone held disgust and impatience. "Yeah, yeah. You don't get it. We've done this already tonight. We told you some shit just can't be explained. But did you listen? Nah. Why the fuck would you listen to us bunch of brainless twits whose collective IQ doesn't total even half of yours? 'Cus you know better. Right, Harry?" Nina asked, handing Carl a head of cauliflower. "And if you touch my zombie, I touch you. Trust when I tell you it won't be like your mother's touch."

Mara's hand flew up before Harry's calmer state became riled again. She liked this Harry much better. He was easier on her shattered nerves. "Stop. Both of you. Please. Harry's exhausted, Nina. He's saying things I'm sure he doesn't mean due to situation normal all effed up. I'm exhausted, too. Please, let's not bicker anymore. Let's not beat Harry up for trying to make sense of all this. Let's just agree to let this sit until tomorrow. Which is in two hours for lab geeks like me."

Harry's delicious ass found one of her padded stools at the breakfast bar. He ran his hand through his unkempt hair when a revelation clearly dawned on him. "Work . . . I forgot about work. How the hell am I going to work?"

"Just like I do," she said, tamping down a new rush of irritation. "You know, you get up, grab a shower. In my case, throw on some lip gloss in a lame attempt to gussy up, blow-dry your hair. Have some coffee, pack a lunch, get in your car, drive, park it in the parking lot, take the elevator—"

"I meant as a werewolf!" he yelled down at her, slamming his fist against the counter, his face again rigid and red.

Carl shuffled, mewling a small groan at Harry's angry words, hiding behind Nina.

Nina took his enormous, gray blue hand and patted it to comfort him before slapping Harry on the head. "Quit goddamn well upsetting my zombie, you loudmouth. He's already freaked out by all the extra stimulus. Stop making it worse. Jesus, Harry. Get it together. You go to work and play with all those stupid numbers just like before you were a werewolf. Stop being a pansy."

"And I hide this"—he tugged at the fringes of his freshly grown, albeit scraggly beard—"how? I get the feeling if I come in clean shaven and by the time lunch rolls around I look like ZZ-Top, I dunno, but I think there might be some uncomfortable questions!"

Nina was in his face in an instant, growling a warning to ease up.

Harry backed right off, as though he were trying to contain himself and his newfound rage. "Apologies," he offered, contrition clearly written all over his face. "It just happens."

Mara let her forehead rest on the cool granite of her counter, her grainy eyes sore. Shit. He was right. His hair growth was out of control, not to mention his mood swings. What if someone added some numbers on an invoice incorrectly, and Harry went ballistic on them?

Worse, everyone werewolf would smell his change. How were

they going to hide that? "Did Marty say how long the adjustment period takes, Nina? I forget . . ." Good, God. She'd ruined this man's life. Intruded, invaded, disrupted his world and completely taken it over. Hell wasn't fit for her.

Nina took Carl by the hand and led him to a stool next to Harry, shaking her finger at him to warn him he should sit and stay. When he reacted appropriately by grunting and giving her that almost endearingly crooked smile, she stroked his stringy hair and smiled back before saying, "Longer than know-it-all Harry has."

"I have to work. I have to take the kids to school. I have to be there for them."

Mara immediately melted again. His dedication to his sister's children outweighed his shitty mood shifts. Sympathy and more remorse than her gut could handle overwhelmed her. "I'll take care of it. You have sick days, right? Call in werewolf and I'll handle everything else. Okay?"

Harry swallowed hard, rolling his thick shoulders. "And the kids? How am I going to explain what's happening to me to them? They're smart enough to know I can't grow a beard overnight. And the car-pool ladies? They're always asking personal questions about me, bringing me casseroles, trying to help with the kids. How do I explain this to them?"

Mara fought a sarcastic, maybe even jealous snort. She'd just bet the car-pool ladies were very interested in Harry. He was single, struggling with two children who'd lost a parent, and he had no idea how ungodly hot he was. He was the perfect prey.

"Don't you worry about shit, Harry. I'll handle the chicks in minivans with the tuna casseroles, and the kids, too. Marty and Wanda'll help. You're gonna stay the hell put here at Mara's, and shut your yap until we can figure this out."

Harry's face held concern. "Will handling them involve crude language and cracked ribs? The ladies of the Cedar Crest Elementary car pool are the only people who actually like me these days. And they bring me food. Sometimes, it's even edible. I don't want to risk a shutout because you beat one of them up. And there are the kids to think of . . ."

Nina chuckled finally, relieving some of the tension between them. "I'll let Miss Clairol Number Two-twenty-two deal with the broads. She's good at shit like that. I won't fuck anything up for Fletcher and Mimi. I like 'em. But I don't like you. Remember that."

"Don't vampires need to sleep during the day?" Harry asked, then made an odd face with a look that said he couldn't believe he was actually asking something so absurd.

"Don't kids go to school during the day, Harry? Marty and Wanda'll take the day shift. I'll handle the night shift. Plus, I got a kid of my own so I'm used to losing sleep. Especially with a vampini who's teething."

Harry's dark head shot up. "Vampini?"

Nina grinned—because it was in reference to Charlie. Clearly not because of Harry. "You really wanna know, dude? Or do you wanna let the rest of this shit sink in before I freak your already freaked-out ass some more?"

Harry shook his head and almost smiled, but he covered it swiftly with a frown. "Full up on the freak, thank you."

"I'll help, too, Harry," Mara assured, rearranging the fake lemons she'd stacked in a black wire basket to avoid the sudden rush of heat her cheeks felt when she thought about working so closely with Harry. "I can watch the kids and whatever else you need."

"No fucking way," Nina interjected with the shake of her finger, slapping lightly at Carl's hands when he reached over her to grab at one of the vases on the counter. "You go to work just like you always do. You want the council up your ass? We need to keep all suspicion off you until we can figure this mad-assery out. Until then, you do what you do and keep it on the down low. That means no nerd-girl confidentials with that weirdo clan of smart broads you hang out with either."

Her fingers trembled, making her drop the lemon. How would she hide this from Astrid, Ying, and Leah? She sucked about as much at subterfuge as she did at playing the role of vixen.

She was going to the werewolf pokey for this, for sure. She'd forgotten all about the council in the rush to convince Harry everything would work out. No. She would own this and pay the consequences. "I have to tell them, Nina. I have to own up to my actions. They'll find out anyway. All the other weres at Pack will smell the change in Harry. I'm headed for the big house."

Harry placed a hand on her arm, the simple action, painfully innocent, sent a rush of blood to all of her limbs, leaving her warm and tingly. "They don't have to know. I said I wouldn't tell them, and I meant it."

Mara shook her head firmly. "Harry? Take a whiff. A really deep whiff like this." She inhaled long and exaggerated for his benefit.

Harry mimicked her, his gorgeous eyes widening. He gripped the edge of the counter to anchor his big body in place, the realization so great.

She waved a finger at him. "See? You can smell everything, can't you? Every last splinter of wood on the floor, every last carpet fiber—everything. There's no hiding your change. The others will smell it instantly. And you then have two choices. Rat me out or let them think you're infiltrating Pack. You so don't want an investigation on where you came from to happen. We know our own kind by scent, Harry. We know fellow pack members. We can identify other weres from other packs, too. All of the people you've worked with for all this time who are were are going to know you've been turned. And then the hunt for the perp begins."

Mara fought a visible gulp. God, that would not be pretty. "So I'm going to avoid that at all costs and confess. I don't want you to suffer any more change or discord in your life because I screwed up."

Nina reached around Harry and yanked Mara's hair. "Shut the fuck up, Short-Shot. You're going to go to work, shut your piehole and let me, Wanda, and blondie figure this shit out. They made an exception for Keegan when he jazzed Marty up, they'll make one for you."

Right. Because Keegan's accident was so much like a baby-making accident. "The council isn't going to like that I was toying with tradition, let alone DNA, Nina, and you know it. I purposely and willfully created a serum to impregnate myself. I didn't wait to find my mate. I didn't procreate the old-fashioned way. I know the council. I'm going to do time for this, and I accept that as my punishment."

Harry jumped up from his stool, outrage on his face, making Carl cringe. "Who the hell is this council? Is it like the FBI equivalent of the werewolf contingency? People are artificially inseminated all the time. What kind of archaic criminal system do you people have in place?"

"Human people do it all the time. Not werewolf people," she whispered, a stupid batch of tears threatening to fall. "Look, Harry. We live by different rules than humans. We live by different rules because we *are* different than humans. We have advantages humans don't. Because we want to live peacefully amongst them, we have a strict code of honor—one I stomped all over in my desire to be a mother. Which I'll tell you all about tomorrow, after I go to work and pretend I didn't ruin your, Mimi, and Fletcher's lives. Now," she croaked, pushing back her stool, "I need to grab an hour or so before I have to get up and go to work, so no one will become suspicious. I'm going to collapse on overload if I don't catch my breath. You do just like Nina said, and after work, we'll figure the rest of this out. But please leave all the worry and planning to us. Deal?"

Harry nodded, that faraway look in his eyes. "I'll do what you ask—*for now,* but I won't let you go to jail for this, Mara—or whatever crazy medieval punishment your people exact to punish you for something very twenty-first century."

She boldly reached forward and pressed two fingers on the warmth of his lips, allowing herself only a brief second to treasure it, her own lips trembling in time with her fingers, and said, "Tomorrow we'll talk, but please, if you do anything else tonight while you're thinking about the day's events, remember I'm really sorry."

She shot a look of thanks to Nina before escaping to her bedroom and shutting the door so Harry wouldn't see her cry like a pathetic weakling.

Diving for her bed, she drove her hands under the yellow and blue eyelet shams and yanked the pillows over her head to cover her sobs.

Mimi, Fletcher, and Harry's face circled her brain, flashing in her mind's eye, still pictures of the moments they'd only just recently shared stamping their imprint.

And she was ashamed. Ashamed her selfish carelessness had created a problem she couldn't take back.

She'd taken from Harry in an even bigger way than just an ordinary accident. She'd involved children he might never be able to tell about his true nature. Might never be able to share with them the rituals of the pack he'd now become an unwilling member of because he'd have to hide what she'd done to him.

And she'd have to go into work tomorrow and hide her gut-wrenching guilt over ruining three lives, and somehow manage to get through the day without exposing herself.

She was a crappy liar.

That was her last thought before she set her phone's alarm and drifted off into a fitful succession of disjointed dreams involving handcuffs and prison guards.

CHAPTER
7

"Where have you been?"

Mara instantly froze at the sound of her friend Astrid's voice, guilt and panic washing over her in a wave of chills.

So, yeah, where have you been, Mara? Have you been with Hairy Harry, helping him accept his werewolf-ism, one you created in a lab like some crazy mad scientist?

She looked down at her phone to read the text Harry had sent her, keeping her eyes averted. "What do you mean, where have I been? I've been here all morning. Right here. At Pack. Doing Pack things . . ." *Shut your piehole,* she heard Nina whisper in her head. *Less is more, twit.*

Astrid placed a hand on her shoulder to thwart her escape up the wide escalator in the center of Pack's busy atrium. She turned her around, her full face, almost always serious and rosy-cheeked, displayed a frown. She sniffed the air around Mara, her round eyes full of skepticism. "No, you weren't. I looked everywhere for you on my morning break. I texted you, called you. No one could find you in the lab either."

Oh, right. That was probably because she'd been in the ladies' room while she pondered the slammer, hurling every last ounce of her morning coffee, vomiting her guilt up in chunks of last night's dinner, one messy heave at a time.

She'd decided to stick as closely to the truth as she could. Astrid was genius-level smart—one little thing out of place on an average day made her paranoid and suspicious.

The magnitude of the secret she had would turn Astrid's world upside down. And she'd be angry if Mara didn't confide in her. Astrid's self-esteem, right along with hers, suffered. They just suffered in very different ways.

Astrid's low self-esteem led her to believe everyone was making fun of her and she was just missing the subtext of their snide jokes. She wasn't good in crowds, she wasn't good with change, and she especially wasn't good at sharing a friend. She hoarded Mara like an intervention was needed.

Sometimes, like today, when panic was clear in Astrid's voice, it choked her—smothered her naturally loner tendencies. Sometimes she also had to remind herself that one-on-one, she really enjoyed Astrid's company. She just didn't enjoy her Saran Wrap–like cling.

A deep breath later and Mara lifted her eyes to meet her friend's, knowing the slightest thing could set sensitive, meek Astrid off. "I didn't feel very well. I was probably hugging a toilet in the bathroom." Mara ran her hand over her stomach. "See? Bloated. Gross." She exaggerated, letting her tongue hang out of her mouth, making a gagging noise.

Astrid's hand went to her forehead, concern in her sharp blue eyes. "You don't feel warm," she commented in a suspicious tone as if Mara'd purposely gone off shopping and lunching without her. "In fact, you feel fine."

Should've felt me last night when I was pressed up against Harry at

Guido's. No. She couldn't say that. Mara forced a smile to her lips. "Do I have to feel warm to not feel well?"

Did that sound defensive? You know, like I'm lying?

Astrid paused, her hand going to the signature butterfly barrette holding her dirty blond bangs off to the left side of her head, a self-conscious gesture she made when she was uncomfortable. She adjusted it and made a face. "Touchy much?"

Mara jammed her phone into the pocket of her lab coat and gave Astrid a look of apology. "Sorry. I'm just tired today."

Astrid nudged her shoulder, shooting her a secretive smile, toothy and wide. "So guess what I know that you clearly don't know, Crabby Patty?"

No. Why don't you guess what I know that you don't know instead? Here's what I know that you can't ever know. I turned my obsession into one of us. Then I stalked him to his house and tried to convince him being a werewolf is super cool.

Then I stalked him some more by hunting him down at the local witch doctor's to convince him being a werewolf isn't so bad for the second time in the span of five hours. And then my friend Nina came home with a zombie named Carl who eats vegetables, not people.

Instead, she just asked, "What?"

Astrid's face scrunched up. "I said guess," she ordered when Mara wouldn't play the game to suit her.

Astrid was also demanding not just as a coworker, but as a friend. However, she wasn't up to the game today. Mara scowled at her, squinting at the bright glare of winter sun from the atrium's ceiling. "I don't want to guess, Astrid!" The moment the words flew from her lips in a resounding echo, making the small clusters of people turn around, she clapped her hand over her mouth. *Way to do covert, jackass.*

Astrid's eyes went round with hurt before she shrugged her shoulders. "Then don't." She turned on her heel and began to stomp off, her white Crocs making a dull thud on the floor.

Regret washed over Mara, prompting her to grab Astrid's arm. "Damn. I'm sorry, Astrid. I am touchy today. I don't feel well, and I didn't sleep very well last night." Truth. Chasing your fantasy man all over Buffalo was a sure way to lose sleep. "So I'll guess, okay? You found a nonsurgical cure for small boobs, right? Phew. Just in the nick of time, too. Maybe bigger boobs are the answer to my manless problems?"

Astrid softened, giggling a low chuckle. "Harry's out sick."

"He's not sick," she was quick to correct until she saw suspicion on Astrid's face. "I mean, he is not? Shut the front door! Really? Harry's never sick." She injected as much disbelief as she could into her words.

Astrid was all things Harry. Knowing Mara had an enormous crush on him, her small group of friends often teased her about it, but Astrid took her job, and Mara's crush, very seriously.

She often reported things she'd heard, seen, thought she'd seen to Mara on a daily basis. Mostly, Mara humored her—today, when she was a liar whose pants were just shy of being on fire, she just wanted everyone to go away and leave her in her guilt.

But Astrid bobbed her head. Once more, Mara's confidante in all things Harry. "I know! But he's out today. Word is, he has a twenty-four-hour flu. I figured you'd want to know so you could make pretend chicken soup in your mind and make a pretend trip to his house to pretend to give it to him," she teased.

"Ha-ha. Funny Astrid. We all know, for as long as I live, I'm never going within a mile of him—ever. It's my own mental restraining order. Not after last year's Christmas party. Never again. No, sir."

Astrid seemed to take comfort in that just by the way she overall relaxed.

Mara often wondered if Astrid could keep her to herself and not have to share her with the other two girls in their hodgepodge of a group, if she'd finally realize that Mara was a loyal friend to her. If that would be enough to fill up her friendship cup.

"Well, anyway, he's not here for you to watch over a cup of steak soup while you pretend you're not really watching him."

"Bummer that. There goes a perfectly good visual lunch, huh?"

Astrid stuck her arm through Mara's. "It's okay. You have me. I'll share my steak sandwich with you. C'mon, let's go find a table in the cafeteria. I'm starved."

"Where are Leah and Ying? We were going to go over the results of those test samples during lunch for the new line of moisturizers Marty wants."

Astrid made a face. "Why do they always have to eat lunch with us? They're simple and crude."

Mara tilted her head. "They're just like us, Astrid. Just as smart, and we have a lot of things in common. That's why they eat lunch with us. Why do you almost always object?"

"Because they're not as smart as us, and you know it."

She didn't have it in her to soothe Astrid's unwarranted ruffled feathers. Today, of all days, she didn't want to cajole and coax her friend into eating a stupid sandwich at a table where two other women sat.

It was ridiculous under normal circumstances. In light of this day's tragedies, it was just intolerable. "Look, Astrid. I don't know why you have a beef with the other girls. They all like you. But it's becoming irritating. Now, I'm going to go find Leah and Jiaying and have some lunch. Either come or don't."

She didn't give her the chance to become angry or petty about the other girls. She turned on her heel and fought her way through the atrium to the cafeteria, leaving Astrid undoubtedly huffy.

Her phone buzzed then, making her frown. God, she hoped Harry was okay. Nina had left him in charge of Carl, so she could grab some vampire sleep, with strict orders to treat the zombie like a mischievous child who needed to be kept on track. Nina had decided Harry needed some sensitivity training where Carl was concerned, and she was throwing him into the training pool whether he liked it or not.

In the last text he'd sent, Harry said Carl had turned to her plastic vegetables and a chair leg to feed his never-ending hunger.

But it wasn't Harry texting her at all, it was Marty. She wanted to see Mara ASAP.

Oh, God. That could mean only one thing. Keegan knew. The wrath of Attila the Older Brother wasn't far off. It was his responsibility, as alpha pack male, to handle things like this, and somehow he'd found out what a dirty, dirty pool player slash baby-maker she was.

She'd been found out. It was over. Hello, orange and bars on your window.

On stiff feet, Mara flew up the escalator, running the steps rather than utilizing the electric movement.

"WE have a problem."

Another alarming thought stole her breath on her way to Marty's office. Harry's niece and nephew. Had they seen something? Her heart began pumping again, beads of sweat forming on her brow. "Are Fletcher and Mimi okay?" She swallowed hard. The last thing she wanted was for her egregious error to harm them.

Marty smiled from behind her large walnut desk. Her smile always warmed Mara. It was as much home as her mother's used to be. With a click of her computer's mouse, she was out of her chair and moving toward Mara, perfectly dressed in an empire-waist blue silk tunic with gold embroidery around the neckline, denim shrug, matching skinny jeans, and black pumps.

The ease with which she crossed the floor made Mara look down at her roughed-up white tennis shoes so Marty wouldn't see her envy. Marty could run a marathon in heels, while Mara would trip just putting them on.

She gave Mara one of her infamous hugs and went to sit on the small couch in the corner of her office. "They're fine. This morning, Wanda and I made pancakes with chocolate chip smiley faces and fresh strawberries, packed their lunches up, braided Mimi's hair, made Fletcher put on underwear, kissed them on the top of their adorable heads, and dropped them off at school. They're great kids, if not still in the business of taking advantage of Harry because he's so uncomfortable and unsure in his new role. But worry not—there was no advantage-taking today. Not with us. They're at school, safe and sound. Though, wow. Those car-pool ladies? You'd think they weren't married women the way they looked at us when we told them we were two-thirds of Harry's ménage."

It sounded like a morning similar to Hollis's, one Mara had witnessed time and again until she'd moved out. Marty was an amazing mother and Hollis was well-adjusted, if not precocious, because of it.

Wait. Ménage. Oh, God. "You did not say that to them."

Marty threw her head back and laughed out loud. "No. But I wanted to. We kept it easy and simple to thwart any questions or create any more lies we'd have to keep track of. But those women." She cringed. "If death by eyeball daggers were possible, we'd be deader than Nina. Oh, they're awful, and obvious. Painfully obvious. Harry should count his lucky stars Nina wasn't there. It would have been far worse than any verbal damage Wanda and I could do. Anyway, that's not the problem I'm talking about."

Terror raced in Mara's veins. Keegan knew. He was going to have to handcuff his own sister and drag her off to lycanthropic prison where she'd eat gruel and pound out license plates between her shifts in the laundry room. "Before you say anything, I know.

I'm sorry, Marty. I swear, I never meant for any of this to get so far out of hand. I know this could be an issue for you and Keegan if you keep it from him. I would never want to come between you two. I don't know what I was thinking. I was just . . ." What had she *just*? Just been looking to find an easy way out of hunting down a real relationship and doing the hard stuff that came with it because she'd been rejected? Just impatient?

Marty patted the red leather couch in her office with a hand. "That's not what this is about. Come sit with me."

Mara trudged to the couch like she was headed for her death and plunked down next to the sister-in-law she loved.

Marty tucked a knee beneath her, her eyes inviting and kind just like they always were. "First, not in a million years would I snitch to Keegan about this because we're family, Mara. Always. And no way am I handing you over to him just because he's the alpha of our pack. No matter what, you're family first, pack member second. Period. I won't hear it any other way. And before you say anything, I console myself with the fact that keeping this from him for a time is what I consider paranormal crisis counselor-client confidentiality. That you happen to be a part of that crisis is neither here nor there."

Relief washed over Mara, relief and gratitude. In this very moment, she was petrified of what would happen to Harry and his children. Her fear of the council was only secondary to helping Harry and the kids overcome their obstacles and adjust. She couldn't do that if she was in the pokey. "Thank you," she murmured low, because it was all she was capable of doing.

Marty lifted her chin, using her thumb to swipe at a stray tear on Mara's cheek. "I want to talk about what you said about me yesterday."

"What did I say yesterday?"

"You said you weren't as good at charming people with your

smile as I am, and that's why you're single. Why do I have anything to do with that?"

Mara let her head hang low with regret. "Poor choice of words. What I meant was, being with the opposite sex is easy for you." She shook her head. "Wait. What I mean is you relate well to those outside of your gender. I guess . . . I guess I envy that. No. That's not true. I totally envy it. Obviously, if I related better, I wouldn't be making werewolf babies in a lab. I'd be rutting until the cows came home, making babies the good old-fashioned way."

Marty chuckled. "And you're smart. I envy that. So there. We should activate our Wonder Twin powers. Imagine the shit that would rain down, huh?"

Mara's eyes filled with tears. She was tired, and worried, and the last thing she wanted to do was hurt Marty's feelings. "I really love you, Marty. I hope you know that. Since you came into our lives, into the pack, everything's been a million times better. *Everything*. I'm just really uncomfortable with men. You know, the norm. Small talk suckage, flirty suckage—I suck at all of it. You're a pro. Which is why you have Keegan and I have a baby-making serum."

"Oh, Mara. I wish you saw you the way we all see you."

"Geeky, nerdy, timid?"

Marty shook her head, the swish of her blond hair artful and perfect against the color of her denim shrug. "Gorgeous, genius smart, so totally unaware you can have anything you want."

Right. It always worked like that for women like her.

Marty cocked her head, taking Mara's hand in her perfectly manicured fingers. "You have it bad for our Harry, don't you, honey?"

"It borders on ridiculous."

"Making this situation a hundred times more uncomfortable for you."

"Times infinity."

"You know, I'd give you tips on how to flirt and all sorts of pointers if I thought that was you, sweetie. But it's not you, and that's okay. I wish you'd see that. It might be helpful when catching the prey, but it doesn't make a damn bit of difference when you want to keep it. What good does flirting do you when the hard stuff in a relationship comes along? Can you flirt yourself out of a financial hardship or a long-term medical issue? No. You need to be smart. You're smart, Mara. So, so smart. You're funny. You're gorgeous. You're gentle, and most of all, you're kind. Don't let that stop you from pursuing the things that you want—even after this is all water under the bridge."

Was there water under the council's prison bridge? Her grainy eyes filled with more unshed tears. She shook it off and laughed in irony, focusing on the flat screen TV in the far corner opposite the couch. "Well, I can want Harry for days, but he kind of has to want me back for it to work out."

"I don't just mean Harry. I'm not talking about a man, hunky Harry or otherwise. I mean wanting to parent."

"But—"

She flapped a hand upward to hush Mara, her chunky costume ring on her finger flashing with the gesture. "Oh, I know what the pack says," she said in that poo-poo way she had of dismissing something she didn't approve of. "The pack says all sorts of things— all sorts of stupid things. Remember the things they said to me? Sure you do. You were there when they carried on about how bad humans mating with werewolves was blah, blah, blah. The pack is all bark and almost no bite. If you want to artificially inseminate yourself, it's your damn body, and I'll fight to the death to see you have the right to do as you please with it as long as you're not harming yourself. The pack can suck it, as far as I'm concerned. Who are they to tell you, by whatever means you wish, you can't have a baby?"

"A baby?" Keegan roared, bursting through Marty's office door. Large and fit, his muscled build barreled to a stop in front of the women. "Mara's having a baby?" he bellowed, which was essentially the Keegan way. If no one answered you, you just yelled louder.

Marty jumped up just as Mara's face flushed red. She shrunk down into the cushiony softness of the couch while she watched Marty set about "handling" her brother. Marty was a pro at soothing Keegan's rougher edges. They offset each other in every way—a balance no one watching the two of them together could deny.

"Is that any way to greet your wife?" Marty purred up at Keegan, cupping his lean jaw and running her fingers through his graying temple.

"Remiss me. Lay one on me, Mrs. Flaherty. Hollis is just outside that door, waiting for me to take her home so we can have princess tea. You know, boas, tiaras, tea in those cups the size of my thumb? So make it count," he ordered on an indulgent chuckle.

Keegan did all sorts of girl-things with Hollis. He let her paint his nails, curl his hair, put makeup on him . . . When it came to Marty and Hollis, Keegan was just a pile of gooey mush. Her brother's family was everything Mara had ever wanted. He was a different man since meeting Marty five years ago.

Marty dutifully lifted her lips for a kiss, her tinkle of laughter sweet and light.

"Now, who's having a baby, ladies?" Keegan said against her lips, leaving one eye open to scan Mara's form on the couch with a critical gaze.

Mara's heart began that fluttering beat again. She was going to have to lie. Keegan would sense something was wrong with her, and then he'd interrogate it out of her. Then he'd know, and he'd have no choice as alpha but to take action.

Panic forced her to repeat the mantra, less is more, Mara. Shut up. Keep it simple.

Marty pulled back, hooking her arms around his waist, giving Keegan a frown, but forcing him and his penetrating gaze to focus on her, taking the heat off Mara. "No one's having a baby, silly. So quit interrupting conversations you're not invited to join. Mara and I are dishing. Girl-talk. Which means none of your business."

Keegan's hard jaw clenched tight. He narrowed his eyes, skeptical. "I feel like there's something going on I should know about. Yet I'm afraid to ask for fear it's nothing, and you'll cancel our wrestling match date to punish me for accusing you unjustly."

"You guys go to wrestling matches?" Mara managed to squeak from the couch, forcing her guilty panic to calm.

Marty swatted at Keegan's shoulder, her eyes full of the kind of affection Mara had grown so fond of witnessing. "No. That's what we tell Hollis we're doing. Let me just say this. Four-year-olds are the most inquisitive, nosy beasts on the planet. She's at the age where all she does is ask a question about everything. Especially when Mommy and Daddy make too much noise while we're, you know, wrestling." Marty winked, her long lashes sweeping her cheek.

Mara hopped off the couch, wrinkling her nose in teasing protest. "Okay. No explanations required. In fact, please don't explain. It's almost like hearing my parents talk about doing it," she joked.

Marty laughed, squeezing Keegan's hand before shooing him toward the door. "Mom's do it, too," she taunted. Turning to Keegan, she pointed toward the outer office. "Go. We have girl stuff right now. But tonight? After we put said nosy beast to bed? You. Me. A T-bone for two?"

Keegan planted a quick kiss on her cheek. "Ludmilla the Russian Spy, willing to do whatever it takes to get the super secret government formula from Heinrich, the suave, yet debonair millionaire? Even interrogate him, you know, wrestling match–style," he said over Marty's shoulder for Mara's benefit, laughing as he sauntered out the door.

Mara jammed her hands into her oversized lab coat, tugging at her lifeless turtleneck. "Well, that explains why I can't get a date. I need to change my name to Ludmilla and practice my Russian accent."

Marty pulled her into a hug, squeezing her close just as her cell phone rang. She dug it out of the back pocket of her skinny jeans and frowned before returning her eyes to Mara. "I've got to take this. But this conversation isn't over. I want to help you, honey. Not just Harry. Okay?"

"You got it. I have to get back to work anyway. See you later, *Ludmilla*." She laughed her way to the elevators, warmed that Marty and Keegan were truly so happy. She'd do anything to protect that—even if it meant lying to Keegan about Marty's involvement in the Harry incident.

On her way out the door, she caught Hollis and Keegan at the elevator. Hollis was the spitting image of Marty. Everything about her screamed "girlie" from her wispy blond hair, caught up in two barrettes with streaming ribbons on either side of her head, to the fashionably red and orange jumper dress she wore with complementing black tights and shiny red clogs. Save her smile. Her smile was all Flaherty. Wide, open, generous. "Aunt Mara!" She wiggled her excitement.

Mara bent down and scooped her up, dropping a kiss on the top of her golden head. "You are the prettiest thing I've seen since I went to the frog store to look at frogs."

Hollis giggled, her chubby cheeks rising upward in an angelic grin. "Frogs aren't pretty because they don't have lips. And frogs can't wear lipstick. See?" She puckered her lips. "I have on sparkly lipstick."

"Okay, fine. You have lips. That means you win the pretty prize!" Mara giggled at their private joke. She would come up with the ugliest thing she could think of to compare Hollis to, and Hollis would respond with something that never failed to make Mara fall more in love with her.

It was their ritual—one Mara cherished. "So, you off to give Daddy some tea and a pretty pink boa? Speaking of, when are you gonna come to Aunt Mara's and have girls' night? We'll watch movies and eat popcorn and stay up really late. Like at least till eight thirty."

Keegan came up behind her, draping his arm around Mara's shoulder. "Hollis has been begging to have a girls' night with you, but we didn't want to cramp your newfound independence."

When she'd made the choice to have a child, she'd also decided to move out of the house where Marty and Keegan still lived, along with, until just a few months ago, her brother Sloan. Keegan had offered the estate's guesthouse after her endless search for a reasonably priced apartment had turned up some questionable properties. While she knew it was due to Keegan's overprotective, bossy nature and the fact that Marty wanted to keep her close, she'd agreed only after Keegan and Marty agreed to accept monthly rent.

Despite what she was sure other employees thought, she was paid what any other lab tech was paid to work at Pack. Keegan had insisted on it, and it had been that way since she'd gotten her degree and come home from college ten years ago. As a Flaherty, you didn't piss away your portion of the proceeds from a Fortune 500 company. You worked to make it more successful.

Hollis wrapped her chubby arms around Mara's neck and squeezed, making Mara sigh contentedly with the scent of cupcakes and little girl. "So can I come over, Aunt Mara?"

Damn. What had she been thinking? *No, you can't come over, Hollis. Aunt Mara's hiding an angry man she's wildly attracted to and a half zombie named Carl under her bed.* Instantly, she fought her body's reaction to the lie she was going to tell. Forcing herself to relax, she smiled—an easy thing to do with Hollis. "Soon, pumpkin. I've got a lot going on these days while I'm fixing up the cottage. Bunches and bunches of stinky chemicals and paints, and I've been putting in a lot of overtime here at work. But I promise to call you soon, and we'll have a girls' night. Okay?" She gave her niece a pinch on the cheek, rubbing noses with her before handing her off to Keegan.

Who was frowning down at her.

He set Hollis down, directing her to push the button for the elevator. When he turned to her, his hard face was tight, his lips thin. "What's going on?"

"What do you mean, what's going on? What could be going on?" Using the Marty tactic, she feigned innocence with wide eyes and an exasperated snort. When being accused of something or asked a question about a situation you were absolutely up to your neck in, behave as though your accuser is crazy.

"I mean, what are you doing with your time these days?"

Also, when your accuser is poking around the accused, use humor. Marty tactic number two. Mara shrugged her shoulders and sighed forlornly. "Oh, the usual. You know, lab tech by day, dominatrix by night."

Keegan tapped the bridge of her nose with affection, but he wasn't smiling. "Funny, you."

Mara rolled her eyes at him and reminded herself to remain calm, but move on to tactic number three: appear irritated with her big brother for behaving, well, like a big brother. "Well, what do you think is going on Keegan? Nothing ever goes on in my life. I work. I go home. I renovate. Wash, rinse, repeat. The most exciting thing I've done this week is refinish the kitchen cabinets and clean my refrigerator."

But Keegan wasn't totally buying it. God, he was a nosy ass sometimes. He sniffed the air, a frown knitting his eyebrows together. "Something's not right. I can smell it."

And tactic number four in the Marty Handbook of Avoiding Getting Caught: get away. "*You're* not right. So knock it off, Keegan. I'm fine. Everything's fine. Look, I have to go. I have a ton of work down in the lab. So quit harassing me about my life and go live yours, pal." She turned to scurry toward the stairs, but Keegan grabbed her arm.

"Dinner tomorrow night? Sloan's coming. So is Jeannie. She's bringing her better-than-crack brownies." He smiled the way he used to when he was apologizing for interfering in her very adult life without actually saying the words.

But she warmed—only because she loved Jeannie, her brother's djinn-caterer wife. She made the absolute best pastries ever. How she managed to run the djinn realm and still keep her catering business going like gangbusters always left Mara so full of admiration. "Text me the time. And I accept your apology for being a nosy ass," she said on a laugh, standing on tiptoe to give him a quick kiss on the cheek before darting off to run for her guilty cover.

As she ran down a flight of metal stairs, her phone chimed a text from Wanda.

She paused to read it, her limbs growing shaky, her eyes widening. Her head swam, the words of the text blurring, then sharply coming back into focus as horror began to settle in her gut.

"Need you here STAT. Fletcher and Mimi are missing!"

CHAPTER
8

"Mimi?"

"Uh-huh?" she asked from the corner of her frightfully pink bedroom as she tried to force a bonnet onto poor Coconut's head. Amidst the clutter of her dolls and assorted play strollers, Mimi played like any other five-year-old would after school on a snowy day.

It was all Mara could do not to rush over to a seemingly unfazed Mimi and smother her with hugs and kisses chock-full of limb-shaking relief. Instead, after spending two hours with the police, being questioned as if she were the criminal, Mara approached her with an easy stride, smiling as she hunkered down next to her and poor tormented Coconut. "Can you tell me again what the lady who picked you up from school looked like?"

"I already told the policeman."

Mara nodded. "You sure did, and you did a great job, honey. I didn't hear all of it, though. So I was just wondering. No big deal."

Mimi shrugged agreeably. "She had hair just like you. Long and swingy," she murmured, stroking Coconut into submission. "But she wasn't as pretty as you are. She was just really nice to us," she assured Mara, her round eyes bright and totally minus the least bit of trauma. "She gave me this." Mimi held up her wrist to show her a bracelet, her name spelled out amongst the beading.

It was all Mara could do not to scream her anguish and horror, but she stayed as calm as possible. "And where did she take you when she gave you that, sweetie?"

Mimi made a face as Coconut began to protest his hat. Mara took her small hand and instructed, "Gently, honeybunch. Coconut doesn't understand what you're doing, and he's afraid. See?" She demonstrated by stroking Coconut's chin, fighting the panic thrashing her heart around like a ship lost at sea.

"I wasn't afraid," Mimi offered, easing her hold on Coconut until he sat in her lap, puffing her chest out to show her valor. "Auntie Nina said I should always be afraid of strangers no matter what, even if the lady didn't scare me, and even if she's nice to me."

So it was someone who had a rapport with children. "So where did she take you guys, Mimi?"

"Just on a quick walk, but we came right back and she said we were really good."

Terror raced through Mara's veins. *Who* would take Harry's children, unauthorized, from school? And where was the sitter, Cora, Harry's designated pickup? "And what did she say to you again?" she asked, her voice unsteady and trembling.

"She said to tell you and Uncle Harry she sees you. I think she meant to say hello. I forgot to tell the policeman about that."

Mara's blood ran cold just as Harry burst through the door, almost knocking her out of the way to get to Mimi. He scooped her up in his arms, pulling her to his chest.

The police had separated the adults from the children when they'd questioned them about the incident, and while Harry had answered questions succinctly and stoically, he was clearly allowing himself to feel the panic now that the dust had settled. "Are you okay?" He held her from him, letting her legs dangle as he assessed her from head to toe with a critical eye.

Mimi nodded, her deep eyes confused. The bob of her curly head was slow. "Uh-huh."

Harry pulled her close to his chest, burying his nose in her hair, taking deep breaths. For a brief moment, Mimi sunk into Harry's arms, giving him the opening he needed to cuddle her closer. From where Mara stood, she saw just the slightest tremble of his fingers, gripping Mimi so tight she then began to squirm.

Mara popped up, placing a hand on his arm. "She's okay now, Harry," she offered quietly.

Harry's lips thinned as he rested his head on top of Mimi's to eyeball Mara, his jaw tight. "Says the woman who used that word just yesterday. I think we have a difference of opinion on its meaning."

Oh yay. Mara-blaming Harry had arrived. She stiffened in guilt as a new fear began to reside in her gut. Did someone take the children because of what had happened yesterday? That made no sense. No one knew what happened yesterday but her, the girls, and Guido. "Listen, we need to set aside some of the other stuff for right now and talk."

Mimi squirmed in Harry's arms again, bracing her small hands on his forearms. "You're squeezing me too tight, Uncle Harry!"

Harry loosened his grip, letting Mimi slide down his legs until her purple-sneakered feet hit the floor and she went off to hunt down Coconut. "Someone, someone unauthorized, took my children, and Cora's nowhere to be found," he said between clenched teeth.

"Yeah. Someone did. And Cora's at home. Wanda checked in on her. She was fast asleep. So, WTF, Harry?" Nina groused, holding her hand out to Mimi who zipped across the room and took it as easily as if Nina had offered her candy.

She swung Mimi up in her arms, wrinkling her nose at Mimi with a warm smile. "So what did we talk about when we talked about strangers? Say it again for Auntie Nina so she knows you get it, pretty princess. It's more important than anything, like, *ever*."

Mimi nodded dutifully, her sweet face expressing thought. "You said no matter what, even if the lady says she knows Uncle Harry or you or Mara or anyone in my family, I can't go with her unless I know her and Uncle Harry gives me permission. And if she tries to take me somewhere, I have to scream like this!" Mimi opened her mouth and let out a squeal, long and high.

Nina winced, placing a finger over her lips to quiet her. "Not ever, ever. Got that? Stranger danger, right? And if someone tries to take you, a stranger or a bad person or maybe even someone who seems nice, but someone you don't know, what else are you supposed to do?"

Mimi paused in thought, her round face scrunching. "Say your name really loud?"

Nina held up her fist for Mimi to knock, popping it open to imitate it blowing up. "Boom, little lady. You remember that all the time, okay? Fletch, too. There are lots of bad people out there. No way I'm gonna let them hurt you, ever, ever. You call, I come, okay? Now, go find Aunt Wanda. She's taking you and your stinky little bro for some dinner and then ice cream."

This time, Mimi's squeal was of joy, but it made Harry blanch as he watched her scurry down the hall to locate Wanda. "You're scaring her," he accused, Angry Harry back at the helm of his I Hate Werewolves Ship.

"Dude, somebody's got to. Jesus. You can't even trust the school to look out for them! The kids need to know this crap, fucknuts. They're never too young to learn there's some bad shit out there. That's your job. If you won't do it, I'll damned well do it for you. You wanna stop me?"

He ran a hand through his hair, inhaling deeply, clenching and unclenching his fist. "We'll talk about that damn school later. For now, you're right. I don't know what made them go with this woman. I know my sister, and if I ever knew anything about her, I know she taught them better. I've taught them better. And who the fuck is this woman?" he seethed. "Wait, I know. Bet she has something to do with all of you."

Whoa. Harry swearing and accusing. Less and less like the Harry she'd once held a wedding, complete with doves and flowered arches, in her mind with. Fatigue, fear, and, in general, Harry's pissy mood left Mara pissy, too. They'd coddled, cajoled, apologized, catered to his grudge against being paranormal long enough.

Harry's poor-baby account was officially in the red.

Pushing Nina aside, Mara went on the attack. "Harry? Shut up. Stop being an asshole, come into the kitchen, sit the hell down, and let's figure this out. Because I'm damn tired of your crappy attitude. Yes. I, Mara Flaherty, turned you, Harry Emmerson, into a werewolf. Boo muthaeffin' hoo. It's done. There's no going back. Now either shut up and lay off the grudging, or I'm going home and leaving you here to your own devices. If you think you got this, then we'll all leave you to the getting. But don't you call me when the full moon comes and you don't know what to do when this," she yanked another stray tuft of hair sprouting from his cheek so hard he winced, "becomes a full-bodied event, because I'm going to tell you to—suck—it!" She spat out her last words in his face, standing on tiptoe, finger wagging under his nose.

Silence settled between them. Awkward and heated.

Nina cackled in Harry's face, clapping her hand on Mara's shoulder. "Nice, Short-Shot. Way to read your man."

Mara pivoted on her heel, staring up at Nina. "He is *not* my man! I'd never have a man as whiny and angry as him!" she yelped before storming off to the kitchen where she had to bite her knuckles to keep from slugging a contrite Harry in the face.

He trudged in behind Nina, his large body slumped, his eyes full of apology when he stood beside the stool in front of his small breakfast bar. "I'm sorry, Mara. The kids are the most important thing in the world to me. I wanted to kill anything in my path to get to them. I reacted badly. In short, I was a jackass."

Mara leaned over the counter, her expression full of outrage. "Like I don't know that? Like any child involved in a kidnapping, especially children I've managed to somehow screw over without even trying, isn't important to me, too, you jerk! You keep saying you're sorry, and I'll grant you some leeway because your hormones are on full tilt, but the hell I'll let you keep throwing this in my face when we have a much bigger problem. Now, sit down and shut it!" She jabbed a finger at the polished wood stool.

Harry did as he was told, making Nina snicker while pointing to a chair indicating Carl, looking sharp, if not still a little green, in his new jeans and sweater, should sit as well.

Rolling her shoulders, she tied her hair up with the rubber band around her wrist, fanning the back of her neck to keep her anger in check. "Now let's try and figure this out, rationally and logically."

Harry drummed his fingers on the counter. "Because there's so much of that involved in this."

His flippant response was the last nail in his coffin. Her temper, usually almost nonexistent, didn't just flare, it exploded. "Didn't I say to lay off, Harry? If not, let me say it again. Lay the hell off!" she roared, unable to stop the forward thrust of her wildly shifting emotions.

Without warning—a rarity indeed—her mouth opened wide before she could stop it.

And then, it was all hair, limbs, and big, snarling teeth. Drool, too. She distinctly felt drool flying from her muzzle.

Right there in the middle of Harry's black-and-white kitchen.

"WHERE the fuck is Carl, Harry?"

Harry had either learned his lesson or he was in a state of quiet terror. He shook his head to indicate he didn't know.

"Damn it, Harry, didn't I tell you to watch him while I cleaned this shit up? Jesus, dude. We can't have a zombie running the hell around your nice suburban neighborhood, loose and shit with humans. Are you nuts?" She stomped out of his kitchen and headed to the door leading to Harry's small backyard, where he'd installed a swing set for the kids.

"You have a zombie, and I'm the one who's nuts?"

"Half zombie," Mara reminded, cracking her knuckles and stretching her arms to readjust in her human form.

Harry nodded while Mara used his Dustbuster to clean up the remnants of her very angry, tumbleweed of hair shift. She dropped it back in its charger and brushed her hands together, before tying one of Harry's shirts tighter around her thighs. "Ready to talk like adults now and figure this out? Or do you want to hold a grudge and sulk some more?" she asked, still angry.

Harry leaned forward on the counter, crossing his lean forearms. His eyes had lines around them from lack of sleep, and his skin was chalky white. "You were naked."

Mara lifted her chin. She would not hide—even if he'd seen every last ounce of cellulite on the backs of her thighs and the dimples on her ass cheeks. She was a werewolf and damned proud of it. Sometimes, when stupidheads like him made her angry and frustrated, she shifted. Too bad. "I was. Bet you'll shut up from now on, won't you?"

"That was insane."

"Me naked?"

"Yes. No. I don't know. It was all just insane."

Mara clucked her tongue at him, strangely empowered now that she'd cleared the air. Children were being snatched. Someone had to take control. "That was me really angry."

"Wow."

Her eyes fell to the floor with her next admission. "That's only happened twice before in my life. I'm usually pretty easygoing. Which means you really irked me."

"Third time's a charm," he quipped, only this time, he actually followed it up with a small smile to indicate he'd mildly amused himself.

She used that as her in to question him. "So let's figure this out. How could the school allow Mimi and Fletcher to leave with someone unauthorized? Don't they have to have permission slips or something?"

Harry nodded, his expression grim, his eyes full of concern. "According to Principal Ditter, no one saw them leave—classes weren't even out yet. They were at recess, which means they were talked into going with this person from the playground, if what the teacher says is right. Principal Ditter sounded the alarms and called me when neither of them showed up for last period. But according to her, no sooner had she sent out a search party than the kids were back on the school's premises. It all happened so damn fast. One minute I was babysitting Carl, the next the principal was calling to say she couldn't find the kids. Who would want to take my kids, Mara, and why?"

Harry's grief, his statement thick with it, shoved the last of her anger aside, letting in sympathy and yet more fear. Mara reached out and squeezed his hand, relishing the warmth of his skin before she pulled away. "I don't know. But we won't let anyone hurt them. I swear that to you, Harry. So, did you notice the bracelet Mimi had on? She said the lady with the swingy hair like mine gave it to her. It had her name on it, Harry. Did Fletcher come back with anything unusual, too?"

Harry shook his head, his eyes bereft, his mind clearly sifting through his conversation with Fletcher. "No. Nothing. And his description of this woman was the same as Mimi's. Except he said when she dropped them off, as she ran away, she got all blurry. He said she was really fast. 'Superhuman fast' were his words."

Mara gripped the edge of the counter. Blurry? What would make a child describe a scenario like that unless the person doing the running wasn't human? Humans didn't get blurry when they ran. "Someone paranormal . . ." The words slipped from her lips before she could stop them.

"So this does have to do with all of you?"

Mara tilted her head, certain she hadn't heard an accusatory tone in his voice, just a simple question. "That makes no sense, Harry. No one knows about you but Guido and us. And he doesn't know about the kids unless you told him. No one at Pack even knew the kids existed. They still don't, as far as I know. How could they unless you told them? HR doesn't even know about them."

Harry's head popped up, his dark hair bristling against the collar of his shirt. "You looked at my file?"

"Before you get all hormonal on me, yes. Once I found out about Mimi and Fletcher, I wanted to be sure I didn't make things worse in case you didn't want anyone at work to know about them. You weren't answering your texts and I was sweating the small stuff. So I peeked at your insurance information to see if you'd put them on the plan. That's it. I was just trying to keep track of my lies."

"Then I don't get it. I just know they can't go back to that school until we find out who this person is. Maybe never, at that. Because after today, it's obvious their security is lax. No way am I taking a chance someone could grab them if it was that easy to do it, and I've said as much to Principal Ditter and the police when they questioned the kids and me."

Oh, she could almost hear the weeping and wailing of the car-pool ladies now. "Okay. So next question. Until we find this person, how do you feel about them staying with Wanda while you adjust? We can't have them witness a shift until we know you can control it."

Harry's head cocked. "But isn't she out on the Island? That's too far from me. I *need* to see them."

Mara shook her head. "What choice do we have? I'd bring them back to Pack, if you'd all just let me. But nooo, everyone's worried about me getting caught for turning you, even though that's going to happen anyway. So we can send them to Wanda. Heath's away right now, so he won't be there to tell anyone. She keeps normal daytime hours, or they can play Count Dracula with Auntie Nina and Carl the Zombie."

Nina barged through the back door, holding Carl by his belt loop. "Sit, buddy. When I tell you to stay with Harry, you stay the hell with Harry. Do you want to end up kidnapped by the bad people? No. You do not. Because then I have to kill the bad people if they hurt you. That's always a shitty mess."

Though his face always had that crooked, almost misshapen turn to it, his eyes said he'd been caught doing something he knew he shouldn't have. He folded his chin to his chest in remorse as he sat on a stool and put his head on Harry's shoulder.

"So the issue of the kids. You wanna see them on Skype for a little while or on a website's sidebar, Harry?" No Holds Barred Nina asked, jamming her hands into her hoodie's pocket.

Harry grimaced, clearly realizing his choices were few, and Nina was only pointing out the reality of it. He reached over and patted Carl's head to comfort him when he stirred. "And how will we explain to the kids what's going on? They hardly know all of you, and I'm just going to send them to stay with Wanda for an indeterminate amount of time?"

Mara's lips set into a firm line. She sighed, releasing the pent up air in her lungs. "Then that settles it. I don't want the kids to be unhappy or usurped. They've had more than enough change in their lives. If you think there's even a small chance that'll happen, let me tell my brother what I've done. You can stay here with the kids. Wanda, Marty, and Nina can show you the way of the werewolf—"

"And you can go to werewolf jail? Nope. Not while I'm still breathing." He gazed directly at her, his eyes capturing hers and holding them.

His answer, so "I dare you to tell me otherwise," caught her off guard. Even Harry didn't look like he understood where this sudden need to keep her out of the big house came from.

Mara's breathing all but halted. There was almost nothing but Harry's eyes locking with hers and the sound of their lungs taking in air. He was protecting her, which wouldn't work for long against the council, but still . . .

Nina waved a hand between the two of them and snapped her fingers. "We have shit to figure out, kiddies. Let's get on with it." She rolled her shoulders, cracking her neck. "I damn well just told Wanda last night this shit would turn ugly. Fuck if I can remember a single time one of our cases hasn't."

"Meaning?" Harry broke the silence between them.

Nina leaned her elbows on the counter, her coal black eyes deep and serious. "Meaning, we've never had a case that hasn't had some whacked motherfucker involved. That includes Marty, and me, too. Don't you remember, Harry, I told you I was the muscle at OOPS? I said that shit for a reason. I thought we were safe this time, seeing as the accident was family related, but somebody took your fucking kids, Harry. I wanna know who and why. Then I wanna eat their legs off."

Harry's ruddy complexion went pale again, the tic in his jaw pulsing. "So you think this was related to me and Mara, too?"

Nina popped her lips, gazing into Harry's eyes. "I think if Fletch said this person ran away 'superhuman fast,' then yeah—maybe."

"You heard me tell Mara that?" Again, poor Harry's face held wonder and horror.

Nina snorted, clapping Harry on the back. "I told you, I hear everything, man. I make it my business to always know what the fuck's going on. That shit, coupled with the "tell Uncle Harry and Mara I see them" thing she said to Mimi, worries the hell out of me."

Mara blanched. "Mimi didn't tell the police the message this woman with the swingy hair gave her. Maybe we should call them and let them know?"

Nina rolled her eyes. "Dude, are you crazy? If this shit has anything to do with the paranormal, who better to handle it? Us or the local cops? Remember how helpful they were when Marty was kidnapped back in the day?"

Now Harry blanched. "Marty was kidnapped?"

Perfect. Just what Harry needed, more stories about the bad paranormals to feed his rampant fears. Mara ran her fingers over her temples, massaging the knot between her eyebrows. "It was a long time ago—early in her turning, and yes, she was kidnapped, but it had nothing to do with us crazy werewolves. It was a shitty human." *So take that, one-time human.*

Nina cracked her knuckles. "Yeah, but guess who took care of it in the end?"

Mara looked Harry directly in the eye. "For now, I think it's better not to stir this up any more than it's already stirred—if it is someone paranormal, Nina's right. It's better we handle it. The children are safe for now, and we'll be sure it stays that way. We're much better equipped to handle this than any human police force. So are you okay with keeping that piece of information from the police for now?" She searched his eyes, praying he wouldn't push this. No human bars in the land could contain someone of their ilk.

Harry waffled for a moment before saying, "Agreed. I think."

Nina slapped him on the back and smiled. "So, lovebirds—

fucking make some choices, would you? Carl's hungry, and I need to know where I'm hangin' upside down to sleep tonight."

Harry made a face at her, tearing his eyes from Mara's. "You do not."

"Of course I don't, wingnut. I just wanted to be sure you were paying attention. So decide, Harry, because once you do, while you guys were fighting like you're married, I thought of a way we can get you back to work so no one sticks their noses in where they damn well don't belong."

Mara rolled up the sleeves of Harry's shirt, fighting the impulse to bury her nose in its collar. "Nina, we're just prolonging the inevitable. I was a nervous wreck today—all day. I couldn't stop worrying about what a horrible liar I am, or about getting caught lying. I'm here to tell you, I'd suck so hard at being a spy. I can't do this forever. I'll end up with a werewolf-sized ulcer."

"We'll figure it out, Mara," Harry insisted, the forceful tone he used giving her delicious chills. "We'll find a way to present this to your brother and whoever these people are you're so sure are going to put you in jail, and we'll *make* them listen. I don't know anything about your legal system, but I'm not giving you up. So while I can't believe I'm saying this, let's hear the Crypt Keeper out." He frowned.

Harry's words, again said with so much conviction he seemed as surprised by them as she was, had her wondering where this refusal to let her pay for her crimes was coming from.

Mara sighed, partially out of relief that Harry appeared to have gotten control of his angry barbs, and partially because there was no convincing anyone this was going to come crashing around their ears sooner rather than later.

"Fine. Shoot, but if the heat gets turned up, I'm turning myself in. I don't want Marty and Wanda in trouble with the pack for protecting me. Fair?"

"Yeah, yeah. What the fuck ever. Now quit clangin' your cup against the bars on your cell and listen."

Harry leaned in, taking Carl, who napped on his shoulder, with him.

Mara leaned in, too, crazy curious to hear her plan to sneak Harry into Pack without every werewolf within two hundred feet of him smelling his scent.

"Short-Shot—meet your new boyfriend." Nina grinned—wide and beautiful.

Well, thank God someone had finally heard her carnal request.

CHAPTER
9

"This is crazy."

"I dunno. Personally, for me anyway, this is the best werewolf day ever."

Mara blushed, her cheeks hot, her mouth like the Mohave Desert. "It'll never work."

"We won't know until we try. Hey, don't forget my back." Harry paused, a low rumble emitting from his chest, sending vibrations of warmth to hers. He lifted his arms high, the stretch of his navy suit spanning the width of his broad back. "Yeahhhh, like that."

"I protest." Well, that probably wasn't being totally honest with herself, but for the sake of her pride, and the maniacal gleam in Nina's eyes, she protested.

And besides, did you hear yourself, Mara? Weak. So weak.

"Really? I don't." Harry's reply was thick and deep, rumbly and delicious-gruff.

"Dude, stop complaining and rub—all over him. Everywhere," Nina ordered, swirling a finger around.

Mara fought a groan as she stiffly shimmied up and down

Harry's body just as they prepared to leave for work. After clueing Marty in on Nina's plan to keep the pack at bay, and finally convincing Harry to let Wanda take Mimi and Fletcher home with her, they'd all gotten a decent night's sleep at Mara's cottage—including Carl, who loved sitting on her enormous cushioned window seat and watching the snow fall outside while snuggling under a down comforter.

Now, they were in the middle of her living room at seven in the morning, leaving her scent on Harry and her acutely aware hormones in a pile of screaming nerves.

The brilliant idea behind it?

To fool all the werewolves at Pack into thinking Harry smelled like a werewolf because he was doing one—the lesser of two evils. Theory being, Mara would probably warrant less trouble from the council if she slipped up and began a relationship with a human.

The pack didn't love humans and werewolves mating. They especially didn't love it in a working environment due to the risk someone would become spiteful and angry in the event of a messy breakup and reveal their status to the world at large out of revenge. But they'd like this idea a whole lot more than they'd like knowing Mara'd turned Harry with a homegrown baby serum.

In short, her punishment would be far less severe. A slap on the wrist at best, versus a prison cell and meals served on a tray with dividers.

Harry wrapped his arms around her, leaving her breathing choppy. He smiled down and winked, his voice all crushed velvet and smoky. "Just making sure we've covered, you know, everywhere."

Everywhere was pretty well covered on Harry's fit, hard, luscious body. If she managed to survive staying out of the council's reach, she was never going to survive claiming every square inch of his rippling mass with hers.

Mara fought the insane, almost uncontrollable, impulse to let loose and rub up against Harry like a cat. His body, thick with muscle, coupled with his new werewolf scent, was driving her hormones to a place she couldn't quite remember ever going. Instead, she tried to appear unaffected, letting her arms fall loose in his embrace.

When what she really wanted to do was wrap her arms around his neck, thrust her hands into his thick hair, and bury her nose in his muscled neck. Nip at his square, freshly shaved jaw as she hiked herself up around his waist and pressed into his . . .

Mara took a shaky breath when Nina poked her head over her shoulder and said, "Short-Shot, make like you like Harry. He's your new boyfriend, right? This is the stage when you can't keep your paws off him. So put your paws *on* him," she demanded, placing Mara's hands on Harry's shoulders. "Jesus. You'd think you've never been stupid in love before."

Point?

Mara gripped Harry's shoulders, for practice purposes, of course, sinking her fingers into his sculpted flesh, making a face at Nina. "You can't possibly believe this will work, can you both? No way are we ever going to make people believe that Harry has the scent of a werewolf on him because we've been . . ." Doing it. Making it. Wonking. Scoring.

Oh, heaven above.

"Fucking," Nina offered without blinking an eye. "A lot. And hell, yes, I think it'll work. Maybe not for long, but at least long enough for us to figure out how we're gonna get your scrawny ass out of this jam. So do you wanna try this and see if it works? Or do you wanna piss away an opportunity, skip this lovebird bullshit, and just call Big Bertha up on the prison love line and invite her to make you her bitch?"

Harry shook his head in vehement gesture, burying his nose in her hair. "Absolutely no Big Bertha. Wow," he said on a deep inhale, his chest rising and falling against hers, making her heart do all sorts of erratic things. "You smell amazing." He drove his fingers into it, drawing the long bulk of the strands to his nose.

Mara's nipples tightened when Harry's breath fanned out over the flesh of her neck. She cleared her throat. "That's just the were-wolf in you talking. Tomorrow, as you adjust, I'll smell like day-old bologna."

Carl appeared behind Harry's broad back, holding up two brown paper bags with his half grin. He struggled to keep his grip on them, his fingers stiff and, in some places, rigid.

"Aw, Carl, did you make us lunch?" Mara smiled her approval. Carl, despite his rather impish behavior and his gray green pallor, was adorable in a weird, sort of dead way. He aimed to please with an air of fear he'd not only displease Nina but end up shunned and taken from these people he'd found who accepted him as is.

Carl couldn't express how he felt in words, but his eyes spoke volumes about his emotions. Mara wiggled her finger at him, drawing him to her and Harry, and pulling him into a hug. He smelled so much better since Nina had insisted he bathe and drink a bottle of mouthwash. "Thank you, Carl. You're awesome."

Carl's eyes went immediately to the floor with a nasally grunt, a shy response to her words of support.

Harry's eyes never left Mara's when he teased, "I hope it's bolo-gna, Carl. Thanks, buddy. That was thoughtful."

After a good night's sleep, Harry's mood had lightened consider-ably. He'd spent a portion of their evening while they ate dinner together listening to Nina explain what she'd meant when she said none of their cases came without trouble.

Nina didn't candy-coat the things they'd experienced since they began OOPS, and while Mara never failed to cringe when she told of the most frightening crisis case of all, involving the turning of Nina's sister Phoebe and her ex-FBI agent husband Sam, Mara knew there was motive for it.

To keep Harry aware. Not only was he now paranormal, mean-ing he had to make conscious effort to pay attention, but his children had been threatened. Paying attention was crucial to figuring out who'd done this.

"All right, let's bust a move, people. You nerds have to get to work, and I need a goddamn nap. Darnell's comin' to stay with Carl while I sleep, so we're covered for now. Just remember what I said, Short-Shot—keep it simple, no deets. Some shit ain't for the masses, ya know? So if people ask questions, play possum. Make googly eyes at Harry here. Hold hands, kiss the shit out of each other behind that stupid fucking palm tree Marty had shipped in from wherever-thefuck in the atrium. Eat lunch together. Make it believable, but keep it simple." She turned to Harry, pinning him with her vampiric gaze. "You got that Harry? Make Mara your bitch and let everyone know you've pissed on her tree."

Harry stiffened against Mara just before backing away from her and acknowledging Nina with a nod. "Right. Kiss. Googly eyes. Kiss. Piss on the tree," he repeated, backing up only to trip over the third pair of shoes she'd tried on this morning and stumble on the edge of her couch before righting himself. "I got this," he murmured when Nina moved to right him.

Mara's cheeks burned. Actually kiss Harry? Like, his lips, touching hers? And she was supposed to keep herself neutral during all of this, knowing full well it was only to keep their cover, how? She was going to end up wearing one of his used T-shirts and sucking down gallons of Ben & Jerry's while she cried herself to sleep about a boyfriend she never had.

Instead of speaking her fears out loud, Mara made another weak protest. "We can't hang all over each other at work, Nina. It's unprofessional." *It's also torture.*

Nina planted her hands on her flannel pajama–clad hips. "Hmmm, let's fucking see. Unprofessional? Soap on a rope?"

Mara threw her hands up in the air with an exasperated huff. "Okay, okay! Unprofessional it is." She snuck one last peek of herself in the oval mirror at her entryway, smoothing her hair over her shoulders and down over her breasts. Her blue eyes had that luminous, wide-eyed look of fear she was fighting to keep in check.

Harry appeared behind her, his large presence filling her senses. He placed his hands on her shoulders, giving them a squeeze. Warmth spread in her belly when he leaned down to her ear, watching her watch him. "You ready to do this?"

"Ready," she whispered, held captive by this sensual side of Harry, who made her insides feel like molten lava and left her body throbbing an excited rhythm.

"Then let's do this." He backed away, popping open her front door, a cool blast of early morning air ruffling his perfect hair.

Carl thumped Harry on the back, lifting his entire arm high in the air to wave them off with a jerky hand.

Mara sucked the cold into her lungs, squinting at the glare of sun on the freshly fallen snow.

Harry made his way along the path, which Nina had dug in a matter of seconds, only to slip on a patch of ice. His feet went out from under him like someone had shot his knees out with a long-range rifle. "I'm okay!" he yelled from somewhere below the line of the wall of snow.

As she made her way to her Smart Car, rushing to help Harry up, she said a small prayer that some dormant thespian skill locked deep inside her would step up to the plate.

Because she didn't know what soap on a rope was, but if Nina did, it had to be ugly.

HARRY caught sight of Mara just as she rounded the corner to the cafeteria. He jumped up, pulling out a chair for her. He'd selected a table in the middle of the room, so everyone would see them together as planned.

And he liked it. He liked it so much he forgot he didn't want to be paranormal and she sucked for turning him into a werewolf, and instead, smiled at her.

As she strode toward him, her almost waist-length hair, cut in layers framing her heart-shaped face, shone a deep, near blue, black, reminding him of her scent. Rosemary and citrus—or something he could now define merely by calling up the memory.

It was driving him out of his mind. He'd thought about it all morning as he'd tried to focus on numbers that swam in front of his eyes; when he'd Skyped with Mimi and Fletcher while Wanda's manservant Archibald oversaw things. He'd thought about it when he'd closed his eyes, breathing deeply to fight that strange tingling sensation in his limbs Mara had told him to expect in times of stress.

He'd fought it while he remembered the curve of her hip pressed to his, her skin emanating heat even from beneath her jeans. The swell of breasts he wanted to cup in his hands and knead until she screamed his name. Uncomfortable things were occurring under the cafeteria table, forcing him to shift positions.

Jesus, she was beautiful. Even in broad daylight, with the sun from the windows blaring down on her gorgeous head, he couldn't find a single flaw. Her skin was creamy and tinted with a peachy glow, her eyes the shape of almonds and so deeply blue they were almost sapphire, making the fringe of her dark lashes striking.

She plopped down next to him, her eyes giving him that deer in the headlights look. He watched her throat work up and down in a nervous gulp, smelled the sweat on her palms when she wiped them on her thighs.

Usually, when he was attracted to a woman, he was the one secretly sweating, forming words carefully in order to keep himself from sounding like a complete ass. But today he was Mr. Carefree?

She'd said someone needed to take charge, and if she was going to handle the adjustment phase of this, he was going to handle the boyfriend aspect—like a boss.

He had a strange rush of confidence he hadn't possessed before this "accident," and he liked it. He had definitely been guilty of missing some very overt signs when it came to a woman, but he knew how to treat one once he had her.

While they were just pretending, he'd pretend they weren't pretending. He sure didn't hate the idea. In fact, this morning he'd awakened ready to get his pretend on.

Still, he heard his sister Donna's warning in his head about what a sorry judge of character he was, and promptly ignored it. *This is all a game, Harry. Remember why you're playing it.*

He was taking one for the team—yeah, yeah. But not a chance in hell was he going to let an opportunity like this pass him by. He didn't want to be a werewolf, and he'd continue to look for ways to reverse that, but that didn't mean he didn't want to explore Mara.

It had hit him like a punch to the kidneys last night, when he'd sworn she wasn't going to jail on his watch. He'd toyed with why he'd developed this sudden protective instinct, put the notion away, then toyed with it again until he had to chalk it up to the unexplainable. He didn't like anything there wasn't a solution to, a logical explanation for—yet, here he was behaving illogically.

And liking it. He was liking it. Rolling around in it like a pig in mud.

Reaching across the white Formica, Harry grabbed her hand and smiled, rubbing his thumb over her silky, porcelain skin, savoring the texture of it. "You look really pretty today."

Mara rolled her eyes. "Really? I'm glad terrified looks good on me. Because that's what made up my entire color wheel this morning."

Her reference to color wheels reminded him of the upcoming

merge between Pack and Bobbie-Sue Cosmetics. "Okay, other than your color wheel issues, how's it going?"

"Which part? The big, fat teller of tales part, or the part where I expect my brother to knock down the lab door at any moment and handcuff me with his infamous 'I'm so disappointed in you, Mara' frown?"

He grinned rather than buy into her panic, hoping it would soothe her frazzled nerves. "Both."

"They both suck."

"Your brother Keegan? He raised you and your other brother Sloan, right?"

She nodded her dark head, a strand of her hair slipping from the thick clip she held it up with—one he wanted to brush from her face. "Mostly, and don't change the subject. We need to plan for a knotted-sheet escape, and in the event we can't figure that out, toilet paper rations. I can't skimp on the TP. Not even in prison."

Nothing about her fear was okay with him. You'd think what she did was on par with murder in her culture. So he had to ask. "Do they really have—" he leaned into her, "a place they keep people who commit crimes in your world?"

Mara's finger slipped to his arm and tapped it. "It's your world now, too, lest you forget. And yep. They really do. We have to. One bad apple could spoil the whole damn thing. We want to live peacefully with humans, not create widespread panic. If someone found out about us, just one cruel or even nutty someone, imagine what they could do. What the government would do. So we have our own secret government. One you'll have to learn the laws of. One of those laws is don't turn someone into a werewolf. Period."

Harry bristled. She hadn't done it maliciously. "But you were trying to create a life. There was no malice in what you did."

His defense reawakened Donna's voice in his head. *Ahem. Excuse me, Mr. I Don't Want To Be A Werewolf, aren't you consorting with the enemy? Wasn't it you, just two nights ago, thinking all sorts of horrible things about the very woman you've claimed today is not only hot, but you've now complimented and admitted a wish to conduct carnality with? Wasn't it you who was blaming her, et cetera, for doing this to you? Now it's okay because her excuse was she wanted a baby? Oh, Harry.*

Shut. Up. Donna. Mara's talking.

He returned his attention to Mara, focusing completely on her and her dimples.

She wrinkled her cute nose and actually smiled, making his gut twist. "Is that you sticking up for me, Harry of the 'You suck so hard for doing this to me, Mara'?"

Though he was pleased she was smiling, and he didn't even know why, he kept his response honest. "I won't lie and tell you I'm not still going to try and figure out how to change this, but I don't think you should go to jail for it. And before you ask, I don't know why I don't. I just don't."

The wheels of her razor-sharp mind turned. He saw it—was suddenly living for it. "It doesn't matter. Or it won't. I don't know if there's a law against what I did yet. I do know the pack wants to keep our bloodlines strong. They want us to mate—with each other preferably. That's how we keep most of the crazy out. By keeping our core pure."

Harry shook his head, loving that she'd finally loosened up a bit. "It's bullshit. Also, medieval comes to mind. Everyone's using surrogates nowadays. I don't get the resistance."

"They're not using them the way I used them."

"I'll never look at another bottle of vitaminwater the same."

Her bright eyes fell to the table again. "I'm sorry, Harry."

He didn't want her to keep apologizing. It was done. Her apologies only reminded him he lusted for someone he was supposed to be angry with. But she was so cute . . . So he changed the subject. "So you want a baby? Single parenthood and all that stuff?"

Mara's eyes went to her lap, her tongue, luscious and pink, flitting over her lower lip in nervousness. "I do. I did."

"So why didn't you just do this mate thing? The one I vaguely remember you talking about at some point during my freak-out?" Those words sounded so archaic and blatantly sexist. Who mated?

Her chest rose and fell in an enticing lift of soft pink turtleneck. "Someone has to want to mate with you for you to do the mate thing."

He paused. *What?* The idea that Mara, gorgeous, curvy, sexy as hell, couldn't find a mate made his mouth drop open, but he slammed it shut before she lifted her eyes. "I find that almost impossible to believe."

"Believe."

She must be as lame about social cues as he was. He could name five guys from his department alone who thought she was hot. It had to be her brains. It scared off the weak. "I think you're just too much woman for this bunch of slackers. I smell a lot of werewolf in this room. Lots of single, available werewolf. Which, as a by the way, freaked me out when I discovered how many of you there really are today as I sniffed my way through just my department alone. Anyway, you're just too smart, and they're all intimidated by you." *Wow, pal. Nice. Smooth, even. Where'd the player in you come from?*

Her cheeks tinted an adorable shade of red followed shortly thereafter by the tip of her nose. "I'm sure that's what the problem is. My oversized brain."

The back of his neck began to tingle, making him take a covert peek around before refocusing on Mara's pretty face. "I think we've been noticed."

She shifted in her chair, *awkward* written all over her features.

"It won't be long now before everyone on lunch break will have to recharge their batteries for the texting they're doing about us even as we speak."

Harry didn't bother to look up again. He couldn't. Now that he'd moved past the initial shock of his turning and his anger had subsided, he was in the process of coming back down to earth. And earth had this gorgeous creature named Mara. He liked earth. "Screw 'em. That's what we want. Them talking. Now look at me like you think I'm the only person in the world, and let's sell this."

Her eyes were shy, her lips pouty and peachy-colored. "Who are you, Harry Emmerson?"

"I'm your boyfriend, Mara Flaherty."

"You're my *pretend* boyfriend."

"So let's pretend," he goaded with a sly chuckle. Somehow, a new facet to his personality had flared up. It was called The Flirty Harry, and it was doing something he'd sucked ass at in his former totally human life. Huh.

"My pretend boyfriend who's suddenly very vocal about the issues at hand. I don't know this Harry Emmerson."

"Did you know the other one?"

Her eyes skirted his, settling on the table again. "I knew enough to know that he was quiet and easygoing. Not opinionated and pushy."

Was he quiet? Yeah. Yeah, he probably was. But he didn't feel like being quiet today. "Well, now you know the werewolf Harry, and it would appear he's got something to say. So, let's make googly eyes at each other to announce our budding relationship."

That demure look was back on her face, in her posture. "You go first."

Harry pulled her hand to his lips, savoring the feel of her flesh against his mouth, and brushed a kiss on her fingers while he gazed into her eyes. "You look like I'm holding you hostage. It's just lunch. Not *Zero Dark Thirty* day," he joked.

She almost laughed before he saw her realize she was doing it and caught herself, but she didn't pull her hand away. In fact, she closed it around his.

It was much smaller than his own; smaller yet callused in some spots from the work she'd so proudly announced she'd been doing all by herself to renovate her frilly cottage.

A cottage he felt like a big oaf in for every basket of flowers he'd tripped over, and all the periwinkle blue and moss green pillows he'd all but annihilated by squashing after sitting on them on her ivory couch. "A lunch of lies. So many lies," she whispered, scanning the crowd of heads dotting the cafeteria.

Ah. She was worried the other werewolves would hear them. "You're making this harder than it has to be." *Literally,* he thought, drawing his napkin over his lap. "Weren't you the one who said most times werewolves block out the sounds around them in order to focus on conversations they're having, and to keep from literally going insane with so much stimuli? I've been practicing it all day. Though I have to admit, I was a little uncomfortable with Esterhazy's story about his hemorrhoids and subsequent visit to what he called a butt doctor. Some things should remain private."

Not even a giggle. In fact, she didn't say anything. She didn't have to. She was throwing off an uncomfortable vibe he could virtually catch in his mouth as if it came in the shape of popcorn.

He tried another tact. He was damned interested in how she'd whipped up a baby-making serum. She was smarter than he'd ever guessed, and it only made him think about her naked that much more—which was an unsettling segue from her big brain.

She could talk with him about the things that interested him, too—theories and equations and *The Walking Dead*. If he were checking off characteristics on his dream list, she was almost perfect.

"So tell me about the, you know, serum. How the hell did you make something so brilliant? It's damn well genius, Mara. Tell me in geek-speak, if you have to, but I gotta know."

Mara scooted her chair closer to his, reaching for the lunch Carl had packed them. She pulled out a sandwich bag with a crushed slice of bread in it to peek inside and find it slathered with mustard and some jaggedly cut carrots on it. "I think we need to order lunch. Carl's intentions, while sweeter than sweet, are geared more toward what he likes for lunch, I think. Besides, hasn't the hunger hit you yet?"

Christ. He could have all but dived on top of the leftover cake Trisha from legal had brought down to their break room, and fighting the temptation to keep his hands off Liam's lunch in the fridge, a thick roast beef and cheddar sub with horseradish dressing, had sent him to the bathroom to splash his face with cold water.

"The hunger's hit, for sure. I usually avoid red meat but maybe once a month. Now I can't stop thinking about a porterhouse— rare. Or maybe just a whole cow." Among other things.

Her shoulders relaxed as she became the Mara he was more familiar with, full of informative tips and directives. She was in her safe zone if she was instructing him on the way of the were. "In the beginning, you need to eat, and eat often. So make sure you come down on breaks and grab—"

He cut off her werewolf tutorial by pulling her to him with merely a foot braced against the leg of the cafeteria chair, and planted a kiss on her pretty peachy lips, so full and glossy he wanted to suck on them, drive his tongue between them as he peeled her clothes from her body.

He couldn't help it. Having her this close to him, smelling her unique scent, feeling all the things he was feeling became magnified, making his nerves raw with need.

If he didn't kiss her, he'd haul her over his shoulder and drag her off to some janitor's closet and have his way with her. This was the next best thing to being labeled a Neanderthal.

Mara's surprise was evident at first, until she appeared to forget they were in the middle of Pack's cafeteria when she nuzzled her jaw into the palm of his hand, skimming her tongue over his lower lip.

While his head exploded, the lunchroom fell silent. So silent he heard heartbeats and blood pulsing through veins.

Until Mara's trio of friends showed up, and the one named Astrid dropped her lunch tray on the table with such force it hurt Harry's ears, leaving a humming vibration in its wake.

He sensed discontent—and something else he couldn't quite pinpoint. It was out of place in the realm of new scents he'd discovered, but it was there.

And it was unhappy.

"So, this is news," Astrid drawled, pulling out a chair and dropping into it, clearly displeased she hadn't been privy to Mara's fantasy crush turning into a reality.

Mara struggled to come back down from the cloud she was on after experiencing her first kiss ever from her pretend boyfriend.

It was everything she'd hoped and more when having her pretend affair with him. Soft, hot, sweet, and sinful in one soul-jarring kiss. Harry's lips didn't just press against hers, they consumed hers, devoured them. She'd kissed aplenty in her time, but never quite like that. The heat between her thighs pounded in time with her heart, still crashing against her ribs. He'd proven the age-old adage—geeks ruled.

Leah and Jiaying, always supportive of her fictional life with Harry, gave her a grin and a thumbs-up from behind him, giggling softly before taking their places on the other side of the table next to Astrid, expressing their open curiosity.

Mara stayed calm, pulling the juice box Carl had packed for her out of her brown paper bag. "Uh-huh. Definitely news," she agreed, forcing her eyes up even while Harry's hand drew tantalizing circles on her back.

Leah was the first to stick out her hand in Harry's direction. Her pixie cut left a swatch of her sandy blond hair hanging over her left eye, but her smile was friendly. "Hi, Harry. I know you, but I don't think you know me. I'm Leah from the lab. Nice to finally meet you."

Harry took her hand and shook it, grinning at her. "We had a run-in just the other day at lunch, right? I tripped, as usual, and you and Astrid were there." He turned to Mara. "Leah helped clean up the coffee I spilled all over everyone and everything."

Leah chuckled. "That was me."

"Thanks for that," Harry said on a smile. "I'm half klutz."

"Anytime," Leah offered, beaming at him and Mara.

Jiaying, petite and plump, held her hand out, too. "I'm Jiaying, or Ying, if you'd rather, from production, and I think we see each other from time to time when I drop off requests to you. You know, for more money," she said on a lilting chuckle.

"Pleasure," Harry said, his gaze stopping on Astrid who was ripping apart a beef shish kebab.

"And this is Astrid, Harry," Mara said as Leah nudged her to get her attention. "Astrid, this is Harry. Remember, we crashed into him in the lunch line a couple of days ago?"

Her eyes, narrowed and shiny, acknowledged Harry before returning to the chunk of pepper on her plate. "I know all about Harry."

Perfect. Astrid was angry. She didn't like newcomers, and she was doing her best to make that incredibly clear.

But Harry wasn't having it. He leaned forward, sticking his

hand under Astrid's bent-out-of-shape nose. "Pleasure, Astrid. You work in production, too, right?"

Mara fought a dreamy sigh while Ying and Leah rolled their eyes at Astrid. "She does," Leah answered for her. "With Ying. Astrid's the socially maladjusted crankypants in our little group."

Harry smiled, lopsided and adorable. "Every group needs one. We can't have too much happy. We need balance in the universe."

Ying giggled, nodding her approval of Harry's sentiment with a warm, wide smile.

"So tell us everything," Leah demanded with a wink and a smile, sinking her teeth into a shiny apple.

"Everything!" Ying chimed in, popping open her bag of chips.

Mara hedged, sipping at her milk, her grin sly. "Everything," she teased.

Leah and Jiaying giggled, but Astrid, not so much. Mara knew exactly what Astrid was thinking. Harry was yet another person taking up time Mara should be spending with her. It was a good thing Harry wasn't really her boyfriend. Soon this would all be over and everything would go back to the way Astrid liked it.

Except, she'd be in jail. Which would probably please possessive, smothering Astrid to no end. All she'd have to do to find Mara was pop in on visiting days at werewolf jail.

Mara caught herself. Yes, Astrid drove her nuts sometimes, and she didn't love to share Mara's attention. But Astrid was also a good friend. Not the kind of friend you did girls' night with—or shopped with. But one who'd text you links to recipes for chicken soup when you were home sick with the flu. Or offer to hack another employee's phone and wipe out their contacts list when you groused about them over lunch.

Her mean thoughts left her ashamed of herself. So Mara reached across the table, tapping Astrid's arm. "Wanna do coffee together later on our afternoon break? I've got the most awesome article to show you on ALMA. You know, the telescope we were talking about the other day?"

"The one in Chile?" Harry asked.

Mara's eyes widened at her pretend boyfriend before she grinned. God. He was so . . . perfectly perfect. "You know about it?"

"You bet. Just read about it in *Popular Science*, I think—"

"I have other plans for my break with another *friend*," Astrid belted out, jumping up from the table, her chair scraping against the floor so hard it made the floor beneath Mara's feet tremble. "But you won't miss me. You have Harry," she spat, grabbing her leftovers and stalking out of the cafeteria—but not before she all but hurled her lunch tray at the top of the trash bin.

Silence prevailed, in all its awkwardness. She'd hurt Astrid. Totally not her intention. But what if Harry were her real boyfriend? Wasn't it okay for her to expect support from her friend? Wasn't it okay to fall in love?

Harry broke the still air with a grin when he said, "So I guess Astrid and I doing Jell-O shots and karaoke is off the table?"

Everyone dissolved into laughter, breaking the tension.

Harry looked at his watch and frowned. "I have to get back to work. Regrets, ladies. I hope we'll get the chance to talk more later. Until then," he said on a chuckle, pulling Mara to stand with him, and tucking her close. "I'll see you tonight for dinner, right?" He didn't bother to wait for her response. Instead, he planted a light but lingering kiss on her lips before scooping up the bag Carl had packed and heading out of the cafeteria.

Her eyes strayed to his tight backside, before admiring the way he sauntered out of the cafeteria like he owned the joint.

Well, until he crashed into the glass door, forgetting to push it open and knocked over a potted palm, spraying the dirt and moss from the base all over the floor.

He bent to pick it up, waving at her with a sheepish grin as the women giggled.

She cupped her chin in her hands and sighed. Even clumsy Harry was dreamy.

Leah reached her hand out and patted Mara's to console her. "Don't let Astrid upset you. She's got a lot of stuff going on I think even we don't know about. It bothers both of us the way she hoards you, and creates drama when there isn't any. If she would just accept the fact that when she's not behaving like she's the antagonist in some psychopathic killer movie, and always worrying about whether we're mocking her in some weird code, everything is okay. But something's not right with her, and sometimes it scares me. I've always said that, haven't I, Ying?"

Ying nodded her agreement, her deep eyes solemn as she twisted the multicolored scarf around her neck. "Um, yeah. We knew you before she did. So if anyone has first dibs on lopping your head off, it's us. But in all seriousness, she can be really lurky and creepy sometimes. I know she's valuable to Pack and the brightest star in production, but she's also the moodiest. I tread lightly because I can never seem to gauge her moods."

Leah patted Mara's hand and smiled, her eyes twinkling. "Either way, if she's not happy for you, we are. It's like your dream come true," she gushed, batting her eyelashes. "And you guys are adorable together. You make a gorgeous couple, so dark and just pretty. And who knew Harry was so funny and charming. Did you, Ying? Up top, girlie. Score for the nerds!"

Mara clapped Leah's hand, but she was uncomfortable brushing aside Astrid's unhappiness. She didn't want to lose a loyal friend due to a lie that would soon end.

Yet she couldn't deny Leah was right. Something was off about Astrid. She'd always chalked it up to her quirky genius, and that intense glare she wore when she thought no one was looking was just her brain in constant overdrive—solving some Rubik's Cube of a problem in the dark corridors of her mind.

But she'd known how nuts Mara had been about Harry for all this time, and she'd supported her fantasy about him—her ridiculous gushing about him—until it had actually become a reality. It stung a little to see a dream realized, even if it was a pretend dream, crushed by Astrid's discontent.

However, the good news?

Mara found herself less uncomfortable pretending Harry was her new BF.

Especially after that Vulcan mind-meld of a kiss.

She'd be fanning her lady-garden for days after.

CHAPTER
10

"Darnell!" Mara cried, lunging at her favorite demon disguised in a teddy bear's body, thrilled to find him looming with a cheerful grin in the middle of her tiny cottage. She hugged him hard, kissing his cheek.

He looked as big and out of place as Harry did amongst the large willow baskets of hydrangeas and overflowing vases of silk peonies, ducking his head when he dropped her to his side. "How are you? How was Carl today?"

Darnell tucked her beside his solid, lumbering girth. "Aw, you know how it goes with ol' Darnell. People always end up comfortable with me. Carl and me made cupcakes today, didn't we Carl? Outta cauliflower and cornbread. He's a good helper in the kitchen, our Carl is."

Carl grunted and groaned, lifting his stiff arm to thump Mara on the back. He drew her into a rigid headlock intended as an affectionate hug, making Mara tug at the arm he'd planted around her neck.

Darnell put his hand on Carl's sweater-covered arm. "Easy now, brotha. I tol' ya, Carl. You gotta be nice to e'rybody, gentle, right? But remember, not just the ladies, the menfolk, too." Darnell tugged at Carl's arm, stroking them with his paw-sized hands until Carl let go.

Carl looked to Darnell for approval, his crooked smile in place, his glassy eyes searching the demon's for confirmation.

"Yeah," Darnell muttered on a grin. "Just like that, pal. You're a good dude, buddy. Now you go do like I told ya and rinse your mouth out with the mouthwash, 'k? Can't have you with death-breath." Darnell waggled a finger at Carl in the direction of her small bathroom. "After every meal—that's the deal if you want ol' Darnell to bring you more cabbage. Now go be a good zombie n' rinse, rinse, rinse."

"Half zombie," Harry piped in, loosening his tie as Carl dragged his left foot across Mara's floor, scattering her white and moss green throw rugs as he went.

Darnell barreled toward Harry, white high-tops thumping, the chains around his neck swaying against his football jersey. "You must be the poor sum-bitch Mara made outta baby juice," Darnell said, putting his wrist over his mouth to attempt to hide his cackle. "I'm Darnell—a demon. Mara can explain the how and why to ya later."

Mara expected Harry to react with anger to the demonic branch of their paranormal group. But Harry didn't look angry. He smiled and laughed, too. Like he and Darnell were old friends, laughing over an inappropriate joke.

Wow. She liked whoever was in charge of Harry's mood swings today. Whoever it was, they were invited to stay the duration of his adjustment period. "I am, indeed, the product of the infamous baby-maker." He shook Darnell's hand with a friendly grin.

And now we were bathing in the fodder of this all? What was with the ha-ha-ha?

"Have you heard anything about who might have abducted the children, Darnell?" Mara asked. All day long, aside from her other worries, it had troubled her.

While they were safe with Wanda, it didn't change the fact that someone had tried to take them. Someone who wasn't a human. Every time she thought about it, she couldn't help but feel completely responsible and sick to her stomach. Maybe someone had seen something the other night in the lab? But who? And what did it have to do with Harry's children?

"Not a rumble," Darnell said, shaking his head, directing his next comment to Harry with a slap on his back. "But you count on this, ain't no one gonna get past me and get yo' kids. I promise ya that. And if I hear anything at all in my world, you'll be the first to know."

Harry's eyes clouded over. "Appreciate it."

"So how ya feelin', man? You got the fever tonight?" Darnell asked on a grin meant mostly for Harry.

Harry's alarm was evident, his lean face losing its easygoing smile and expressing concern. "Fever?"

"Yeah, buddy. Mara ain't told ya about the fever yet?" Darnell whistled, rubbing his hand over his shortly cropped hair.

Mara's sigh was meant to grate on its way out. It wasn't really a fever. It was more like a really extended hot flash. No big deal. "I was getting to that." Because it was touchy and shouldn't be explained in a rush. Or without the purchase of condoms or maybe a dirty magazine.

Darnell pointed to the window where darkness began to fall. "Well you better get the gettin' on. Tonight's the full moon."

Harry looked to Mara, his eyes narrowing. "It's not really like the myth is it?"

"Do you mean like the *American Werewolf in London* myth? Or like myth-myth, folklore-myth?" she hedged, backing away from him and bumping into Carl who thumped her on the back just the way Darnell instructed. Mara grabbed Carl's hand and let it rest on her shoulder to show him he'd done good.

Harry's approach was swift, leading Mara to believe he'd been trying out his new werewolf powers. His face hovered above hers, making Carl's feet shift in a nervous shuffle. "I mean, am I going to . . ." He paused, clearly searching. "Do that thing . . ."

"Shift," Mara filled in his blank.

His lips, lips that had touched her soul, thinned in disapproval. "Yeah. That. Then turn into some werewolf version of a mad dog and eat a herd of cows?"

Mara laughed. "No, silly. Yes. You'll shift. No. You won't eat cows. We don't allow that. I mean, you'll want to, but I'll make sure you consume plenty of food beforehand so the hunger doesn't eat you alive. It won't be easy to fight it off, but you'll learn. I'll help."

His expression was bland. "How accommodating. So that's it? There's nothing else I should know about other than my body is going to be ripped apart in an agonizing grip of twisting flesh and shattered bones?"

She'd always wondered what it was like to not have the urge to shift. Or for that matter, to never have shifted at all. She'd been doing it since birth, with no recollection of her first time, much like a human baby doesn't remember abruptly leaving the womb or the pain of teething.

But to have it occur, and actually remember the first time, was, if Marty and Harry's descriptions weren't an exaggeration, quite painful.

Mara winced at his description and made a mock pouty face, hoping to coax him back to the place where he wasn't scowling at her. "Oh, c'mon, Harry. Was it really that bad?"

"Bad? Are your bones grinding together and your flesh splitting apart bad? Is feeling new follicles form under your skin, then sprout thousands of tiny hairs like they're each individual razor blades bad?"

Mara put a hand up, resisting the urge to place it on his chest. Because here at home, he wasn't her pretend boyfriend. "I can help with that, Harry. My brother helped Marty, and she shifts like a champ now. It's just about breathing and focusing."

"Sounds more like giving birth."

Okay. So that analogy had been bandied about once or twice during Marty's adjustment—or maybe it was a million times. It was Marty. Of course it was a million times. "Well, Marty did make that comparison."

"Great," he said between clenched teeth.

Carl mewled, reaching over Mara's shoulder, putting his fingers on Harry's lips.

Harry let his head drop; regret slashing his eyes just as his chin hit his chest. He sighed. "Okay, Carl. I get it. I'm sorry, buddy. I didn't mean to upset you. I'm just a little tense."

Carl reached out and ruffled Harry's hair, lifting his chin with a grunt.

Harry gave his hand a quick squeeze before asking, "So is there anything else I need to know about the full moon thing?"

"Hoo, boy," Darnell said on a whistle. "I'mma go make ya'll some dinner fit to feed an army. C'mon, Carl. You can peel potatoes so you don't have to hear what all goes on up in here." Darnell held out his large hand to him. "There's gonna be some outside voices."

Harry glowered at Mara.

Funny that.

She shrunk against the wall. Okay, fine. So she'd left the part out about how his hormones weren't just going to run rampant, but explode—maybe it was implode? Whatever. They were going to be hard to teach him to contain.

When a human was turned, not only did they experience the

rush of hormones, exaggerated by their new inner werewolf, but according to Marty, it was magnified tenfold. Full weres were taught from a very young age to control their powerful urges—over time, and with much preparation.

It wasn't always easy—sometimes it was like a sixteen-year-old in the backseat of a car with a willing girl times a million, but it was manageable when you knew what to expect.

If Marty's account was right, for a human who hadn't grown into their were status over time—it could be an all-out hormonal war.

Harry crossed his arms over his chest. "Outside voices? Hmmm, Mara—why does Darnell think we'll be using our outside voices?"

She sighed, letting her shoulders sag. "Well . . ."

He glowered harder, the lines on either side of his mouth deepening as his lips curled inward.

Mara's gaze upward was tentative. "So, orgies? What's your take on them?"

"ARE you ready, Harry?" Marty asked.

Harry nodded. Hell no, he wasn't ready. But he wasn't going to share that with the group. Not out loud. Not if his life depended on it.

"Are you okay, Harry?" Marty tilted her head, her eyes concerned. "We have to do this soon, Harry, or it'll happen anyway. Let's make it as pleasant a journey as possible, yes?"

Harry heard Marty. Yet he couldn't look away. He knew his eyes were wide with geek wonder, but holy shit. The land surrounding the Flaherty estate and Mara's cottage was crawling with werewolves. Crawling. Small, short, burly, wide, all sorts of various shapes and sizes of people who'd shifted just like Mara had—right before his eyes, running, trotting, intermittently stopping in small groups to mingle. It was like a paranormal church picnic or something.

Jesus Christ. He was watching, from a distance, while tucked into a cluster of towering pines, actual *people* turn into werewolves.

The rolling hills and frozen landscape, dotted by stars and trees, were beautiful, leaving him irrationally angry. He didn't want to appreciate this. He didn't want to live this life thrust upon him because of some mistake. Yet, the call of it, the allure of superhuman power, and his newfound, almost cocky confidence tempted him, tempted him until he had to clench his teeth to stave it off.

Where was this gig when he'd been an awkward fifteen-year-old with a retainer, Coke-bottle glasses, and only a hundred and twenty pounds at almost six feet?

But then there were the kids. How could he possibly explain something like this to them without scaring the hell out of them? He couldn't raise his sister's children if he was turning into something kids had nightmares about. How could he explain this eternal life deal? How would he explain that as they aged, he wouldn't, or rather, the process would be much slower for him.

It was incomprehensible that he'd outlive the kids.

And that was the angry part of all this. If it were just him, he'd figure it out. But ending this crazy as soon as possible so the kids could return to their lives was the only way. If that meant shifting comfortably rather than having his face ripped off until he could find a way out, he was in.

"Harry?" Marty poked him in the arm, her pretty smile encouraging and warm. "We have to do this before Keegan notices I'm missing, if we hope to keep Mara out of trouble and keep you away from the rest of the pack while we do it."

Marty had kindly offered to help Mara with his shift, her understanding of his dilemma keener than that of Mara's. The damned trouble with these people was they were so nice. So ready and willing to stop their lives, mid-living, and help out a perfect stranger. Darnell was a demon, yet he'd offered him comfort like they'd been friends for life. Even Nina, ghastly, foul-tempered beast that she was, had held out her hand for him to grab on to. He'd been despicable concerning Carl's existence. Regretted it the moment it had come from his lips. Hated that he'd sounded like an ass for the ages.

Yet each of them expressed their emotions, got it out, and considered it done. Like a family.

That tempted him, too. This sense of family, the solidarity they all shared. It was just he and the kids. No remaining relatives, no friends of theirs close enough to be counted on. What if something happened to him? Who would take them then? The state? The kids needed a strong home base, a soft place to fall—a network of soft places to fall—and Mara's pack offered that.

"Harry? I need you to really focus. We don't want to draw attention to my absence or you. So remember what I told you, okay? Just let it happen. The first time you fought it because you didn't know what was happening. This time, you're going to relax into it and focus on the change in your body."

Mara stood just behind Marty, beautiful in the glow of the moonlight, hesitation and uncertainty shadowing her eyes, and he felt that fever thing she'd told him about.

For her.

Every breath she took, he smelled, savored, wanted to inhale by pressing his mouth over hers. He wanted to tear her clothes from her body, lick her from head to toe, bury his face between her legs, taste every inch of her.

It was goddamned uncomfortable, and as the moon rose while they'd eaten dinner, full, buttery soft, pulling at him like it pulled the tide, his need had become almost unbearable. Mara was the last person he wanted close because of this strange, pulsing lust, yet the only person he thought he'd die of wanting if she wasn't near.

There weren't really any orgies, but there was uncontrollable lust, compounded by the fact that he hadn't grown into this were lifestyle like the others. More adjustments to be made.

Followed by more anger because he had to adjust to anything. Mara had felt the brunt of his brooding silence at dinner while he stuffed himself with a savory sirloin stroganoff, a porterhouse, and an entire pot roast lathered in rich wine gravy.

Shoving all that food down his throat only minimized this hunger Mara spoke of by a little, but it did successfully keep him from dragging her across the table and burying himself deep within her. How did all these male werewolves manage to control that, even if their lust was only half of what he was experiencing?

"Okay, Harry, here we go," Marty said with a smile, reminding him he had to protect Mara from the others finding out. "Close your eyes. Feel the pull of the moon. Let your limbs go limp, and breathe with me. Trust me, Harry."

He took a deep, long breath, fighting the shudder of it, hoping to relax to the sound of Marty's instructions, when a searing lick of flames accosted his gut. He fell forward, hissing as though he'd been burned from the inside.

Marty stroked his back, her fingers, though meant to soothe, like nails on a chalkboard. "You're fighting out of fear, Harry. It won't be like last time if you don't let it. Please trust me."

He pulled more air into his lungs, forcing himself to stand erect, hearing Marty's words become warbled and distant. Fighting to find this focus they talked about.

Another slash of pain ricocheted across his face and tore at his neck muscles, making him reach for the tree trunk to keep from screaming and humiliating himself in front of two women who did this like they were changing their clothes.

He gripped the trunk of the tree, his fingers clenching a branch, shredding it, the pine needles stinging his hands.

Marty bent down low, her perfume, floral and light, mingling with her unique scent. "You're fighting it, Harry. It's because you're angry you're a werewolf. You don't want this. You want everything to be the way it was. I get it, but the harder you fight, the harder getting to the end result will be."

Yes. By fuck. That's exactly what he wanted. He wanted to go back to his average, if not boring and predictable, life.

The tearing of his biceps followed that thought and more slashes of white-hot agony, ripping at his flesh. It was like being stabbed with a poker freshly pulled from the fire over and over again.

"Too bad, Harry!" Marty's whisper came from some far-off place. "You're a werewolf now. There's no going back. Own it, Harry," she sang in his ear.

He fell to his knees hard, snow and leaves swirling around him, his body twisted and misshapen. One glance at his hand, almost entirely covered in fur, gnarled and forming the shape of a paw, made him growl, low and fierce.

"Harry?" Mara called. Kneeling down beside him, she bracketed what was left of his human face. "Shhhh. Listen to me," she soothed, stroking his hair, her lips moving slow and precise. "Listen and watch. Listen to me, *hear* my voice."

He stopped struggling quite so hard, the tight pull of his tendons easing ever so slightly, his spine no longer like the stretch of a tight bow.

"Did you know that you have a third eyelid? It's called *plica semilunaris*. It's a tiny fold of tissue at the inside corner of your eye. I read that it's the remnants of a nictitating membrane, most commonly found in birds, fish, and reptiles. Crazy, right?"

That caught his attention. Really? Shut the front door. He had no idea. Harry moaned, more because she was red-hot when she was spouting obscure data than the fact that he was in pain.

Mara's hands continued stroking him, soothing, calming as she spoke. Her hair brushed against his face, soft and smelling of rosemary and mint. Her breath made clouds of condensation in the almost-below-freezing temperatures. "And, ohhh, just the other day I was on Twitter. I follow *UberFacts*, and I read the first couple to ever be shown in bed together on prime-time TV was Fred and Wilma Flintstone. Yabba-dabba-do," she said on a laugh seconds before she let go of him with a gasp.

Just like that, Harry rolled away from her and rose on all fours, stretching his neck, testing his new body, sniffing at the air, taking in the delicious scents of the world around him.

"Well, Harry Emmerson," Mara murmured, husky and deep into the lush velvet of the night, her hair merely an outline of shiny folds against the backdrop of darkness. "Look at you."

Striding toward him, she rolled her shoulders and her flesh began to melt away until she, too, was in her were-form.

He hadn't been able to appreciate the beauty of it the other night in his kitchen when she'd become so angry with him. He'd been too caught off guard. Too freaked out.

But tonight? Jesus. She was beautiful. Sleek, her coat thick and shiny just like her hair, her eyes glowing and elongated, her stride confident and lithe.

Turning her head, she lifted her muzzle and howled into the rising wind, the majestic tilt to her ears, the sweet caress of her tone, all mesmerizing him.

She called to him, trotting off into a light jog, encouraging him to follow.

And he damn well would.

But he forgot he now had four legs.

So of course he did what he always did when Mara had him transfixed.

He fell.

Over a rock, cracking his jaw on the sharp edge.

Yeah, you got this, right? Such a stud, Emmerson.

CHAPTER
11

Mara burst through her cottage door, invigorated from her shift and Harry's triumphant foray into his transformation. Harry burst in behind her, almost knocking her down, his laughter rich and hearty.

He grabbed her at the waist to steady her so she wouldn't fall into Nina, and she found herself leaning back into her pretend boyfriend's embrace.

Nina stood waiting for them in the middle of the living room, her eyes marred with worry. "When you two ass sniffers were out in that frozen tundra of the great beyond, all runnin' around like you were auditioning for *Wild Kingdom*, did you see my Carl?"

"Wasn't he with Darnell?" Harry asked, pulling his gloves from his hands and laying them on the bleached brick of her hearth.

Nina nodded, popping her lips. "Some kinda goddamn babysitter that demon is. He fell asleep and lost the little fucker."

Harry began to pull his gloves back on. "We'll go look for him."

Mara almost sighed at his offer. Chivalry. It wasn't dead.

Nina dismissed him with a wave. "Nah. Darnell's out there

looking. You stay here. After all that hills-are-alive bullshit, it bein' your first time and all, you need to rest, and you need Short-Shot to stay and keep you from acting on any impulses."

Mara winced—Harry wasn't the only one who might need to fight impulses tonight. Thank goodness for her vivid imagination and a crazy apparatus called Bendy Bob.

Nina took long strides toward the door, leaving her image a blur. Popping open the front door, she stuck her head out and yelled, "Carl? Where the hell are you? Swear to sweet baby J, you're gonna get grounded!"

At just that moment, Marty stuck her head in the kitchen door, strangely unlocked. Mara could have sworn she'd locked the back door before they'd left . . .

Marty peeked around the kitchen doorway, shaking her hair out with a wide smile. "Oh, Harry, you were magnificent tonight! Bravo!"

Harry took a small bow, clearly pleased with himself. "Thanks for your help. I appreciate the kindness you've extended to me—an outsider and all."

Marty waved a white-gloved finger. "Oh, no, no, no. You're family now, pal. Love it or leave it, you're one of us. We just have to explain that to my husband."

All the joy of her shift seeped right out of Mara's body and was replaced with that jittery nervous twitch she was developing. "We have to tell him soon, Marty. I was a nervous wreck all day today. I'm a crappy liar. You know it, I know it, and my scent on Harry is only going to take us so far before the others will be able to distinguish. Besides, the guilt is eating me alive."

"Then let it feed, young lady," Marty said, crossing the room. "No way am I giving you up. The hell. I'm not letting your brother pull some sort of pack-law move on this. He did turn me into a werewolf, didn't he? Oh, yeah, he did. So there'll be no stone throwing in my family. He started this. Now, I just came to check on you two and be sure everything went well after I left. Give me a hug, and no more crazy talk. I'll figure this out. Just give me some time, okay?"

Mara went willingly into Marty's vanilla-and-snow-scented hug, squeezing her extra hard. "Okay."

As Marty pulled away, she cocked her head in Harry's direction. "How do you feel?"

The fire Darnell had lit before dinner blazed, its shadows playing on Harry's stiff jaw. "Unwillingly exhilarated."

Fuck chivalry. It had only been momentarily alive before Harry stomped all over it with his grudge. Mara fought the roll of her eyes, throwing her knit hat at her overstuffed armchair. She'd been trying to give him the benefit of the doubt. It had, after all, only been a couple of days. But for all that was holy, couldn't he just enjoy the moment?

Marty giggled, burrowing her chin in her fake fur coat. "Then you're right on track. But it gets better, and look at it this way, you got all of us in the process. Anyway, I'm out. I need to get back and spend some time with Hollis and Muffin."

"Thanks again, Marty," Harry said, almost smiling.

Marty gave them a wave before heading toward the front door. "Did you fucking see Carl on the way in?"

Marty shook her head. "Not a fucking Carl anywhere."

Nina rolled her eyes. "Jesus, he's like a greased cat. He's always wandering off." She pulled Marty out into the darkness. "C'mon, help me find him. Two noses are better than one. We gotta find my flippin' zombie before one of your crazy pack eats him."

Marty followed Nina out into the night, closing the door behind her, leaving them alone for the first time since this had all begun.

Harry shuffled his feet, stooping to unlace his work boots. "Marty's nice."

Now she was grudging. "Most *werewolves* are."

He dropped his shoes by the fire to dry, giving her a fed up expression. "Look. I told you, while this is what it is, and I have no choice in the matter right now, I don't want to be one of you."

Her mouth dropped open in outrage. She was tired of his werewolf blaming. Jerk. And no more of the poor Harry, he's just hormonal bullshit to excuse his rude behavior. "One of *you*? What the hell does that mean?"

He shrugged his wide shoulders, shaking off his down vest like he hadn't just insulted her family. "It means that it was pretty cool what just happened out there, I appreciate everything you and all of these people have done for me, but I'm still going to try and find a way to reverse what's happened."

Zing. Her temper shot through the top of her head. Tearing off her jacket, she dropped it on the floor and rounded on him, backing him into a corner. "You know what, Harry? You go right ahead, genius! Nay, I *dare you* to try and find a way to reverse this. I'm tired of you insulting *my* people, my family, who've been nothing but kind to you, like we all have some incurable disease, you jerk!"

Harry remained unruffled and unapologetic. "I can't wrap my head around why you're insulted. I'm not insulting you or your family or even your way of life. I'm just stating a fact. It's impractical for me to remain a werewolf. That's all there is to this."

Yet, Mara was still insulted. Rather than respond, she glared at him.

"And seeing as you found a way to create a werewolf, why can't I find a way to uncreate one?"

"Because it takes an open mind and a whole lot more smarts than you've got!" she yelled up into his face. Arrogant jackass.

Harry's eyes glittered, his chest rising and falling. "Did you just call me dumb?"

"No!" she shouted, rising on tiptoe. "I called you not as smart as me." So there!

His chest puffed out when he leaned down and jammed his face at her. "What's your IQ?"

She made a face at him. "What are we using as our source of measurement, your penis?"

"Are you now attacking my manhood?" He virtually squealed the question as if it were incomprehensible she'd do such a thing. Or maybe it was just that she was behaving like a child. Whatever.

"You have to have one to attack!"

Now Harry's temper was flaring, too, his nostrils following suit. She smelled his anger, wanted to bathe in it for the insults he kept hurling her way. "Quit the low blows. How am I less of a man because I don't want to be a werewolf, Mara? Because I don't want to have to figure out a way to explain to the kids about full moon jaunts, fevers, inhuman amounts of consumed beef, eternal life, and the fact that Uncle Harry wants to have his way with the nice Miss Mara until she begs for goddamn mercy?" he seethed, then pulled up short.

His face no longer a hard mask, but sheepish.

"Shit. I just said that out loud, didn't I?"

Mara's mouth was dry. She licked her lips with a nod. "You even spit a little, too." It was just the full moon calling. He'd get over it.

He leaned in even closer. "Really? Where?"

She reached upward, forgetting she felt insulted and attacked, and wiped at the corner of his lips. "Riiight there. Okay, all gone."

Harry's mood swung wide and wild again when he caught her thumb between his teeth and wrapped his arm around her waist, crushing her to him. "Mara?"

"Harry?" she whispered, her breathing coming in gasps.

"I have to," he said between the sudden clench of his teeth.

Mara's mood did the same. Her hand somehow ended up on his chest. The insane urge to dig her fingers into his pecs verging on desperate. "I have to, too."

Harry hoisted her up until her feet were off the ground and his rigid cock rested at her cleft. Even through his jeans, he was stiff and ready. "You're supposed to teach me not to give in to my impulses. Do it. Do that *now*, Mara." His demand was husky, tight with restraint, riddled with his fight for control.

All of her pent up emotions, her desire for Harry, her days and nights of fantasizing about him came down to one thing. She could either fulfill the fantasy and recognize that's all it was, all it would ever be, or she could "teach" him to control his inner sex demon with breathing techniques and finding other vices, like a *Deep Space Nine* marathon.

Deep Space Nine—sex with Harry.

Damn. You. Choices.

Harry's lips were but a half-inch from hers. "I think this is where you tell me not to give in, Mara. *Say it. Say it fast*," he ordered, his tongue striking out to caress the corner of her lip, his hot breath fanning her face.

Her chest became tight, the blood in her veins throbbing, leaving trails of white-hot heat as she warred with her primal urges. As hard as she tried to force the words from her lips, she couldn't say it. Full moon lust induced or not, she wanted this. She'd always wanted this. From the moment she'd laid eyes on him.

Harry. All of him.

Harry hiked her higher, backing them up until she was pressed against the wall in her living room. Now his lips touched hers, just the hint of a graze, but it made her rear up against him, fighting the natural urge to grind against him. It was painfully sweet and sharply hot, gripping her and holding on tight.

Her chest heaved up and down, rising and falling with harsh gasps for breath.

When she squirmed, Harry's rigid flesh rubbing against her, her eyes almost rolled to the back of her head with the exquisite pleasure the sensation wrought.

Harry's groan came out on a gasp as he tried to process what was happening to him in words. "I feel totally out of goddamn control. I know it. I can feel it. But it's almost like I don't give a damn. Jesus, every nerve I own is on fire right now. What if I hurt you? I wouldn't be able to live with myself if I hurt you, Mara."

Mara's breathing was ragged when he thumbed her nipple through her shirt, drawing it to a tight peak, but he pulled his hand away as if she'd bitten him. "I can handle it. Promise."

His lips took a tentative nip at her neck and her spine began to melt. Yet, he planted his hands flat on either side of her against the wall. "I don't know if *I* can," he growled, the scrape of his nails against the wall grating in her ears.

"Should we see?" Mara clung to his waist, her feet hooked at the ankles, her arms tight around his neck. She was baiting him, encouraging him, and she was going to do it without regrets.

"I can't promise flowers and candy the first round."

"I have allergies. Not a huge fan of sweets."

His body trembled against her, rock-hard, rippling, fighting for control. Yet, still he managed to say, "Have you tried that new allergy medicine everyone's been talking about?"

"Do you care?"

His chest continued to rise and fall, the friction of it delicious, teasing her nipples through her shirt until it was an all-out effort not to scream her pleasure. Harry shook his head and huffed out, "Not even a little. Not right now. Promise I'll care later, though. During the flowers and candy stage."

"You do this in stages?" she squeaked.

He rolled his head on his neck, sucking in air before responding. "I want to do this in one fell swoop, but then I'd be an inconsiderate lover."

Need clawed at her gut, yet she managed, "Inconsiderate is a matter of opinion."

"Oh, no. Not when it comes to a woman."

"Sexist."

"Truth-ist."

Impatience, longing, need made her curl her fingers into his hair and clench a fistful of it. "That's not a word, Harry."

"I'm running out of them at this point."

"Then don't say any more of them." *Please.*

"You're sure?" he ground out, his powerful body, fit and hard from working out, quaked.

She swallowed hard. "That I don't want you to talk anymore?"

"No. That you'll be able to handle what I think is going to happen."

"I got this."

Those words triggered his response—forceful and teetering on the edge of uncontrollable.

Harry's hands went to the front of her shirt where he placed his fingers between her breasts and tore the flimsy material, dragging it down and pushing it away. The filmy fabric ripped easily, turning her on almost as much as the brush of his fingers on her overheated skin.

Next, he popped the clasp on the front of her bra, groaning his appreciation when she ripped open the front of his flannel shirt, too, driving her hands inside, placing her fingertips on his flesh, pinching his nipples.

And it was exquisite madness, the hard planes, the sprinkling of hair between his pecs, the crash of his heart against her palm. She grabbed a fistful of his skin, kneading it, driving her hips against his, writhing with so much desperate need it was almost more than she thought she could stand. His skin was like rough satin, smooth, overheated from the need to mate. Mara wanted to burrow inside him, consume him until they had no beginning and no end.

Harry's lips went to her neck again, licking the sensitive flesh, nipping at it, creating wave after wave of heat between her thighs. And then he was shoving her legs from around his waist, tearing at the button of her jeans before giving up and simply removing them with a hard yank.

The rip of denim, her nipples scraping against his chest, his sinfully thick groan in her ear when he first touched his finger to her swollen flesh, made her howl her pleasure. She clung to his neck when he began to move toward her bedroom, kicking her refinished coffee table out of his way as he went.

He stopped momentarily at the entry to her bedroom, scanning the room for her bed with, as he'd dubbed jokingly, a million unnecessary and much too impractical pillows on it. "Condoms," he rasped, running his hands up and down her spine, along the curve of her hip, whispering over the tops of her thighs.

"We don't need them now. My cycle doesn't begin until January or February. It's only November," she somehow managed to force the words out against his neck.

He grabbed a handful of her hair, tugging her head upward to spear her with his intense gaze. "Cycles?" Even in his fight to keep control, he managed to question everything.

"Reproduction is cyclical for female weres."

Even as Harry muttered how crazy it was, he was dropping her to the bed, dragging his jeans off and kicking them aside, his face hard, his focus intent.

Her first quick glimpse of him naked stole her last breath. Harry's silhouette in the moonlight, streaming into the arched stained-glass window just above her bed, was as magnificent and perfect as she'd always thought it would be.

His shoulders, bulky and firm from working out, tapered to a narrow waist and an abdomen so flat, her mouth watered. His thighs were thick and bulging, straining with corded flesh, his hips lean, the sharp line of his hipbone, lickable. His cock was long, jutting upward, thick and impossibly hard. It brushed against her thigh, hot and rigid when he lifted her knees.

Harry's eyes glittered, staring down at her. He clenched his teeth together, gripping her knees with crushing fingers. "I want to devour you, Mara—every last inch of you," he almost spat. "But I'm still afraid I'll hurt you."

Mara put her hands at his wrists, clenching them, pulling him to her until their bodies were pressed together. His thighs pushed into hers, lean muscle against softer flesh. Hard chest against aching breasts. Abs that rippled, flexing against her abdomen.

Mara heard his heart crash, felt the tight hold he had beginning to crumble, weakening his resolve until he was unable to move. His fists clenched into tight balls of restraint, his chest heaved with effort.

So she reached between them, stroking the length of his shaft before lifting her hips and placing him at her entry.

Harry clamped his lips to hers, possessive, demanding, he drove his tongue into her mouth as he drove his cock into her desperate, aching body.

The impact of his thrust upward tore through her, making her gasp out loud, claw at his back until her fingers dug into his muscles. His cock stretched her and she welcomed it, welcomed the rigid invasion of heat.

Harry spread her wide, hiking her legs up with a hiss when he penetrated her deeper, harder.

Slick with desire, Mara reveled in his forceful thrusts, drove her hips right back at his, matching his speed, insisting with her body he take her higher, harder.

He suckled her tongue, slipping his over hers in a rasp of silken flesh, while his hands clutched fistfuls of her hair, pulling at it to expose her throat. He tore his mouth from hers, nipping at her jaw, moving to her ear, rimming the lobe.

Mara's need grew, frenzied, wetter, rising upward, and when Harry cupped her breast, she almost lost total control, bucking against him. His mouth encompassed her nipple, licking it until it turned hard, blowing on it only to warm it again with his tongue.

Harry's strokes began to pick up speed, his hips crashing against hers while he sucked her deeper into the vortex of climax.

Lights flashed behind her eyes, brilliant streaks of white and blue. Her clit throbbed an achy rhythm, scraping against his crisp pubic hairs as he rolled up and down with each thrust.

His last drive into her seared her, branded her forever. They came together in a long howl of vocal pleasure. White-hot and desperate, their movements so in sync, it was as if they'd always done this.

Harry's head reared upward, the lean corded muscle beneath his flesh tight when he screamed her name.

As long as Mara lived, she'd never forget Harry inside her, obliterating her sanity, stealing the last protected piece of her heart.

A loud bang of a fist at the bedroom door brought them both crashing to reality. Harry wrapped his arms around her waist and rolled with her until she was on top of him. He cupped her breasts, skimmed his hands over nipples, slipped his fingers into her wet cleft. Harry was still stiff, making it an effort for her to answer the knock on the door.

Still shaky, Mara called out, "Yes?"

"Hey, lovebirds! Knock off the sexy times—we got fucking trouble!" Nina yelled.

Harry's lips were at her breast, licking, teasing, enveloping her nipple. Her fingers automatically went to his hair, driving her fingers into it and fighting a long moan of satisfaction.

Nina knocked again—this time harder. "Did you fucking hear me, nerds? Put your clothes on and your private parts away. My Carl's really missing!"

CHAPTER
12

Mara, Nina, Marty, Darnell, and Harry scoured the woods, calling out Carl's name.

"Motherfucker—where's my freakin' zombie! It's cold out here, right?" she asked Marty. According to Mara, Nina had no sense of the temperature as a vampire. She couldn't gauge how cold it truly was.

Marty gave her a squeeze, rubbing Nina's arm. "It is, but Carl's dead, honey. I don't think he can feel it. Much like you can't."

Nina made a face, kicking stray limbs out of her way in anger. "Have you seen his damn arms and legs, dude? They're stiff as shit from rigor mortis. The cold can't help that. What if he's just out here, wandering around all alone? He doesn't know his way. He can't even talk, for fuck's sake. And who the fuck's gonna talk to him anyway? He's dead. Like scary dead."

"Which only makes him that much harder to sniff out." Marty remarked what they'd all forgotten earlier. If Carl was dead, he was almost impossible to smell. He didn't have the stench a rotting body should have due to the baths Nina insisted he take.

"I ain't nevah gonna forgive myself, Nina. I'm damn well sorry,"

Darnell said, letting his head hang low. "I don't know what happened to me. One minute we was watchin' Walter make crystal meth on *Breaking Bad*, the next, I woke up and found Carl gone. Swear I don't know what happened."

Mara reached around the enormous demon and gave him a hug, patting his shoulders. "Carl's hard to keep track of. We know you'd never let anything happen to him intentionally, Darnell. We'll find him, I know it."

Mara's conviction, her determination, settled deep in his bones. Harry watched these people from beneath the brim of his knitted hat, people he barely knew, band together to find Carl, and he found himself full of yet more wonder.

No matter the situation, no matter the time of day or night, they were always there for each other. Always. Everything stopped when one of them needed the other.

And then there was Mara—one of the first to insist they all scour the area. She was warm, soft, compassionate, gentle, fiercely protective of her family and friends.

And he wanted her almost more than he had earlier.

Making love with her had been mind-blowing. But it wasn't just some of the most incredible sex he'd ever had, or the fact that he'd experienced it on a hormonal high. It was afterward, when she'd sat atop him, the mixture of strong and shy, confident and vulnerable as she gazed at him with a smile that made his gut twist and ache.

Shit. Shit. Shit.

He didn't want this. He didn't want to want her. Not given the fact that if he found a way out of this, nothing between them could ever work. She was dead set on believing it was some kind of insult not to want in on the way of the werewolf. She'd resent his choices. He'd only end up stomping all over her lycanthropic sensibilities like the clod he was.

Yet, the idea he'd never experience Mara again, left him empty.

Not the kind of empty he felt when Brigitte had broken it off with him, or for that matter, the kind of empty his bank account had felt. Not the "Damn, it sucks to eat alone" kind of empty. It was the "I don't want to think about a day when I don't see your face" kind of empty.

Shit, shit, shit.

Harry stopped dead in his thoughts, cocking his ear. While the women fretted out loud over Carl's disappearance, he listened.

To everything. Caught up, now he couldn't stop the noises. Leaves rustling, crisp and rubbing against one another in the freezing cold wind. He *heard* the foliage, deeply imbedded in the soil, most of it dormant now in winter, resting until spring.

He felt the pulse of everyone's anxiety, heard snowflakes gather and fall in swirling patches. Felt the vibration of forest animals, their blood coursing through their veins, their small hearts pounding out steady beats.

It was like seeing sounds. And it was madness. He put his hands up to block the stimuli, shaking his head as though it would knock the noise out of his brain.

But then he remembered what Mara said. Focus on your subject, force the everyday sounds of life, conversations and such, out.

Harry squared his shoulders and focused so hard he broke into a cold sweat. Clammy chills chased up and down his spine, but he managed to block out Nina's anxious worry, Marty's need to soothe and pacify her, Mara's muttered worry, Darnell's huffing body as he lumbered over fallen logs.

Because there was one he heard above all else.

Carl. That was Carl's moan, a stilted grunt, a low whimper of fear.

And it was close. So close, it became all Harry heard.

Carl was terrified. He smelled it, almost tasted it, and it was nearly more than Harry could bear. Helpless, alone in the dark,

Carl's pitiful snuffle grew weaker. He was giving up hope anyone would find him, jarring Harry into action.

Harry began to run, jumping over a fallen tree, knowing it was there before his eyes even saw it. His running turned into a gallop—a blurring gallop of colors and sounds, swooshing past his sharp eyes. His ears twitched, burned, ached with the strain to hear Carl.

Hang tough, Carl—I'm coming!

Left! Carl was to the left—in a patch of thick pines. The clank of a chain vibrated in Harry's ears, resonating until his head throbbed, threatening to explode.

And then he saw Carl, as clear as day. Gaunt and still, pale with that greenish tint to him, eerily glowing under the moonlight, and slumped against a tree in his rigid, postmortem pose. The new shirt Nina had bought him torn, his eyes wide and glazed, his mouth slack in defeat. Closer inspection showed he'd been tied there with a heavy chain of some kind.

Son of a bitch. Whoever did this would pay.

His heart crashed in his ears, his fury rose to a higher level, one he hadn't experienced quite this way, one that had him gnashing his teeth on Carl's behalf.

Skidding to stop, he opened his mouth to soothe Carl and realized he couldn't speak. What the hell?

Harry looked down.

He had paws. Big hairy, black paws.

Holy shit—he'd shifted. No help from the shifting gurus. No big drama. Just boom. Full-on werewolf.

Carl moaned again, fretful, keeping him from wasting time marveling about the ease with which he'd shifted, and turning all his concern toward Carl.

Trotting over to him, Harry used his muzzle to nudge Carl's stiff hand, running his nose along it with a gentle sniff. Carl shrank back in fear, his body banging hard up against the trunk of a gnarled tree as he used his stiff legs to try and scurry around the base of it and away from Harry.

Shit. He had to find a way to show him he was just bologna-sandwich-loving Harry—or shift back. Which he wasn't entirely sure he could do just yet. For now, he had to convince Carl he was safe.

So he rubbed his large head against Carl's knee then rolled over on his back to show his submissive nature. But Carl howled in response. More terrified than ever by the look in his usually dull expression, now wide with fear.

It was while he was on his back he realized that Carl wasn't just tied to the tree, he was rigged to it. Jesus Christ. As Harry got a better look, he found Carl's arms were high above his head, one wrong move and Carl could loosen those chains and . . . If Harry used his super-strength to yank the chain off, it would trigger an ax, high above Carl's head, effectually swinging down and embedding in the zombie's skull.

He was a huge fan of zombie apocalyptic fiction. Not a fan of it when a sweet, if not precocious, man-child he'd like to think he'd bonded with over heads of broccoli and carrot sandwiches would end up eradicated with one wrong move.

Who would do this? It would kill Carl if the evil, glinting ax fell on him. Wasn't that how you killed zombies? Slicing off their heads?

Who else knew about Carl? Guido? He was the only other person who knew of Carl's whereabouts aside from the girls. And what was his motivation for killing him?

Rage burned in the pit of Harry's gut as his suspicions turned to the witch doctor. But Carl had something else attached to him, a rumpled note in the pocket of his dirty, torn shirt.

Harry decided it was time to let everything else go and focus on keeping Carl from jerking the tightly wrapped chains. He hopped up, using his hind legs to anchor his feet before placing his paws on either side of the tree and willing Carl to look at him—feel his emotions—see Harry meant him no harm.

Instead, Carl keened a high wail of terror. Harry licked his face to get his attention, forcing himself to forget it was dead flesh he was licking, willing Carl to understand. *It's me, buddy. Harry.*

He stared harder.

Carl stopped attempting to release himself and cocked his head.

Sort of. It was a slight shift to the left, but it was definitely inquisitive in nature. He thwarted all motion and stared intently at Harry for a brief moment, as though he got the message Harry was trying to send with his werewolf mind-meld, but then terror streaked his face again, and he began to wail.

"Carl?" He heard Mara call out from the darkness, her voice full of anxious worry.

"Where the fuck are you, Carl?"

Nina. That was Nina. And some fear. Nina was afraid for Carl. He smelled it.

Christ, this was crazy.

Snow crunched beneath several pairs of feet as the women and Darnell hit the thick patch of trees where Carl was tethered. Harry hopped down, unsure how to warn them about Carl's precarious position, seeing as he wasn't quite sure how to shift back.

Carl saw Nina first, his cries easing and his face going slack again, the relief on his face evident.

Nina made a dash for Carl just as Mara and Marty approached, her feet moving in a blur of motion.

"Harry?" Mara asked, surprise riddling her question. She reached a hand out to cup his muzzle, gazing into his eyes. He bumped her hip with his hindquarters, nudging her in acknowledgment.

"You shifted? All on your own? Holy cow, look at you!" There was a hint of pride in her voice, and it made him want to stomp around and crush beer cans with his bare hands, shred a big steak with his teeth, howl with smug satisfaction.

As he gazed into her beautiful blue eyes, something in Harry shifted. He got lost in the orbs, and he had no rhyme or reason for it. It just happened, deepening his earlier feelings until his chest ached.

"Hold tight, buddy," Nina reassured Carl. "I got this."

Alarm and panic seized Harry all at once. He tore his muzzle from Mara's warm hand, whipping around in just enough time to see Nina begin to grab on to the chains tying Carl to the tree.

And she wasn't gonna like it, but he had to take her out.

Or she'd kill Carl.

Apologies in advance, Crypt Keeper.

WITH a deep growl, Harry went for Nina. His leap in the air, silhouetted by the buttery moon, executed to perfection. He arced up and over, ramming his enormous body into Nina and knocking her almost clear across the large group of trees.

The sharp crack of wood reverberated through the trees, pinging against them, followed by her angry grunt.

"Harry!" Mara yelped in surprise. If this was another one of his angry outbursts because he was a werewolf, blah, blah, blah, she was going to show him what being-around-for-as-long-as-she-had was like when she wiped the wooded floor with him.

Nina rose like the Terminator, angry and snarling, her fangs sharp and gleaming. One minute she was down, the next she was up, launching herself at Harry and screaming, "I'm gonna cut a bitch!"

Marty flew between them, catching Nina by ramming her hands into her chest. "Knock it off, night dweller!"

"Hold up!" Darnell shouted, his large hand pointing upward. "Harry's just doin' right by Carl. Look up."

All eyes followed Darnell's finger.

Mara gasped when she saw what he was pointing out. "What the hell is going on?"

"Goddamn it, who the hell has it out for my zombie? Swear to Christ, when we find out who's messin' with us, somebody's gonna fekkin' well die," Nina seethed, shaking off her anger with Harry and stomping toward a petrified Carl.

Mara gasped again when she saw the tree limbs above Carl's head. Someone had rigged the chains binding Carl. If they'd tried to free him without seeing . . . She blanched, shivering harder. "Nina! Keep Carl still. I'll get this."

As Harry paced and huffed and Nina and Marty stroked Carl's hands, still high above his head, Mara scaled the tree. If she was nothing else, she was a proficient tree climber after having two brothers to keep up with.

As the ax hanging over Carl's head came into view, Mara cocked her head at the intricate, almost guillotine-like maze of chains and her brain raced. Who would go to this much trouble to hurt someone so helpless? What did Carl have to do with anything?

She began to attack the mess, carefully pulling and unwinding. "Hold on, Carl—I'm almost done!" she called down to the whimpering zombie. Her hands, though ice-cold, managed to move quickly, unlacing the chains and yanking the ax up and off the limb above Carl's head.

Carl made a strange sound of relief when Nina pulled the remaining chains from his hands, lifting an arm and thumping Nina on the shoulder in his trademark sign of affection.

Nina pulled him into a hug, stroking the back of his head, her voice holding a hint of a tremble as she consoled him. "Jesus, dude. Who the fuck did this?"

Mara hopped down from the tree, reaching down to grab on to Darnell's hand as he helped her off the last limb.

Carl grunted upon seeing her, dragging his stiff foot behind him; he fell into her in his zombie embrace. She gave him a gentle hug, pulling back to look into his fear-glazed eyes. "You okay, Carl?"

Carl tucked his head into her and snuffed against her shoulder before lifting it and giving her his lopsided grin. Then he set his sights on Harry; tripping and stumbling, he made his way to him, thumping him on the back, using the side of his hand to stroke Harry's fur in jerky fashion.

Harry's big body began to tremble and quake and in mere seconds, he'd shifted back to his human form without so much as a protesting groan.

And he was naked.

Even in the height of this madness, Mara found a way to appreciate Harry's gorgeous physique. It made her shiver.

Harry, on all fours, didn't even open his eyes, and he didn't look up at the group. "I'm naked, right?"

"Like the day you were born," Marty said on a snort, averting her eyes.

"Dangly bits and everything, dude. Look away, Carl—stranger junk alert," Nina cracked, grasping Carl's hand and using it to cover his eyes.

"Shit," Harry mumbled at the snow-covered ground.

Darnell was the first to react. He yanked off his sweatshirt and covered Harry with it, holding out his hand to help him up.

Harry tucked himself inside the sweatshirt, tugging it down over his muscled thighs as he rose.

Mara fought a girlish sigh and instead smiled at him. "You were awesome! You found Carl."

Harry nodded and smiled back. "Yep."

She wrapped her hands together behind her back as they began to walk back toward her cottage behind the others. "And how ever did you do that, Harry Emmerson? Was it due to your uncanny powers of deduction?"

"Nope," he muttered low.

"Your superior detective skills, *Castle*?"

"No again."

Mara mock gasped. "Wait. Could it be it was because of those werewolf abilities you so despise?"

"Maybe."

"Aha!" she shouted before giggling. Score one for lycanthropy.

Harry paused, barefoot and almost naked, and grabbed her arm. "Look, Mara, I told you it's no insult to you and your family, pack, whatever. It has nothing to do with this not being amazing, because it is, and under any other circumstance, I'd be all for it. I'm sorry if you feel insulted. That's not my intention. And I don't despise these abilities. I just don't want them."

Mara decided they had bigger fish to fry tonight than Harry's inability to accept his fate. "And I'm just saying it isn't all bad. However, that's all I'll say for now."

Harry grabbed her hand and pulled her close, wrapping his arm around her waist. He looked down at her, a smile flirting with his lips. "Really?"

"Really," she confirmed, putting her hand on his chest. "And thank you. We were all so caught up with worry we forgot to listen for Carl. You, on the other hand, were brilliant."

Harry's smile was warm. "I'm just glad he's okay. He was pretty scared."

"None of this makes any sense. First the kids, and now Carl."

"You think they're related?"

"I think it's pretty strange that there've been two instances so close together, and so similar, don't you?"

He shook his head, his lips thinning. "Yep, and I keep trying to make the connection between the kids and Carl, and I can't. The only thing I can think of is Guido."

No. That didn't add up. Guido didn't even know about Harry's niece and nephew. "But what does he have to do with Mimi and Fletch?"

"That's where I lose the connection, too."

"Hey, lovebirds!" Nina called out. "Step that shit up. We need to stay together, and we need to get back before Harry's man parts freeze the fuck off."

Harry looked down at Mara, the crinkle of his eyes showing his amusement. "She has no filter."

Mara giggled. "Nope. For as long as I've known her, she's always just said it."

He shrugged his shoulders and chuckled, the deep vibration of it tickling her hand. "It's rather refreshing, if obnoxious and crude."

"But you have to admit it's better that she's on your team. Imagine her on the opposing side."

Harry mocked a shudder. "I'll take the zero on that. So, question?"

"Make it fast, or she will get angry. Angry Nina is scary Nina."

"Are you upset that she knows what we were doing . . . you know, before? I don't want to embarrass you."

She was a million things in the aftermath of their lovemaking, but upset that Nina knew what they'd been up to was the least of it. She almost avoided his eyes, then internally voted for complete honesty. How could she be ashamed of such an amazing experience? Mara shook her head. "No."

He let his head drop, lowering his lips and resting them just tantalizing inches from hers. "You're kinda smart and hot."

Now she was embarrassed. Mara let her eyes fall to his chest, their cold noses pressed together. "I'm mostly not," she denied.

Bracketing her face, Harry lifted her chin, forcing her to rise on tiptoe, and claimed her lips in forceful possession, sending that same rush of heat straight to the place between her legs he had but an hour ago. He swept his tongue over hers before releasing her. "For the record," he whispered, "I emphatically disagree, Mara Flaherty, and I don't get how you can't see it. But I want you to know I do. I see it. I see *all* of it."

His words, said with such forceful conviction, made her shiver, but her response was guarded. "Duly noted," she murmured, taking his lead on the path back to her cottage, fighting the impulse to read too much into Harry's words.

CHAPTER 13

Upon their return, Carl safe and warm, wrapped in a cocoon of blankets and pressed against Nina's side, they all hovered over Mara's kitchen table. Marty had gone home to keep Keegan from growing suspicious in her absence. Now, with Wanda and Archibald, her husband's manservant, on Skype, silence prevailed.

Harry's good mood had turned sour when he'd remembered the note he'd seen tucked into Carl's shirt pocket. He'd yanked it from Carl's pocket, hissing his anger after reading it.

After careful examination, including sniffing the paper and studying the handwriting, none of them could figure out what it meant. No scent on the paper that was recognizable, nothing special about the handwriting.

It left them all not only stumped but on high alert. Everyone was edgy, but no one was edgier than Harry.

"Who the hell is doing this?" Harry said between thin lips, swiping the note up with an angry hand.

Nina flicked the note with two fingers. "Dude, somebody knows about you two, and whoever the fuck it is, they don't like it. But

I'll tell you this, the dickknuckle responsible for stalkin' kids and stealin' my zombie's gonna fucking pay."

Mara's veins had turned to ice, the heat emanating from the nearby fireplace doing nothing to warm her. *Tell Mara and Harry I see them . . .* " The words on the spiral-pad notepaper sent cold chills up her arms and alarm bells screeching in her brain.

Nina's hand slammed down on the table, the brunt of it knocking the vase of silk flowers over. "Bet it's fucking Guido. Why the fuck he'd be doing this, I got no clue, but he's the only other person who knows about Carl being with us. We need to go get his ass and shake it out of him."

"And if it's not him?" Harry asked, his voice rising. "Then what?"

Nina slammed her fist on the counter, making Carl bury his face in her neck. "Then we goddamn well do what we always do in every other case like this. We figure it out—together—and we don't stop till we take a motherfucker out."

"Nina!" Wanda yelled from the laptop on Skype, her fuzzy pink bathrobe tucked around her chin. "Before we get too crazy, how about we poke around and see if maybe it's an old girlfriend of Harry's? Jealous or something." Her eyes fell on Harry. "So you have any of those, Harry? Maybe someone who saw you and Mara together yesterday?"

Harry shook his head. "I don't date anyone at work for a reason. Secondly, whoever this was took Mimi and Fletcher before Mara and I introduced ourselves as a couple."

Mara sat silently. She didn't want to know about Harry's ex-girlfriends. Not if they weren't important to finding out who'd taken Carl and the children.

Archibald stuck his shiny head around Wanda's shoulder and peered at them. "I'm Archibald, sir," he addressed Harry with a smile. "Might I say your children are delightful. We've had a lovely time these past days. We've baked, we've indulged in song and even some dance, for which I'm no match for the lovely Miss Mimi. Then Mimi and I had a divine traditional English tea. Sir Fletcher and I battled the evil dragon with our makeshift swords made of cardboard and tinfoil. Truly, they are superb, precocious, well-mannered children. They have asked to call me Grandpa Arch, as the others do. Shall I give them your permission?"

Harry's hard swallow tore at Mara's heart, his grief biting her hard. He loved those children, and despite their rocky start, he missed them. "Of course. I'm glad to hear that, Archibald," he said, his voice husky and low. "They're a handful sometimes. I appreciate your help."

Arch held up a finger with a refined chuckle. "Ah, you mistake a handful for insightful, curious minds. Their energy, if I might be so bold, is simply misdirected. And of course, there is the issue of the loss of their parents. My deepest condolences to you." Arch bowed his head momentarily.

Harry swallowed again, his fist clenching around the note. "Thank you."

"However, Sir Harry," Arch said, his weathered face changing from light to dark. "On one of our nature walks, wherein we chatted about things such as the dormant state of Miss Wanda's vast gardens and the reason for said state during winter, as well as Mimi's unwavering love of the color purple, we did discuss this woman who came to their educational facility and took the children."

Harry sat up straight, leaning toward the computer. "And?"

Arch scowled. "As we walked, Sir Fletcher made mention of something I noted but made no impression on me until just this moment. He said the woman who took them on their walk had whiskers. Now, while I found that unusual, and of course, I wanted to remain calm and not cause greater concern for the young lad, I quite passively asked him what he meant. He said her *chin* had whiskers—bushy whiskers. I don't think I quite understood what that meant, other than certainly, some women of a certain age," he paused to clear his throat, "need more assistance than others in maintaining their grooming habits. Yet now, I question whether this is a factor, a *paranormal* factor, in your quest to consider all possible suspects."

"Whiskers?" Mara repeated, putting together what a child of eight would interpret as whiskers. "So potentially, she had unsightly hair?"

Arch shook his head. "No, miss. I don't believe it was simply a female issue. I did not press Sir Fletcher so as not to frighten him. Yet I firmly believe this was something he considered out of the ordinary. Not simply because it was so pronounced on a woman, but just that he'd made note of the very fact that they were *bushy* whiskers. Along with, as you already know, Mimi's description of her 'swingy' hair. He said it as though he knew it was rude to speak of out loud, yet appeared to find it rather important, now that I reflect."

"So we're lookin' for a bitch who has a beard?" Nina crowed.

"Oh, Miss Nina," Arch said on a chuckle. "I do so miss your presence. Tell me, when will you bring me my sweet Charlie? Surely, she's overdue for some of Grandfather Archibald's spoiling?"

Nina held up her knuckles to the screen for Arch to bump, her grin wide. "She doesn't need another fucking toy, Arch. Jesus, you and the stuffed unicorns. She's got a hundred of 'em in her damn crib. Promise, once shit cools off, I'll bring her over, and Carl, too."

Carl's glazed eyes had brightened while he watched Archibald talk. He thumped the screen with the side of his hand in his attempt at a wave.

Archibald waved back. "Hello, Sir Carl! Aren't you a fetching fellow? Come soon to visit, won't you? I shall make you a broccoli soufflé so light and airy, you'll surely float."

Carl grunted his approval, but swiftly became distracted. He stood still for a moment, his head cocked at an awkward angle as though realization had just hit him, then began to hop around in his stilted fashion.

He grabbed a handful of Mara's hair and tugged at it. Due to his stiff limbs, what Mara was certain was meant to be just a tug turned into a full-on wrenching. "Ow! Easy, Carl. It's attached to my head," she reminded him with a smile.

But Carl wouldn't let go. He clutched her hair tighter, drawing her to his chest.

"Carl!" Nina jumped up with a shout. "No hair pulling, buddy. Do you remember our list of rules and personal space?"

Carl began to make new sounds, anxious and frantic. He loosened his grip, but refused to let go.

Mara's ears twitched. "I think he's trying to tell us something," she said on a wince when he lifted the rope of her hair higher and shook it.

Carl bounced once more, spewing forth short, excited grunts.

Harry rose from the table and put his hand on Carl's. "Carl, easy, pal," he soothed, easing the thick strands from Carl's grip. "First, are you trying to tell us something you think is important?"

Carl hopped again, snorting and huffing with a wheeze.

Harry smiled his encouragement. "Okay, good. So, obviously, it has something to do with Mara's hair?"

Carl went straight for her head again, but this time Mara ducked him. "My hair, right, Carl?"

"Wait!" Wanda yelled from the laptop screen. "Archibald just said Mimi mentioned the woman who took them had swingy hair like Mara! Is that what you mean, Carl?"

Carl thumped the counter with the side of his hand.

"Good job, pal," Harry complimented with a gentle pat on the back and a warm grin. "Now, what about Mara's hair? I don't get it, but I will, okay? Just give me a minute, and if you understand what I'm saying, bang the counter, okay?"

Carl banged the counter, his grunts becoming more expressive.

Mara squeezed his arm and grinned. "Oh, Carl, you're so smart! So, does my hair have to do with something you know?"

Carl whacked the countertop so hard that he knocked one of his fingers off. It rolled to the end of the counter and dropped to the floor with a light thud.

"Shit," Nina muttered. "I'll get the duct tape."

"Easy, Carl," Mara coaxed with a smile. "Don't hurt yourself. So you know something that we need to know to help us find out what that note you had means?"

Carl thumped, only this time, with less vigor.

"Did you know the person who took you, Carl? Was it Guido?"

Carl stood stock-still.

Not Guido. Hold on. *Her hair.* She twisted the length of it, her eyes widening. "My hair . . . do you think the person who took Mimi and Fletcher was the same person that took you, Carl? Did she say something about the kids to you?"

"Christ, this is like goddamn zombie charades," Nina muttered, reentering the room with silver duct tape. She began to wrap Carl's finger back on, while Carl thumped his other hand in answer to Mara's question.

Harry sat back in his chair, his shoulders sagging. "So the person who took Carl is probably the same person who took the kids."

Carl thumped once more.

"Do you know this person, Carl? Have you ever seen this person before?" Mara asked, pressing the edges of the duct tape on his finger to secure it.

Carl didn't move.

No. Damn. "Did she talk about me and Harry, Carl? Did she talk about the kids?"

Carl thumped once more.

"Maybe we should be more direct rather than generalize? My

gut says whoever this is, even though she took Carl, she wouldn't let slip much that was important. Not if she's a smart kidnapper, anyway, even with Carl unable to speak," Harry suggested. "Did the lady say anything else but our names, Carl?" Harry asked.

Carl played statue.

Damn, damn, damn.

"But *who* is this woman? How are Carl and the children connected in her mind other than to both of you?" Wanda chirped from the laptop, straightening in her seat. "I go back to my original theory, Harry. Do you have any ex-girlfriends with the potential to do harm? Whatever this is about, part of it is about you and Mara being together. That much is obvious."

Harry shook his head. "I've only had a couple of serious girlfriends, and I think I can quite honestly say with no disrespect intended, they wouldn't go to these lengths to catch my attention. I don't think they're capable of putting something like this together."

Mara's heart sang a stupid song, giddy over the fact that if nothing else, she won the biggest brains contest. *Knock that off, Mara. It's catty and petty.* "So for now we rule out a jealous ex and focus on what? None of this makes sense. I certainly don't know anyone who cares one way or the other about our pretend relationship."

"Astrid," Harry dropped the word like a bomb.

Mara's head swung upward. She was definitely smart enough, and she'd certainly expressed her displeasure about her and Harry dating. "She doesn't have swingy hair like me."

"A wig?" Wanda suggested.

Mara shook her head. "Astrid's quirky and even sometimes possessive, but she's not—"

"Nutty as squirrel shit, Short-Shot? I'm here to tell ya, I've met that wingnut a time or two at some of Pack's company picnics. Bitch is one screw shy of coming unhinged, and I'm not just talkin' brainy kinda wingnut like you two. I'm talkin' full-on, all in her head, crazy-ass nutcase. I did the potato sack race with her. You learn a lot about a whack when your ankles are tied the fuck together like drumsticks on a roast chicken." Nina nodded her dark head to confirm her statement.

Mara was quick to defend her friend. "But she's known all along about my crush on Harry. She supported it. I would daydream all the time with her . . ." Oh. Oh, God, why, why, why were her emotions suddenly like a babbling brook?

Harry's eyes found hers, but his words didn't belie his feelings on the subject, nor did they mock. He was All Business Harry. "So you've talked with Astrid about this—I mean, me? She knows how you feel, felt . . . whatever?"

Nina's mouth began to open, but even from the distance Skype created, Wanda was on watch. Her finger flew upward before tapping the screen. "Nina! Do not. I'm warning you. Do not open your big mouth, or I'll drive over there tonight and stuff one of Fletcher's dirty socks in it."

Nina smirked, using her fingers to indicate she was zipping her lip and throwing away the key.

Mara looked down at her hands and swallowed. How could she admit she'd fantasized loud and proud over many a lunch with Astrid as her compadre in lust. How could she divulge that all her secret desires had been shared out loud? But she had to. If Astrid was suspect, and she'd had anything to do with taking the children or Carl, they needed to look into all aspects of her—even the most unbearably uncomfortable. "Yes. Astrid knew."

Harry lifted her chin, forcing her eyes to meet his, his gaze intent. "Then we need to investigate, okay?"

Mara clenched her eyes shut, hoping her utter humiliation would go away if she just willed it gone. When she popped them open, Harry was still gazing at her. No such luck. "Okay. But please let me talk to her first? Astrid's an odd bird, and I know that. I've always known that, but I don't want her to feel cornered if she had nothing to do with this. She's already low in the self-esteem department. She thinks no one likes her no matter how openly we say we do. It could really hurt her if she's not responsible."

Harry gave her chin a gentle squeeze. "Deal."

"All right, ladies and gentleman," Wanda interrupted with a warm smile. "It's late, and I have children to get up with in the morning. So I'll say goodnight, but we'll see you on Friday night for sledding. Oh, and the kids miss you, Harry. They said so just tonight after snack and bath time. I'm really enjoying them. Thank you for sharing them with me," she said with a warm smile.

Harry's expression went humble. "Good to know. Thank you, Wanda, for watching out for them. You, too, Arch. I don't know what I would've done without all of you."

You just don't want to be one of us. Ugh. Why did that trouble her so?

Wanda and Arch signed off with the promise they'd give the children Harry's love.

Nina dropped off the stool, holding out her hand to Carl. "You two keep the screeching during the sexy times down, would ya? Carl's fucking freaked out with all the stimuli. All that 'do that to me one more time' shit's bound to rile him." She cackled at her joke, taking Carl off to the lone guest room.

Mara's face went red, her cheeks burning, but Harry scooped her up from behind, nuzzling her neck. "Don't listen to the cranky vampire. 'Do that to me one more time' is perfectly acceptable bedroom talk. Succinct, yet super seductive and sexy. And a song, I think, right?"

Mara stifled a giggle, allowing Harry to lead her into the bedroom.

Tomorrow she'd talk to Astrid. Tonight she'd try to forget that Harry didn't want to be a part of the pack, and that it bugged the hell out of her.

Tonight was for living in the moment.

The moment with Harry in it.

"MARA!" Astrid flagged her down in the hallway as she approached the lab. Mara fought a visible cringe. She'd spent all morning trying to find the words to cobble together in order to avoid coming off confrontational, but still get some answers from Astrid.

She sucked at confrontation. Hard. The last thing she wanted to do was accuse Astrid of something so horrible without sound reasons behind it.

Sucking in a breath, she plastered a smile on her face and waved as Astrid approached.

Astrid was all smiles today. If she was upset that she'd missed their usual morning coffee break together, she didn't show it. "Hey! Missed you at morning break."

Mara fought a look of confusion. What? No interrogation. No wisecracks about her and Harry in the janitor's closet? Who was this cheerful, friendly soul? "Sorry about that. I've been so backed up in the lab, I totally lost track of time." *Liar!*

Astrid smiled again, brilliant and wide. Two times in as many seconds? "Listen, I wanted to talk to you about something. Got a sec?"

And here it came. Mara braced herself for Astrid's anger. "You bet. Bathroom?"

Astrid led the way, her white Crocs following a precise pattern on the floor, her soft counting just above a whisper. She propped the door open and smiled again, letting Mara enter first.

Mara leaned against the ceramic row of sinks, forcing herself to look Astrid in the eye. "What's up?"

Her return gaze was contrite. "Look, I know I behaved badly about

Harry and you. I kinda took all the fun out of your announcement, didn't I? I suck, and I feel like shit about it. I know I'm insecure and moody and difficult, but I acted like a total jerk. There's no excuse for it. I can only say I'm sorry."

Mara frowned, readjusting her position against the sink. She opened her mouth to speak, then snapped it shut while Astrid waited for her response. Yesterday Astrid had behaved like they were in grammar school, but today she was an adult? Maybe she'd just had a bad day? But Astrid always had bad days. More often than not.

Mara's voice was tentative when she finally replied. "So you're okay with it?" She couldn't believe she was asking her friend if she was okay with her dating Harry. Like Astrid was her mother and she needed permission. But here she was, not rocking the friendship boat.

Astrid gave her a sheepish look from behind the glasses she wore for no other reason than to hide her eyes from the world. "It's not for me to decide, Mara. And of course I'm okay," she said with warm conviction, reaching out to squeeze Mara's arm. "I think it's great that your dreams suddenly came true. I guess I was just caught off guard by it. I felt like we spent so much time talking about it that when it happened, and when you didn't tell me, I was really hurt. It was like planning a wedding with your friend and then not being invited, ya know? You know how lame I can be about stuff like that. I'm stupid insecure. You know it. I know it. Everyone knows it. So I was a bitch because of it."

This was more like the Astrid she'd learned to appreciate early on in their friendship before they'd teamed up with Leah and Ying. Mara let out a breath. "I'm so relieved. I worried about it all night. I didn't call or text because I didn't want to push you." Mostly true. She had worried Astrid would hack off her limbs and use them to make a Mara marionette. Relief flooded her from head to toe, almost making her shaky.

Astrid waved a dismissive hand and smiled. "I'm really happy and excited for you. All the time invested finally paid off. So, if you don't mind me asking, when did this happen? How did I miss it? Was I being selfish again?"

Now the lying began—again. She turned to wash her hands in the sink, letting the disinfectant soap pile into her hand until it looked like soft-serve ice cream. "Just two days ago. Harry asked me out, actually kind of suddenly. I never picked up the vibe from him. Well, you know that because we talked about it so much. So I was surprised, but I said yes, of course, and we just sort of clicked. It's nothing official yet. But we figured it would be stupid to try and hide it."

Astrid nodded her consent, a smile still fastened to her face. "Definitely not easy with the kind of gossip that goes on here. How are you going to handle that, by the way? The human and werewolf thing? I mean, the humans won't think anything of it, but the werewolves will be curious. I know the rule no longer applies to us dating humans, but you know, the old order still exists in some narrow minds. Everyone knows you're my friend, so I want to give the kind of answers you're comfortable with. Just say the word."

Mara paused for a moment, trying to pick up any sign Astrid was just giving good face, but there was nothing. Not a hint of dissent. She turned to face her to find Astrid smiling. "For now, we're just trying to see what happens. Day by day thing. So maybe just say we're taking it slow and that's all you know?"

"You got it. And I'm still sorry I kind of ruined the intro bit."

Mara gave her a sudden, grateful hug, partially out of relief that she was pretty sure Astrid wasn't the one who was snatching people out of their lives, and partially because when she tried, she was a really good friend. "It's all good. Forget it and come have lunch with Harry and me today, okay?"

Astrid smiled again, holding the door of the bathroom open for Mara. "You bet. Save me a seat."

On another sigh, Mara waved to her and skipped off to her beloved lab, happy in the knowledge she had Astrid's support of her new relationship with her pretend boyfriend.

She ran right into Leah on her way back down the hall. "Hey? You okay?" her friend asked.

Mara forced herself to look her directly in the eye. "Yeah. I'm good. Why do you ask?"

Leah rolled her eyes, brushing her sandy hair away from her face. "I just saw you leave the bathroom with Astrid. Is she giving you shit about you and Harry? Because I know what she's like, and she'll suck the life out of all the fun. Just like she does with everything else that even remotely smells like happiness."

Mara squeezed her arm. "Actually, this might surprise you, but she apologized for being so awful to Harry yesterday. Said she was happy for us, and that she was just upset because I didn't tell her about us first."

Leah made a face. "She's a nut, Mara. You be careful around her. Who says she should have been the first to know anyway? Is she like your mother now? That's why we stopped indulging you at lunch when you talked about Harry—because Astrid always acted like it was just a secret between you two instead of all of us. She got mad at Ying once because she mentioned something you'd said about Harry, and Astrid didn't know about it. It made Ying and me uncomfortable. It's like she wants to wear your skin or something."

Mara made a face, taken aback by this new information. "Grim."

Leah snorted. "No kidding. But anyway, as long as you're

okay—just know we're happy for you. He's hot. So, so hot. I'd be jealous if not for the fact that you've been crushing on him forever."

Yeah. Forever. And now here she was. At the end of forever. Instead of divulging that, she smiled at Leah, grateful for her support. "Thanks, Leah. Thank Ying, too."

Leah squeezed her arm. "Will do. Gotta run—see you tomorrow. Don't do anything I wouldn't do with your hot new boyfriend, huh?" She chuckled as she turned to leave.

If only he was really her hot boyfriend.

A big hell yeah for all things fake.

HARRY fought to concentrate, loosening his tie and ruffling invoices needing approval on his desk. He was still working at blocking out the overwhelming buzz of voices in the office, but it was distracting and took all of his effort to focus on the task.

Add in the effort to work the numbers swimming before his eyes and his mind's eye straying to Mara, naked and supple on top of him, and he was losing the fight.

His eyes fell on the oval-shaped, silver-framed picture of Fletcher and Mimi with his sister—smiling, laughing, happy, making his heart feel like a heavy weight in his chest. For all the hardships they'd endured as they attempted to bond, he loved them, wanted to understand how he could help them heal.

Hearing Wanda say they missed him reminded him he needed to get things in order—for them. If he did nothing right from this point on, he'd do right by them if it was the last thing he did. He was sick with worry about their safety and determined to do whatever he had to in order to keep them safe.

But how, when the unknown entity was still at large, and worse, it was unknown? They had next to nothing. The person responsible for kidnapping the kids and Carl was a woman with "swingy" hair like Mara. According to Mara's texts, it wasn't Astrid. There was nothing swingy about Astrid anyway. She was just gloomy.

So who? Why?

He'd been chewing on potential suspects all day long. If it wasn't Astrid, who'd become the likely suspect due to her Mara fixation, then who'd go to such lengths to make their displeasure about he and Mara known in this format?

He gripped the pen he used to sign invoices. Couple that with trying to find a way to get his old life back, with absolutely no luck, and he was doomed to never concentrate again.

In order to get things right, he needed to find a way to reverse this. No one thought it was possible, but then, who thought it was possible for Mara to make baby juice?

Anything was possible as far as he was concerned, now that he'd seen what he'd seen. Demons and vampires and werewolves were just the tip of the iceberg, baby.

"Yeah, no shit, man! She's a hot piece of ass. Can't believe Emmerson was the one who nailed her."

Harry's head shot up, his fingers gripping the pen he held. His eyes searched the small cluster of desks in front of him, mostly empty due to an afternoon break, and zeroed in on Lloyd Beecham and Gary Lingfeld.

In short, of the two, Lloyd was the asshole. He used women like he used his overbearing cologne: liberally and without any sort of discrimination. They were nothing more than a depository for his limp dick to find solace.

Both were werewolves, a trait he still couldn't believe he was capable of assessing.

And if he didn't like the smug asshole before, he sure as hell didn't like him with Mara's name on his lips. Yet he stayed seated in his chair, forcing himself to focus on numbers and block out the voices.

"She's got an ass I'd tap so fast, it'd beg for mercy," Lloyd bragged, his snicker rubbing Harry's nerves raw.

Harry's pen snapped in two, bits of the fallout flying across his desk. He fought a snarl, gripping the edges of his desk. He cracked his neck, considering a good hard workout tonight after work. Just to relieve the unbearable tension in his muscles.

For a moment, Lloyd and Gary's voices became muffled. But then, they drifted back to his highly attuned ears, crisp and sharp.

One more word . . .

"You'd better shut the hell up, Lloyd. If boss man heard you talkin' about his sister like that, he'd eat your sorry ass for breakfast," Gary warned, his chair squeaking as he began to roll back to his desk.

Harry's eyes narrowed in the direction of Lloyd's smug face, his throat squashing a low grumble.

Lloyd guffawed at the idea Keegan would kill him. "Please. Keegan Flaherty's all talk. He should be grateful I'd pork her. Even though I don't get it, nobody else seems to want to. Why else was she single for so long?"

Motherfucker.

And that was it. It was the last semi-functioning, almost rational thought he had. Before he'd even realized he was doing it, he'd done it. And he didn't just do it a little, he went all the way. Best news? He didn't stumble once on his way to kill Lloyd.

Lloyd was up against a wall with Harry's fingers digging into the flesh of his throat until it compressed and turned red beneath his grip. Desks had been scaled; papers, calculators, files, assorted lunches, and Gary were all knocked over like bowling pins in the process, but he hadn't fumbled once.

"Were you talking about my girlfriend, Lloyd?" He gripped his neck tighter, jamming his face in Lloyd's, begging him to give him a reason to kill him. *"My girlfriend?* I sure as hell hope not, limp dick, because if you were, I'd have to kill you."

Lloyd collapsed against the wall, his lean, spray-tanned face going pale as he held his hands up to signal his surrender. "Dude! We were just bullshitting. You know, just us boys. Calm down, man!"

Harry fought the very urge he was about to express—with every ounce of will he possessed. He let Lloyd drop hard, righting him when his legs began to crumble. "Get one thing straight, you piece of shit: I ever hear my girlfriend's name on your lips again, I'll tear them off your face. Now shut your mouth or I'll damn well shut it for you. Clear?" Harry seethed down at him, his muscles rigid and ready to spring into action.

Lloyd's deep gray eyes, wide with terror, and probably confusion, over quiet, unassuming Harry making a threat to take him out, warred with pride and the idea that he'd been checked in front of Gary. "It was just a joke, Harry," he attempted to make light.

"Don't joke about my girlfriend—ever. In fact, quit talking about women like they're monkeys meant for your amusement. It offends me, and when I'm offended, *this* is what happens. Got me?" Harry roared in his face.

Lloyd gave his chest a halfhearted shove, slipping out and away from Harry. But he took a parting shot to save face. "Whatever, man. It was just a joke. If you can't take a damn joke, I get it." He made a fast exit, the sound of his hurried footsteps satisfying to Harry's ears.

His vision cleared in that second, leaving the impact of what he'd done crystal clear. With a wince, he picked up a chair and held out his hand to Gary. "Sorry, pal. I don't know what came over me."

Gary's eyes went wide with shock. "What the fuck was that, Harry?"

Harry jutted his hand forward at him again, insisting he take it.

Gary's gaze was hesitant, his grasp tentative. "So? What the hell, buddy?"

Harry yanked him up and righted him while he thought about what to say next to explain how mild-mannered Harry had turned into the Hulk.

He jammed a hand through his rumpled hair while Gary waited, blotting his coffee-covered tie with a napkin. "Lloyd's an asshole. That's what that was about. He's always talking shit about women. But he can't talk about mine."

Gary backed up. "I gotcha. But Lloyd's always been an asshole, Harry. You've heard his sexual exploits since day one. I get that he was talking shit about your girlfriend, but that wasn't like you at all. Even when you're pissed off, you're never that pissed off."

Harry shrugged his shoulders. "This is different." And it was. Fuck, it sure was. He couldn't remember anyone he'd spent so much time not only conflicted about, but thinking about, quite the way he did Mara.

"So is it serious?" Gary asked with a grin, smoothing back his blond hair and brushing at the seam in his tan trousers.

He didn't want to talk about Mara. Not right now. And it wasn't like this was all real anyway. For all he knew, her crush from Christmas was long over. He hadn't exactly been crush-worthy these last few days. Not to mention, they were only doing this to keep up pretenses. He found himself wishing it were real. But he didn't reveal that to Gary. Instead he shrugged with a smile. "I don't know."

Gary slapped him on the back, letting him know he understood. "It damn well must be for you to get so worked up. Now quit talkin' and help me clean up. Then we'll superglue Lloyd's *Playboy* pages together. He'll never know what hit him."

Harry chuckled, shaking his head and stooping to pick up a batch of papers when his phone rang with the theme song from *Star Trek*, the song he'd chosen to alert him it was Mara.

But it wasn't Mara. It was Nina, her voice brisk, her statement, as always, littered with bad language and to the point. "Brainiac? Get your fucking ass up to Keegan's office now. Nine-one-one, buddy."

CHAPTER 14

Harry burst through the ornate double doors to Keegan's office, tripping over the plastic runner and almost falling. "I'm okay!" he yelped, righting himself with his hands against the dark oak paneling until he caught his balance.

His eyes, fraught with worry, flew past Keegan, Marty, Wanda, and Nina, and sought Mara. His hair was mussed and his shirt was torn, but he stood strong and tall, his expression a question. "What's going on?"

Nina popped her lips, pressing the heel of her hand to her forehead. "Jig's up, Harry. We're fucked."

Marty flicked Nina's tie on her hoodie with a snort of disgust. "Nina! Why must you always be so crude? Could you just once find your sensitive bone and make use of it? We have a serious crisis here!"

Nina flipped Marty the middle finger. "I'm just callin' it like I see it. Why bullshit? We got trouble. Big, big, ugly, hairy, pack trouble. I'm not butterin' up my fist to jam a painful truth down his throat."

Wanda, stately as always, dressed in a red cowl-neck sweater and black trousers, ironed to within an inch of their life, held up her hand, as always, the calm in their crazy storm. "Nina, I'll say this once." She snapped her fingers under Nina's nose. "Shut it."

When Keegan's secretary had called Mara up to his office, she hadn't thought much of it until she'd gotten a slew of texts, one after the other, from Marty, Nina, and Wanda, all with the ominous words, *"He knows."*

Apparently, Keegan had received an anonymous tip earlier this afternoon from someone who had details of Harry's turn. Details she'd thought only the group knew about.

Whoever this person was, they knew everything about the night Harry had been accidentally accosted by Mara's serum. The revelation left Mara not only stunned but petrified this same person was responsible for taking the children and Carl.

According to Keegan, "Anonymous" promised to reveal to the council what happened that night in the lab if he didn't do it first.

Cue spooky organ music.

So with shaky words and trembling limbs, she'd confessed everything in the hopes that even if she went to pack prison, Keegan would be able to protect Carl, Harry, and the kids.

Marty sat at the edge of Keegan's desk, her eyes filled with concern. She took a deep breath and addressed both Harry and Mara. "So like Nina said, we have trouble."

Mara watched Harry stiffen, still so solid, still trying to keep their secret. "I don't know what you mean," he said, moving to stand behind Mara, placing a hand at her waist.

But he sucked at subterfuge as much as she did. His lie was written all over his adorable face. Mara put her hand at his wrist, fighting the possessive pride filling her heart. "It's okay. Keegan knows about you, Harry. He knows I'm responsible for what happened to you."

Harry looked at Keegan, his gaze direct. "It's my understanding you're the alpha male of your pack. What kind of action do you plan to take? Because while I don't want to be disrespectful, or cross any employer-employee boundaries, I'm not letting you punish her for something that was an accident. You know what those are like. That's how you ended up with Marty as your wife."

Mara's heart shifted and fluttered at Harry's noble gesture. He might not always be terribly coordinated, but he was nothing if he wasn't all about doing the right thing. She turned to him and patted his warm chest, ignoring the tear in his white shirt. "Harry? Someone tipped Keegan off anonymously. It's not his fault he has to do what he has to do."

Keegan, despite his anger, stuck out his hand. "We've met, Harry, on several occasions."

Harry nodded, shaking Keegan's hand before placing it back on Mara's waist in a protective gesture. "We have."

Keegan nodded, his head full of thick, dark hair. "You have children, right?"

Harry's answer was guarded. "I do."

"So then you know they're always protected within the confines of the pack, correct?"

"It's what I've been told, yes."

"Then for the moment, I don't want you to worry about their safety. It will be handled. We have other things to focus on."

Harry stayed silent, really taking Nina's "less is more" lecture to heart.

Keegan waved his finger at Mara with a shake of his dark head. His smile could have been tagged as ironic if his eyes weren't filled with what smacked of betrayal. "You and that brain of yours."

Yeah. Her and her big, big, brain with the big, big ideas.

She let her eyes fall to the floor, but her words were fierce. "I'll just say this—I won't apologize for wanting a family of my own. I won't. I want children. So, so much," her voice hitched, going gravelly and full of the emotion she'd tried too hard to keep to herself, before she cleared her throat and let her eyes meet Keegan's. "The pack says I have to mate with my own kind if at all possible. But none of my kind was all that interested, and there weren't many I was interested in either. So I took matters into my own hands. The only thing I regret is involving Harry and his children. But I'll never regret making a choice that might not have been with my head, but was definitely with my heart." End impassioned plea. She wouldn't say she was sorry for something she was only half sorry for.

Keegan crossed the room, dragging her into a hug, making her eyes sting with tears. "Jesus, kiddo. What the hell am I supposed to do?"

She heard how torn he was, listened to the ragged release of his breath. Struggling out of his strong embrace, she cupped his jaw and patted it. "You're supposed to treat me just like everyone else, Keegan. It's the only way to keep the respect you've earned. Just because I'm the alpha's sister doesn't mean I get special treatment."

Harry was beside her again, standing just on the fringes of her and Keegan. "I won't let you do that, Keegan. I know I'm crossing a line here, but it was an accident. Period," he said with clenched teeth.

Keegan's gaze, usually so serious and fierce, was torn. "I can't do it, Mara. I *won't* do it."

She gave him a shove, regretting the instant she left the security of his arms, but determined to keep his good name and reputation as alpha intact. "Oh, no, brother. You will do it. You will, or I'll give myself up to the council and pretend like you never got this anonymous tip. I'm not jeopardizing the faith these people have in you. So either you hand down the edict and turn me in, or I go myself."

"Goddamn it, Mara!" he thundered, his face a tight mask of myriad emotions. "Why didn't you just come to me? Tell me what was going through your mind before you made a baby potion?"

Marty was all flapping hands and accusatory tones as she hopped off the edge of Keegan's desk, her kelly green pumps clacking on the hardwood of Keegan's office floor. "Because sometimes, darling husband, you're a total Neanderthal. How uncomfortable would it have been for her to come and tell you she wanted to become a mother, but without the aid of a penis? Wouldn't you have spouted these ridiculous, Victorian era rules you've all set forth within the pack? What would you have said, Keegan? 'Oh, sure, kiddo. Go on and make some baby juice'? Hah! And I'm here to tell you right now, if you don't, at the very least, attempt to convince those council members your sister has every right to do as she pleases with her body, I will leave you, Keegan Flaherty. I'll take Hollis and go to Nina's dark, dreary castle, and I won't come back!"

"Fuuuck, Marty," Nina complained, clucking her tongue. "Why didn't you pick Wanda? She has Arch, ya know. He likes you a shitload more than I do."

Marty's eyes blazed, her ringed fingers flying upward in Nina's face. "Shut it, vampire. I'm making a point!"

"Couldn't you make it the fuck at Wanda's?"

"Nina! Shut up!" Wanda yelled, slapping Nina's arm with her gloves. "Don't make things worse."

But Nina slapped Keegan on the back with a roll of her eyes at Marty and Wanda. "For what it's worth, dude, I'd let her bring the kid and all her girlie guru crap, and her chest full of hair dye, because a personal choice like that shouldn't be up to a bunch of dicks who have no idea what it's like to have a vagina. This rule you ass sniffers have about keeping the bloodlines pure is one thing. Yeah, it makes sense to avoid hooking up with a human if you can to keep everyone safe. The rest is just goddamn ridiculous. Short-Shot found a way to make little werewolves. She wants a little werewolf. She can take care of the little werewolf. I don't see the fucking problem. So I hate to be a bitch, 'cus mostly I like you, pal, but I gotta pick Marty over you, or Wanda will never let me hear the end of it."

Keegan's lips thinned when he planted his hands on his hips, staring them all down. "You women and your conclusions. Did it occur to any of you that, Neanderthal that I am, I might actually agree with your stance on Mara's wish to have children without the benefit of a mate?"

Oh. Mara'd never given that even a little thought. Her brother enlightened? God, Marty really was the Caveman Whisperer.

Guilty looks passed amongst the women.

Marty gave him a sheepish glance. "Hadn't gotten that far, Neanderthal."

He held out his hand to Marty, which she immediately took without a single word spoken, meaning all was well with Team Flaherty. "That's not my dilemma here, honey. I don't even know if that's going to be the issue with the council. Insemination is one thing—a separate issue all unto itself. The issue is Mara was careless, and someone was unwillingly turned as a result. Yes, it was an accident, but it was much different from ours. It's a dangerous thing to create babies in a lab. What if someone got hold of her serum—or her and that genius brain of hers? Some shithead who wanted to make a buck—or a hundred million bucks? We'd be exposed, Marty—exposed and used. Potentially harmed."

Mara let her chin drop to her chest. Damn all that big picture, long-term-effect thinking. Harry tapped her wrist, pulling her hand into his and squeezing it.

"But the worst of this?" Keegan said. "My dilemma in having to turn in my own sister for something I think is just as ridiculous as all of you just because I'm in charge. It's not like I can hide the fact that Harry was a human and now he's suddenly a werewolf. You knew damn well it wouldn't be long before rubbing your scent all over him, or whatever crazy plan you hatched to keep him hidden, wouldn't work anymore. You were just buying time. If I don't do something about this, they'll launch an investigation and corner Harry to find out how this happened, if they don't already know."

Harry shook his head, his jaw tight. "The hell they'd get it out of me. I'll just act like I don't remember. They can't make me confess something I refuse to confess."

Mara's heart beat a tribal call of love for Harry. Even though he hated the idea of being one of them, he was protecting her anyway.

"And that's all well and good, Harry, but is it fair? To you? To put you through a rigorous investigation, have the council invade your life? Mimi's and Fletcher's lives? Because that's what'll happen."

Harry squared his shoulders, his jaw tight. "I don't care. I'll do whatever I have to do to keep Mara safe."

"You know," Keegan shook a finger at Mara, "if you'd come to me sooner, Harry's suggestion might have worked, Mara. But you didn't. You didn't trust me enough to handle this—or to help you. Now, what if this information I have is leaked, accusing you directly, and it spreads like wildfire through the pack? You know what gossip is like. It's hard enough to deal with weres and humans working together side by side. Then there's the fact that in the thirty-five hundred employees we have here, there are a total of twenty or so humans."

"Actually fourteen, if my records, and my nose, are correct," Harry offered.

Keegan nodded. "There's a reason for that. First, office affairs happen whether we like it or not. There are some pack members who are single. Single plus working closely together can create trouble and unwanted drama. Add in paranormal trouble, and we've got a problem. We're careful about who we hire, not just because of this purity law, which I also think is ridiculous, but because what if the wrong human, one who becomes involved with a were, finds out, freaks out, tells the world?"

"We end up an episode of *The Werewolf Diaries*?" But her attempt at the joke fell flat. Much like most jokes fell flat with Keegan.

"No, funny girl. We're a little sunk. You know why the rule to keep to your own was implemented in the first place. Sure, it's a little more lax since Marty and I happened, but we didn't just do it to protect our own kind. We did it to protect humans from the trauma Marty, and now Harry, have experienced. We're as equal opportunity as we can be in the situation without risking the well-being of thousands."

Everyone stood silent. No one could deny Keegan's logic.

Tears streamed down Marty's face. If Mara regretted one thing, it was that Marty had brought them all so close together, and now she was ripping them apart, leaving Marty the challenge of making peace with both sides of the issue, Keegan's duties and her friendship with Mara.

Wanda held out a hand to Marty, squeezing it, just as Nina grabbed a tissue and blotted her friend's tears before shoving it under her nose and dabbing. "Don't cry, blondie—you get all blotchy and it's damn ugly," Nina snarked, pulling Marty into her embrace.

But Keegan wasn't done. Yet Mara saw the effort it was taking for him to steel himself against his wife's tears. "Harder still is keeping our paranormal business from leaking to the outside world. If pack members are all abuzz about this, what if someone slips? It isn't like employee A slept with employee B and folks are whispering about it behind their hands. That's harmless gossip about an act with consequences meant only for the two people involved. You created a *baby-making formula*—or at the very least, a formula that produced an actual werewolf. How can I hide that from the council? Pack members will want answers, and as well liked and respected as you are, you have a dangerous mind. What that mind made in a lab with some hormones and whatever else you used to do this will scare the hell out of everyone. I'm scared by it."

The lump in her stomach hardened until she thought she might vomit. The chaos she'd created had a domino effect she had, in all her smarts, never considered—making the choice she'd been toying with in her head since Keegan had called them up here clearer. "Which is why I'm turning myself in. No guilt. No conspirators. No blame—just me," Mara said before breaking away from Harry and jumping out of the fourth-floor window to the tune of crashing glass and Harry's howling roar of protest.

"DUDE!" Nina roared in Harry's face as he struggled to break her grip, clenching his wrists so tight he forgot all about the badass he'd been back at the office today with Lloyd.

Fighting a very unmanly wince, he relaxed like he was the one who'd decided to give in, rather than Nina forcing him to submit. "If you don't sit the fuck down in this chair, I'll break off your nerd fingers one by one and you'll never play *Call of Duty* again. Got that, dork?"

Oh, no. Not the dreaded threat. Hah! Nothing would stop him from trying to find Mara.

It's Call of Duty, *Harry. Dude—think hard.*

Wait. What was happening here? Why was he so enraged about Mara's sacrifice? You'd think he liked her or something.

Shit. He liked her.

He liked her enough to want an opportunity to see if they could find their way through this together. Maybe date. See a movie. Have a pizza with the kids.

The kids. He was thinking about Mara with the kids.

Harry tipped his head back and grinned up at Nina, fighting the urge to stick his tongue out at her. "But I'm a werewolf, Crypt Keeper. That means I heal quickly. Break away." Hah, and hah again!

Nina flicked his hair. "Let's hope your pride heals as fast after I wipe the joint with you, Square Root Man."

Marty stood before him, one hand on her slender hip, the other holding her dog Muffin like a football under her arm. "Harry? Chasing after Mara is a sure way to garner your own trouble with the council."

Wanda sat on his lap hard. She wasn't heavy by a long shot, but she was as strong as, if not stronger than, Nina, judging by the grip she had on his face.

Her usually serene features remained as such. There was little strain in her effort to keep him seated, which was totally affecting his manhood. "Look at me, Harry. Look and listen. You'll only make things worse if you try to find Mara. Now, hear me, Harry. You're not going anywhere. We absolutely won't make things worse for her. There are rules and protocol when addressing the council—rules I won't allow you to break with your poor imitation of the Hulk. So, we're going to use our big brains and talk this through rather than Nina it, okay?"

Nina let go of one of his hands and gave Wanda the middle finger. "Fuck you, Wanda. My way gets results."

Wanda's gaze narrowed. "Your way gets us kicked out of places and shunned by the socially acceptable. I will not risk Keegan's status or Mara's future because Harry's gone all rage-ish. Got it? No muscle today, Elvira."

Nina rolled her beautiful eyes. "Fine, but if he keeps this shit up, I'm gonna clean house." She gave Harry one last shove. "Now knock it the fuck off, or we're gonna tango. You cool?"

Wanda patted his face and smiled, giving his cheek a pinch. "If I let you up, you have to promise not to bolt. I take a man's word very seriously, Harry. Plus, I know your ego can handle only so much.

Two women dragging you back here by force will only make your self-esteem cry salty tears of regret. So, you in or are you out?"

Harry lifted his chin, yanking it from Wanda's grasp, and puffing his chest outward like any man who'd just cried uncle to two women would. They knew these council people better than he did. The last thing he wanted to do was rock the boat for Mara. "I'm in. I apologize. I'm still dealing with my hormonal surges. Sometimes they get the better of me."

She ran her finger down the length of his nose, popping the tip of it. "I get it. So, let's put our heads together." Wanda hopped off his lap and smoothed her hair from her face.

As the women kept a cautious eye on him, they scattered to different areas of Mara's cottage, settling in for some brainstorming.

But Harry couldn't sit still and let Mara take the hit for him. He also couldn't go back on his word to the girls. At all costs to their personal and even professional lives, they were always there for him.

Instead, he paced the floor of Mara's cottage while Nina taught Carl the art of duct-taping his limbs back on if the need should arise, frantic with worry about this council that Marty had flat out refused to allow him to surrender himself to.

Damn Mara and her sense of honor. If she could have just held out for a little longer, maybe they could've found the person who'd ratted her out and stopped this all before it got any worse.

He could have made something up for this crazy council, and kept them from ever knowing Mara had anything to do with it.

And now, she'd been gone ratting herself out for over four hours. He was going to lose his mind.

Yet, here everyone was, all in a huddle of support for Mara. Christ, he admired their unity.

Marty sat on the couch, hugging one of the million pillows Mara had flung all over while Wanda held Muffin, Marty's poodle, and the catalyst for this whole string of accidents.

"Anyone hear from Keegan?" Harry asked, fighting the lump in his throat.

"Nothing yet. Hey, Harry?" Wanda called out. "Come sit, would you? You're going to wear a hole in the floor with all this pacing, or wear me out in the process." She reached over the back of the couch, holding her hand out to him.

Harry squeezed it before dropping to the raised hearth in front of the fireplace. "We need to figure out who sent Keegan that anonymous tip." He was damned if he even knew where to begin. He'd never been in trouble in his life, nor could he remember anyone hating him so much they'd want revenge. He was a nerd, for Christ's sake.

"Swear it, as sure as I sit here before you, Harry, if I find out who did this, I'll kill them myself. Pack laws be damned," Marty spat, running a weary hand over her eyes.

His head throbbed when he dropped it into his hands. "I keep going over and over it in my mind, and I can't even come up with one person who could have seen what happened that night. The whole damn place was deserted. Even Cal had gone home for the night," Harry said, referring to the janitor at Pack. "I saw him on my way down to the lab."

"I'll tell you this much, dude. Whoever the fuck this is, it's the same assclown who took the kids and Carl. I can smell it," Nina said, pulling Carl to the small window seat and handing him the duct tape to practice.

"It makes sense, but it doesn't make any sense. Where did this grudge for me and Mara, or whatever we're calling it, suddenly come from?"

"Hey, Harry?" Marty's head popped up. "Question? Did we ever ask you why you were in the lab? I mean, you're in accounting. What were you doing in the lab to begin with?"

Huh. He'd never given thought to that. How could he have

missed it? "I was meeting Jeff Grandy. He texted me and asked me to meet him there so he could pass on an expense report to me. Said he was too wrapped up in a project, and didn't want to leave the lab. You know how the lab group is—always wrapped up in one thing or another. They get in deep. Jeff and I worked out together all the time at Pack's gym. He was always talking about his projects."

"And where was Jeff when all of this went down?" Wanda asked, her hand cupping her chin. "Where is Jeff now, for that matter? Did you ever see him that night?"

Harry bolted off the hearth, startling Carl. Shit. "I never saw him that night. I'd just finished working out, which is why I had the vitaminwater. I dropped into the lab to find all the lights on, but nobody home. Went to Jeff's desk to see if maybe he'd left it there, but nothing. That was when I drank the baby-making juice by mistake."

Marty sat up straighter, tucking the pillow closer to her chest. "And have you seen Jeff since that evening? Since you've been back at work?"

Shit. Sounds of alarm clanged in his head. "No. No, I haven't." He reached for his phone with hasty hands, scrolling back to the texts for that night. It had definitely come from Jeff's phone.

Whether he'd been the person using that phone was another story. "Let me text him now and see if we get a response. I forgot all about it with everything else going on." He sent off a text to Jeff and waited, clutching his phone with tight fingers, pacing once again.

Marty scrolled her phone, her brow furrowed. "I'm checking to see if Jeff's been in this week."

Shit, shit, shit. Why hadn't he thought of this sooner? He'd been so wrapped up in his own bullshit he never considered he hadn't seen Jeff since this began.

His phone remained silent. Damn it.

Marty slid to the end of the couch, the pillow dropping from her lap. "Jeff hasn't been in since the night of your accident, Harry."

"Christ," Harry murmured, running his hand over his jaw.

"But wait," Marty interjected, her face smoothing from a frown to a smile. "Jeff has the flu, according to his mother who called him in sick. Phew. Okay, then. All's well. Bet he's just in bed and not answering texts. That makes sense, right?"

"Well, it would."

"I feel a fucking 'but' coming on, Harry. So say it," Nina ordered.

Harry took one last hopeless glance at his phone before shaking his head. "But . . . Jeff's mother is dead. She died when he was in college."

MARA laid her head against the cottage door before opening it, loving the smooth surface of it, the reflection of the lights pouring through the oval stained glass in the center.

All of her hard work, all of the long nights she'd spent renovating a space to call her own would be replaced by a dank, square cell in werewolf prison, if the news from the council was even close to correct.

Maybe she could be like the Bill Nye version of Martha Stewart while she served out her sentence? Teach her fellow inmates about DNA strands and evolution? Because learning was so popular in prison.

Her ears caught the sounds of Harry, Marty, Wanda, and Nina, voices raised in panic and anxiety, filtered through the door.

She just needed a second to process where she stood, and then she'd face the next hurdle. Just a second . . .

Snowflakes began to fall, dusting her nose and cheeks as tears welled in her eyes. She'd really done it this time. For all the times she'd been as close to perfect as she could get, mostly because her brother Sloan had been so out of control, and Keegan was always caught up in dealing with his antics, she'd made up for it on one fell swoop.

She'd trashed Harry's life, and now it was in total upheaval. He couldn't go home. He'd been taken from his children because someone had lured them away, and that was probably indirectly related to her, too. Worse, he didn't want to even consider the idea he'd remain a werewolf. No offense, of course.

When she made snowballs, they turned into avalanches.

There'd be no babies, no strollers in the park, no midnight feedings, no scouring baby name websites.

There'd also be no Harry, and that hurt so hard she almost couldn't breathe from the pain. Despite his wildly swinging moods, and his resentment toward what she'd done, she still liked him. His deep sense of honor, his love for his sister's children, his work ethic were all things she admired in a man—in Harry.

He'd really stepped up to the plate for her today, leaving her not just grateful, but even more deeply enamored than she'd already been.

Which wasn't good, considering she was going to end up clanging a cup against some cell bars, and he'd probably go on to accept his fate, find a rich supermodel werewolf who was five-ten and gorgeous, marry her, and live on her private island where Mimi and Fletcher would body surf and be homeschooled by the natives.

The voices behind her door rose, forcing her to wipe her eyes and set about confronting whatever was going on inside.

Mara closed her eyes one last time before reentering the madness that had become her life.

Taking a deep breath, she sent up a wish, *I don't care what happens to me. Put me in the clinker, leave me to rot in solitary, whatever, but please, please, please, keep Harry and the kids safe.*

CHAPTER 15

"How could I have missed the fact that Jeff was absent from the lab?" Mara groaned into her hands. Harry was crammed into the driver's side of her Smart Car, his large body filling the small space, navigating the back roads of Buffalo behind the Jeff Gordon of the paranormal world—aka Nina. The race to get to Jeff's house was on.

Every nerve in her body screamed for relief from the tension she felt just thinking something had happened to Jeff. Who would use his phone to text Harry and summon him to the lab if it wasn't Jeff?

"How were you supposed to know it had anything to do with this, Mara?"

In exasperation for her selfishness, coupled with yet another blunder on her part, she snapped. "Oh, for heaven's sake, Harry! He's a coworker. He works closely with me in the lab, and I didn't even realize he was out for almost a whole week? I'm as selfish as they come. Always too wrapped up in some chemical for a product we're creating to pay attention to the people I respect and work with on a daily basis!"

"Baby-making juice can be distracting and taxing." His smile glowed against the rush of oncoming headlights.

Mara turned her body to face him, angry he was making light of yet another aspect of her brainy paranormalness. "Being reminded is taxing."

He gave her a look of apology. "I'm just trying to lighten things up a little."

"Stop lightening at my expense. I wanted a baby. Is that a crime?"

Harry reached over and stroked her arm. "No. It's amazing. What you did, aside from the trouble it seems to have cause with your family and this council, was amazing and brilliant. And it worked."

She rolled her eyes. "We don't know if it worked. You're not craving formula and baby strollers, are you?"

He shrugged his shoulders. "In the beginning, I had a twinge of a craving for those pureed carrots in a jar. Who's to say what the long run will bring?"

She couldn't even giggle. Instead, she buried her face in her hands again.

"It's not like you were wrapped up in you, Mara. You were wrapped up in me and the kids and Carl being taken."

"And why am I wrapped up in you, Harry? Because I created you. That's why!" She tugged on her seat belt, snapping it back into place.

Harry reached over, grabbing her hand and running his thumb over it in circular motions meant to soothe. "I'd like to think there are other reasons now."

She couldn't address her other reasons at this point, her stomach was too twisted in knots. "What if something's happened to Jeff? Why didn't I think to ask you why you were in the lab? Who am I, Harry? I'm usually smart and intuitive and I can always figure out whodunit on *CSI*. Why can't I figure this out?"

"You're not the only smart one in the Smart Car right now, Mara. I'm just as guilty."

His joke whizzed right past her. "You're supposed to miss things. You've been traumatized. By me! I did this!"

As they pulled into the driveway of Jeff's small ranch house, Harry flipped the car into park and reached for her with hands she didn't even see coming. Even in the midst of her worry for Jeff, she had to admire how he was growing into his abilities.

Pulling her close, Harry mumbled into her hair, "We still have to talk about the council. What happened?"

Tears stung her eyes, and the comfort of Harry's embrace was so tempting. It would be so easy to focus on her fears, tucked against him. "We have a fellow geek to find. We'll talk about it later."

Kissing the top of her head, he let her go and popped open the door just as Nina approached them. "It's goddamn dark out here. What is it with you dorks and the deserted locales?"

"Smaller radius of stupid people in a square mile," Harry joked on a chuckle.

Mara ignored their banter and made a beeline for Jeff's red front door. The house was entirely dark except for the small LED lanterns along the paved path to his house. She ran up the small set of steps and rapped her knuckles on the door. "Jeff?"

Nina was right behind her, grabbing her hand before she could knock again. "Shut the fuck up," she hissed in Mara's ear. "You wanna tell the world we don't know where the fuck your fellow nerd is? Lay off." Nina shoved her out of the way, cupping her hands around her eyes to peer into the small arched window above Jeff's front door. "It's damn dark in there. Looks like stuff's been knocked around."

Mara's stomach began to flutter with nerves. She tugged her beret down over her forehead with nervous fingers.

Harry trotted up the steps, putting his hand at Mara's waist again. "His car's in the garage."

"So what do we do now?" Mara asked, turning to Nina for an answer.

"We break the fuck in," she said, popping the door open with a quick flick of her wrist. It creaked as it opened, revealing the landscape of what was supposed to be Jeff's living room. But it looked more like a disaster area.

Four computers littered several tables, all turned off. Printers held reams of paper with Jeff's notations along the columns of numbers in black ink. His furniture was toppled over as though there'd been a fight. But no sign of Jeff.

"So either he was a total slob or some shit went down. I smell shit, you, Short-Shot?"

Mara lifted her nose and sniffed as she made her way to two of the bedrooms in the back of his house. "Something's not right. That's all I can smell. His bathroom's clean as a whistle," she said, giving the guest bath a once-over.

Towels in earth tones neatly lined an organizer over the toilet, and the soap dispenser and a small plant lay squarely on either side of the sparkling white sink. This was the Jeff she knew. Orderly, calm, not the Jeff of the living room full of toppled furniture.

"So what do we do now? Sift through his personal belongings?" She scoured the bathroom one last time before making her way back to Harry, turning to him for advice. She found him with his mouth open, swinging like it was hinged.

"Harry? What's wrong?"

"Jesus," he whispered, holding his hand in front of his face. "It's like having night vision goggles. I can see *everything*. I don't think I realized it until just now. We don't even need to turn on a light. I think I can see sounds."

Mara smiled up at him, ticking off another pro for team were-wolf. "I told you so would be trite, wouldn't it?"

Nina clapped both of them on the shoulder. "Lovebirds, quit with the starry-eyed bullshit and let's roll. Your fellow nerd was a slob—look at this place."

Harry's gaze said he was skeptical. "Truthfully, I didn't know Jeff outside of the Pack gym and work. We didn't go out for beers or whatever. I was too busy with the kids to get out much. So I can't say for sure if he was disorganized." His gaze went to Mara in question. "Mara, were his work habits like this?"

She shook her head. No. Jeff was meticulous, not only in his research, but his physical belongings at his desk and at his worktable in the lab. His beakers were always crystal clear, his portable scale shiny, and all of his acid-base indicators aligned. "Jeff was neat as a pin at work. That's not to say it wasn't just for show, but he was pretty thorough. His desk and lab space were always pretty neat."

"Lovebirds?" Nina called from the kitchen just adjacent to the living room.

Harry and Mara's eyes shot across the room where Nina stood by Jeff's shiny, silver fridge. She held up another of those now familiar slips of paper.

Mara's heart began to crash against her ribs in a painful beat.

It was the same handwriting, the same lined notepaper torn from a spiral notebook.

"Tell Mara and Harry I see them."

MARA tucked her hair up in a knot on the top of her head before placing a knitted cap over it, trying to shake off the fear eating her alive.

For now, because Jeff had been missing for over forty-eight

hours and he was a human, they'd filed an anonymous missing person's report, realizing the police would eventually show up at Pack and question his coworkers.

Harry had been the voice of reason on Jeff's disappearance. Their chances were better if the police didn't immediately put Harry and the kids together with Jeff's vanishing. How did you explain that since you'd become a werewolf, your wards and one of your coworkers had gone missing all in the space of a week? Not to mention identical messages had been left both with the kids and at Jeff's place—key pieces of evidence.

The common denominator in all this was Harry.

But they were only buying more time at this point. The police would have to show up sometime, and if they were smart, they'd eventually string together the relationships between Harry, Jeff, and the children, and then the heat would be on.

They'd also searched Jeff's house, something she, Nina, and Harry had done before letting the police in on his disappearance. Nothing.

Absolutely nothing, other than the scattered furniture, said this person who was snatching people up had wanted something important from Jeff's personal research. Jeff was a respected scientist, but to her knowledge, he wasn't working on anything for Pack that would change the world.

After a lengthy discussion, they'd all nixed the idea that Jeff's kidnapping had anything to do with his work, and had everything to do with his connection to Mara and Harry and that damn lab. What had Jeff seen that would make someone want to tear his place apart or worse, hurt him?

Jesus. At this point, was Jeff even alive?

Mara's stomach coiled into a tight knot of fear. Someone had lured Harry to the lab, and that someone had seen what had gone down that night. There was no escaping that.

She'd worried all last night about Jeff, wracked her brain to find his connection to this, other than that he was a convenient way to get Harry to the lab.

She'd notified Keegan and the council about Jeff, who was very human. If Jeff was hurt, or even if he wasn't, the council had been clear, this revelation could lead to more charges. The only solace she took was in Keegan's words that he'd do whatever it took to find Jeff.

She sighed, forcing her fears to quiet. Today, Mara was determined to enjoy Mimi and Fletcher for their short visit to tube along the hills behind her cottage. It was a rare opportunity for Harry to spend some time with them in this madness, and it was important.

With nothing else to go on, no clue where to look for Jeff, they'd entered the frustrating land of limbo.

And if she didn't find something else to focus on, she'd go crazy.

Mimi's and Fletcher's excited voices drifted in from the living room where Nina made them hot chocolate with marshmallows and explained why Carl was such a strange color and couldn't speak. She didn't balk at their questions. She didn't chastise them for being curious.

She invited them to ask her anything and everything to create an open dialogue about his differences, yet alleviate the fears they surely experienced upon seeing him for the first time.

"Fear created chaos" was Nina's motto, and while she didn't exactly tell them the truth about Carl, she was as honest as the situation allowed, telling them only that Carl had been in an accident that left his skin a different shade than what was considered normal and his limbs stiff and difficult to use.

As they giggled and chatted, she'd encouraged them to hold Carl's hand, and when he'd grunted his pleasure, they'd all gone about their giggling and chatter like they hadn't just met a real, not so alive, zombie.

"I have to give it to Nina, she's an amazing guide to parenting," Harry said, wonder in his voice. "The kids have accepted and moved on to the topic of what would happen if you woke up and there was an alligator on your floor."

"We can all only aspire," Mara said on a forced smile.

He grabbed her hand to prevent her from avoiding him, warm and reassuring. He stroked the skin between her thumb and index finger. "So we still haven't talked."

She squeezed it, loving the feel of it, the calm strength of it. "We will."

"When?"

She didn't want to spoil this precious time with Mimi and Fletcher. Avoiding his eyes, she said, "Soon."

His handsome face filled with admonishment. "You said that last night after we got back from Jeff's."

"And I meant it. But I was so tired from the day's events, I passed out. Sorry."

Harry eyeballed her, and it was full of his skepticism. "No. You're avoiding."

She gave him a shy smile. "And I'm good, right?"

"So good I almost believed you were actually passed out last night when I got into bed—or not."

She'd feigned sleep when Harry had finally stopped trying to figure out what the note meant and whom it was from and had come to bed. He hadn't pushed about her meeting with the council, just gathered her in his arms and stroked her hair until she'd fallen into a fitful sleep.

She loved that he'd come to her room without hesitation, as if their lovemaking hadn't been only rise-of-the-full-moon related. Whatever the reason, she'd treasure that memory. It was clear, strong, and easy to recall how he held her like no other man before him.

If she had the power to freeze that one moment in time with him—stay in his arms forever, she'd have made it so. "I had a headache."

"You had avoidance aches."

Mara sighed, refusing to spoil this day. "Listen, you haven't seen Mimi and Fletcher in days. They need to see you. They need to spend time with you, and you need to focus on them, nothing else. Everything's going to go to hell in a handbasket when the police start questioning the connections between Jeff and us. For the moment, while it's quiet, let's just let everything go and have some fun. Okay? I promise I'll tell you everything tonight."

Harry smiled his beautiful, fabulous, heart-wrenching smile. "Swear it?"

Mara crossed her heart over her oversized down jacket. "On my *Dr. Who* DVDs."

Harry wrapped an arm around her waist, hauling her to him, his smile full of amusement. "You watch *Dr. Who*?"

"All while I drool over the TARDIS."

"God, you're hot," he mumbled before he lowered his lips to hers, claiming them in a kiss that made her toes curl.

Laughter from the doorway made them both break apart in guilt.

"Uncle Harry's kissing Mara—so gross!" Fletcher shouted before hiding his embarrassment by running at Harry and grabbing onto his forearm, burying his face in it. Harry pumped his arm up and down while Fletcher clung to it and laughed.

Mimi's eyebrow was comically raised, her tone sassy. "Do you loooovvee Uncle Harry, Miss Mara?"

Mara scooped her up, swinging her in a circle to the tune of more raucous giggles. "I love that we're going tubing! So how about a lot less talk and a whole lot more snow, huh?"

Mimi's face lit up, her angelic features full of chubby delight when

Mara hauled her upward and wrapped her legs around her waist. "Last one to the top of the hill smells like Uncle Harry's stinky socks!" she hollered, taking off out of the bedroom with Mimi still in her arms.

She bolted out the front door into the cold, clear day, Harry's and Fletcher's laughter just behind her, filling her soul.

MIMI latched on to Mara's hand as they made their way back up the winding hill to grab another tube for one last trip down. Snow crunched beneath their feet, Mimi's purple boots, courtesy of Marty, made Mara smile. "Are you having fun, Mimi?"

Mimi bobbed her head, her grin wide; her cheeks dusted a healthy red from the cold air. "Can we have hot chocolate and marshmallows again when we go inside?"

Mara tugged at one of her springy curls poking from beneath the purple hat Auntie Nina bought specifically for this tubing occasion. "Wouldn't miss it. You can help me make it. But remember, I like lots of marshmallows. So no skimping," she teased.

Wanda's excited scream as she whipped past Harry and Fletcher, racing the pair on her tube, echoed in her ears.

Archibald, in his comical combination of red galoshes, hat with earmuffs, and stately black manservant uniform, chided Wanda for being so competitive with the shake of his finger until she began throwing snowballs at him.

"Miss Wanda, I fear I must exact revenge upon you! Duck, Sir Fletcher! Bombs away!" he shouted his devilish delight, landing a snowball in the middle of Wanda's back.

Mimi stopped walking, watching the four engage in an all-out snowball fight. Yet her mind was still somewhere else. With Donna. "My mom used to make hot chocolate for us when it snowed. I miss Mommy. Daddy, too," she whispered as though it

were a secret she'd kept to herself and she was embarrassed to say
the words out loud.

Mara's heart felt like it was in a vise grip. She knew what it was
to miss the influence of a female presence at a young age. She ached
for Mimi and the loss she'd suffered.

But she decided not to avoid the issue of talking about Donna
the way her brothers had avoided talking about their parents' death.
In their efforts to soothe her, they hadn't allowed her to mourn.
They'd rushed in to protect her, but sharing her feelings with two
boys was awkward, and while they hadn't discouraged it, they
hadn't inspired it, either.

So Mara followed Nina's lead in, believing that silence led to
fear and misunderstanding. She wanted Mimi to remember, and
when the pain wasn't so fresh and she understood loss from a more
mature perspective, she hoped Mimi would fondly recall sharing
all the wonderful things she'd loved about her mother. "You absolutely can miss her, fancy pants. She was a great mother. Your Uncle
Harry told me. Maybe sometime, you can tell me all the things
that were great about her, too. I'd love to hear them all."

Mimi set her gaze toward the purple streaks blazing across the
sky, signaling that nightfall was coming. Her lower lip trembled.
"Do you think she can see us?"

Mara squeezed Mimi's gloved hand, tucking her jacket around
her neck. "I think she can. I think she can see that you're trying so
hard to be good for your uncle."

Mimi nodded, but it was slow. "Uncle Harry's always too busy
to talk about Mommy."

Ah, the run, hide, and divert tactic. To avoid experiencing his
own personal pain, Harry'd shut everyone else down in the sharing
process, too. "Know what I think? I think Uncle Harry might not be
so good at talking about your mom because he loved her so, so much.
For some people, it hurts to remember. But he told me she was the

best sister ever, and he really liked your daddy. So next time you want to talk to him about your mom, how about you just ask him if it's okay for you to miss Mommy together? Oh, and be sure to give him a big hug when you do. He loves hugs."

A tear slipped from Mimi's eye, making it painfully clear she was trying to remain stoic in light of the fact that the one person left in the world who was closest to her couldn't open up. "Bet Mommy has the biggest, sparkliest angel wings ever."

"Bet where Mommy is they have purple wings that sparkle, all shiny when they flap." Mara made a flapping motion with her arms, making Mimi giggle.

Moments later, the floodgates opened, her round eyes fell to the snow-covered ground. "I miss her."

Mara fought a wave of her own tears. Mimi was so small against the backdrop of the enormous landscape behind her, her genuine sorrow making her look even more vulnerable. Mara gathered her close. "So why don't you tell her that?"

Mimi shrugged as if the idea were pointless—useless. "She can't hear me."

"I dunno. I talk to my mom all the time. She might not answer, but I like to think she hears me."

"Did she died-ed, too?"

Mara's heart shifted, but she smiled anyway, caught in the grip of this child's desperate wish to find peace. "She did die. My father, too. I was sad just like you."

Mimi's gaze up at her was full of innocent hope. "But you seem really happy now."

If only happiness were as simple at her age as it was at Mimi's. She wanted Mimi to always have that. No matter what life threw at her, it was okay to hope love would always win. "That's because I know my mom's keeping your mom company, and they're up there talking about sparkly wings and wishing us happy thoughts while they miss us, too."

Mimi let her head rest against Mara's hip, putting her arm around her thigh. "I like that."

Mara squeezed her shoulders and fought a shudder of breath. "Me, too, Miss Mimi."

"I like you."

She blinked to erase any sign of impending tears, glancing down at this small child, fighting to find a way to survive such tragedy. "Really? You do? I guess I like you okay enough," Mara teased, dragging a finger down Mimi's freckled nose, making her squeal. She held out her hand. "C'mon, let's go back to the cottage and see if Carl's made us some cabbage soup for dinner. Yum-yum, cabbage. Whaddya say to that?"

She wrinkled her bright red nose and made a face. "That is so gross. Cabbage is stinky. But I like Carl, even if he is a weird color."

Mara burst out laughing at the irony of her childish statement.

If Mimi only knew the half of it.

WITH the children gone back to Wanda's, and Nina and Carl visiting with Marty and Keegan, the silence of the cottage became profoundly obvious.

Harry was lost in his thoughts on the couch, staring off into the roar of the fire he'd built.

But they had to talk before . . .

Wiping off the last remnants of a very messy dinner made up of cheeseburgers and Tater Tots from the counter, Mara poured him a mug of coffee and took a deep breath before making her way to the couch to join him.

He smiled up at her distractedly when she offered him the steaming mug. "Thanks."

Pulling a throw from the back of her couch, she settled in, crossing her legs beneath it. "Penny for them?"

He shook his head, his eyes distant. "I didn't think I'd miss them this much."

"They're amazing kids. I had a great time with them today. Who knew Arch was such an ace snowman maker?"

His smile, when it happened lately, changed the landscape of his face, taking it from hard and cold to boyishly sweet. "They had a great time, too. It was probably the happiest I've seen them since . . ."

"Donna died." No holds barred, time to get it out in the open while she still had the chance.

He nodded his dark head, cupping the mug with a firmer grip. "I guess I got so caught up in Donna's death, and I was so over-whelmed by all the little details of running a household with two active kids, I forgot to enjoy them the way I used to when I was just plain old Uncle Harry. We used to have some really fun times. Lately, I've been nothing but an internal wreck or a badger about bedtimes and structure."

The struggle Harry fought so hard to hide made him so much more endearing. Each second she spent with him, every word he spoke about the children, left her wanting to peel back yet another layer of his personality.

But they didn't have time to indulge in anything other than the facts. "You were just trying to do the right thing. Get them settled. Your whole life was turned upside down, too, you know. Single man suddenly raising two children who are so young. Be fair to yourself in the assessment process."

"I want to do right by Donna. I need to."

"You will. You are. You're adjusting. But do me a favor?"

"Name it."

"Let Mimi talk about how much she misses Donna. Fletcher, too. Speaking as a kid who lost her parents, distraction so you don't have to face your own pain isn't the answer." And it bred all sorts of coping mechanisms like avoidance, solitude, and most importantly, a voice unheard.

Harry scowled, making his "Nina" face. "Fear breeds confusion, misunderstanding, and eventually gives you fucking kids who act like they're entitled to shit in gold toilets while they text their friends on their fancy iPhones they don't deserve and didn't goddamn well earn."

Mara laughed and nodded, letting her cheek rest on the cushioned back of the couch. "In the words of Countess Dracula, yes." Reaching out, she grabbed his hand in impulse, forgetting everything but her mission. "Don't let that be a part of what keeps them from sharing with you, the fear they'll upset you. I know they see a therapist, and that's healthy, but the therapist isn't you. She didn't love Donna and her husband like you did."

Harry looked away from her and out the window, his fingers twitching beneath hers. "I'm shitty at sharing my feelings."

She snorted. "Oh, please. How quickly we forget. You've been very share-ish about your reluctance to be one of us. You sure didn't hold back when you were reminding me about how you were going to find a way out of this."

"Dig, dig, dig," he teased, leaning closer to her.

"Hide, hide, hide," she reminded him, staying the course of her mission.

His throat worked, the strong column of muscle beneath his sweater, tensing. "Losing Donna was even worse than when I lost my parents. All we had was each other."

No excuses. No compromises. She couldn't explain why, but she needed to know he'd nurture Mimi and Fletcher's desire to remember their parents, encourage them to share the good and bad. "Too bad. The kids shouldn't have to hide their anguish, Harry. It's part of the reason they're acting out. For someone so smart, you're a little dense. Just promise me this, and I only ask you because Keegan and Sloan did the same thing to me that you're doing to the kids. They diverted, they coaxed, they gave me things. Lots and lots of *things*. They never talked to me. But nothing makes up for losing your parents, Harry. Not a bike or a dog or the best prom dress money can buy. What helps is expressing it. Don't ever give up. Because you can't throw your hands up in the air and pretend like you don't know what's wrong when they act out and you're part of the explanation. No more excuses." More tears had begun to form in her eyes at her own personal memories.

Harry swiped at them with his thumb. "Your parents died when you were a kid, right?"

"Not as young as Mimi and Fletcher, but yes. I was almost thirteen, and it was awful. Keegan did all the right things, but because he claimed he sucked at expressing himself, too, I felt the brunt of it. There was nowhere to go with all the pain of losing my mother and father."

He grinned suddenly. "But look at you. You turned out pretty good."

Anger made her lash out at him. It wasn't something to joke about. "If by good you mean in the future you're comfortable with Mimi making baby potions because she's single, lonely, and can't find anyone who wants to start a family with her, keep this up."

"I'm sorry. You're right. I mean, not about how pathetic you've made yourself sound. That's just not how everyone else sees you, me included. I mean about listening to them and talking about Donna. I'm bottling up all the memories because they always lead back to the same thing. She's gone, and she's never coming back." Harry paused, his voice raw and low. "Sometimes it's almost more than I can handle feeling all at once. She was a great mother, and that makes her a hard role model to live up to, but worse, it hurts to talk about her in the past tense."

Her heart pulled again, clenching and unclenching. "And you're going to be a great father. Don't doubt that, Harry. I don't."

His eyes remained blank, his head cocking in question. "You say that as if you won't be around to see it."

Her eyebrow rose when she poked a finger playfully at his chest. "You say that as if there isn't a conflict between us. Aside from everything else, you don't want to be like me, remember?"

He gave her the look. The one that said he was tired of her razzing him. "Just because I don't want to be like you, doesn't mean I don't want to be with you."

She smiled the smile of someone who had a secret. His words brought a girlie high, but then she remembered two things: her age and tomorrow. "Do you know how old I am, Harry?"

"I know all about the eternal thing. You're not going to scare me off with that."

"Good. Then how old am I?"

Harry frowned, a crease cutting across his forehead. "Nothing but trouble can come of that question."

"Oh, stop. You can't offend me. Just give me a number."

"I dunno. But you don't look a day over twenty-five."

She snorted.

"Good save, right?"

She giggled. "Super save. But here's the deal. Around everyone who's human, I'm technically thirty-five. But in reality, I'm sixty-five."

Harry's mouth fell open in that adorable way it always did when he was trying to process something he just couldn't wrap his mind around.

She patted his hand. "We age very, very slowly, Harry. So we won't age appropriately together. I'll look like this for a long time to come—you, not so much."

"You could be my mother . . ." His revelation appeared to stun even him.

"Well, at least I'd be *someone's* mother."

"I was joking. Wait. No. I wasn't joking, I was opening my mouth before I thought about it. I can stick my foot in it myself," he teased with a grin.

Mara laughed at him, rubbing his arm, loving the feel of his muscles encased in a sweater. "It's okay. Technically, it's true. No hard feelings, or feet either."

He let his cheek fall to the cushion along with her. "Did I ever tell you my mother named me after Ralph Waldo Emerson? Harry was my father's name, but she loved Ralph—quoted him all the time. He said, 'As we grow old . . . the beauty steals inward.' I don't much care what you'll look like. Sure, you're beautiful on the outside, but that's not the most important factor with you, Mara. Not by a long shot."

Her heart stirred again, this time deeply, shifting, changing, opening up, and as much as she wanted to fight it, she couldn't. It was so rare, such a gift, she chose to accept it. "Well, you say that now, and those are very pretty words, but you can't possibly know what the future holds. Everything's in too much of a jumble."

Instead of acknowledging her truth, Harry changed the subject. "You really wanted children pretty bad." It wasn't a question. It was a statement. One he'd clearly given thought to—wondered about, if his expression was any indication. One that sounded as though it came without judgment, even if in her want, she'd run amok in his life.

"I really do, er, did. Now I just want everything to be okay, and for you and the kids to be okay, too."

"Are you rethinking your stance on it now?"

"I'm rethinking everything right now," she told him truthfully.

"I realize I didn't give a lot of thought to the idea someone could steal the formula and create utter havoc for us paranormals. Why I didn't think about it is the question. I'm usually pretty thorough. I never would have let anyone have the formula for it. I almost can't believe it worked."

Harry's smile was wry. "I guess we can only surmise it would have worked. You sort of started with a living, breathing guinea pig. But I don't doubt it would've worked because you're brilliant. Yet, I've wondered something . . ."

"Shoot."

"If this pack of yours is so strict about mating and all these rules, how would you have explained how you got pregnant?"

Mara sighed, looking down at their intertwined hands. "I never got that far in my mind, I guess. I wouldn't let myself get that far. It took me months to get as far as I did."

He gave her one of his sweetest smiles, making the grooves on either side of it deepen. "So are you willing to share how you got as far as you did?"

"Not if you flayed me alive and poured vinegar on my open, raw wounds. If I don't ever tell, no one can ever steal it."

He chuckled, rich and full. "Damn. Fair enough. Either way, I think you're an amazing human being, and you're really good with kids. I think the pack should let you have a dozen. I know my kids like you a lot. I'm impressed."

"I like them, too," was all she could manage around the lump in her throat.

"So, sixty-five, huh?" he asked, low and husky.

"Total GILF."

He leaned into her, nipping at her jaw, brushing her hair aside, his breath hot on her neck. "Total package, if you ask me," he murmured on a rasp of a breath before removing her coffee cup from her hand, then taking her lips.

CHAPTER 16

Harry slanted his mouth over hers, slipping his tongue between her lips, stroking it until Mara had to grab hold of the front of his sweater to keep the world from tilting.

He bracketed her face with his hands, driving his fingers into her hair, pulling the clip that held it up out so the strands fell over her shoulders and down her back. "Hearts and flowers this time—promise. We'll go slow. Really slow," he muttered between kisses.

Her heart raced with need at his words, so much gentler than the last time. Her answer was to move closer to him, burrow into the warm shelter of his chest, savor the friction of her nipples, drawn tightly in her bra.

Harry's hands slipped under her sweater, caressing her skin, drawing out the agonizing wait for him to unclasp her bra and touch her naked flesh.

He drew her to him, pulling her top over her shoulders, teasing her with his tongue, caressing the sensitive flesh of her neck while exposing her flesh to the cool air.

He groaned when he pulled away, scanning her in nothing but

her bra and jeans. "So beautiful," he whispered, popping the clasp on her bra and brushing it off her shoulders.

Pushing her back against the couch with a hot moan, Mara tugged his shirt off, too, dragging it upward, relishing his heated flesh against her fingertips.

She ran her fingers over his nipples, moaning her satisfaction when he hissed into her mouth, sliding down along her body until he was at her breasts.

The brief moment before he wrapped his lips around the tightened bud was full of exquisite agony. Suspended by his dark head against her pale skin, his molten-hot tongue rasping along her collarbone, settling between her breasts, and nipping the underside of one.

She arched against him, rearing up when he enveloped her nipple, wetting it, blowing on it just before capturing it again. Heat, white and thick, spiraled in the pit of her belly. Her cleft grew wet with anticipation, the rib of Harry's chest between her legs, excruciating.

Mara's hands gripped his shoulders, digging her fingers into his flesh as he gathered both of her breasts together; he laved each nipple to a tight peak, making her writhe beneath him with the scream of his name.

And then his hands were dragging her jeans off, unzipping, tearing until there was nothing left between her and complete nudity but her lace panties.

Harry slipped a finger into the triangle of material, drawing his finger between her swollen lips, stopping only briefly to drag his index finger over her clit.

Desperation warred with her wish to make these moments last as long as she could. Yet, with a will of its own, her body bowed against his touch, begged for it, each stroke he took, each whisper of his breath across her thigh, made her need deeper, harder.

Harry slipped his tongue along the crease where thigh met hip, teasing, taunting until she had to clench her teeth to keep from ordering him to pleasure her.

His mouth inched closer, sliding her panties over until each increment of movement became a carnal act all unto itself.

He was delivering the hearts and flowers he'd promised slow and deliberate, driving her not so quietly insane.

When Harry finally plunged his tongue into her wet folds, she bucked beneath him with a wild abandon she'd never encountered. The combination of his hands stroking her thighs and his tongue deep within, skimming her clit in hot pass after pass, made her come in a flash of brilliant color and lights.

Mara strained against him, rising up and driving herself against his mouth, spreading her legs and wrapping them around his neck.

It was then Harry drove a finger into her, deep and hungry, and as his lips consumed her and his tongue devoured her, she came again.

Her chest heaved, her lungs begging for air as she rode his mouth, curling her fingers into tight fists.

Harry drew his finger from her slowly, caressing and kissing every inch of available flesh while he did. Whispering, soothing, when she whimpered the loss of his body pressed to hers. He rubbed his cheek against her calf wrapped around his neck, the bristles of five o'clock shadow sending shivers along her spine.

His fingers, now gentle and tender, continued to stroke her, skimming across the tops of her thighs as he made his way up along her body.

Mara tore at his jeans, desperate to touch him, feel the weight of his cock in her hands. Harry helped, driving them downward until he was naked.

His beautifully maintained body gleamed in the firelight, lush with muscle and endless razor-sharp edges of bone pressing against flesh.

Mara's breath caught in her throat when he slipped entirely from her grasp and pulled her upward with him, leaving them standing face-to-face.

Harry splayed his hand across her lower back, driving her up against him hard, curling his other arm around her shoulders until their chests crashed together.

Mara reached between them, cradling his shaft, stroking the long column of it, lingering over the tip, reaching around him and cupping his ass to knead the muscled flesh.

Harry's lips sought hers again, his tongue driving into her mouth until she almost couldn't breathe from the newest round of heat between her legs. He pulled away with a suddenness, drawing her to the floor and splaying his large frame in the small space between the couch and the fireplace hearth.

Mara's heart jumped at the sight, crashing and pounding in her ears. His thick thighs, dark with a sprinkling of hair, his lean calves, tight from working out, all made her mouth water. The ripple of his abs and the trail of hair led to his erection, stiff and waiting.

"Sit," Harry demanded, his breathing harsh, his words not a request as he positioned her atop him, her back to his face.

She gasped when their skin met again, leaning forward when Harry placed his large hand under her ass and lifted to hold her just above his cock. Her fingers dug into his thighs with anticipation, luxuriating in the flex of tight muscle.

When he centered himself at her passage, Mara almost wept a plea. Instead, she bit her lip and savored his entry, a slow push upward of thick, hot cock.

Her gasp echoed in the room, the pleasure so intense. Yet Harry lingered, lying still beneath her until she wanted to scream a demand to drive deeply into her. He placed one hand at her waist, stroking the curve of it, slipping it around until he found her throbbing clit.

Mara jolted when he began that torturous stroke of the sensitive nub, her hips began to writhe, moving up and down, slow, steady, and that white-hot need grew in her again.

Harry drew circles on her spine, pushing her forward inch by inch until his hand was under her ass again. Mara lifted her hips to give him access while she clung to his hand, encouraging him to stroke her cleft, moaning long and low each time he hit her sweet spot.

She braced her hands on his thighs, using her core to rock with him, savoring the thrust of his cock, slick from her desire.

Each thrust made Harry hiss, sounding out his pleasure, making Mara smile with the joy being a woman brought her tonight.

She cried out when his thrusts became more forceful, welcoming the stretch of her muscles, gritting her teeth when he sat up and pulled her tight to his chest.

His hands went to her breasts, rolling her nipples between his fingertips. His words, hot and hushed, spurred her on. "Christ, Mara. I can't hold on much more, but I don't want this to end—ever . . ."

Her arms went up around his neck with a cry of completion, tears stinging her eyes. This—this moment with Harry—one she'd never even considered; it was so tender and right it left her weak with need. She clung to him as he took a final drive upward, exploding into a million pieces when he demanded she come with him.

He held her tight. The hot press of his chest against her back, his arms around her, all drove her right over the edge into the blissful relief of orgasm.

Harry moaned long and low in her ear, nipping at her earlobe before finding his own release. His arms tightened, his muscles rigid, before he relaxed into her, letting out a long breath of air.

The expansion of his chest against her back made her cling tighter to his neck, her fingers tugging on the wisps of hair at his damp neck.

"Who knew GILFs were made of so much awesome? We didn't break a hip, did we?" he teased, nuzzling her neck.

Mara laughed, forcing air into her lungs, letting her arms drop to squeeze his forearms. "It's the Bengay massages and calcium tablets. They do a GILF good."

Now Harry laughed, the deep rumble vibrating against her back. "You're amazing, Mara Flaherty."

"In the sack?"

"In the everything."

Her cheeks grew hot. "Yeah, yeah. Bet you say that to all the geeks you woo into your web of love."

"Nope, I really don't. And you're my first geek in the sack, thus proving geeks rule."

Leave it to Harry to mix his blatant honesty with a compliment. "You're not so bad yourself."

"Not so bad? Not—so—bad?" he mocked, tickling her and forcing her to roll away from him. He pinned her to the floor while she giggled uncontrollably, placing his large body squarely upon hers. His eyes captured Mara's, glittering with amusement. "So, say again? Not so bad?" He drew her thigh around his waist again, slipping his cock between the folds of her flesh.

Mara giggled from beneath him, loving this version of Harry, playful and light. "Isn't improvement always the goal? If I tell you how incredible you were, you'll never work harder."

He leaned down and nipped at her bottom lip, sending another small wave of heat throughout her body. "So improvement's what you're looking for? Tell me, fellow nerd, what can I do to improve this?" he asked, slipping back down to find her breast, lashing her nipple with his tongue until it ached.

She hissed her pleasure, fighting to find words. "More of that could improve your game," she teased, cupping the back of his head.

"More," he murmured, trailing his fingers along her stomach before skimming the place between her legs. "Like this?"

Her hips moved to the rhythm of his fingers. "Definitely more of that," she said on a shuddering sigh, dizzy from the talent of his hands.

Harry's words grew fewer and farther between when she stroked his cock, pulling him back up into her arms to place his heated shaft between her legs, loving that he wanted her once again.

When he drove into her this time, she opened her eyes, watched each move of his muscles, memorized each clench of his jaw and stroke of his hand. And when he came, she clung to him and held him close so she'd always have this night.

No one could take that away from her.

Not ever.

"CARL? Close your eyes, buddy. Mara and the brainiac are doin' stuff your delicate orbs shouldn't bear witness to."

Mara's eyes popped open at the sound of Nina's voice to find her and Carl in the middle of her living room, Nina's hand over the zombie's eyes.

Harry sat upright, too, grabbing his discarded sweater and dragging it over his head in a rush. His hair stuck up at odd ends, and his cheeks were tinted an adorable red.

"Carl?" Nina swished her finger in their general area. "This is what not to do when you have houseguests." Nina cackled. "We stayed at Marty's last night to give you two some time alone. Get dressed lovebirds. Stop exposing my zombie to the nasty," she ordered, guiding Carl toward the guest bedroom.

As they passed, Carl lifted his hand and gave them a stiff wave of his arm, eyes still protectively covered.

Harry stretched and yawned, pulling the throw from her couch and covering her with a kiss. "Morning," he hummed against her lips.

"*Afternoon*, lovers. It's afternoon!" Nina bellowed from the back of the cottage. "Do you have any flippin' idea how long you two went at it? We thought you'd never get 'er done. It's a damn good thing I learned to tolerate daylight hours."

Mara hid her face in the throw, then in Harry's shoulder with a giggle, forgetting everything but waking up beside him and the intense joy that feeling left in its wake.

Nina reentered the living room, hand now over her eyes. "One more thing, lovebirds. Jeff called in to the police today."

Mara cocked her head, unsure whether to be relieved or concerned. "*What?*"

"Yep. At least he said he was Jeff. Anyway, the cops called Keegan to let him know that according to Jeff, he's safe and sound. Gave them some bullshit story about a bender in Vegas. Sounded too goddamn *Hangover*-ish to me, but the cops fell for it."

Harry shook his head. "Jeff wasn't a Vegas kind of guy. A tech convention in Vegas, maybe. But a weeklong drinking spree? Not a Jeff thing."

Nina nodded. "I said the same damn thing to Keegan, nerd. I don't know shit about Jeff. I do know it's fucking convenient, and I don't give a shit if his story checked out with some hotel on the strip. My spidey senses tell me someone made him call in. Like by force. The same someone who took my Carl and the kids. His story ain't sittin' right with me. So today, while you two make googly eyes at each other, I'm goin' back to Jeff's and seeing what I can sniff out. I'm also callin' that hotel in Vegas. If I have to, I'll fly on over there and knock some heads together. Somebody has to save the nerds of the world."

Mara's hands shook. If what Nina said was true, and someone

had Jeff, they had him because he'd been in the lab that night. The same person who'd anonymously called Keegan. But why? God, she was tired of asking why. "I don't understand why someone would want to harm Jeff? Just to use his phone and keep him from telling Harry about it?"

"Maybe this person thought Jeff knew about the serum? You sure you never let a word about that crazy shit slip, Short-Shot?"

Oh, there was no doubt in her mind. "Absolutely sure. All my notes were in my head. I have a photographic memory. So as I wrote them down—on paper, not an electronic device—I memorized them, and burned the notes afterward. Also something to note, I didn't do it because I thought enough to worry about someone getting their hands on the serum and wreaking havoc. I did it because I didn't want anyone to know pathetic Mara couldn't find a mate to create a family with."

Harry pulled her hand into his. "It isn't pathetic to want to find the right person to mate . . . spend your life with. I'm damn tired of hearing you say that. You might not have seen how many men were interested in you, but everyone else damn well did. You were just being discriminatory. There's a difference. So knock it off."

Carl groaned from the other room, prompting Nina to snap her fingers. "You two heathens get dressed, and we'll figure out where the fuck to go from here. I call we go back to Jeff's and poke around some more. If he's in Vegas, I'm America's Next Top Model." She stomped off to tend to Carl while Mara huddled into the throw.

"How'd you sleep?" he whispered into the top of her head, the scent of his sweater comforting against her nose.

Mara closed her eyes and savored Harry, his arms, the beat of his heart, for one more brief moment. "Well, I know I did a good job refinishing the floors. They're as hard as floors should be," she teased.

Harry reached around her to find his jeans, dropping hers in her lap. "They're definitely hard. What say we do this on your bed next time?"

Slipping her jeans on and recovering her sweater, she let her eyes fall to the bottom of the couch and gulped. There would be no tomorrow. But Harry didn't know that. "Bed it is."

Harry rose, holding his hand out to her. He smiled down, warm and sweet, his teeth perfect and white. "If we can do, you know, *that* again, I'll even put all those frilly pillows back on the bed afterward."

Mara took the offer of his hand, allowing him to sweep her upward in his embrace. She laughed, forcing herself to ignore the numbers on her microwave's clock and focus on the visual of Harry, his clumsy fingers trying to arrange her pillows the way she liked them. "I think it's only fair. I put out. You pick up," she teased, squeezing him one last time, refusing to linger too long in his embrace, before making her way to the kitchen to brew a fresh pot of coffee.

But Harry grabbed her hand and took the lead. "I'll make coffee. You grab a shower first. I'd join you, but you know, Carl. Impressionable zombie and all . . ." he added with a wiggle of his eyebrows, his husky voice full of suggestion.

As the microwave's clock struck one, she realized this Harry, the one not overcome with testosterone, was sweet and accommodating; this Harry was considerate.

But she didn't have time for a shower, and she wouldn't be able to help Nina scope out Jeff's house.

When the doorbell rang, Nina whooshed by in a blurry vision of arms and legs, her eyes bright and aware, her words protective. "I got this. You two stay put. Harry? Just in case this isn't the motherfucker kidnapping people right out from under our noses, brush your hair. You look like you used a hand blender on it."

Harry's hand self-consciously went to his hair. He licked his fingers and smoothed it down with a cheesy grin in Mara's direction.

It was adorable and so Harry it hurt her heart. That was exactly as she wanted to remember him.

Squaring her shoulders, Mara sucked in a breath when Nina popped open the door.

The face on the other side of it was stoic, reserved, maybe even a little remorseful against the backdrop of the gloomy sky. Cooper Beaman held his hat respectfully in his hands.

Nina grinned, acknowledging one of many she'd defeated at Pack's annual touch football game. "Cooper? How the fuck are you, dude? You here for a little rematch? How many times I gotta kick your ass before you accept I'm a chick and I rule the field, buddy? Go home and iron your pom-poms." She slapped him on the back good-naturedly.

Mara watched Cooper, his eyes looking past Nina's shoulder. Usually, Cooper was all about a good ribbing, especially when it came to his rivalry with Nina. But not today. He cleared his throat. "I'm here for Mara, Nina. Official business."

Harry was instantly at her side, pushing her behind him before she had the chance to object. "What official business?" he demanded.

Mara let her forehead rest against his broad back for only a moment before she said, "It's okay, Harry. I knew Cooper was coming."

Harry whipped around, his eyes searching hers. "*For what?*"

Nina's face went from playful to angry in an instant. "What the fuck's goin' on, Coop? What official business, dude? Spit it out, or you're gonna find out what it feels like to be annihilated by a chick, ass sniffer!"

"Pack business," Cooper said, straightening his spine before pulling a pair of handcuffs from his belt.

"Hold on a minute, Cooper, is it?" Harry stepped between Nina and Cooper, his hand on the man's chest. "What the hell is this about?"

"Harry!" Mara grabbed his arm, scenting his anger. "It's okay. Cooper's here for me. I knew he'd be here. The council gave me twenty-four hours to get my personal affairs in order as consolation for turning myself in. I said I'd go peacefully, and I will."

Stepping around Harry, Mara held her wrists out. "I'm ready, Cooper." While she forced her voice to calm, her stomach threatened to empty itself.

"Hold the hell on!" Harry roared, pushing her hands away from Cooper, his eyes angry, his jaw tight. "The hell you're taking her anywhere. Take your hands off her, or I'll put mine on you!"

Mara's heart swelled, hitting her ribs with a hard knock. Her hands shook when she took the handcuffs away from Cooper and slapped them on herself.

"Cooper, I'm gonna beat your ass bloody, motherfucker!" Nina yelled in his face.

"Nina, Harry! Both of you stop!" Mara shouted. "Please stop making this harder than it has to be. I thought you'd both be gone. I didn't think that Harry and I . . ." she shook her head, fighting back tears. "I didn't think you'd be here, Harry. I turned myself in the other day. There's just no other way. Eventually, the pack would have found out you're not a human anymore. How would you explain that? Should you lie for me? I had to take responsibility before you were considered a conspirator. Add in that someone's bound to mention Jeff's been gone from the lab. The Vegas story isn't going to work a week from now when Jeff's used up all his vacation time. To make everything so much worse, what if someone in Jeff's family, or maybe a friend we don't know about, begins to wonder where Jeff is and contacts the police? You said it yourself, Nina, human interference is always a problem. We can't keep running behind this broken story, gluing the fallen pieces of it back together only to find more of it has chipped away. The pack will know how to handle both Jeff's disappearance and the police. But I have to take responsibility for Harry's turning. It doesn't matter that it was an accident. It happened and it happened at my hands. Period. The council has to investigate in order to protect everyone. You included, Harry. So, please, *please*, just let me go with Cooper."

Nina's fists clenched and unclenched before her barely contained rage exploded. "Fuck you and your stupid goddamn pack, Cooper!" She flipped up both middle fingers. "You and all your fucking rules and bullshit. Mark my words, Cooper, and tell all your freakishly, old-ass comrades in crap, too, I'm comin' for her. And when I do, you damn well better hope you're not in the way," she snarled down at poor Cooper, making his ruddy face go white.

"It's my job, Nina."

"Fuck you and your job! That you're even a part of enforcing this kind of middle-age shit makes you a sissy-ass follower, collecting a paycheck at the expense of someone else's life. Fuck. You."

Aw. Nina really liked her. She'd linger on that revelation a little longer, but the color orange was in the distance, calling her name. "Nina," Mara soothed, brushing her cheek on Nina's shoulder. "I offered myself up, to keep Harry from having to lie and make up some wild story, and to keep us all free of guilt. Now let him take me, and let him take me peacefully. Don't shoot the messenger."

Nina hissed in Cooper's face, flashing her fangs in protest, but she didn't try to stop him from taking her.

Harry put a hand on Cooper's shoulder to thwart him. He loomed over Cooper, almost twice his size and bulk. "Just give me one minute, okay?"

Cooper nodded moving toward the opening of the door. "One minute. That's it."

Harry pulled her to his chest, kissing the top of her head. "I'll come get you. Swear it. No way am I letting you take the fall for

this, Mara. I'll lie. I'll tell them I drank the serum on purpose
because I wanted to know what it was like to be a werewolf. They'll
believe it because I'm King of Geeks. Whatever it takes. But the
hell I'm letting you go to werewolf jail. Hear me?" His breath shuddered from his lungs, making the width of his chest brush against
her cheek.

She shook her head hard. "Don't you dare do that, Harry! Stay
with the kids. Hear me? They need you so much right now. Please,"
she begged before pulling away, more tears threatening to escape.
She rose on tiptoe and pressed a soft kiss to his cheek. "No matter
what, they need you to be there. Don't let them down," she whispered before pushing her way past everyone and flying out the door
toward Cooper's waiting car.

The last thing her sharp ears picked up was the sound of poor
Carl, wailing his discontent at Mara's departure while Nina and
Harry tried to soothe him.

CHAPTER 17

"Fuck!" Harry roared in impatience, making an already on-edge Carl jump.

Marty's mouth was a thin line, her eyes rimmed with red as she, Wanda, and Nina gathered in the small cottage to formulate a plan to help Mara. "Keegan's meeting with the council tonight. He'd better find a way to talk them out of this, or I'm going into full-on assault mode and storming the castle!"

Wanda squeezed Marty's shoulder, her elegant face full of sympathy. She wiped a fresh batch of tears from Marty's cheeks. "They're really going to put her on trial?"

"Ain't that some shit? Kid makes an honest mistake, one even Harry will tell them was without malicious intent, and still they have to try her in front of a jury of her peers. Some goddamn bunch of jackasses you got in your corner, blondie," Nina growled.

Marty nodded her head. "You know what, Elvira? Today? Today I won't disagree with you, and if I knew there was a way to take my family and get away from this ridiculous rule the council's set forth, don't think for a minute I wouldn't!"

Mara had been gone for ten hours. Ten long, painful hours they'd waited to hear what the council's intent was regarding Mara's arrest.

Ten long hours wherein Harry kicked himself for not seeing the signs, the hidden messages she'd left him like a trail of bread-crumbs. She knew damn well he'd have found a way to try and stop her from handing herself over like she was guilty.

Wanda came up behind him. Grabbing his hand, she pulled it to her chest, as though she were trying to absorb some of his pain. Her voice was raw when she whispered, "Promise you, we'll figure this out, Harry. No matter what it takes, we'll find a way. Please believe."

Nina clapped him on the back. "Goddamn right, we will. Don't you worry, nerd. I'll get her out of there if I have to chew my way through the motherfucking doors."

He'd done all the believing he was capable of. Now he just wanted everyone to get the fuck out of his path while he got to Mara.

At that moment, Keegan walked through the door, his face grim, his eyes lined from exhaustion.

Marty didn't rush to his side the way she normally did whenever her husband entered the room. She lifted her eyes to meet his, and Harry knew as the look passed between them it wasn't good.

Harry stiffened and growled, stunning even himself with the level of his anger.

Wanda gripped him harder, holding him in place. On tiptoe, she whispered in his ear, "Harry, I'm begging you, think of the kids. *Please*. They need you so much. They adore you. I know you can't feel that sometimes because they've struggled, but I've been with them almost every night since this happened, and they cling to your memory. Please, don't be rash. We'll help you. We'll help the kids. Archibald's fallen in love with them. Don't deny him the chance to fall in love with you, too, because you did something stupid."

He breathed deeply, forcing down the urge to break free of Wanda's iron grip and bust Mara out. Nothing was more important than the kids, but Mara had taken a spot right alongside them. "Okay." He cleared his throat, and his murderous thoughts. Turning to Keegan, he asked, "So what happens next? Tell me what we do?"

Keegan ran a hand through his dark hair, his eyes finding Harry's. "She goes to trial in front of a jury of her peers. It goes the same way it does with humans."

"How can she go to jail for an accident? This was a goddamn accident!" How the fuck was this happening?

Keegan's head shook, slow and weary. "We have no precedent for this, Harry. It doesn't matter that you don't want to see her punished. The problem is she has, in that mighty brain of hers, the wherewithal to create a formula that makes werewolves. That's dangerous to the pack. It's dangerous to everyone concerned. She created you. If she can do it, and she gets away with it, who's to say someone else won't do it and think they can get away with it?"

Harry's jaw grew tight. "So they think if they lock her up it'll keep some other lunatic from creating a serum just like it? Did it stop serial killers when they jailed Jeffrey Dahmer? That's ludicrous!"

Keegan pulled off his knit cap, pinching the space between his eyebrows. "It sends a message, Harry. It's a deterrent of sorts. Just like prosecuting anyone who's broken a law. Mara knew what she was doing was an iffy proposition. She knew it could lead to trouble if she got caught." Keegan held up a hand to keep Harry from protesting. "But don't think I don't understand your point. I do. I made it myself to the council. Still, they've decided to allow Mara's peers to vote whether she can be trusted to never reveal the ingredients of that serum. She has a solid reputation in the community, mad scientist that she is. That'll go a long way in keeping the council from believing she would sell this serum to someone." He shook his head, sorrow streaking his eyes. "If she could have just waited, I would have found a way—something," he murmured, worry lining his face.

Harry looked down at the floor, his gut in a knot. No way was he going to sit around while Mara was in jail. "She hated the lying. She knew it was only a matter of time before her scent on me wouldn't fly anymore. She also knew she had to keep your alpha position safe. She didn't want you to be accused of favoritism."

Keegan approached him with clear hesitation. "In all this, I've forgotten to ask how you are. Marty tells me you want out no matter how you find it."

"What if I find a way to do that? Will this council arrest me, too?" He was provoking unnecessarily, and while it was rude, Harry couldn't stop himself.

"He's not the fucking enemy, dude. Step off," Nina said with a warning.

"What can the pack do to help you adjust, Harry? At least until you figure this out." Keegan persisted, obviously not put off by his angry words.

Harry took in another deep breath. "My apologies. I'm taking this out on you when it's not your fault. Just tell me what this proceeding is like. Can I be there?"

Keegan nodded. "You have no choice. They'll call you as a witness. You just tell the truth and relay what happened the night you were turned."

Harry scoffed without even realizing it. "Will it even matter? Will they take into account my testimony? They don't seem to care much that I, the alleged victim, am just damn fine with the idea of being a werewolf. If I don't want to press charges, there shouldn't damn well be any." It was all he could do not to break something, hit someone.

And he'd just admitted, out loud, he'd come to terms with being a werewolf.

It meant he could be with Mara. For as long as she'd have him. *If* she'd have him. He'd decided last night when she'd given him the speech about her age and all the kooky bits of information about werewolf-ing. He wanted Mara. Period. If that meant baying at the moon and living forever, he'd find a way to figure it out where the kids were concerned.

In this precarious situation, one he was told he could never change, he'd rather have Mara and the kids together than have them without her. He didn't ever want to think about a time when the kids weren't a part of his world. However, the cards he'd been dealt left him little choice but to accept what fate had handed him.

But he had to make one thing clear to Mara. If there ever came a time when he could reverse this, he would. Not because he hated the idea, but because Mimi and Fletcher were the most important things in his life, and to watch them leave this earth before him was unthinkable.

He ran a hand over his grainy eyes. "How can I make these council members understand?"

Keegan cleared his throat. "I'd like to think they will, Harry— if they hear it from you. They didn't love Marty and me at first either. I was meant to mate with someone else entirely."

Harry held a hand up. "Hold up. This pack chooses your mate? The hell I'll be told who to spend my life with," he grumbled. "Do they even know what century we live in? Next you'll tell me dowries and goat exchanges are involved."

Keegan barked a harsh laugh. "You know, there was a time . . . Never mind. The point is they adjusted. They're not unreasonable. They're just from another era, one where humans and werewolves don't mix under any circumstances. So yes, I'd like to think they'll find a way to understand how this happened."

"*Think* they will, Keegan?" Marty erupted in a yelp, disbelief riddling her question. "You have some pull, Keegan! Use it, damn it. I'm not going to sit back and let Mara go to prison because the council thinks she's a crazy, werewolf-creating little Frankenstein. You know that's not true! Surely her good reputation within the pack lets them see she'd never hurt a soul? What's being a good girl for, if not for it to work in your favor? Jesus Christ!" Marty yelled up at him, her face contorted in fear and misery, her fists clenched at her side.

But Keegan didn't shoot back like one would expect. Instead he pulled Marty to his chest and let her cry into it, releasing her ragged sobs of frustration.

Her raw, agonizing wail made his chest uncomfortably tight. Harry gripped the back of Mara's couch.

The very couch he'd made the most incredible love with her on. And he was determined, despite their enormous differences, to have the chance to do that again.

Nina knocked his shoulder with hers and hitched her jaw toward the small hallway dividing Mara's bedroom and the bathroom.

He followed without question. "Say something good, Nina. Say something that'll keep me from blowing this whole thing for Mara by doing something unreasonable."

Nina held up her phone, tapping it with a short nail. "Your favorite lame-ass witch doctor Guido just left me a voice mail. I think we got a lead on who snatched the damn kids and Carl. Listen." She held her phone up to his ear.

Harry grabbed the phone, his eyes going wide as he heard what Guido had to say.

As she entered the council courtroom, rich with miles of crown molding and an imposing judge's bench that appeared a mile high, Mara lifted her chin, refusing to be ashamed of her prison garb.

This might be, by far, one of the least flattering outfits she'd ever worn, but Marty's words, as crazy a time as it was to actually remember them, still rang clear. "Even if it's the worst fashion faux pas of your life, wear that bitch like you intended it, honey."

Okay, so that had been in reference to the ugly oversized tie-dyed T-shirt she'd worn with a pair of red leggings and yellow ballet slippers, which Nina had promptly banned, but her jailhouse jumpsuit was sort of on the same level. She just wasn't a free woman making the choice to wear something so ugly.

Clinking her way to her seat, along with what felt like an endless aisle of pack member after pack member in the crowd, she passed Marty and Keegan. Marty, threats of no contact to the prisoner be damned, reached out and grabbed her hand just before one of the council's prison guards tried to prevent it, her eyes irate and sad at the same time.

Nina was up and out of her seat in a flash, almost making Mara smile. Except she was on her way to being tried for werewolf-making, and maybe a life sentence. That wasn't cause for smiling.

Nina lifted her sunglasses and growled at the guard. "Touch a bitch, and I kill you, weasel. You got that?" She leered at him; despite his size, he had to clearly fight to keep his ground. "You're draggin' her around like you just caught Charlie Manson the Second. Take it down a notch, brother. You didn't train at Quantico, and she ain't some mass murderer. So step off. You do not want to see my vampire rage, poser."

Mara, after a long sleepless night next to a snoring fellow were-wolf inmate doing time for killing a neighboring farm's cows, almost giggled. It had to be from lack of sleep and maybe a touch of delirium, but somehow Nina ignoring the long arm of the law was a million shades of awesome. "Nina," she whispered, remembering where she was. "It's okay. Sit down before they give me extra time for friends behaving badly."

Nina turned to her, putting her hand up in the guard's face before he could protest. "You okay, Short-Shot? Anybody bother you in the big house? You say it, I'll kill it."

Mara nodded on a gulp. She'd never doubted Nina was a marshmallow on the inside. When her favor shone upon you, it was like Mother Teresa herself had taken your hand and told you everything was going to be just fine.

"I'm fine. Swear," she assured like she'd spent the night glamping instead of lying on a hard cot, in a cold, sterile cell, beneath a woman whose snoring rivaled ten grown men with deviated septums. "Are the kids okay?"

Harry, big, handsome and, even in her predicament, still stealing her breath with his handsomeness, rose and stood up behind Nina. And then he tripped over something, probably his big feet, almost falling into the vampire and the others seated beside them.

Someone reached up to offer assistance, but Harry held up his hand. "I've got this!" he whisper-yelled, gripping the back of the wooden pews set up in the courtroom to steady himself. When he looked at Mara, his eyes were warm. "The kids are fine. They're with Arch while we're all here."

Mara glanced over past Harry and Nina to find Wanda, Ying, Leah, and Astrid all in solidaric attendance. Astrid and Ying raised fists of support while Leah dug in her purse.

Darnell stood at the back of the courtroom, his face somber even as he nodded his head in her direction. Her brother Sloan and his new wife Jeannie, a pretty petite blonde who adored her husband, sat in the middle of everything, holding hands, worried expressions on their faces.

The cold glare of sunlight filtered in through the high row of windows to their left, lining the interior of the courtroom, highlighting their faces, so pale and full of fear. Mara's heart warmed with undying gratitude for the people who loved her and supported her, even in an act of stupidity.

Jeannie wiggled her nose a la *I Dream of Jeannie*, using the joke they all teased her with as a signal to Mara she could make this all go away by using her magic if necessary. Genie magic trumped everything, but that would only bring huge disorder to Jeannie's reign as head djinn. Never would Mara risk her sister-in-law's position for her own benefit.

Mara gave her a subtle shake of her head, shooting her a glance filled with gratitude.

Harry reached over Nina's shoulder and ran a tender finger along her cheek.

"Has anyone heard from Jeff?" she asked him, still sick with worry he was hurt somewhere.

He passed Nina and shook his head. "No. Not yet. And for now, the police seem satisfied he's in Vegas. We spent all night trying to find clues to his whereabouts, but nothing turned up. Not even in Vegas—which will never be the same after Nina. But right now, I need you to just listen, say absolutely nothing, and keep your expression unreadable. Second, if all hell breaks loose, just go with the chaos, okay? Oh, and go team werewolf," he said on a smile— one that was steady and sure.

Her face curled into his touch without a moment's hesitation. She stared right at him, trying to read what his cryptic message meant. "Thank you," was all she could manage before the guard pulled her away toward the high back chair she was to sit in for judgment.

Settling herself as comfortably as she could with handcuffs on, Mara waited for the council to begin the proceedings. Oddly, while the elders of the pack assembled and situated, she wasn't at all fearful for her future or their scowling frowns. Not the way she'd once been as a child anyway.

When she was little, the council was a group of people who watched over you from on high, larger than life, and scarier, too. You never saw them. They were, for all intents and purposes, invisible; chosen for their superior observation skills and wise handling of pack issues. You never knew how they were always watching. You just knew they were.

Sort of like Santa Claus, minus the cute, fun-loving elves and flying reindeer.

And she'd always behaved accordingly—with the idea that at any moment, one of them would pop up and catch her doing something wrong, like writing on the bathroom walls or smoking weed. Her fear, the fear they'd instilled, had always been with her, albeit subconsciously. It was the silent force that drove the good girl in her without ever having to say a word in reprimand.

Today, as she focused on the faces deciding her future, aged by centuries of life, gray and allegedly wise, as she watched the group of her werewolf peers file in and take their places in the jury box, she saw them for what they were.

Really old guys with dusty robes and a bunch of people she used to see in the halls of her high school who knew nothing about her. Not a single thing. They didn't know how deep her desire to have a family of her own ran.

They didn't know a single personal detail about her because she'd spent most of her time studying, learning, dreaming of going places and discovering something besides keg parties and bongs.

Sure, she could go to the slammer for life because of these people—in her case, that was a long, long time—whether they knew those things about her or not.

But she'd damn well go with the knowledge she'd finally gone after something she really wanted, and she'd go with no regrets.

She was taking one for the single girl werewolf team.

She hadn't done anything horrible, per se. She'd found a way to take control of her life, of her deepest desire, without the aid of anything other than her brain. She'd followed her heart. For the first time in forever, she'd done something on impulse.

Sure, her impulse was a whole lot bigger than most whims. It wasn't like buying an expensive sports car or even having a one-night stand on impulse. Yet what she'd lacked in her impulsivity, the forethought to consider the far-reaching consequences of making the serum, she more than made up for in sheer determination to have a family of her own—on her own terms.

No matter what happened to her during this proceeding, she'd never regret pursuing her dreams.

Just before the eldest council member, somber, stoic, ancient by human terms, dropped the gavel, Mara heard a rustling of paper, making her turn around.

Marty, Nina, and Wanda whipped up signs made of poster board with big, bold red letters that read MY UTERUS, MY CHOICE!

The crowd, along with the council and members of the jury, let out sharp gasps.

Mara closed her eyes, shrinking in her chair. Marty absolutely had to stop watching televised court cases on her lunch break, but their support meant the world.

As the gavel swung hard, cracking in her ears, she readied herself.

Let the games begin.

"I object!" Marty yelped from the crowd.

All eyes swung to Marty, beautiful and sunshiny-blond, dressed all in her "protest pack authority" black, the clang of her bracelets reverberating through the cathedral ceilings of the courtroom.

She climbed out of Keegan's grasp like she was made of melting butter and hopped over people in the crowd as though she'd been possessed by a high school hurdle jumper.

She flew down the long aisle toward the council bench, evading three guards and the pack's version of a bailiff. "I said I object!"

"Marty . . ." Griffin Atkin, second elder of the council used his warning tone when speaking into the mic. "We have yet to speak a solitary word. There's nothing to object to."

Marty ignored the loud protests of Keegan. She narrowed her eyes, gazing up at the row of eight council members, hands on her hips. "The hell there's not something to object to! I object to you telling my sister-in-law, or any female pack member, what she can do with her uterus! When—and only when—you have a vagina, and not some dried-up, old—"

Keegan was right behind her, scooping her up and placing his hand over her mouth to quiet her. Marty flailed in his grip, but Keegan was stronger, wrestling her back to their places in the crowd with an apologetic look to the council members.

Charles Knotts, council member number four, glared down at Keegan, disapproval all over his stately, intricately lined face. "I trust you'll control your mate from here on out, Keegan?"

From the corner of her eyes, Mara saw Wanda pop up from her seat, waving her poster board with a flutter. "Control?" she yelled in outrage. "Did you just use the word *control* regarding a woman from *this* century, sir? I'm offended. I demand that," she paused a moment, frowning as though she wasn't sure what to demand. Stomping her foot, her tastefully made-up eyes shot them all condescending glares. "How dare you order a man to control his mate in the presence of so many of the female persuasion? I demand that statement be stricken from the record!"

Charles Knotts pursed his lips, giving his fellow council members a roll of his eyes. "There is no record as yet, Ms. Jefferson. We can't have a record if no one has said anything to be recorded," he offered dryly, followed by a grating sigh.

Wanda shook her finger at the council members, using her stern mommy face. "Then let it be recorded that no one's said anything worthy of recording!"

Yeah. You go, halfsie. Mara silently cheered Wanda, now really unsure where this was going. They were clearly trying to distract and delay, but for what? Yet she did as Harry asked and remained expressionless.

Council member number seven, Thomas Carson, leaned forward and spoke into his mic. "Silence!" he thundered. Thomas, one of the more easily agitated, stuck in his eighteenth-century ways, sent Wanda the imposing glare of death before waving a finger at the guards to escort Wanda out.

Nina leapt over the pew and was at Wanda's side before anyone could say differently. "Hey, old dude! Tell your goon to back the mutha—"

"Your mouth, Nina—mind it!" Wanda reminded with a shout, even as they attempted to drag her out of the courtroom, the heels of her midsized pumps digging into the floor. "Remember, you're in a court of foolish law!"

Harry was there suddenly, shoving his way past the onlookers to shield her from the quickly growing chaos of the crowd. She tugged at his shirt. "What's going on?" she yelled up, panic rising in her chest as people began to react.

But Harry didn't answer. He just looked over his shoulder and smiled at her, then pointed to the courtroom doors.

Mara's eyes flew to the opening where Darnell stood, holding on to the arm of none other than . . .

Uh . . .

Wait. Who the hell was that?

The courtroom erupted in loud bursts of outrage and overall chaos as Darnell tugged the man toward the council.

One of the council members grabbed the gavel and pounded it hard, holding the microphone to it in order to amplify the sound. The screeching echo of gavel against wood had everyone scrambling to see what was going on. The crowd settled, leaving only a distant hum of curious whispers.

"Identify yourself!" Griffin demanded with a harsh order, pointing his knobby finger at the stranger.

Darnell patted the man on the back, and gave him a toothy smile. "You up, brotha. Time to sell it."

"*Who are you?*" Charles Knotts roared, making the man's spine almost crumble. But Darnell stood behind him, giving him an anchor to hold on to. His big hand clamped on to the gentleman's shoulder, resting there to keep him upright.

The man with the raven hair looked down at his feet, his hands trembling, making his overly large gray suit ripple. "Guido. Um . . . Guido the Witch Doctor."

Mara's eyes flew open, then upward at Harry. *"That's Guido?"* she mouthed, shocked.

Harry nodded with a wide grin. But his smile held a secret she didn't understand.

She'd have never recognized Guido without his witch doctor getup. He looked so vulnerable, afraid—entirely different without his head full of feathers and garish makeup.

"Just wait and trust me, okay?" Harry murmured, running a hand over her head.

"What brings you to disrupt this proceeding?" Griffin demanded with another crash of the gavel. "This is official pack business. Not witch doctor business."

As Guido shuffled his feet, searching for his words, Nina, Marty, and Wanda lined the back of the courtroom by the entrance. How strange . . .

Mara shot a question with her eyes up at Harry, but he simply smiled and squeezed her shoulder.

"I'll ask you again. What brings your disruption to this proceeding?"

Guido's Adam's apple bobbed along his reed-thin neck when Darnell nudged him again. "I have information about what happened the night Harry Emmerson was allegedly turned by Mara Flaherty."

More gasps erupted from the courtroom, forcing Mara to gasp with them, until Charles smacked the gavel against the wood surface again. "There will be silence in this courtroom, or I'll have you all removed at once!"

Guido sucked in a gulp of air, fidgeting with the buttons on a suit that hung off him like it belonged to his father.

"Explain," Charles prompted, raising his bushy eyebrows in question.

"So it went like this. I was all doin' my witch doctor thing a few weeks ago when I got a call from this lady who wanted a love potion. You know, I love him, he doesn't notice me, make me irresistible to him, right?"

Each council member leaned forward in their seats high above Guido, anticipating his next words.

Griffin gave him a sharp nod. "You have our attention."

"Anyway, she sounded pretty desperate, and even though I suck royally at witch doctoring, it's like I told your wingnut friends back there." He hitched his thin jaw over his shoulder in the direction of Nina. "I gotta eat. So I told her to c'mon over. And she did." He paused, shuffling his feet until Darnell patted his shoulder to reassure him. "Wow. All I gotta say is holy nutballs. You people sure make 'em crazy."

"Meaning?" as yet unheard from council member number six, Davis Eaton asked.

Guido held up a thin, pale hand. "No disrespect to your kind, but man, this lady was certifiable. She kept going on and on about how she was sick of hearing her friend talk about this guy all day long. How she was tired of pretending her friend was right for this guy when she was the one who was right for him. She said she was sick of keeping her love for him a secret while her friend blathered on about this guy. All this while she was sweating and pacing, her eyes all round and wide."

Davis frowned, tugging his gray beard. "And then?"

Guido's eyes expressed guilt. "Look, I just wanted her to get the heck outta my shack. One minute she was smiling all nice and polite, and the next she was ranting like she was possessed, knocking things over, hissing like a wild animal. All *Carrie*-like. See where I'm going?"

Mara couldn't pull her gaze away from Guido. Yet deep down inside, she knew it was because she didn't want to address what he would say next. Hear what she was almost certain he'd say. Her breathing had almost completely stopped even as Harry kept his hand firmly on her shoulder, holding her in her seat.

"I think we see where you're going. Please continue."

Guido scrunched his nose up as if something distasteful had passed under it. "Like I said, she wanted a love potion. Something that would make this guy fall over the moon in love with her. She had this big plan. She kept calling it her life plan. I called it a batshit plan—in my head, of course. I'd never say it out loud. You couldn't even say boo to her without setting her crazy off. But she said she was going to turn this guy into a werewolf, slip him the love potion, and then they were gonna ride off into the sunset in his Volkswagen. She said it wouldn't work if he wasn't a werewolf like her because only the purest of pure could be her mate."

Mara's stomach dove to the floor as she began to gag, clamping her hand over her mouth to muffle it. No. No. Please, God, no.

"So what did you do next, Guido?"

"Are you kidding me?" he squealed as though everyone should know the answer to that. "What would you do? I gave the nutball a grape soda with a bunch of herbs and dead seeds from my garden out back mixed into it, told her it was my strongest love potion ever, took her money so I could grab a burger, and got her the heck outta my shack! I don't have a lot, but the way she was carrying on, knocking things over, I wouldn't have had anything left if she kept it up. So yeah, I lied."

Davis lifted his chin from high atop his council perch. "And what does this have to do with the pack's case against Mara Flaherty?"

His next breath shuddered, wracking his slight body. "Well, like all nutballs do, she came back, and holy man alive, was she on fire! She woulda spit flames if she could've. I don't think I've ever seen anybody as hot as she was."

"Because I'm assuming this love potion of yours didn't work?" Griffin asked, his eyes sharp and assessing Guido.

Guido scoffed and rolled his eyes. "Of course it didn't work. I'm a hack. Total hack. So she comes back, right? Madder than ever, if that's possible with lunatics like her. She was screaming and throwing things, said that she'd done exactly what I told her to do *after* she turned him into a werewolf. Got up the next day to the tune of rainbows and mystical sunsets, totally expecting the love of her life to come to her house with candy and flowers and fall down on one knee or some kookiness, but that didn't happen. Instead, he fell in love with her friend, the one who liked this guy, too. The friend nutso was sick of hearing talk about the man she knew was really meant for her."

No one moved in the courtroom, the air thick and stifling. Mara's pulse raced, she sat frozen in place, hearing Guido's story. Her icy fingers, clamped together, wouldn't move.

"So this woman claimed she'd turned someone into a werewolf. Did she reveal how she'd gone about doing that?" Davis asked.

Guido's head bobbed up and down with a furious nod. "Oh, you bet, she did. Don't all nuts like to brag about how smart they are?"

Griffin pursed his lips, tapping his mic. "If we could refrain from coloring the description of aforementioned with the word *nut*, and stick to facts, this council would be most pleased."

Guido'd gained some steam now, his confidence still tentative, but certainly not as fragile as it had been when Darnell had all but dragged him into the courtroom. He rolled his neck. "You can color her anything you want, my friend. Nuts is nuts, and that's how I'm callin' it." He gave the council members a no-apology look before continuing. "So, yes. She definitely bragged about how she'd scratched this poor dude in the cafeteria where she worked with her fingernail. Said she'd created a distraction by tripping someone so they'd fall into this poor sucker, then, in the chaos of scattered lunch trays and spilled hot coffee, she said she reached right down and nicked him with her fingernail. According to her, that's all it takes."

Mara's mouth fell open—it was all she could do not to gasp out loud. She hadn't turned Harry into anything. By the time he'd gotten to the vitaminwater, he was already a werewolf. She was almost too afraid to believe it was true.

"And then, sir?"

"And theeennn, she says she knocked out her supposed soul mate's friend, used his phone to send this guy a text, asking him to meet in some lab. I don't know what lab or where that lab is. She said she did that so when lover boy turned into a werewolf, she could be there to douse him with the love potion."

If not for Harry, Mara would have slipped right out of her chair. Jeff. This friend's phone was Jeff's phone. Her head swirled with questions. How had Jeff called into the police just yesterday? Oh, sweet Jesus. She had Jeff.

"And where is this *friend* of this nut's, er . . . the accused's alleged soul mate?"

Guido looked at Davis like he was insane. "Man, you think I was askin' questions? I dunno what she did with the guy's friend. She said she knocked him out in order to get his phone. I figure he's doin' what he does, never the wiser. Least, I hope he is. All I know is, she was PO'd. Like crazier mad than the last time I saw her. She was hatin' on me. She was hatin' on this chick she called her friend. She was hatin' on her soul mate, too—because he liked her friend better. She said when she was angry she did bad, bad things. That *they* made her do bad things. I don't know about you personally. Me, on the other hand? I know me. I'm not into bad, bad things. But I knew she'd come back because the love potion didn't work. The crazies always want revenge on me. So, I was ready for her. I got a gun—one with some silver-tipped bullets. Told her I'd blow her crazy out of her crazypants if she ever came back again. Not a fan of violence, but no way was I waitin' around to see if she was gonna chew a hole in my intestines."

Davis cocked his head in question. "And how does this all lead to Mr. Emmerson and Mara Flaherty?"

Guido's eyes bulged. "Hello. Harry showed up at my place two nights after wingnut came callin' for the love potion, right? I thought Mara was the one who'd turned him into a werewolf with her baby juice. He said she did."

Mara winced, scrunching her eyes shut, her hands trembling until Harry placed his over them, warm and supportive, stilling her shaking.

"And why did Mr. Emmerson come to see you, Guido?" Griffin asked.

Guido flapped his hands. "Oh, you know, the usual. Because he thought I could turn him back into a full human. Like reverse the werewolf thing. Of course, I couldn't. Like I told you, I can't do anything but screw up."

The crowd rumbled their disapproval, glaring at Harry.

"Continue," Griffin encouraged into the mic.

"I didn't make the connection between the nut and Harry until quacky flakes came back a few days after Harry and Mara and that seething, fanged lady on legs left. Like I said, she was screaming at me and calling me all kinds of names, then I threatened her with the gun—so she hightailed it outta there. I was still shaken up, you see. I didn't make the connection between Harry being turned in an accident and the flippy broad turning some unknown guy on purpose. I did think it was weirder than weird that two people had recently been turned into werewolves so close together, but what do I know about werewolves and what they do? Maybe you people do this stuff all the time . . ."

Council member Samuel Cross spoke up for the first time, clearly offended. "We most certainly do not. We absolutely do not advocate turning anyone into a werewolf! I suggest you finish, sir. My patience has grown thin."

Guido shook his head, his sleek hair, shiny under the glare of the overhead harsh lights, combed neatly. "I don't mean to offend. I'm just sayin' I didn't wanna know what you all do after crazy lady left. I just wanted her to leave. But she said something before she ran screeching outta my place that freaked me out. I couldn't sleep all night last night because of it, and that's when I called the spittin' mad vampire back there." He thumbed in the direction of Nina, who stood, imposing and tall, at the exit to the courtroom. "She's the only person I know who knows other werewolves, and after my experience with loony-loon, I didn't want to talk to any more werewolves. So I called a vampire. She was friends with Mara and Harry, and I figured if I gave her the heads-up, she could get the word to someone for help if mush-for-brains really meant what she said." As he finished, Guido began to shake, making Mara begin to shake all over again right along with him.

You could've heard a pin drop as everyone waited to hear what this woman had threatened that left Guido shaking so visibly.

Darnell gave Guido a nudge with his sneaker. "Go on now, little man."

Guido's breath shuddered in and out. He hunkered closer to Darnell. "I don't know who these people she was talking about are, but I don't want anyone to get hurt. Especially . . ."

"What did she say, Guido!" Samuel demanded.

He looked to Darnell, his eyes round with fear spawned from terror.

"S'okay. I got yer back. Ain't nobody gonna hurt you."

Guido looked up at the council, his face ashen. "She said she'd kill them all: the kids, her friend, and this guy who didn't love her . . ."

More chaos ensued as everyone processed Guido's words. Pack members jumped from their seats—words of outrage flew in jumbled clusters of voices.

To threaten someone's life without fear for your own was a serious werewolf offense; to threaten the lives of innocent children—heinous and forbidden under any circumstance. That she'd done this over a lover was just like Guido had said, quacky flakes. The shock and astonishment rippling through the crowd mirrored Mara's scattered thoughts. Her blood raced through her veins, ice cold with fear.

He'd said she'd kill the children? Mimi and Fletcher . . .

Her heart began a whole new kind of crashing, almost fighting its way out of her chest. But then she remembered they were safe with Arch. It was then Mara thanked whoever was in charge that Harry's children were with Archibald.

"Silence!" Samuel roared to the out-of-control crowd as guards raced up and down the aisle, warning everyone to be seated.

When silence once again prevailed, Davis looked to Guido, flattened to Darnell's large frame. "Who is this woman you accuse of such a heinous crime, Guido?" Davis asked, his face tight with anticipation, his eyes icy ships of ire in his head.

Guido gulped. "Look, it's not like she came in and said, 'Hey, I'm so-and-so, and I'm a bag full o' nuts who wants a guy who doesn't even know I like him, let alone want to have his kids, and I'll kill anyone that gets in my way to do it.' Be real here. People don't leave their names with me. Scratch that. I didn't want to know her name. I can only tell you what she looked like. I mean, aside from crazy. Because I just wanna remind you again, she's nuts."

"You can identify this woman?" Griffin asked, his eyes piercing Guido's.

"Yep. I dunno who she thought she was foolin' with that weird disguise she had on. Her wig was crooked the whole time she was wearing a hole in my floor." He held his hand up. "Now let's be clear. I'm not sayin' I want to identify her, see? Not without the cover of some protective glass and maybe a Glock, her bein' fifty shades of lunatic, but I will because if I don't, and someone gets hurt, I won't be able to live with myself."

"We'll see to your protection. I promise you," council member Samuel assured. "Can you describe her for the council, please?"

Mara held her breath, gripping the chains dangling from her hands until they cut into her fingers. Oh, God. She knew. She didn't want to know, but she knew. It was why the women of OOPS had lined the exit to the courtroom.

Guido looked to Darnell, his face once more riddled with fear.

Darnell just nodded his assurance while Nina yelped from behind them, "Do it, dude!"

"I . . ." He cleared his throat. "I don't have to describe her. I can point her out. She's here."

"In this courtroom?" Griffin asked in outrage, rising from his seat, his gnarled hands planted on the surface of the high desk.

Guido nodded with a wince. "Yep. She's right over there."

As Mara's gaze swung to follow Guido's finger, her stomach screaming out in protest, the blood in her veins rushing in her ears, her heart stopped.

And she had one brief thought when it did.

As smart as she was, how was it she was always wrong when it came to a good whodunit?

LEAH jumped up from the row she sat in with Astrid and Ying, moving to the side of the courthouse where the room was lined with windows. Her eyes were wide, just like Guido had described them, wild and glazed.

In her hand there was a shiny gun, rock steady and aimed directly at Mara. "Nobody move or I'll kill her—hear me?" she screamed. "I've got silver bullets in this, and I'll shoot anyone who breathes the wrong way!"

Everyone ducked for cover, falling to the ground and scrambling under the wooden pews, crawling across the floor to make themselves as small as possible.

Everyone but Mara and Harry. As the room filled with panic-laden heavy breathing and the scent of sweat, Mara refused to back down. She sat straight and tall, glaring at Leah. God, how could she have kept something like this hidden for so long?

But Harry stepped in front of her, shielding her from the barrel of the gun. With a hard shove, he knocked her to the floor before she had the chance to brace herself. "Leah," he used his rational tone, stepping over people, looking her directly in the eye. "Don't do this. Just give me the gun, and we'll talk."

Leah screamed her rage, and Mara caught Guido cringing from the corner of her eye, probably in the same way he had when she'd come to his shack. Her howls pierced Mara's soul. Her mouth was wide open, strings of saliva stretching from the corners, her usually pale face red with fury, and her body tight and tense—ready to react.

Tears streamed down her cheeks in fat droplets, streaking her pretty features. "You were supposed to fall in love with meeee, you dirty man! Me! I loved you, Harry. I loved you so much, but instead you fell for a weak, sniveling entitled brat who has everything she's ever wanted but a baby! Poor Mara. Boo-hoo-hoo!"

Harry was moving forward now, pacing himself, his arms spread wide in helplessness. "But I didn't know, Leah," he said, impassioned and pleading. "You never told me. How could I know if you didn't tell me? *Why* didn't you tell me? Maybe I feel the same way, Leah. Let's talk about it, okay? Just you and me. No one else."

As Harry moved closer to her, Leah began to back away, her arms trembling. She waved the gun wildly, circling the air with it in frantic gestures. "No, Harry! No, no, no!" she moaned with an agonizing screech. "You've soiled yourself with her, you pig! All men are dirty, filthy pigs! Oink, oink, oink!" she squealed, her eyes huge orbs in her head, her face changing from rage-filled to child-like and innocent in a matter of words.

She backed up some more toward the windows, her shoulders sagging. "But I thought you were different," she sobbed. "You're smart and goofy, and you weren't like all the other men. Until *her*! Then you became just like them, always thinking with your dirty impulses." Her voice became a harsh whisper, her face one moment ago stricken with anger, now full of sorrow. "We could have been together, Harry. You and me and Mimi and Fletcher. I sent you a message. I told the children. But you've ruined everything! You should have known, Harry. You should have been able to tell!"

The kids. Mara froze on the hard floor, her hands stopping the task of trying to unlock the handcuffs with the key from the guard who lay beside her, trembling.

Leah had been the one who'd snatched the children from school. Taken Carl.

The world had gone mad.

Harry froze now, too, but he didn't stop talking. "Sometimes I just don't see the signs, Leah. I'm a dolt when it comes to women. Ask anyone. But we'll get the kids and we'll all go somewhere together, somewhere far away from Mara and everyone. Okay? Just give me the gun, and we'll go. Don't hurt anyone, please. Just come with me." Harry's voice was husky as he tried to sound convincing, husky and stilted as he searched for the words to convince Leah to let him help.

"You're never going anywhere with your children, Harry—never, ever again! I've hidden them far, far away where you'll never find them!" Leah roared, shooting the gun into the air to the screams of the crowd, backing up, kicking at the people on the floor before launching her body into the row of high windows and smashing through them.

Glass soared through the air, pelting everyone in its path just as Mara freed herself from the cuffs. Screams echoed in the drafty room, bouncing off the high ceilings, vibrating in her ears.

She didn't stop to see anything other than her family members and friends all racing toward the windows right behind Harry.

But she was faster, and even in her panic—in her utter surprise Leah was involved—she knew somehow, some way, Leah had gotten past Arch and to the children. This was no bluff.

Liken it to whatever one did in times like these—the adrenaline a mother experiences when her child's trapped under a car, and she somehow manages to lift tons of weight to save her baby. Or maybe it was sheer panic that set her feet into motion.

Whatever it was, Mara passed Nina, Marty, Wanda, and Harry like they were all moving in slow motion.

And when she got her hands on the bitch—she was going to kill her.

CHAPTER 19

Mara flew into the thick of the trees behind the courthouse, ignoring the sharp sting of pine needles raking her skin, scratching her bloody, her eyes on Leah's retreating back.

Leah has the kids.

She didn't think about the fact that she had a gun. She didn't think about the fact that she'd die if Leah let loose with that gun.

She didn't think.

She ran with only one thing on her mind.

Leah has the kids.

She didn't think about anything but killing Leah. Making her suffer for creating a situation that was no mere accident, but done purposely in some mad bid to win a love that didn't even know she'd existed until just a few days ago.

She wanted to rip Leah's limbs from her body and beat her bloody for giving Harry no choice when it came to Mimi and Fletcher and the fact that someday, they would leave this earth before him.

And when she was done tearing her limb from limb, she was going to choke her with her entrails.

Mara cleared a cluster of rocks, jumping over them and landing with a hard grunt. She knew these woods like she knew the back of her hand. She'd hidden here as a child. Come here to study and read endless books. Dreamt up foolish scenarios about Harry, with her back leaning against a big oak tree. Taken long walks as she pondered motherhood and what she was about to do.

Ignoring the screams of Harry and the rest of the gang, her focus on nothing else but wrapping her fingers around Leah's neck and squeezing the very life out of her, she moved in closer to Leah, pushing her way past a thick pine into a clearing where there was nowhere to hide.

Sharp rocks lined the far side of the clearing—rocks she'd hidden behind when she and the other children of the pack played hide-and-seek.

There was nowhere for Leah to go, though surely she smelled Mara. There was no way to sneak attack her. No way to fool her into dropping her only defense.

Mara approached her, her chest heaving from the run. She didn't put her hands up in defeat. Instead she stalked toward her prey. "You have Mimi and Fletcher, don't you, Leah?"

Leah's hair was drenched in sweat, her upper lip dotted with perspiration. She swung around, aiming the gun at Mara and laughed—girlish, almost giddy. "I do! I have them somewhere you'll never, ever find them, pretty, precious Mara!"

Mara pushed her hair from her mouth, clearing her eyes of the heavy strands, sniffing the air. It would do no one any good if she attacked. As much as she didn't want to play Leah's game, whatever it was, she didn't want to provoke her into doing something foolish. She had the kids.

She sniffed again. But if Leah had them, why couldn't she pick up their scent on her? "Why—why didn't you just tell me, Leah? Why didn't you tell me you loved Harry, too?"

Now her laughter turned maniacal, scraping from her throat in a harsh wheeze, as she, too, tried to catch her breath. "You knew, Mara. You knew!"

Mara shook her head, her heart racing. Guido hadn't been far off the mark when he'd said she was fifty shades of lunatic. Speaking of Guido, where was everyone? It was damn quiet behind her. "No, Leah! You never said a word!"

"I told you the night of the Christmas party, Mara—I told youuu," she wailed, heartsick and long. "I told you when I drove you home because you were too drunk to do it yourself. I told you, and you ignored me!"

Mara's head swirled. There wasn't a lot she could remember after she'd made a fool of herself in front of Harry and her coworkers. She'd chosen to forget by drowning her rejection in spiked punch. Yet, she didn't recall a single word about Leah's love for Harry. In fact, in all the time she'd gushed, fantasized, spoken her daydreams aloud, Leah hadn't even twitched, making her the consummate nut. Clever, and totally insane.

Leah used the heel of her hand to press her temple, banging it hard. "I told you, and you said it was okay because you said Harry didn't want you anyway. I asked before I took, Mara." Her features changed with her words, becoming wide-eyed and passive. "Just like I was always taught. Always ask before you take something, Leah. Always ask!" It was almost as if Leah was confessing to a parent rather than her longtime friend.

Mara shook her head, her cold lips forcing the words out. "I don't remember, Leah. I was drunk. It's my fault. I'm sorry. But we're good friends, Leah. Let's start over, okay? You can have Harry. All yours. No backsies."

"No!" she roared as though being given what she finally wanted was pure agony. Her hand clenched around the gun, her free fingers tightening into a fist she pressed to her chest. "I don't want your sloppy seconds, you dirty girl! You know that can't happen anyway. The council knows it was me who turned Harry now. They'll punish me just the way they were going to punish you."

There was madness here. So much madness, Mara almost couldn't breathe from it. Her chest tightened with each word she attempted to speak. Her feet froze in place, her heart crashed so hard, she wondered if it would push its way out of her chest.

She was staring into the face of insanity. Leah, easygoing, sweet, never a cross word, was standing before her, gun loaded, threatening to kill a pack mate over a relationship she'd created in her head. And Mara had never once suspected. During Guido's confession, she'd all but tried and convicted Astrid in her head.

So Mara shook her head again, desperately trying to sniff the air around Leah without getting caught while she did it. She was still unable to smell the children on her. There was nothing but Leah. "I won't let them, Leah. I'll protect you."

Leah fell back against the face of the rocks, her face contorting, her shoulders slumped in defeat. "No one can protect me now. Not even pretty, precious Mara with all the nice toys and her cute cottage and her new boyfriend, Harry."

Mara inched forward. If she could get the gun, she could take Leah. Then a thought occurred to her. "Harry's not really my boyfriend, Leah," she offered with as much calm as she could muster. "We made it up. All of it."

Leah's head shot upward on her neck, her glazed eyes flying over Mara's face. "What?"

"It's true! We didn't want anyone to know Harry was a werewolf. We were trying to keep me out of trouble with the council. So we made him smell like me so no one would pick up his true scent, and then we told everyone we were dating. Crazy idea, right? Nowhere near as smart as yours. But it's not true, I swear. We're still just Harry and Mara—separate." The word hurt, rolling off her tongue, but she said it anyway.

Leah shook her head while she processed Mara's words. She began to sink against the rocks, sliding down toward the ground, giving Mara hope she'd get lost in her confusion. "No . . . I saw you together. I've watched your every move since that night."

"So you called Harry to the lab with Jeff's phone? You saw him drink the water?"

Leah smiled, smugly satisfied. "I knew he'd come. It was the perfect plan until Jeff came along and caught me with his phone. Stupid, stupid Jeff," she murmured, appearing as though she were back in the moment. "He kept me from getting to Harry before he turned. I had to do something with him, right? And then you and your dirty sister-in-law showed up and ruined it all. You took the credit for what I'd done!"

Mara swallowed hard. "But I didn't do it, Leah. You did. Because you're smart. *So smart.*" God forgive her, but she'd do whatever it took to get to that gun.

Leah's voice began to rise again. "You're lying. Liar, liar, liiiar! You don't think I'm smart. You think I'm sick, just like that disgusting witch doctor!"

Mara shook her head hard again. "No! For example, the ax you put over Carl's head—it was genius, Leah. How did you do such intricate work with that chain? For that matter, how did you get past Darnell?"

The gun shook in her grip, but she smiled like a Cheshire cat. "I watched and waited. I'm good at that. I saw Darnell drink tea. So when he took Carl out for a walk, I swapped out his tea bag for one made especially with him in mind, and voila."

Good, this was good if she could just keep her talking. "And the kids?"

"No!" she screamed, waving the gun in the air. "I don't want to talk about the kids with you. You're dirty, dirty, filthy! You slept with Harry!"

If she went too deep, tried to lie her way out of sleeping with Harry, it would only make Leah angrier. So she changed tactics. "Why did you do it, Leah? Why would you turn a human?"

Of the many sides of her personality, indignant was the one Leah projected best. Her spine stiffened, her chest rose from her core. She shot Mara a look that said she should know why she'd turned a human. "Because my mate needs to be pure, of course. Pack law says so, no matter what that half-human slut Marty and her mate Keegan do. Your mate should be a *werewolf*. But you wouldn't understand that, would you, Mara? Because you're a whore—a disgusting slutty-slut whore!"

It was all Mara could do not to tear Leah's throat out. Her comment about Marty and Keegan made her see red. But she had to find the children. *Stay calm. She's cracking.* If she could just get a fingertip in that crack, she could break it wide open. "Why did you hurt Jeff, Leah? The police said he called them. How did you get him to do that?"

Leah's eyes shone, her gaze sly with her brilliance. "I made him call the police after I saw you go to his house. It was easy."

This had all been some bizarre game of cat and mouse? "He's alive?" Oh, thank God Jeff was alive.

Her chin lifted, the silhouette of it against the coming night sharp and sure. "For now . . ."

Panic began to rise in Mara's chest, so tight she was afraid it would explode. "Why did you send Harry to the lab that night, Leah? You could have chosen any other venue. Why at Pack?"

She rolled her eyes as if it were obvious. "Because, you dimwit, I couldn't let him go home to Mimi and Fletcher when he was going to turn. What kind of mother would I be if I let them see that? It would frighten them, and I wanted to be there with him when it happened. And Pack was the perfect place. It was where we met— where we would have fallen in love if not for you!"

Mara heard nothing else but one word. Mother? Leah thought she was Mimi and Fletcher's mother? If she was granted more time, she was going to kick herself for never picking up on a single clue about just how disturbed Leah really was. She kept her next question as casual as possible. "So are the kids with Jeff?"

"They're hiding," she taunted, grinning wide, her eyes flashing like they were playing out some game.

Hiding. Okay. Mara fought to stay sharp—aware, flexing her fingers to keep the ache of the cold away. "You did such a good job of hiding them. You're so smart." Praise—validation—recognition. Wasn't that what every mad genius secretly wanted?

Leah was back at attention again, standing erect, waving the gun at Mara under the setting sun. "You don't mean that, liar! You want the children. You want to be their mother. I saw you tubing with them. I know! But I won't let you, Mara! You're dirty, so dirty! If I can't have them, you can't have them either!"

Mara held up her hands. "No! You don't have to give them to me, but don't you want to tell Harry where they are, Leah? You can't be a whole family without him, right? He completes the picture." Just saying those words made her want to gag, retch until her stomach was empty—she fought the bile rising in her throat.

"He's so handsome, isn't he? We'd make a perfect couple," Leah cooed, her eyes far off and glazed now, a teenager this time. One with a crush no one had ever suspected.

Darkness was coming, and the temperatures would drop to the teens. If the kids were somewhere around here, they'd freeze to death.

Praying for patience, Mara continued to play the game. "You would. So let's go get the kids and you can bring them to Harry yourself. He loves them so much, just as much as you do." Mara moved even closer, pressing her knuckles against the rocks inches from where Leah stood. She held out her hand, forcing it to still. "Why don't you give me the gun, and you can go find Harry, okay?"

Leah stiffened, visibly tensing. In a flash, the gun was pointed at Mara's chest. "You lie, Mara! You're never going to let me go. I could've made Harry love me, but you ruined everything. You took him from me. You used your slutty charms and stole him away. You're unclean, dirty, dirty Mara. I hate you!" she screamed, her finger reaching for the trigger.

"Nooo!" a familiar voice bellowed. Just before Leah screamed her rage, a body fell from high atop the crag of rocks onto her.

Leah was knocked to the ground, the gun dropping from her fingers, her head crashing against a sharp edge on the face of the rock.

Mara went for the gun just as Guido rolled to his side and grabbed it, but Leah was stronger—so much stronger than him.

She rose and pounced on him, fighting him for it, clawing at his fingers until she had it aimed at his chest. Her screams angry, her howl frenzied—she pulled the trigger before Mara could blink— the blast of the gun earsplitting, cracking and echoing in the open space.

Guido's anguished cry rang in Mara's ears as a pool of blood began to form at his shoulder.

Sorrow at Guido's still form mingled, danced, warred with rage until rage won the battle. "I'll kill you!" Mara howled, racing toward Leah's back, preparing to launch herself at it.

Out of the inky darkness, Nina was there, her warrior cry a high-pitched roar of wrath. She fell on Leah, tearing her from Guido's body just as Harry ran to his side, ripping his shirt off and pressing it into the oozing wound.

Wanda and Marty pulled up short behind him, dragging him from Guido and replacing his hands with theirs. "Go!" Wanda ordered with a harsh bark. "What Leah says is true. Arch says she has the kids! Find the kids and Jeff!"

Nina hauled Leah up by her neck, shaking her like a rag doll. "Where are the kids, you fucking fruit loop?" she hissed in her face, jerking her body, flashing her fangs.

Leah hung almost lifeless, her eyes half-mast. Yet she summoned the will to spit in Nina's face. "I'll never tell you. Never, ever!"

Mara's rage spread through her limbs and tore at her self-control. She shoved Nina hard, dragging Leah from her grasp and wrapping her fingers around her neck. "Where are Mimi and Fletcher? Tell me, damn you!" she screamed, curling her fingers into Leah's hair and drawing her head back until her body bowed.

"Let's play a game, Mara," Leah choked out with a grin. "I'll give you a clue, you have to . . ." She swallowed, blood from her split lip seeping from the corner of her mouth. "Guess. You have to guess!" She began to laugh; whatever was broken in her was pulling away, leaving nothing but fragments of the Leah Mara thought she'd always known.

Mara's teeth clenched, her nose flared again. Still no scent of the children. Suspicion began to claw at her gut. "Liar!" she hollered. "I don't believe you have them, Leah. You don't smell like them. Now who's the liar?"

Leah laughed, sputtering a cackle. "I have them. Yes, yes, I do! Olly olly oxen free!"

"Tell me where the children are, Leah, or I'll kill you myself!"

Leah struggled against Mara's grip, her hands clawing at Mara's. "You'll never find them," she said on a harsh gasp for air. "You're not the only one who's smart enough to create a serum. I made one, too. I took away their scent. You'll never find them without me . . ." She was bragging, taunting, and it only made Mara want her dead—pummeled so far into the ground, no one would ever find her remains.

Mara's other hand went to Leah's neck, she squeezed until her eyes bulged and unconsciousness was almost upon her. Her hands shook from the force she was using, her head pounding, screaming the wild rage erupting in her.

"Stop!" Harry yelled, putting his hand on hers, pulling. "Stop, Mara," he said quietly. "She's the only one who knows where the kids and Jeff are. Stop now!" he bellowed in her ear.

Leah's eyes popped open when Mara's grip eased, focusing on Harry, becoming soft. "I loved you, Harry," she said on a gasp, her chest pumping up and down. "But . . ." She hacked a cough, a tear, glistening in the moonlight, fell from the corner of her eye. "You never even knew I existed. We would have been good parents together. I would have taken good care of them."

Harry gritted his teeth. Mara watched him gather himself, batten down the hatches on his fear and anger. He ran his hand over Leah's hair, soothing her, gazing into her dull eyes. "You can still do that, Leah. Take me to them. Good mothers want to protect their children, right? Let's protect them—*together,*" he forced the word out as though it tasted sour.

Mara's eye caught something on the ground, a familiar piece of spiral notebook paper just like the one they'd found at Jeff's. She scrambled to pick it up, kicking up dirt, ignoring the gash in her forehead she'd somehow acquired. A map. It was a hand-drawn map . . . One Leah had probably made in order to remember the spot where she'd left Mimi and Fletcher. She stared hard at the paper—a piece of it missing. It was torn, frayed, probably from Leah's fingers worrying the edges.

But it looked familiar.

Her eyes widened. She knew where this was. She and her brothers had played there often as children. The kids were . . .

No. Jesus. No. Not there.

There was nothing there for miles and miles but a grouping of caves and frozen ground and rocks—so many rocks. Even with the strength of their paranormal skills combined, as cold as it was, and the amount of time the children and Jeff had been missing, they'd never find them in the masses of rock before they froze to death. If they hadn't already. Oh, God, how long had they been there?

Mara's heart screamed in her chest. *Think, Mara, think!* There had to be a specific reason Leah had chosen this area. Everything she'd done so far had been carefully planned—meticulous. All of it geared toward an obscure message she wanted to send. A game she wanted everyone to play, to recognize and validate, while she sat back and reveled in her superior intellect while no one had a clue she was the one pulling the strings of this marionette.

And then she knew. Without a shadow of a doubt, she knew.

"I know!" Mara screamed into the night, holding up the piece of paper. "I know where they are!"

"Where?" Harry rasped, his voice tight.

She couldn't say it—she couldn't say the words out loud. She'd rather die than say the words out loud. Turning her back to the group, she forced herself to speak the next words calmly. "Get Guido and Leah and follow me. Do it now!"

Mara took off, pumping her legs harder than she ever had in her life. Harder than when Sloan and Keegan had raced her to home base when they played tag. Harder than when she'd run track against Lavinia Meyers in high school, her toughest opponent in all of paranormal-ville.

She ran harder because she knew—she knew what Leah had done, and there couldn't be much time left—if there was any at all.

If she let it, the horror of it, the sick, twisted plot involved to pull it off would thwart her, wear her down until she wouldn't be able to move a muscle.

Leah had buried the kids and Jeff alive.

THEY all came to a screeching halt in the exact spot marked on the map. Harry flung Leah's semiconscious body down on the ground, the air wheezing from his lungs.

Nina had wrapped Guido's wound with Harry's shirt, pulling it tight under his arm to stop the bleeding.

Wanda grabbed Mara's hand with trembling fingers, looking out at the vast expanse of nothing but snow-covered ground and miles of rock. "Where are they, Mara? I can't smell anything! I know these kids now. I know their scent!"

Marty lifted Leah up by the front of her shirt, shaking her so hard Mara heard her teeth rattle, then hurled her back to the hard surface beneath their feet. "Tell us where the children are *now*!" she screamed down at a broken and battered Leah, her hands balled, the wind pushing at her slender body.

"You'll never find them. Never, ever." Leah wheezed a giggle from the ground before Nina planted a foot on her chest and drove it into her flesh, making her scream in pain.

"Shut the fuck up, fruity, or I'm gonna shoot your ass myself!"

Harry began to pace, his heart thudding in his ears like thunder itself. He sniffed the air—nothing. Jesus Christ, there had to be at least a million square miles of rock. Piles and piles of rocks. It was getting colder by the minute, and he couldn't smell them. What good was this damn werewolf thing if he couldn't smell them? "I don't get it, Mara!" He yelled the words over the wind that had begun to swoosh in heavy gusts. "How can they be here? I can't smell them either!"

Mara dropped to the ground on all fours by the first grouping of rocks, stacked taller than he was. She placed her ear to it, her hair flying around her head in a tangled mass of ebony. "She's covered their scent with something. Now, shhh! Listen, Harry! We have to listen! Listen and look—look for anywhere the dirt is soft."

The stacks of granite were endless. Why weren't they ripping them apart? What good was all this superhuman strength if they didn't use it? Harry's hands reached to the top to begin pulling the rocks down, away from their tiny faces.

"No!" Mara screamed, bolting upright and pushing at him. "Don't just start haphazardly throwing things around! What if they cave, Harry? If I'm right and they're under this mess, we can't afford for it to collapse!" Squeezing his hands, Mara fell back to the ground, pressing her ears back to the sharp edges of the rocks.

She was right.

Fear clawed at his throat, terror ripped a hole in his gut, but he dropped on all fours right along with her and listened.

"They're going to die. Everyone's going to die." Leah laughed on an ugly gurgle of blood. "There'll be no playing mommy for you!"

Harry's eyes flew to Leah's body but feet away from him and he fought the urge to rip her face off.

Nina leaned down next to her, raising her fist up high, she brought it down on Leah's jaw, the crack of impact slipping to his ears on the wind. She hauled Leah with her, clamping her ankles as she, too, dropped on all fours and listened.

His chest was tight—so tight he thought he'd never take another breath again without laboring.

Focus, Harry. Find the kids. Donna will kill you if you don't find the kids.

He began crawling along the face of the rocks, his ear scraping the ground as he went, inching his fingers across the rough edges, willing himself to focus.

Donna's gone, Harry. She's never coming back. You're all they have.

They need you. Find the kids, Harry. If you do nothing else with this werewolf gig, use it to help you find the kids. Listen. Listen for Mimi's breathing—you know it. You've heard it a million times while she napped on your lap. You know the pattern.

But what if she wasn't . . .

Don't think about it, Harry! Find the kids.

And then he heard it. That slight hitch, the adorable little hiccup Mimi always made when she was sound asleep.

Use your ears, Harry—follow the sound. He crawled. He crawled for all he was worth.

His eyes grazed something—something plastic—caught up in the formation of rocks. His eyes focused on it, rounding in horror.

He yanked it from between the rocks, examining it. It was just like the straw from the juice boxes the kids were always trying to convince him that Donna had let them have.

He'd have never seen them without his new eyesight. Not in a million years. And in that second, he was grateful—so grateful.

He couldn't stop the mere second or two of horror—at the mental instability it took to do something like this, but when it passed, he began screaming, his voice hoarse and raw, the cold wind biting and unforgiving. "Here! They're here!"

CHAPTER
20

All at once, five pairs of hands began digging; dirt flew in frozen clumps, tearing at Mara's knuckles, ripping her flesh. Shards of rock broke and scattered, and she had to remind herself to slow down. If this caved in . . .

"Slowly!" she screamed, remembering the intricate way Leah had designed Carl's trap. If this was anything like that, Leah would have designed it to fall on the kids and Jeff. "We have to be careful not to jar it or it will cave!"

Oh, God. Please, please don't let it fall.

Marty was bleeding, too, tears streaming down her face, flecks of dirt in her blond hair, as she dug right alongside Wanda.

Wanda's nylons were shredded, her shoes lost, her prim driving gloves falling away from her fingers with each drive of her hand into the wall of rocks.

Harry began screaming Mimi's and Fletcher's names while Nina anchored Leah with her knee in her chest. She yelled into the face of the crumbling tower, "Auntie Nina's coming, kiddos! Hang tough, Jeff!"

As they widened the hole around the straw, Mara caught her first peek of Mimi's purple hat. Joy welled up inside her, the most unbearable joy she'd ever experienced. "Here! Mimi's here!"

"Fletch!" Nina called out next. "I found Fletcher!" she hollered above the screeching wind.

"Jeff!" Wanda and Marty screamed simultaneously, digging faster.

Leah's head lifted suddenly, howling her rage. "They're all dead! Dead, dead, deader than doornails!" she keened.

"Shut up, you crazy nutbag!" Guido screamed before the final shot of the night rang out, scoring Leah's skull. He fell back on the ground with a grunt, the gun falling to the frozen ground.

Tears stung Mara's eyes, but she looked straight ahead, steeling herself, willing herself to dig until her hands touched flesh. Mimi's flesh.

She tore at the dirt around Mimi, reaching for her body, hauling her out of the clump of heavy rocks, unsettling the ground with the force of her pull. She dragged Mimi to her and began tearing at the duct tape over her mouth, ripping it from her hands and feet while Harry did the same with Fletcher.

Mara frantically put her fingers to Mimi's throat, feeling for a pulse. Her skin was ice cold, her lips almost blue, and then she was yanking off her prison garb, removing Mimi's sodden clothes with swift hands. "We need to warm them!" she yelled above the howling wind.

Skin-to-skin contact, wasn't it? Mara began to rock, whispering into Mimi's ear. "C'mon, princess. Please, please wake up for me," she sobbed. "Coconut needs you. Uncle Harry needs you. *I* need you. We'll have hot chocolate and marshmallows with Carl, if you'll just wake up!"

Nothing. Mimi remained lifeless, her bare arms icy cold. God only knew how long they'd been down there. Fear ripped through

Mara, bringing hot tears to her eyes while the freezing air tore at her exposed flesh.

No, no, no. This would not happen. She hugged her tighter, curling Mimi's small body into her own as she rocked. "C'mon, sweetie. Time to wake up now. We have so much to do. I need you to help me pick out the color purple for your room. There are so many shades. We want the right shade, don't we? And we can't let Uncle Harry pick it. Look what he did to your room the last time."

Still nothing but Mimi's thready pulse ringing in her ears. Panic began to take over. She had to force herself to keep it together. "Wake up, Mimi!" she whispered fiercely, leaning back into Nina who'd come to sit behind her, throwing her hoodie over Mara's shoulders and pulling her flush to her chest.

Nina began to rock, too, reaching around Mara and squeezing Mimi's limp hands. "C'mon, pretty girl. Auntie Nina misses you. You haven't even met Charlie yet. She told me just the other day she needed a new friend. I need you to be her friend. You love *Dora the Explorer*, right? If you don't wake up, I'm gonna have to watch it with her. I don't like Dora. Help a mommy out, huh? So wake up, Mimi! Wake up!"

From the corner of her eye, she saw Harry haul Fletcher's half-clothed body to his bare chest. Wanda was there, throwing her coat over his shoulders before pulling Jeff with her while Marty brushed the dirt from his nostrils.

Wanda pulled Jeff to her like he was a rag doll. She opened her shirt, never once stopping at how awkward it was to have a fully-grown, strange man who wasn't her husband, naked and in her arms. She began rubbing Jeff's arms, speaking to him in words Mara couldn't hear, her fear Mimi wouldn't wake up pounding in her ears.

"Fletch—it's Uncle Harry. Wake up, buddy. I need you, Fletcher. I need you so much, pal. Please, wake up!" Harry's frantic plea, gravelly and raw, tore at Mara's soul.

Scooting near Harry, she huddled against him, both of the

children on their laps, their heads bent as they whispered to them. Tears fell, but Mara couldn't be sure if they were hers or Harry's.

And the wind howled while Nina knelt in front of them and sheltered them from the chilling cold, clamping her hands on their shoulders, kneading their flesh to keep them as warm as a vampire could.

Marty came up behind them, stretching her arms across their backs, rocking, whispering prayers, soothing.

Mara's heart crashed as they rocked, her hand reaching for Harry's. *No, God, please, please no.*

He clamped his hand around hers, pulling her and Mimi tight to him.

And they rocked. They rocked while Nina spoke hushed words of encouragement. While Marty, tears falling from her face to Mara's naked back, pressed closer, rested her head in the space between Harry and Mara.

"Uncle Harry?"

All of their heads shot up. Eyes met, wide and in wonder.

Fletcher, sleepy-eyed and drowsy, looked up at Harry and Mara. "Where are we?"

Harry gathered him up, hauling Fletcher's weak body to his chest, burying his face in the boy's neck. His shoulders shook in silence as Marty stroked the top of Fletcher's head. "Oh, thank God. Thank God," he husked out, his voice tight and raspy.

Fletcher didn't fight him. Instead, he snuggled closer, letting his cheek rest on Harry's shoulder with a weak sigh.

Mara froze when Mimi stirred, reaching for Nina's hand to help keep her upright.

Nina flopped to the ground, her beautiful face a mask of relief. She tugged on one of Mimi's curls. "Well, look who's awake? 'Bout time, little lady. You sure are lazy," she teased, running her finger along Mimi's pert nose.

"Mara?" she whispered against Mara's skin—the most beautiful whisper in the world.

She gulped, fighting the onslaught of tears while Marty dabbed at her cheeks, silent tears of her own coursing down her face. "Yes, Mimi?"

"Where's Uncle Harry?"

Mara's breathing hitched, but she fought the lump in her throat. "He's in Africa, playing with the elephants. You want me to tell him you called?"

Mimi giggled—it was weak and it was thin, but it was a giggle. That was all that mattered. "He is not."

Mara nodded, fighting a cringe when the wind tore through her flesh. "Is, too," she said, smiling down at Mimi's beautiful, precious face, fighting the urge to squeeze her hard.

Mimi reached upward, her hand slow and shaky. She touched Mara's cheek with a finger and smiled sleepily. "Do you think Uncle Harry would let us have an elephant?"

Harry pulled Mara and Mimi closer, cupping Mimi's rounded cheek with a smile, his eyes glinting in the dark. "He will not, Miss Mimi." With another shuddering breath, Harry let his head fall back on his shoulders and blinked his eyes for a long moment before finally lifting his head.

The sound of a helicopter roared above them, lights shone down, coming from all directions in the sky.

Harry looked at her, his teeth beginning to chatter. His eyebrow rose in question.

Mara rolled her eyes, fighting the violent shudder of cold ripping through her. "Keegan. He can smell Marty from a hundred miles, and he'd rent a jetliner to get to her, if that's what it took."

Nina knelt beside them, looking down at Fletcher and Mimi. "Hear that, dudes? That means it's time for you to go to sleep now.

So close your eyes." She ran light fingertips over their eyelids. "And dream sweet dreams for Auntie Nina."

Both children took deep breaths before their eyes fell closed and they slumped against Mara and Harry.

Harry looked to Mara again, though it was with complete trust, melting her heart. "Should I ask?"

"She's erasing their memories. So they'll never remember . . ." Mara closed her eyes trying to regain her composure. If she let the horror in—even just a little—she'd close her eyes and never open them again.

"So they won't remember that fucking loon and what she did to them," Nina finished for her. "Kids should stay kids for as long as they can. I'm just doin' my part to keep it that way."

Harry reached up, grabbing Nina's hand, pulling it to his cheek, his words trembling. "Thank you. *Thank you.* I'll never, ever be able to thank you."

She squeezed it before she took a swipe at his head. "Shut the fuck up, nerd, and let's get these monsters and your lady love the hell home. I've had enough drama for today. Carl's waiting, and I need me some zombie-time."

Just as the helicopter landed, and Keegan burst out of the door, Jeff woke up.

His eyes were wild, even if his body was weak, when he realized he was in the arms of a semi-naked woman. "Who . . . the . . . hell . . . are . . . you?" he screamed at Wanda. "And why are we . . . *naked?*"

Nina strutted over to Wanda and looked down at Jeff. "She's Wanda, I'm Nina, and I bet you don't wake up naked to a broad as hot as this very often, do ya nerd? Sorry you won't be able to enjoy it longer. Shhhh, Jeffie, it's night-night time." Nina quashed his protests by leaning down and repeating the act of erasing his memory.

Keegan ran toward them, his long legs covering the area in seconds. He didn't say anything—he didn't have to. His face said it all. There was worry, fear, a million questions on it when he looked at Leah's lifeless form, and Guido, his teeth chattering, his body quaking.

He gathered Marty into his arms, pulling her close and breathing deeply as though he hadn't taken a breath until she was with him again. "You worry me, honey," he muttered, fierce, possessive. "Stop damn well worrying me."

Marty reached up and tweaked his jaw, following it up with a kiss. Her words shook on the way out, the fear of their nightmare obviously catching up with her, too. Collapsing against him, she said, "Don't ask questions. For now, just take us home, and let's have the kids checked by Dr. Field."

As everyone made their way to the helicopter, and Sloan, waiting inside, began to pull each of them in, covering them in blankets, Harry handed a sleeping Fletcher and Mimi over to him and turned to Mara.

He drew her to his chest, his hands like ice, his words hushed. "Thank you. I'd have never found them without you. Jesus Christ, I don't know what I would have done . . ."

She put her fingers to his lips, letting the tears of relief slip from her eyes. "Then don't. Don't wonder. Please don't or I'll make the Crypt Keeper erase your memory."

He chuckled, his mood shifting instantly. He swung her up into his arms. "Would I forget the other night?"

She grinned, burrowing closer, breathing—just breathing. "You mean when we . . ."

"Yeah. When we," he teased.

"You might."

His arms stiffened around her, tightening. "I *never* want to forget that, Mara. Not ever."

Nina slapped his shoulder from behind, Guido in her arms. "Then shut the fuck up and get in the damn helicopter, or I'll make you forget the dates for the next Trekkie convention."

Harry laughed, sliding Mara into the helicopter. "God, she's mean. So mean."

Mara giggled, pulling her legs in and holding her hand out to him. "The meanest."

He took it, settling in beside her. "Will you come with me when this doctor checks on the kids?"

Mara fought the burst of joy exploding in her heart, but she kept her reply simple before she pressed her lips to his. "Wouldn't miss it—not even for my very own TARDIS."

HARRY stood beside Mara as they watched Mimi and Fletcher sleep—safe, warm, loved. Carl slept on the floor on a blow-up mattress, Coconut curled up in the crook of his stiff arm. When they'd arrived back at her cottage with the children, Darnell told them Carl had been fidgety all night, nervous and jumpy in a way the demon said he'd never seen before. Until the kids were carried in and put in bed, that is.

He'd then dragged the mattress Nina'd been sleeping on in the closet and placed it next to the bed, covered the children and lay down next to them, patting Fletcher's hand before nodding off to a sound sleep.

After they'd arrived at the hospital, while Dr. Field examined the children, the council had questioned Mara, deciding to let her go for the moment, but leaving the discussion about her serum still a question.

Nina, Marty, and Wanda had taken a sleeping Jeff home, straightened up his house, and Nina erased all traces of Leah and the torture she'd so clearly put him through during the time of his captivity from his memory. Whatever had happened, maybe after seeing what they'd seen tonight, it was better they didn't know.

Guido, the hero of the night, received more than one kiss of gratitude from the women of OOPS, which he'd accepted humbly before heading into surgery. Except Nina. She'd slapped him on the back and told him the next time she said create a distraction, yell or some such shit. Don't jump on a crazy bitch with a gun. Because she'll use it.

Guido had shaken his head. He'd done it for a reason. For all the wrong he'd done, for all the money he'd taken from others when he knew he couldn't provide the service he'd promised, had left him empty. Just this once, he'd wanted to do something selfless.

Yet, his simple act of loyalty had helped save the children, and that was something none of them would ever forget.

"I'm afraid to leave them," Harry murmured against the top of her head.

Mara nodded, her throat tightening up. The sight of them vulnerable in sleep, the complete abandon as they sprawled out in all their innocence, made Mara send up a silent prayer of thanks: for friends like Nina and Wanda—for Marty and Keegan—and Guido, too. "Ditto."

"I was so scared we'd never find them."

His gruff confession made her smile. She loved that Harry wasn't afraid to say it out loud. "But we did. That's all that matters." She squeezed his now-healing hand, tucking it close.

"You didn't turn me."

"Phew. What a relief, right? All that shift-shaming was wearin' me down," she teased.

Harry chuckled, pulling her from the entry to her guest bedroom and closing the door. He led her into the bedroom and patted the bed where he sat down, his eyes lined with weariness. "I'm sorry."

"Don't be. How could you have known Leah was the one who'd turned you by scratching you? You have nothing to be sorry for." Mara still couldn't reconcile the Leah she knew and the one she'd seen waving a gun in her face tonight. It would be a long time before she was able to connect those dots. Her cluelessness. How completely unaware she'd been of Leah's insanity.

Harry ran a hand over his eyes. "I didn't even remember all the details of that lunchroom incident until Guido talked about it today. I knew Leah and Astrid were there, but . . . Right up until that point, I thought he was going to tell us it was—"

"Astrid," Mara finished for him with a nod. "Me, too. She's pretty moody and temperamental, very possessive of me. It made complete sense she'd be the culprit. Especially after she behaved the way she did when we told her we were pretend lovers."

"Speaking of that," he wiggled his eyebrows.

Mara fought a sigh of happiness, full of hope. "Not before we talk about a couple of things. First, I want to apologize to you for being so offended by the notion you didn't want to be one of us. I get why. Because of Mimi and Fletcher. I realized it after I told you how old I was." She turned to him, cupping his face. "You'll outlive them. I wouldn't want that for my children either."

His hand circled her wrist, bringing her palm to his cheek and planting a kiss on it. "But being one of you tonight was a gift. If not for these ears that can hear Nina grousing under her breath here at the cottage when I'm at Pack, I would never have heard Mimi's breathing. If not for my uncanny eyesight, I wouldn't have seen those straws."

Mara's breath hitched on its way out. "If not for Leah, none of this would have happened."

"But then I never would have known you fantasized about me all day long, if not for Leah."

Her cheeks flushed. "Oh, stop patting yourself on the back. It wasn't all day long. Couple hours, tops," she joked.

"You liked me all that time, and you never said a word."

She wiggled an admonishing finger. "Not true, Mr. Emmerson. I said a word, or ten drunken words to be precise, at the Christmas party last year. You just didn't take heed."

Harry scratched his hair and grinned. "Have I mentioned I'm not so good at hints—flirting—especially when they come from women as hot as you?"

She giggled, with ease, with joy. "So you thought I was hot, but never said a word either? You're just as much to blame."

"I suck at striking up conversation—especially with a woman."

"Stalemate then. But look at us now, all small-talking."

His face took a serious turn, but he put his arm around her, sliding her near. "What will the council do now, do you think?"

"What can they do now? Officially, there is no serum. If you did drink it, it clearly didn't matter because you were already a werewolf. The only turn that counts is Leah's."

"Then they can't still have a trial over a serum we don't even know really works, can they?"

"I'm sure the council will investigate. It's what they do. But they'll never get the formula out of my head. I didn't give some of the factors that Keegan pointed out the importance I should have, the serious thought I should have given creating a child in a cup, for gravy's sake. I didn't even know what I'd do if it worked. How I'd explain it to everyone. But the council's right when it comes to someone getting their hands on it. Someone could really make a mess of things. Maybe sell it to someone. It's unthinkable. So no more serums for brainy Mara. My baby-making days are over." The words brought with it great sadness—the loss of a dream.

Harry kissed the tip of her nose. "I don't think you should give up, honey. Maybe it would have worked. Maybe you can go to the council with the idea of a surrogacy plan in place for others just like you who want babies but haven't found their mates. The idea that pack members pick out someone you have to live with for the rest of your life is nuts. I'm totally against it. But if you were up for it, I'd help you with all the details of surrogacy for paranormals. We'll map out a, for lack of a better word, business plan, and present it. And maybe, if things go well between us, you won't need to create babies in a lab," he finished on a grin.

Her heart throbbed with excitement at the proposal Harry was making. "And Mimi and Fletcher? How will you explain what happened to you someday?" This troubled her a great deal.

Seeing him tonight when the children's lives hung in the balance made her more sure than ever the next toughest road of all would be explaining Uncle Harry's new lot in life.

He smiled, but it was tentative. "I can't promise if there were ever a way I could change this, that I wouldn't. The idea of being left here without the kids . . ."

Mara squeezed his hand. "No explanation necessary. I'd feel the same way." And she would. To lose a child would be to lose the will to go on.

But Harry's next request was simple. "Will you do it with me when the time comes? When they're old enough to process it."

"Why, Harry Emmerson, are you asking me to help you with a sensitive family matter that might not happen for *years*?"

Harry stared down at her, his gaze no longer playful, but very serious. "I think I am."

The fluttering of her heart, the butterflies in her stomach were hard to hide. "Sure. I'll help."

"You know what that means, right?"

"I'd better put my speed-reading skills to good use and find a book on therapy for the family of a werewolf?"

"Nah. It means we'd better invite the Crypt Keeper, too. She's a badass parent."

Mara's head fell back, her laughter ringing in her ears. "Point."

Harry pulled her down to lie on the bed with him, tugging her to a sitting position on his hips. He began to unbutton the shirt the hospital had given her after a warm shower. "So you'll show me?"

She planted her hands on his chest, her breathing labored when he pushed the shirt aside and cupped her breast. "Show you what, Harry, not Harold, Emmerson?"

"How to be a werewolf. You know . . . all the tricks of the trade?"

Mara flashed him a smile before gripping his wrists as his hands roamed over her breasts, his fingertips tweaking her hard nipples. "Only if you promise to do this in return."

Harry groaned, pulling her forward, licking her nipple until heat pooled like lava in her belly. "Scout's honor," he teased, lifting his head and giving her body a shove until their lips were inches apart. "Open your eyes and look at me, Mara."

She obeyed, finding his eyes were full of a million emotions.

Harry's fingers stroked the back of her head. "I want you in my life, Mara. I want you to get to know Mimi and Fletcher better. I want you to help me get to know them better. I want *you*. Period. Any way you'll have me. Before we go any further—before we do or say anything else, I need to hear you want that, too."

In all of her wildest dreams, in all her fantasizing with Astrid about Harry, never had she ever believed any of it would come true.

And now it had.

Whatever it meant—whatever happened—she was going to go for it. No regrets. No waffling. No factoring in all of the things that had held her back before.

With one kiss, one searing, soul-offering kiss, she said, *"Yes."*
Yes, yes, yes.

Harry captured her lips, slipping his tongue between them and stroking her mouth, groaning into it as he pulled her shirt off.

Her fingers found the waist of the scrubs the hospital had given him, pulling at the tie and slipping them down his rock-hard thighs. He was naked beneath, gloriously, fabulously naked.

As she tore her lips from his, she rolled down along his body, pressing her heated flesh to his, moaning her appreciation for the hard lines of his abs, the trail of hair leading to his cock.

Her hands found his shaft, hot, silken, stiff, and without hesitation, she let her lips skim the rigid line. Harry's hiss and low groan made her nipples harden, scraping against the comforter as she settled between his thighs, kneeling there, encompassing his cock with both hands.

Harry's fingers scored her hair, clutching fistfuls of it when she speared him with her mouth, letting her tongue slide along the heated column, cupping his balls, rolling them with gentle fingertips.

His hips crashed upward, his body tensing and flexing as she swirled her tongue around him, along the throbbing vein just beneath the head of his shaft. His knees rose up and Mara slipped her hands under him, cupping his ass, lifting him higher, driving him into her mouth over and over until he pulled away from her with a hiss of a groan. "No more!" he rasped out, grabbing at her shoulders, his fingers digging into her flesh.

He hauled her upward, rolling her to her back, taking her breath away with the force of it, driving his hands into her hair until her back arched and he was kneeling over her, burying his face in her neck, trailing hot, wet kisses along her neck, down over her breasts.

His teeth grazed her nipples, making Mara fight not to scream his name. Her hands clenched the bedding beneath her, tearing at it for the sweet agony he evoked as he slid down her body. Without the pretense of their last encounter, he spread the lips of her sex, wet, slick with a need so intense her heart surely stopped.

Harry ran the length of her slit, entering her with a digit, then two, driving into her and placing his mouth over her clit. He dragged his tongue over the swollen bud, licking, sucking, thrusting his fingers into her until the heat searing her veins exploded.

Mara jammed her hips downward, lifting them again and again until her orgasm tore at her, reaching deep within her, ripping it from her body with a scream she had to bite her tongue to keep from leaving her mouth.

Her chest heaved. Her hands went to Harry's head, threading her fingers into his thick hair as she whimpered his name.

Harry slid up alongside her, turning her to her side and sheltering her with his chest. He raised her thigh high, hooking it around his thighs, spreading her, placing his hot cock at her entrance.

Mara reached a hand between them and stroked him, encouraging, silently begging before his first upward thrust into her.

He nipped at her shoulder, cupping her breasts, rolling her nipples between his fingers to hard peaks, moaning at how easily she accepted him.

Mara's hands went up around his neck, arching into him, loving the feel of her ass against his hips, rolling with him when he splayed his large hand across her abdomen, cupping the heat of it, whimpering again when he let his middle finger slip into her wetness.

They rocked together, Harry deep within her, thrusting, stiff, hot, creating a fire so hot it consumed her.

Their thrusts increased, the spiral of desperate lust Harry evoked in her deepening, crawling its way upward until her body went rigid from the pleasure, tensing, feeling Harry tighten beneath her.

She ran her hands along his muscled arm, abandoning everything but the drive to find her release.

Harry's body seized, his strong, warm arms tightening, his pelvis tightening along with hers until he took one last thrust. One last, silken, wet thrust, so deep everything stopped but Harry within her.

His moan in her ear was husky and raw, her whimper of satisfaction mingling with his.

Harsh air escaped their lungs, rasping into the silence of her bedroom. Harry stroked the curve of her waist, tracing the indentation with his palm, soothing away the vestiges of her frenzied orgasm until she melted back against him.

Harry nuzzled her neck, the stubble on his chin from the long night, scraping her skin with delicious possession. "Werewolf sex rocketh," he murmured, slipping his arm under her and turning her to face him.

Mara giggled, wrapping her arms around his neck and lifting her lips for a tender kiss. "I couldn't say for sure, Harry Emmerson. I've never had human sex. But I think this'll do for now," she teased.

"For now? Fickle, aren't we, Ms. Werewolf?"

She gave him a grin full of the devil. "You'll just have to work harder then, won't you, Mr. Werewolf?"

Trailing kisses along her jaw, Harry chuckled, a deep, contented rumble. "Always with the work. Why is everything with you people so much work?"

Her neck arched into his lips and she hummed her approval. "Something worth winning is always work, don't you agree?"

"I'll work hard, Mistress Mara," he joked, pulling her hand to his thick shaft.

Giddy with joy, she giggled again then sighed. "I'll count on it."

"Uncle Harry!" a small voice cried out in the darkness.

"Mimi," he whispered down at her. "I'll be right back. Go nowhere, woman. Got that?" As he rose, his warmth leaving her embrace, his body hard and supple under the moonlight, it was all Mara could do not to shout her joy before rising, too.

She grabbed her bathrobe as Harry pulled his T-shirt over his head. Tightening the belt, she slipped around the side of the bed and grabbed his hand. "I'm coming, too," she assured.

Harry looked down at her, running his palm under her chin. "I'm a little nuts about you, Mara Flaherty."

"Yeah? I'm a lot nuts about you. Let's go be nuts about the kids—*together*." She pulled him with her out of the bedroom and across the hall where Mimi sat up, Coconut tightly pressed to her chest.

Her face began to crumble and the tears began to fall. "I had a bad dream, Uncle Harry," she muttered.

Mara hopped over her where Fletcher stirred, sitting between the children. She pulled Mimi close and hugged her. "Was it about elephants?" she asked, kissing the top of Mimi's freshly shampooed hair.

Mimi giggled her innocent, sweet giggle. "No, silly."

"Because you know, I've been talking to Uncle Harry, and I think, no promises, but I think we can talk him into an elephant. The only problem is where to put him. You think he could fit in the bed with all of us?"

Fletcher grunted a sleepy giggle of his own. "Elephants don't belong in beds, Mara." He shifted a little when Harry nudged him to sit next to him on the bed, tugging the child into his arms and smiling.

Mara reached over and ran her fingers along Fletcher's exposed belly, making his eyes half-open as he squirmed and laughed. "Said who? Shouldn't all elephants have beds? If you can have a bed, why can't an elephant? Are you special or somethin'?"

Harry looked over at Mara, his wide grin as endearing as it had always been, stretching his fingers to meet hers alongside of Mimi's arm. "I'm the boss and I say no elephants in the bed! They poop on the floor, not to mention they'll turn the bed into a total pancake."

Mara gripped his fingertip, smiling back at him. Her heart so full, she had to fight tears. "Okay, partners in elephant crime, on three." She squeezed Mimi to her, snuggling her close. Grateful. So very,

very grateful. "Ready? One, two, three! Oh, Uncle Harry!" they all groaned simultaneously.

The children fell into fits of giggles while Mara and Harry cuddled them near and Carl snored softly on the floor.

As she gazed upon this new adventure beaming at her from beneath the moon shining into the window, full of giggling, happy, healthy children and a hot nerd of a man, her heart welled with gratitude.

And really, Mara thought, what better way to begin her fairy tale than with two small children, a sorta zombie, a cat named Coconut who wore dresses under protest, and a handsome prince named Harry who had two left feet?

It was everything she'd ever dreamed of and more.

So, so much more.

EPILOGUE

*Seven Months and Twelve Days Later—Eight and
Counting Quacky-Wacky Paranormal Accidents, a
New-ish, Albeit Not As Reluctant As He Once Was
Werewolf, One Incredibly Smart, Suddenly Childless
No More Werewolf, Two Precocious, Very Active
Human Children, Three Doting, Constantly
Interfering Aunties, A Manservant Grandfather, One
Half-Assed Though Totally Endearing Witch Doctor,
and a Demon Who Could Push a Swing Like No
Other, attended a wedding beneath a pine tree in a
clearing on a beautifully perfect summer day . . .*

Mara smiled up at Harry and over at his children—*their* children—
when Charles Knotts pronounced them husband and wife.

Harry kissed her soundly, encompassing Fletcher and Mimi in
his embrace as everyone cheered.

Marty cheered, dabbing at her cheeks and blowing Mara a kiss.
Marty had been her surrogate mother during the planning of the
Flaherty/Emmerson wedding. She'd held Mara when she'd cried
because her mother wouldn't see her marry, given her endless

advice on raising two small children, worried over her—coddled her—made her man up when the going got tough with Harry and the kids.

Cried like a child when Mara, in a simple white, sleeveless silk gown with an empire waist and a small broach tucked between her breasts, one Marty had given her as her something borrowed, had entered the room just before the ceremony.

She'd cooed over Mara's hair, flowing down her back in soft curls, placing the wreath of freshly picked flowers on her head, straightening the ribbons so they flowed over Mara's shoulders just so.

Marty, though not much older than Mara herself, had taken on the role all pending brides relied on, and she'd done it like she did everything else where her family and friends were concerned.

With love.

Nina poked her head over Harry's shoulder, pinching Fletcher and Mimi's cheeks before Harry set them down to run off and play with the other children in the pack.

Nina gave Mara the look of death. "It's good I like you, Short-Shot. This fucking dress sucks ass. Christ, all I did was itch during that whole thing."

Mara giggled, happier than she'd ever been in her life. Nina was gorgeous in the ivory sheath Mara had chosen for Ying, Marty, Wanda, Jeannie, Astrid, and Nina. Gorgeous. Alas, she couldn't see it because she couldn't see her reflection. "But you look sooo pretty, vampire!"

"Fuck pretty," she groused. "I'm burnin' it when this shindig's over."

Marty wrapped her arms around Nina's waist from behind and squeezed. "Oh, thou art a cranky Mistress of the Night. Leave it to you on such a beautiful day to complain."

Nina flicked her fingers at Marty's hands—even though she followed it with a chuckle. "Get the fuck off me, ass sniffer. No hugging. I'm on fire in this goddamn frilly shit."

Wanda, her hair atop her head cascading in loose waves about her face, her expression serene, landed a rare kiss on Nina's cheek with a chuckle. "Hush, Elvira, and come with. You need more SPF one bafillion on that nose of yours."

Before Wanda pulled her away, Nina clapped Harry on the back with a grin. "You, make sure you do this right." She waggled a finger at the space between Mara and Harry. "Got that? Or I gotta kill ya. Ugliness—this I promise. So much ugliness."

Harry cocked his head, so handsome in his dark suit and tie. "Is that your way of saying congratulations, Crypt Keeper?"

Nina grinned, taking Wanda's hand. "Whatever, nerd."

Wanda gave them each a hug, squeezing Mara extra hard. "Happiness. I wish you both so much happiness," she whispered as Nina dropped a kiss to the top of Mara's head, then let Wanda lead her to the shade of a pine tree where more sunblock awaited her.

Carl waited patiently, as he'd been taught over the months, putting his stiff limbs on Harry's and Mara's shoulder. "Hoppy," he said, that awkwardly stiff grin wreathing his face.

He was handsome in his suit and tie, picked out by Mimi and the other girls on "Carl Day"—a day created specifically for their zombie to spend getting to know his new extended family and friends.

And once a week, he sat with Mimi while she practiced her spelling words, and unbeknownst to them, had begun to absorb Mimi's homework.

Mara patted his face, making sure he had his duct tape tucked securely in his inner pocket in case of an accident. "Yes! We're happy—very happy you're here, Carl," she praised.

"Thanks, buddy," Harry said with a warm smile, rubbing Carl's shoulder.

Carl wandered off to find Charlie, one of his favorite people in the whole world. He found her under a tree with Greg and, with Greg's help, settled beneath it, shaking toys to interest her.

Charlie clapped her chubby hands and laughed, her dark curls draping on Carl's arm when she fell over on him, her balance still unsteady. Carl stroked her head the way Darnell had taught him—gentle and soft.

Werewolves bandied about, threading in and out of the ornately decorated trees, eating, laughing, chatting.

Harry sighed, pulling Mara close, surveying the people he'd come to love and trust. The people who'd helped save his children—who loved them almost as much as he did.

Keegan surprised them by pulling Harry into a hug, bumping shoulders with him. "You make sure you take good care of my sister and those kids. Or I'll eat your liver."

Marty burst out laughing, roping her arms through Mara and Harry, her eyes full of the not-so-quiet tears she'd shed during the ceremony. "I'm so happy for you both. We're all so happy you're here, Harry. You and the kids—it's all just right, isn't it?"

Harry cleared his throat. "Yeah. Yeah, it is, Marty. Thank you," he said, his voice tight.

Jeannie rushed up to them, fresh and pretty in her gown, a spot of batter on her face. She grabbed them both up in a hug. "So beautiful—it was all so beautiful. Mara! You're a vision. Have you ever seen a more beautiful woman, Harry?"

Harry agreed warmly, kissing Jeannie on the cheek. Jeannie was one of Harry's favorite people aside from the girls. He'd never admit it had anything to do with her divine apple turnovers or the most amazing dumplings he claimed to have ever had. "Never."

"Except for you," Sloan added, leaning in to gather Mara into a hug and shake Harry's hand. "Welcome to the state of servitude, pal," he joked, handsome in his gray suit.

Jeannie wrinkled her nose, grabbing Sloan's tie and giving it a yank. "Speaking of servitude, I need help with the side of beef I have cooking over there for you carnivores. So move it, husband," she said on a laugh when Sloan scooped her up, twirling her around toward the general direction of an open pit where the most enormous amount of beef, skewered and turning slowly, roasted.

Harry cupped her face. "She's right. I've never seen a more beautiful woman than you. Never. I think I love you, Mara Flaherty," he murmured, tracing her lips with his tongue.

She shivered in response. "You think? It's a little late to be unsure, huh?" She chuckled, holding up her ring finger.

"Fine, fine, fine. I love you—and that's my final answer."

"I love you, too, Harry Emmerson." *So, so much.*

Since the night Leah had taken the children, they'd overcome so many personal obstacles. Helping the children adjust to losing Donna the right way. By remembering her.

Once a week, just before bedtime, while they had milk and cookies freshly baked by Mara, she had instituted "Donna Day," wherein they looked at old pictures of Donna and Harry growing up together. Pictures of them as babies, with their parents, smiling in the bathtub, with their first birthday cake slathered on them from head to toe. Swinging in the swing they'd once had out in their old backyard.

They were encouraged to talk to her—tell her how much they loved and missed her. Sometimes it hurt. Sometimes Harry struggled with the words of his memories. Sometimes they cried—all of them. But they did it together—as a unit, learning to bond, finding their way out of the darkest night of their lives and knocking hard on happiness's door.

And little by little, week by week, while they all repainted Mimi's room purple as a family, when they read books together at bedtime, when they played laser tag or had a picnic in the park with Grandpa Arch, the open wounds began to heal. Nowadays, there wasn't nearly as much sadness as there was great joy and laughter in honor of Donna's memory.

Mara smiled as much as Harry and the kids—she smiled because it was during "Donna Day" that she relayed memories of her own mother and father. And one night she invited Keegan and Sloan to join them—and together, as a growing extended family, she began to heal her own private wounds by sharing her own pain with her brothers. By finding peace with their pain, too.

And it was good.

Adjustments had been a little tough at first. Harry had to learn to be a parent, not the fun uncle, and Mara had to help. They'd spent long nights, researching parents' blogs, reading, laughing, making incredible love, and in all of that, they found a deeper love than either of them could have ever imagined.

It scaled the walls of the role Harry had been thrust into and the one Mara had always yearned for. It was full of mutual respect, communication, admiration, and most of all, trust.

Mara had been cleared of all charges in Harry's turning, and with the promise that the serum she'd created would be brought to the council to discuss the possibility of beginning a surrogacy program.

Score one for female werewolves everywhere.

Guido had become a constant in their lives as of late. After all, he had, in fact, thrown his life in the mix to distract Leah and save Mara. Neither Harry nor Mara would ever forget that. And as he came around the cottage more and more often, showing up suspiciously when Astrid was around, Mara grew to love him.

It seemed his witch doctoring ways didn't go so awry when he was around those of his own paranormal ilk—not to mention, he and Astrid were cute as a button together.

Astrid was like a whole new woman as she fell in love with Guido. Her insecurities, the ones that had made her so touchy and moody, seemed to melt away beneath the glow of Guido's smile.

They'd spoken of Leah and that horrible night once—after going to her parents to tell them of her death. No one understood what in Leah had snapped, or if she'd always been in the process of breaking. Not even her parents knew what had created the Leah they'd witnessed that dreadful night.

But none of them were enough amateur-psychiatrist-curious to find out. Instead, they all talked about it—together, alone, in various groupings, and then each of them opted to move forward—let go.

They were all also there when Harry, Mimi, Fletcher, and Coconut asked Mara to marry them—at a mini *Deep Space Nine* gathering with some of Harry's online friends. There were tears, smiles, laughter, and so much happiness, Mara couldn't help but cry when they all got on one knee and asked her to be their mommy-wife.

And here they were today, on a gorgeous day in late June, with their family and friends, laughing, smiling, celebrating.

Mara tugged at Harry's tie. "So I guess this means I'm Mrs. Harry, not Harold, Emmerson now, huh?" She stood on tiptoe and kissed him, sighing when he wrapped his arms around her waist.

"Mrs. Harry for short, don't you think?" he asked, cupping her to his chest as she watched children in their Sunday best play in the sunshine, Guido and Astrid huddled in a corner sharing a glass of purple punch Mimi herself had created with Aunt Jeannie.

Nina batted at Wanda's hands, lathering her up with sunscreen, complaining as she did until her mate Greg brought over little baby Charlie and handed her to his wife with a doting grin. Chubby and the spitting image of the dark, beautiful Nina, she swung her up in the air, making baby Charlie melt into a fit of giggles.

Keegan and Marty danced slowly to a song the pack band played on a floor especially made for their wedding spot, their hands entwined, heads together.

Heath, Wanda's mate, moved through the crowd toward her, grabbing her hand and twirling her in a spin to the dance floor where he dropped kisses on her lips.

Jeannie and Sloan teased and flirted, despite the fact that they were married now, giggling as though they had a secret only they knew about. Archibald chased after children, his aging cheeks red, his belly full of hearty laughter.

And Mara nodded. Yes. Yes, yes, yes. Tears stung her eyes—tears of complete peace and happiness. "Mrs. Harry, it is."

"So, Mrs. Harry, you wanna go and see about making some babies the old-fashioned way? You know, no vitaminwater. Just you, me, and some serious naked."

"Are you kidding me? If there's no vitaminwater in the mix—I'm out. Where's the fun in that?" she teased.

"Well, maybe I can convince you?" he uttered against her lips, running his hand over the swell of her hip.

She sighed into his mouth, bracing her hands on his chest. "Oh, I dunno, Mr. Harry. You'll have to work hard. So hard."

And as Nina once more called out the question they'd all grown used to, "Where's Carl? Has anyone seen Carl?" and as Wanda fussed over Archibald secretly giving the children too many sweets and as Marty yelled at Nina not to rip her dress, Mara decided there was nothing in the world that compared to this.

Harry released her lips and pulled her toward their secret spot, a spot they'd found one night on one of their full moon runs—secluded and hidden. "Hard you say? No worries, honey, *I got this,*" he teased with a grin, using the familiar phrase they'd made their own.

As Mara followed behind him, his back wide and strong, his hand firm, she prevented him from almost tripping, and listened with satisfaction for his familiar, "I'm okay!"

Giggling and completely forgetting how naughty it was to run out on their wedding reception, she smiled.

Yeah.

They had this.